I0984488

PALM BEACH
COUNTY

Palm Beach County
Library System

Room 13

Also by Henry Garfield

Moondog

Room 13

Henry Garfield

St. Martin's Press
New York

A THOMAS DUNNE BOOK.
An imprint of St. Martin's Press.

Design by Nancy Resnick

Library of Congress Cataloging-in-Publication Data

Garfield, Henry.
Room 13 / Henry Garfield.
p. cm.
"A Thomas Dunne book.'
ISBN 0-312-15203-5
I. Title.
PS3557.A7152R6 1997
813'.54—dc21 96-47862
CIP

First edition: July 1997

10 9 8 7 6 5 4 3 2 1

To B. Rose Anderson,
member in good standing
of the Grammar Police

Acknowledgments

Many people helped in the shaping and reshaping of this novel. Barbara Markowitz and Ruth Cavin, my agent and editor, respectively, provided lots of constructive criticism without skimping on encouragement. Thanks to Mike Sirota and the Thursday-night crew, who heard early versions of much of this and offered comments and suggestions; to everyone who read early drafts and talked to me afterward; and to those who helped with computer matters along the way: Richard and Lois Miller, Robert Mitchell, and Larry Johnson. Special thanks to Susan Brock, my best critic and favorite redhead, for the many insights and the occasional kick in the butt.

Finally, thanks to the people of Julian for having a sense of humor about the first book. This one should be even more fun. Aah-ooo.

Author's Note

The setting for this story is the mountain and high desert region surrounding the unincorporated town of Julian, California, in San Diego County. Names of geographic locations have not been changed. In places, the geography of the area has been altered in small ways to fit the narrative.

Room 13 is a work of fiction. Drew Bailey Memorial High School, the Julian men's baseball league, Pala Meadows Hospital, and the various Julian business establishments are the author's fabrications. Names are either invented or used fictitiously. Any resemblance of characters herein to actual persons, living or dead, is coincidental.

The period between full Moons, called the synodic month, is approximately twenty-nine days. While full Moon occurs at a precise moment, there is a period of two to three consecutive nights each month during which the Moon appears "full" in the sky and werewolves transform. Thus, although the werewolf cycle in this story does not follow exact twenty-nine-day intervals, no laws of celestial mechanics have been violated.

1

The Werewolf of Pismo Beach

Across several months and several hundred miles, Marilou McCormick would cling to the belief that the thing that killed her boyfriend was a fog-induced hallucination.

After all, the fog could play tricks on a person's mind, especially when that mind belonged to an impressionable woman of twenty-five whose education had not been able to erase the superstitions her mother had taught her, or to prevent her from inheriting her mother's impulsive taste in men. That the latest man wound up bleeding in the sand, his head nearly severed from his body, would not send Marilou searching for answers, but, rather, running headlong away from them. They would find her anyway—and the mountains of Julian had no nightly fog to shroud the Moon and conceal the truth.

It had been Gary's idea, the midnight joyride down the beach, but she had readily gone along. She liked him and his bike, a KZ-125, which he sometimes let her ride by herself. "It's strong, but not too much bike for a chick," he'd told her proudly. Motorcycles and pickup trucks—the men in her life seemed to have had one or the other. Her father had told her once that she treated boyfriends like vehicles, and she had cried, because it was true.

The fog had rolled in at sunset, as it usually did in summer, lolling atop the waves and in front of the hills back of the Pacific Highway, but the sky overhead was clear and the full Moon reigned there unobscured, a skylight for the gray-walled world. It was illegal to ride on this part of the beach, several miles north of the State Vehicular Recreation Area, in front of the town and the tent-and-trailer campground. Farther south, the sound of motors would rend the night until dawn. Marilou had been down there once, two boyfriends ago, cavorting around the dunes on one of those three-wheeled things with the big tires, somehow managing to avoid a collision in the dark. She preferred Gary's motorbike, the empty stretch of beach before them, and the small but significant act of rebellion in using it.

Their assailant had been stalking them, Marilou would tell the police. On their first run down the beach, she had seen a huge shadowy figure moving stealthily between the grass-topped moguls of sand up near the trees. She clung to Gary's waist as he skimmed the bike just out of reach of the waves; occasionally, he'd run it through an inch-deep skein of seawater, and she would taste salt spray. She laughed and brushed a strand of long red hair away from her mouth. Tossing her head to one side, she caught a glimpse of the tall silhouette between two dunes, its head higher than the tops of both. When Gary stopped the bike to admire the surf a little farther down the beach, she looked over her shoulder and saw it again, this time behind a dune, half in shadow. Probably somebody from the campground, she thought, out for a late-night stroll. Pismo Beach got a lot of visitors in the summer. She had been coming here all her life, and strangers on the beach were nothing new. She did not think it important enough to mention.

They rode up and down the beach for a while, until they came upon a fire ring piled high with driftwood. Gary parked the bike, and she watched as he built a tepee of small sticks, snapped a plastic lighter in half to spill the fluid on them, and lit the fire with another. She laughed softly and snuggled close to him as he gradually added the larger pieces. "I've never seen anyone start a fire that way before," she said.

"Pays to keep these things handy," he told her, running a hand through her hair. He produced two cigarettes, and they smoked in silence for a while, feeding the fire with fingers, then wrists and arms of driftwood. He was a big man with rough edges, a leather jacket, toothpick in the mouth kinda guy, and a keen disappointment to her father, for that was exactly the sort of man Marilou's mother had run off with. Jack McCormick had been there through her adolescence, paid for her education, and steered her into his own profession—teaching. In her public life, she had made him proud; at the school in San Luis Obispo where she worked, she was every bit the young professional—poised, conservatively dressed, liked and respected by her students and her peers. At the college, her father's colleagues spoke highly of her, and her success was a great joy to him. And she worshiped her father. Why, then, did she feel compelled to hurt him?

"I don't understand, Lou," he had said after the last breakup. (He had called her Lou for as long as she could remember, a token of affection.) "You have so much going for you. You're pretty, you're well educated, and you've got a good job. There're plenty of good men out there. How come the guys you hook up with seem to be in training for the next bar fight?"

Marilou couldn't explain it, either. She didn't consider herself a particularly loose woman—most of the girls she still knew from high school had had a comparable number of lovers. The others were married. That was probably what her father hoped for, even though his own marriage had spectacularly failed. Instead, Marilou tended to choose unmarriageable men, and to grow restless and bored within weeks.

She had forgotten all about the stranger in the dunes as the firelight blazed before them. Gary moved his hand skillfully underneath her shirt. They had this part of the beach to themselves (at least it seemed that they did), and Gary had spread his leather jacket on the sand beneath her. It would not be the first time she had made love on this beach. He had her shirt and bra off and was working on the top button of her jeans when they heard the low growl behind them.

Gary took his hands off her and turned quickly. "Hey!" he cried. "Get away from there!"

The bike stood a short distance away from them, and Marilou could see a huge dark shape poking around it. Later, she would say that she did not get a good look at it, for she had been gazing into the fire, and the fog smudged sharp outlines. The only thing she would remember clearly about the assailant were its eyes, which reflected the firelight with an unnatural reddish glow as it stared at them. It did not back away.

Gary stood up. "I said get out of here!" he shouted, taking a step toward the bike. The intruder rose also, and Marilou knew it was the thing that had been watching them.

Thing—for it was surely not a man, though she would try hard in the coming months to forget that brief but unambiguous moment. It was covered in black fur, and more powerfully built than any human she had ever seen. It had pronounced haunches, a tree trunk of a torso, and a monstrous head full of pointed teeth. It leveled its eyes at Gary and snarled.

Gary stopped in his tracks. He was six foot three, but the thing before him stood at least six inches taller. The creature sprang away from the motorcycle, toward him.

"Holy shit!" Gary said in a queerly small voice. He did not have time to say anything else before the beast was upon him.

The intruder lifted Gary off his feet and slammed him into the sand. It pounced on him, and Marilou screamed. She saw its jaws close around her lover's neck. She was still screaming when the creature raised its besmirched face and looked at her, its horrible eyes catching the firelight. Then it lifted its head to the full Moon and loosed a full-throated howl.

Marilou saw that she could get to the bike. She raced for it, kicked it into life. The creature roared. Marilou gunned the throttle. The bike leaned crazily in the soft sand. She put out her foot and pushed off. The attacker roared. Marilou gained control and raced down the beach toward town. Her heart in her mouth, she imagined the creature's hot breath on the back of her neck as it chased her down. She anticipated sharp, hot, bloody death. Her screams harmonized with the whine of the engine.

When she finally dared a backward glance, she saw that the thing had indeed run after her but then had stopped. She heard it howl again in frustration. The next time she looked, she saw it lumbering back toward their fire, and its hideous feast.

The talk the next day in the bars of Pismo Beach, and indeed all over the greater San Luis Obispo area, was all about the brutal murder—and about the young woman, a teacher at one of the local junior high schools, who had come riding into the police station on a motorcycle, naked to the waist, crying hysterically about a monster on the beach. Even before her sad-eyed father had arrived at the station to pick her up and take her back to his house, where he would spend the next several days consoling her and shooing reporters from the door, Marilou knew that she would have to leave. Gary's death meant the death of her dual life in the area, as well. Her students, her colleagues, her father's colleagues, and most of her friends would never look at her in the same way again. It was time to go somewhere new and make a new beginning.

In the days before she left, Marilou completed a pretty fair job of denial, convincing herself and the police investigators that Gary had been attacked by a very large man, possibly black, possibly bearded, who may or may not have had a knife or some other weapon. It was the only rational explanation, and she clung to it, for, unlike her mother, she was a rational woman.

Two weeks after Gary's death, on a beautiful late-August

morning when the fog had rolled several miles out to sea, she packed her few belongings into her baby blue Volkswagen Bug, said good-bye to her father, and headed south.

She went to Julian because a job awaited her there, a position teaching English at the local high school, a job that had been suddenly vacated. They seemed pretty desperate to hire someone, and her father's list of references proved impressive enough to get her in.

It was a small town, four thousand feet high in the mountains northeast of San Diego. Main Street was perhaps a quarter of a mile long, lined with old false-front wooden buildings. The town was surrounded by pine woods and rolling meadows, and in the winter, there would be snow. It promised a quiet life, far from the horror she had witnessed that night on the beach, and the demons of her own past.

2

The Room

The room was dark. It was windowless save for the back wall, to Marilou's immediate right, where long sets of tightly drawn venetian blinds shut out the Southern California sun. The room smelled musty and close, as if it hadn't been opened in weeks.

But it was also considerably cooler than the blazing summer day beyond the walls, and Marilou was grateful for that. She wasn't used to the kind of unrelenting heat that wafted up to Julian from the desert in late summer. But the nights were cool, and she had found a nice place to live a few miles from town, in a guest house on the property of some Los Angeles movie mogul whose huge house next to it was almost always empty. She liked the land and the quaint little village. And the people seemed friendly enough, if a tad aloof, as people in small towns are likely to be toward newcomers.

"Here it is," said Steve Dakota. "Your new home." Drew Bailey Memorial High School's superintendent walked the few steps to the wall switch and flipped on the ceiling lights high above them. They cast a wan glow over the rows of desks and the dingy green carpet.

Steve Dakota stood by the light switch as Marilou surveyed her new classroom. He was an awkward-looking man, she thought—tall, with outsized hands and a mop-top haircut like the ones the Beatles had sported when they first became famous. He was young for his job, and he probably took it too seriously, for he had hardly cracked a smile all morning. And he was making quite a show of not looking at her. He was, though. Men looked at her—it came with the territory. She knew she was a good-looking woman, though she thought she had too many freckles, didn't like the bump midway down the bridge of her nose, and as a teenager had wanted more than anything else to be blond. She was dressed much as she would dress for teaching, in a loose-fitting blouse that deemphasized her curves and a skirt that ended below the knees. She had found that things went better for her in the classroom when she dressed conservatively. A pretty face and a nice figure had been assets in college; in high school classrooms full of pent-up testosterone, they were definitely a distraction.

"What do you think?" said the superintendent from his post by the light switch.

Marilou had hated the room immediately. But she also knew that what she thought did not matter one whit; the question had been asked only to vibrate the dead air.

They had entered through a small alcove off the main hall of the Annex, the primary outbuilding on the small campus. The door swung inward into the room; immediately to the right was the wall of blind-covered windows, extending upward from a small sill at waist level all the way to the high ceiling. At the opposite end of the rectangular room was the teaching area, well-defined by two long steps that elevated it from the main body of the room. A stage of sorts, it was deep enough to accommodate her desk, a row of bookshelves along the opposite wall, a long table, and a lecture podium. Her massive desk, its solid oak bulk defying anyone to move it, sat stage right. Directly above, a crooked wood and metal ceiling fan had begun to stir lazily when the lights came on. Attached to the wall behind this area was a huge boxlike dinosaur of a heater, which emitted occasional clicking noises.

The superintendent stood by the near wall. The light switch and thermostat were set in the middle of an unbroken expanse of pale green paint. Marilou thought it strange that the light switch was not immediately inside the door, but a few paces away from it, so that one had to enter the room in the dark. Between the switch and the stage, a doorless closet filled with bookshelves disappeared far back into the wall and around a corner. It was very dark in there, darker than the room had been before Dakota had turned on the lights. She assumed that the closet had a light as well and that she would soon be familiarizing herself with its contents.

"Room thirteen," she muttered, looking around. The number, painted in black on the outside of the door, had struck loathing into her heart even before Steve Dakota had turned the key.

"You're superstitious?" the superintendent asked her, amused.

"A little," she admitted. "It's nothing."

But it was not nothing, the sixth prime number, just as black cats and certainly mirrors broken in anger were not nothing. Thirteen was how old Marilou had been when things had begun to fall apart, when her mother had left, when her sexuality had come in a torrent, when she had sneaked her first cigarette from the pack her father kept in the top-right drawer of his writing desk. She had thrown a hand mirror at her father that year, and she had now been smoking, off and on but mostly on, for nearly half her life. Her father had been so appalled when she had started to smoke openly in front of him that he himself had quit the habit while she continued to smoke. The last thing she had done before hugging her father and getting into the Volkswagen was to ceremoniously throw away her cigarettes. It had been four days, six hours, and twenty-odd minutes now, and she was dying for one.

But the far wall, the other long side of the rectangle, wrested her attention from her cravings. A chalkboard stretched like a highway across the middle of the wall. Around and above it were some two dozen portraits, harshly rendered in pen and ink, of famous authors. Each was about the size of a *Life* magazine cover, and each bore a small paragraph describing the author's life and work, below the name and the dates of birth and death. Jack London headed the cast, at the upper corner nearest the raised area; the others were arrayed in a loose rectangular pattern beside and below him, ending with F. Scott Fitzgerald and Mark Twain at the other end of the board, nearest the windows. Marilou noticed immediately that only two women—Edith Wharton and Willa Cather—broke the gender line; a minute or two later, she realized that they were all Americans. But her immediate, visceral dislike of the posters did not stem from feminist or globalist leanings. There was something disconcerting about the portraits themselves, the way the unknown artist had rendered them. Hemingway scowled from his spot next to London; Poe glowered from near the center of the wall. The faces, every one of them, looked tormented, trapped, malevolent. Steinbeck bore a Satan-like look, with his goatee and heavy eyebrows. Not even Twain was smiling.

And the eyes—the eyes were too intense, staring pitilessly out into the room. They followed Marilou as she walked slowly along the wall. She decided at once that she would take the posters down. Authors are supposed to be admired, she thought, as cultural beacons, carriers of the flame, storytellers, and curators of collective memory. This bunch, in these renderings, looked more like the faces on the WANTED posters at the post office.

"I'll want to do some rearranging in here," Marilou said,

turning to face the superintendent, who hadn't moved from his position by the light switch.

"Absolutely," he said. "It's your classroom."

"For starters, let's let some light in." Marilou strode purposefully to the wall of windows, looking with her hands and eyes for the string to raise the blinds.

"Uh, they're broken, I think," said Steve Dakota.

She turned to face him, her eyes meeting his. He looked immediately away, squinting at the top corners of the windows as though trying to determine what the problem was.

"You're kidding," she said flatly.

"No." He looked at her chest, then, catching himself, at her forehead. "Don't worry. It's on our custodian's list of things to do."

"Good," she said. "Otherwise, the kids'll go nuts."

"Maybe they'd pay more attention," he answered, with just the hint of a smile.

She shrugged, giving him a nothing smile in return. She remembered her year of student teaching, at a new school where none of the classrooms had windows. Every building was built like a barracks; the rooms were square and identical. Marilou had thought the effect prisonlike, anticreative, like that old Pete Seeger song her father sometimes sang: "Little boxes, made of ticky-tacky, and they all look just the same." She would rather have kids looking out the window, daydreaming, than watching the clock, mindlessly counting down the minutes to freedom.

"Well, at least I can redecorate a little," she said. "Get a little color around here. God, whoever was in here before sure liked it gloomy."

"This room has looked like this ever since I've been here," Dakota said. "That's four years. We've had . . . a bit of turnover in this room. There have been several teachers. It's strange, now that you mention it, that none of them really changed it."

"Well, this one's going to," she declared. "This place looks like a dungeon."

She saw his serious look, and she couldn't arrest the small laugh that slipped out. Embarrassed, she kept talking. "Here I am, the first day, wanting to change everything. You probably think I'm nuts. But these posters—I mean, they're so *severe,* don't you think? All black-and-white images—and there's nothing else on the walls at all. What I'd really like to do is take them all down and start over."

"By all means," Steve Dakota said, "do whatever you want. Like I said, it's your classroom. We can always give the posters to the library."

And scare little children away, Marilou thought. She reached out for the corner of the closest poster, which bore the face of William Faulkner.

The big heater roared into life.

Sudden pain slashed through Marilou's hand. She recoiled from the poster with a sharp cry. Looking down, she saw that she was bleeding from a deep paper cut along the side of her index finger. A drop of bright red blood welled quickly up from the slice and plopped onto the carpet at her feet.

"Ow!" she cried again, squeezing the cut. It hurt like hell.

But the sudden noise of the heater had grabbed Steve Dakota's attention. "That thing should not be on," he said, his back to her as he fiddled with the thermostat. She realized he hadn't heard her. The heater groaned as it pushed the stale air around the room; there was a faint metallic clanking sound behind the constant rush.

"Mr. Dakota . . . I . . . I think I'm going to need a Band-Aid."

"Huh?" The superintendent turned around, and the heater shut off as abruptly as it had started. He looked at the big silver-gray box with a puzzled expression. "I wonder why it did that?" he said to the room itself. "The thermostat's turned all the way down."

"I'm bleeding," Marilou said.

He turned and saw her upraised finger. A small stream of blood flowed over the back of her hand toward her wrist. "Oh my goodness, you are." He hurried over to her. "What happened?"

"Paper cut," she said, moving her arm about so that the blood would not run onto the two silver bracelets around her wrist. She hoped her voice didn't sound too alarmed. There was a lot of blood—more than there should have been from such a small wound. "I think I ought to clean it up and put something on it."

"Yes, let's go," he said immediately. "The bathroom's down the hall, and there are some Band-Aids back at the office." He fumbled in a pocket of his trousers and came up with a rumpled handkerchief, which he handed to her awkwardly. "Here," he said.

"Thanks." She wiped most of the blood from her hand and then wrapped the cloth around her finger, which still hurt. She smiled at him and he hastened toward the door.

As he was locking up, she noticed again the number painted on the door, and she experienced a moment of worry that the new job was starting off ominously, with an assignment to room 13 and a paper cut that bled longer and harder than any paper cut she had ever experienced or seen. Ridiculous, she admonished herself. Superstitious nonsense, and an especially sharp-edged kind of paper. That was all.

But she could hear the big heater making soft clicking noises from the other side of the door. Waiting for me, she thought. Waiting for me to return.

Stop it, she told herself silently. It's a new life, a clean slate. Everything's going to be fine. Her finger throbbed steadily beneath the bloodied handkerchief as she followed the superintendent down the hall.

3

Robert

Robert Rickard had arrived early for his first day on the job. His years of toil for CalTrans, keeping the California freeways clear of debris, pedestrians, and other hazards, had trained him to get up with the Sun, which was just poking its face above the mountains east of the small campus when Doug, his boss, rolled up in his old Mustang and parked in front of the Annex steps, where Robert sat smoking a cigarette.

The big Indian lifted one side of his mouth in a wry half smile as he got out, and Robert knew that his punctuality on this, the day before the official start of the school year, had scored him points. He was lucky to have the job, really—even if it was only part-time and at a considerably lower salary than he'd earned on the highway. Fifty-five was a hard age at which to be starting over, especially for a guy who hadn't finished high school and wasn't, by his own admission, an intellectual ball of fire. Not that he was hurting financially—the early-retirement package had been more than fair. Government jobs were being cut all over the place, and the state had little use for aging bodies near the top of the salary structure when younger and stronger workers could perform the same labors at far less cost. Robert understood all this. Still, it amounted to a forced layoff, and his pride had been wounded. But he and his wife would be all right, as long as Jimmy, his twenty-three-year-old, ambitionless, crystal-sniffing son, got his butt out of the house and into some useful livelihood sometime soon. Robert tried not to think about Jimmy too much; thinking about his son made him mad.

"Mornin'," Doug said as Robert stood up and snuffed the butt beneath his shoe. Doug eased past him up the four stone steps, unsnapped a ring containing some two dozen keys from his belt, and unlocked the heavy double doors. "Best time of day's right now, buddy," he said. "The whole place is ours. No students or teachers around to fuck everything up."

Robert laughed dutifully as he followed Doug into the cool, dark building. Robert was a little guy, about five foot four, with a wiry build kept thin by a lifetime of manual labor. Next to Doug, he was a featherweight. Doug was perhaps thirty-five and built like a football player, with wide shoulders, virtually no neck, and a low center of gravity. Most of the Indian's six-foot height was in his back; he had short, powerful legs encased in a pair of blue jeans, which hung low on his hips around a plain olive-green T-shirt. His face was round and intelligent; his midnight black hair, graying at the temples, was pulled tightly back behind his neck in a single thin braid that nearly reached his waist.

"We'll need to get you a set of keys," Doug said as Robert followed him into the building. The double doors opened onto a short lower hall between two classrooms whose windows faced the parking lot. Doug unlocked the two doors, revealing similar and very typical-looking learning spaces, with the standard off-white linoleum floors, wraparound chalkboards, and soft-tile ceilings. Four steps led from the lower hall to the upper level of the building. The long main hall made a right angle with the lower one, and the janitor's closet was exactly at the intersection, at the top of the stairs. Next to it were the two bathrooms, a drinking fountain, and a fire extinguisher encased in glass. Standing in front of the closet, Robert could survey the entire topography of his job—he could look out the double doors into the parking lot and down the long hallway that led to the building's other two classrooms.

"You'll be responsible for keeping the parking lot clean, plus the gym and the four rooms in here," Doug told him, striding down the hall. "They're all pretty easy, except the art room. That can be a pain in the butt, 'cause kids spill paint sometimes, and they use clay and glue and all that other shit. The teacher ain't much help."

The hall was well lit because it had windows two thirds of the way down the right-hand side, the back wall of the building. The windows were interrupted by a back door, which opened out onto a cracked patio area and a gravel pathway up an embankment into the woods. Though not blessed with an especially active imagination, Robert knew immediately that this was the route kids would use when heading out for an illegal cigarette or joint break. The other side of the hall was bare wall until it reached a small alcove leading to a third classroom. At the left, on the far side of the alcove, were more windows, through which in the distance Robert could see the baseball field, its surface a haphazard checkerboard of weeds and bare ground. At the very end of the hall, on the side opposite the alcove, was the art room. One could see into it from the hall through high windows at the junction of wall and ceiling; paintings from the previous year were still taped to the part of the wall that sloped down from the ceiling at a forty-five-degree angle. The room itself was huge and tidy, with long tables arranged dominolike around the perimeter. The paints and clay and other janitor's enemies were neatly stored in a row of tall metal cabinets against the far wall. A pair of industrial-size sinks had, over the years, accumulated many colors.

"The teacher's supposed to make sure the kids don't trash this room," Doug said. "But she doesn't have much control over them. Let the small stuff go. If it gets really out of hand, let me know and I'll talk to her."

Doug opened the room off the alcove—room 13—last. Robert had noticed that the two lower rooms bore numbers 10 and 11; the art room, though it had no number on the door, must be room 12. Doug unlocked the dead bolt, swung open the door, but he made no move to enter the room itself.

"The light switch is down the wall to your left," he said.

It was dark in the room, but not too dark to see, and Robert located the light switch easily. He noticed immediately that the ceiling was much higher than in the other rooms, and bare, with strips of peeling paint hanging down. The carpet had wanted replacing for some time; it was ragged, threadbare in spots, and stained. From the far wall, two dozen pairs of eyes seemed to stare at him. Robert stared back at the posters, shuddering involuntarily.

"This room's different," he said, his voice echoing in the stillness.

"Well, it's the only one with carpeting," Doug replied, still standing by the door. "There's a carpet sweeper in your closet, and a vacuum cleaner. You should sweep it every day, and vacuum once a week."

"No, I mean it's *different,*" Robert said, awkwardly, not sure what he meant. "Older, or something. It's got a different feel to it."

"Just another classroom to clean, as far as I'm concerned," Doug said. "New teacher coming in here this year. Hope she sticks around longer than the last couple of airheads. Come on, I'll show you the supply shed."

Robert wanted to look around the room some more, but Doug was already moving off down the hall. With one more glance at the strange posters, Robert followed him.

"You'll need to get here around six-thirty," Doug said over

his shoulder as Robert hurried to catch up. "First thing you do is put up the flags. Then if there's a major disaster in the parking lot, like a whole bunch of trash or broken beer bottles or something, get that cleaned up. Minor shit outside, you can do later. The rooms need to be cleaned by eight-fifteen, 'cause classes start at eight-thirty."

The parking lot was now bathed in full sunlight. In front of the Annex, a low circular wall surrounded the central flagpole. This wall was thigh-high to an adult, filled with hard-packed dirt, from which a few blades of grass timidly poked sunward. At the front of the parking lot, the long, low-slung hulk of the main building faced the highway. Between the side of the building and the side of the lot where the buses would load and unload at the beginning and end of the school day was a wide grassy area with a few scattered benches and trash receptacles. Across the parking lot, to Robert's right as he and Doug exited the Annex, were the tennis courts and, beyond them, the baseball field. At the near end of the Annex, the lot narrowed to a paved driveway that led past the gymnasium to a back lot where the buses parked, and the elementary school was beyond that. Off toward the east, beyond the main building, stood the supply shed, the auto and wood shops, the agricultural barns, a fenced area for goats and sheep, and the football field. Beyond that were trees and mountains, providing a scenic backdrop to this center of Julian teenage life.

Robert followed Doug across the parking lot, heading toward the back door of the main building and a cement walkway that led along the side of the gym to the supply shed. The day was already warming—September can be the hottest month in the Southern California mountains, and Robert knew it would be in the nineties before noon. Suddenly, an engine that had been quietly idling roared into action from somewhere behind them. Robert turned just in time to see a school bus swerve around the corner of the gym, its back tires skidding sideways, kicking up gravel and dust.

He had to hustle to get out of the way. The driver saw him and blasted the horn. As the bus sped past, Robert got a quick look at the man behind the wheel. He had dark shoulder-length hair, a thick mustache, and a strange gleam in his eye as he glanced at Robert, hit the horn again, and gunned the bus toward the twin stone pillars that marked the entrance to the parking lot from the highway.

"Damn!" Robert said, catching up with Doug. Barely slowing down, the bus made a right turn onto the road, and Robert could hear the tires squeal in protest. Its wide rear fishtailed out into the center of the road and into the path of a Jeep Cherokee in the oncoming lane. Both drivers hit their horns. The Jeep skittered over onto the gravel shoulder, bounced heavily a couple of times, and regained the road in the dust trail of the bus. The bus swerved back onto its own side of the road, picked up speed again, and rambled off toward town.

"Where's he going in such a hurry?" Doug said, squinting after the bus as it disappeared beyond the baseball field.

"Damn!" Robert said again. "Who the hell *was* that?"

"Our new bus driver," Doug told him. "Cyrus something or other. Calls himself 'Moondog.' "

"What is he, a nut?"

"Don't know," Doug said, still looking at the road where the bus had been. "He's got a license, though, and we needed a bus driver."

"How many kids did he kill on his last job?"

Doug chuckled. "He won't drive like that with kids in it," he said. "At least he better not."

Doug showed Robert the supply shed, the teachers' lounge, where he could take his coffee breaks, and the gym, which would be his responsibility to sweep and clean up before the end of second period. He then led Robert down to the office at the front of the main building and introduced him to Valerie, the school secretary, an attractive middle-aged woman who, like Robert's wife, was fighting a losing battle against creeping obesity. Doug and the secretary exchanged a few sentences of flirtatious banter—Robert took this to be a routine with them—and then the secretary issued Robert a set of keys.

"Any questions about the job?" Doug asked him.

"Nope," Robert replied. Piece of cake, he thought.

"Good. On normal days, you can leave at eleven. You get a fifteen-minute break whenever you want. What I want you to do today is just check over the rooms up there in the Annex and make a list of anything that's broken. The rooms're all clean, but you might want to dust off the chalkboards and tabletops, just for show. Some of the teachers will be in later. They've each got their pet peeves—just do what they ask. They're usually pretty nice about it."

"Okay, boss," Robert said, and plucked the keys out of the air as Doug tossed them to him.

"And put up the flags," Doug added. "You should do that first thing when you get here in the morning. The superintendent likes to see those flags up."

When Robert returned from the supply shed, with Old Glory and the Bear Republic flag folded under his arm, the school bus that had nearly run him down was parked by the side of the main building, and Doug and the driver were leaning against the grille, conversing. Robert clipped the flags to the halyard, hoisted them aloft, and approached the two men.

"Thanks for letting me live," he said to the bus driver.

The newcomer looked at him, his eyes dark and expressionless. The pupils were exceptionally large, the irises dark, dark brown, the color of a well-oiled hardwood floor. But Robert detected the hint of a smile behind the mustache. "Who are you?" the man asked.

"Robert Rickard. I'm the janitor in here." He nodded over his shoulder at the Annex.

"Cyrus Nygerski. My friends call me Moondog." The driver held out his hand; Robert hesitated a moment before taking it. The man's handshake was firm; Robert noticed that the fingernail on his index finger was entirely black.

"Do you always drive like that?" Robert asked.

"I'm from Boston," Nygerski said.

"You almost ran that poor sucker off the road," Doug commented.

The bus driver chuckled, then kicked at a small rock. "He'll watch out for me now, though, won't he? Besides, the ass-end won't kick out like that when the bus is full of kids. When there's some weight in the back, she'll hold the road better on the turns."

"When the bus is full of kids, you'll slow down," Doug said seriously.

"Relax, boss," Nygerski told him. "The little terrorists will be in good hands. The ones you'll have to worry about are the kids who drive themselves to school. There are few things scarier than a seventeen-year-old driver."

Robert, who had taught his son to drive, had to admit that the weird bus driver with black holes for eyes had a point. "Duty calls," he said, and moved off toward the Annex.

"Listen, I just remembered something," Doug called after him. Robert turned in front of the Annex steps and looked at him questioningly.

"The blinds in room thirteen don't work," Doug said. "You handy with fixing stuff like that?"

"I can give it a shot," Robert said. "What's wrong with 'em?"

"Dunno," Doug replied. "Superintendent told me they were broken, asked if I could get 'em fixed. I ain't got time to do it. There're ladders and everything in the supply shed."

"Okay. I'll see what I can do."

"Be careful of the windows," Doug said. "They're old and

funky. I think only the center section works. The others—the tracks are all rusted out. You try to open one of the windows on the side, it'll fall right out."

Robert checked room 13 last—not because of any superstition, but because that seemed to be the logical order in which to do things. As he unlocked the door, Robert looked up and noticed that the alcove abutted the roof at an odd angle, an angle that no architect would have designed in. The roofline had been there first. So the room was obviously an add-on; it was newer, rather than older, than the rest of the building, despite its rather decrepit appearance.

Aside from the grim faces on the opposite wall, there wasn't a shred of decoration anywhere. There were, however, plenty of books. They filled the shelves inside the dark closet; they stood in rows on the bookcase opposite the teacher's desk, and in piles on the nearby table.

Robert, who had never been much of a reader, paid little attention either to the authors or the books as he steered the aluminum stepladder through the door and set it up next to the wall of windows. When he touched the blinds, dust came off on his fingers. It had evidently been quite some time since they'd been opened.

Robert frowned as he searched the sides of the windows for the string that would open the blinds. Not finding it, he soon discovered the problem: The string had broken, and its frayed remains poked out of the little gizmo at the top that was supposed to hold the blinds open. Robert positioned the ladder and climbed to the very top. Taking out his Swiss army knife and flipping up the marlinspike, he began working at the jammed string.

Robert thought he was being careful. His lack of height made standing on the top of the ladder a matter of necessity rather than safety. He had no sense that he was in danger of losing his balance until it happened.

There was nothing to grab for except the blinds themselves, and Robert missed. He dropped the knife as he fell; his elbow banged the ladder and sent pain shooting up his arm. He managed to land on his feet, however, and sank immediately to his knees, cursing and clutching his elbow. The ladder swayed but did not fall on top of him.

He was more stunned than hurt. He knelt there for several moments, rubbing his elbow, wondering what had caused him to be so clumsy. As he did so, he noticed anew how faded and stained the carpet was. It really ought to be replaced, he thought. And then he saw the book.

The thin paperback lay facedown on the carpet near the back row of student desks. Robert crawled over and picked it up.

As he did so, the large heater behind the teacher's desk emitted a short series of clicks. Robert looked up at it and frowned.

He sat on the floor and turned the book over in his hands: *The Old Man and the Sea*, by Ernest Hemingway. Robert had never paid much attention to books. He'd been a slow learner in school, and his teachers, thinking him dumb, hadn't encouraged him. He'd dropped out at seventeen to join the navy, and his reading since then had consisted of newspaper sports sections, pornographic paperbacks his coworkers at CalTrans had left in the men's room, and the occasional magazine article his wife pointed out to him. He could not remember ever having read a real book for pleasure.

Robert recognized the author's name—he'd watched a young actress named Hemingway on HBO some years back in a soft-core film about lesbian runners that he had liked but that his wife had dismissed as perverted. Without thinking, he turned toward the far wall, and located the portrait of Hemingway within seconds. The scowling, bearded figure looked ready to punch somebody. Robert scanned the other posters, realizing that they were all writers. A few of the names were vaguely familiar to him; most were not.

Robert examined the book. The heater clicked softly; already, he did not notice the sound. The cover art showed a grizzled fisherman in a skiff, fighting a large swordfish or marlin that was easily as big as the boat. The fish, halfway out of the water, had the fisherman's line in its mouth, and the man was standing amidships, harpoon at the ready.

Robert opened the book to the first page. He read the first paragraph, then read the second paragraph and turned the page. Halfway through the third paragraph, and without looking up, he moved to the nearest desk and continued reading. Had he thought about what he was doing, he might have realized that he was engaging in what, for him, was extremely unusual behavior. But he was too absorbed in the story's simple, solid prose to observe himself.

He was on page five when a female voice behind him brought him out of it. "Hi there," the voice said, and Robert jumped.

The book fell to the floor as he stood up. The owner of the voice smiled at him, and Robert swallowed, for he was face-to-face with quite a lovely young woman.

"Hi," he said back to her, feeling sheepish for having been caught goofing off. "Are you the teacher in this room?"

"That's me," she said. She was professionally dressed, and she held a large briefcase in one hand and several bulging file folders in the other. Robert watched her as she carried briefcase and paperwork to the huge desk in the raised part of the room. Her eyes did a quick survey, feeling into the corners, measuring the rows of desks where tomorrow her students would sit, and stopping briefly to acknowledge the authors on the wall. He averted his eyes when she looked at him, not wanting to be caught staring.

"I'm . . . I'm supposed to make a list of anything that's broken in here," he stammered. "If you . . . need anything, you just ask me." He looked down at the book but made no move to pick it up.

"You're the janitor, I take it."

"Yeah."

"Well, you can start with the blinds," she told him. "I'd like to let some sunlight in here. You think you could fix them?"

"That's what I'm doin'," Robert said, nodding at the ladder. "I mean, that's what I *was* doin'."

"Wonderful," the teacher said.

"I gotta find some line to replace the string with," Robert added quickly. "I'm still learnin' where everything is. I'm new here."

"That's okay," the young woman said, flashing him a smile. "Today's my first day, too. I'm Marilou McCormick."

"Robert Rickard."

She stepped down off the raised area and offered her hand. It was cool to the touch, adorned with two thin silver bracelets but no rings. She had good teeth, Robert noticed, straight and white. She gave the impression of tallness, but almost all women looked tall to Robert Rickard, especially the pretty ones. His own wife topped him by an inch and a half, and this woman was probably no taller. She wore a green blouse open at the neck, a plaid skirt ending in fringes below the knees, and western boots that augmented her height. Robert guessed that she was at most a few years older than his son. Her blue eyes looked unabashedly into his when she spoke to him.

And she had red hair, lots of it, nearly reaching her waist. Robert was a sucker for redheads. He'd watch any movie in which Ann-Margret appeared, no matter how contrived the story or how much grief he had to take from his wife, whose hair had once been dark brown but was now mostly gray. Over the past several years, he had been secretly in love with Sarah Ferguson, the fallen Duchess of York, whose picture lay around the house in several back issues of the *National Enquirer*, which his wife brought home with the groceries.

"What are you reading?" the teacher asked him.

"Huh? Oh." Robert bent down and picked up the book. He

held it up so that she could read its cover. "I found it on the floor. Someone must have dropped it. Here." He held it out to her.

"You looked like you were really into it," she said. "You've never read it before?"

"Nope. I guess I don't read much."

"Too bad," the young teacher said. "I've always loved reading. My father's an English professor."

Robert shifted his weight self-consciously from one foot to the other and examined the book in his hands. He *had* been into it, and that was really, really strange. Had Marilou McCormick not walked in on him, he would be reading still. What was going on here?

"Would you like to borrow that book?" she asked him. "I have plenty of copies."

"Um . . . Sure. Thanks."

Marilou returned to her desk and began arranging several of the papers from the file folders on top of it. "Personally, I find Hemingway pretty dull. All that macho male stuff. 'Pain does not matter to a man' and all that. It seems so Neanderthal. And it made him miserable in the end."

"In the end?" Robert asked.

Marilou stopped shuffling papers and flashed him a quizzical look. "You do know that he killed himself, right?"

"No," said Robert. Next to this polished, educated young woman, he felt like an idiot. "No, I didn't know that."

The heater behind her desk clicked twice, then whooshed on, startling both teacher and janitor.

"What's wrong with that thing?" Marilou put down the papers and strode to the thermostat. "This thing's turned all the way off," she said. "It's plenty warm in here, don't you think?"

For Robert, whose palms were sweating, it was plenty warm indeed. "I'll add it to my list," he said.

The heater shut off abruptly.

"Weird," Marilou said.

"Yeah." He scratched a spot behind his ear.

"Somebody's taking about you," the teacher said.

"Huh?"

"When your ear itches, that means someone's talking about you."

"Probably my boss," Robert said. "I bet he's wondering where I am."

It wasn't a half-bad exit line, and Robert was feeling more than a little awkward. The appearance of this very attractive young woman, and his sudden desire to read a book, had given new dimension to the routine job for which he'd signed on. Something in his life had irreversibly changed. Had he been a more introspective man, he might have realized that the book had caught his attention before the teacher had, and that his unexpected interest in it had nothing to do with her. He might have wondered what happenstance had put it there, and what sort of subtle manipulation had occurred for him to overcome, at least for a few brief minutes, a lifetime of indifference to the printed word. He might have wondered whether Marilou was being manipulated, as well.

"I'll go see if I can find some string," he added on his way out the door.

An hour later, he had untangled the frayed mess and replaced the old string with one he'd found on a set of broken blinds in the back of the supply shed. When he opened the blinds, a cloud of dust billowed out into the room. The sunlight streamed in accusingly, accenting not only the dust but the stains on the carpet, the peeled paint, the warped fan, the bent chalk trays, and every other imperfection that had been muted by darkness. Perhaps the light shows too much, Robert thought.

He was halfway home before he felt the bulge in his back pocket and realized that he still had the book. And that night, instead of watching *Wheel of Fortune* and *Married with Children* with his wife, he sat out in the kitchen with a beer and plowed methodically through ten or twelve pages. Something indeed had changed.

And change is almost always frightening.

4

The New Kid in Town

Marilou wasn't at all sure she was going to like Donna Hurley, the senior English teacher and head of the two-person "department." She had been cool to the point of frostiness during Marilou's interview, and Marilou suspected that the decision to hire her had been less than unanimous. Though Steve Dakota had clearly been behind her, and the two members of the school board who had participated in the interview had seemed less interested in her background than in filling the position with a warm body, Marilou knew that school districts, especially small ones, had unofficial pecking orders, wherein lay the real power. Donna Hurley had been teaching at Bailey High for twenty-five years, and she took orders from no one. Had Marilou's father not done such a thorough job of calling on references, she figured she would still be looking for work.

As department head, Donna Hurley would get the upper classes and honors divisions, leaving Marilou with the freshmen, the jocks, and the kids with concentrations in auto shop, agriculture, and the woods. Donna's classroom was on the lower level of the Annex, on the right as one entered the building. She also ran the school library in the main building, which doubled as a meeting room for the school board. Marilou guessed that she was about sixty, with light skin and a hint of Hispanic ancestry in her features. The black hair permed atop her head was rent along one side by an inch-thick streak of white that looked like a bolt of lightning.

Their initial conflict came shortly after the staff orientation meeting, at which Marilou was the only new face in a room of a dozen teachers, whose easy camaraderie suggested that they had been working together for years. The clash was probably inevitable, for the two women were of different generations and philosophies. Donna Hurley seemed bent on establishing very quickly who was in charge. At the end of the meeting, she handed Marilou a reading list for each of her classes for the fall semester and said, "You'll find all these books, I believe, in your closet."

Later that morning, Marilou knocked on the door of Donna's classroom. The older teacher was putting up one in a series of small signs bearing maxims in black letters on bright orange posterboard. The one in her hands when Marilou entered read: "Sorry to write you such a long letter, but I didn't have time to write a short one." The room was austerely decorated; words, rather than pictures, were the focus. But sunlight streamed through the large windows, and the room felt a good deal cheerier than Marilou's.

"What can I do for you?" the senior English teacher asked.

"I wanted to talk with you about this list," Marilou said, taking several tentative steps into the room.

"Is there a problem?"

God, does this woman *ever* smile? Marilou thought. Aloud, she said, "Well, I think there is. I mean, these are all good books by renowned authors—Twain, Hemingway, Jack London. . . ."

"Yes?"

"But it's the old boys' club," Marilou said. "There isn't a

book by a woman or a person of color on this whole list."

"For the fall, we stick to the classics," Donna Hurley said. "And it so happens that nearly all the classic literature in the English language was written by white men. There's no bias about it. That's just the way it is."

"But don't you think the focus is kind of narrow?"

"No, I don't," Donna Hurley said, moving to put up another black-on-orange poster. "Students need a good grounding in the classics before they can appreciate other types of writing. They need that foundation."

"Too much of a good thing is still too much," Marilou maintained. "This is the nineties. You can't expect every student to relate to Okie farmworkers and runaway slaves on the Mississippi. Can't we sprinkle in a few modern books? I'd be happy to make up a list for you to choose from."

"Maybe in the spring," Donna Hurley said, moving away from Marilou toward her desk.

"But . . ."

Donna turned to face her. "Look," she said, "this is the way we've always done it, and I'm not about to change the whole curriculum the day before school starts. We'll have all year to discuss this. And I'd be happy to discuss it with you once we get into the school year a little bit and things are running smoothly. Now isn't the time."

Bitch, Marilou thought to herself. But she realized it would be futile to press the issue further, for Donna Hurley was obviously used to getting her way. Dealing with her would require tact and time, and maybe an ally or two among the other teachers.

One potential friend was Mimi Anderson, the large, fortyish art teacher, whose blond hair was not entirely contained by the single braid in which she wore it. Marilou imagined her sitting over a potter's wheel, periodically brushing back the renegade wisps as she worked. She had the artist look; Marilou was sure she was a working painter, potter, or sculptor for whom teaching paid the bills, much as marginally successful writers often settle at universities, teaching two or three classes and holding limited office hours.

"Lunch," the older woman suggested after Marilou's unsatisfactory talk with Donna Hurley. "I'll treat, since you're the new kid in town."

The art teacher was a fellow Volkswagen owner, but hers was an old white-on-red bus. Stretched canvases, tools, and boxes of assorted junk filled the back, where there once had been seats. On the way to Mariah's Café, she gave Marilou a tour of downtown Julian. This did not take long, for the town proper had only three or four streets. They drove past the Ghetto, a collection of shacks and trailers two blocks behind Main Street. Three half-naked children chased each other around a gravel play area, in front of a shirtless man drinking a beer on a dilapidated couch faded by sunlight. Anderson pointed out the library, the Catholic and Baptist churches, the town hall, and the graveyard. The dead occupied the honored spot in Julian, on a hill overlooking the entire town. "I suppose that's proper," Mimi Anderson commented. "A town as in love with its past as this one is ought to have a prominent cemetery. The main part of it, up at the very top, dates back to the 1870s. You need to have connections to get buried in there. You have to be related to somebody from the mining days. They're running out of room."

"What's that?" Marilou asked as they drove through the town's main intersection. Three corners were occupied by the town hall, the old Julian Drugstore, and a grocery store. The fourth corner looked as if it had been bombed. A chain-link fence surrounded an expanse of hard gravel, littered with broken glass, discarded cardboard boxes, and several small piles of scrap metal.

"It used to be the Chevron station," Anderson explained. "A few years ago, they discovered that the town's water was poisoned. Gasoline was seeping into the wells. Chevron said they didn't do it, but out of the kindness of their corporate hearts, they paid for a whole new filtration system. Then about a year after that, they announced that it wasn't profitable for them to run a station up here anymore, so they just tore the whole thing down and pulled out."

"I see they closed the bank, too." The redbrick Home Federal building, near the other end of Main Street, stood vacant, the automatic teller machine boarded over, a chain across the entrance to the small parking lot. Marilou had been forced to open an account in Ramona, twenty-two miles down the hill.

"Times have been tough," her companion said. "This is a tourist town. It depends on good publicity. The drought hurt us, and so did the poisoned water. It's also a little bit violent. You don't hear much about that. But every redneck up here has a gun, and is willing to use it."

She pulled the bus to the side of the street, in front of a stone wall and a three-tiered shopping complex built to look like a nineteenth-century mine building. Marilou sat motionless in the front seat.

"Did I say something wrong?" Mimi asked her.

"Oh . . . It's all right," Marilou said. "I guess I'm surprised. It looks so . . . quaint, though. I'd expect a town like this to be quiet and peaceful."

"Yeah, well, appearances can deceive. Come on."

The restaurant stood next to the tall commercial building. It had a wide deck, but since the temperature outside was in the nineties, they decided to sit inside. The young waitress greeted Mimi Anderson by name. "Smoking or nonsmoking?" she asked brightly.

Mimi turned to Marilou. "Do you smoke?"

"Not anymore," Marilou declared, laughing nervously.

"Let me guess. You just recently quit?"

"A whole week now," Marilou averred. "They say you haven't really quit until you stop counting the days. I'm still counting the hours."

The interior walls of the café were filled with colorful paintings that suggested Picasso. There was also a Richard Nixon campaign poster from the forties, hung at an angle, a Fabulous Furry Freak Brothers cartoon poster, and a framed newspaper clip featuring a photo of a slightly overweight, ponytailed man with a beard and round wire glasses seated at an outdoor café table between Jerry Garcia and Bob Weir of the Grateful Dead. The art teacher fit right in, Marilou thought, with her long paisley skirt and big hoop earrings.

The menu, crammed with sixties-style cartoons like those on the Freak Brothers poster, boasted a long list of mostly vegetarian omelettes and sandwiches.

At a nearby table, two men and two women talked animatedly about a house burglary that had occurred the previous night somewhere in the Julian area. "What you oughta encourage these absentee homeowners to do, Frank," one man said to the other, "is lay out some land mines for these little pukes."

"How much was taken?" asked one of the women.

"A TV, VCR, some jewelry, some food. . . ." The man called Frank, who Marilou saw was wearing a Sheriff's Department uniform, ticked off the items on his fingers. He was a young man, good-looking in a vaguely nauseating Steve Garvey–like way. "But they trashed the place up real good. Threw stuff around, broke things. Punks."

"Yeah, well when one of these junior hoodlums gets shot, I guarantee that'll make his cronies think twice about breaking into any more weekend homes." The second man was small, balding, bespectacled, bearded and intent. "That's all it'll take. One armed property owner."

"That's Harry Osterman," Mimi Anderson explained quietly. "He runs the newspaper in town. He's also a card-carrying member of the NRA."

"Is crime really that much of a problem here?"

The art teacher shrugged. "This is the nineties," she said, reminding Marilou that she had used the same line on Donna Hurley earlier that morning. "And we're only two and a half hours from L.A., and one from San Diego. Only tourists and people who just moved here see Julian as some sort of romantic rural idyll."

"Tell me more about this cute little town I've moved to," Marilou prompted.

"Well, I've been here for only seven years, so I'm still considered an outsider myself, I guess. Small towns are like that."

"But what about the violence?" Marilou asked, looking worriedly over at the other table.

"Well, this was a mining town," Mimi Anderson said. "That's why it's here—there's gold in them thar hills. And like most mining towns, it had its brief boom, and for a while, I guess, all kinds of nefarious characters showed up to seek their fortunes. A lot of their descendants still live here. Back then, the only justice was vigilante justice. To some extent, that's still true."

"Really?"

"Really. A couple years ago two guys ended up dead at a mine that hasn't operated commercially for a hundred years. There was some sort of dispute over mineral rights on the land. Some bigwig in L.A. bought a permit from the Bureau of Land Management and hired two local guys to keep an eye on the place for him. Apparently, they came across this family group, out for a picnic and a little target shooting with assorted automatic weapons, and told 'em to get off the land. No one really knows for sure what happened, but the two guys were kinda like local drunks, and apparently one of them brandished a rifle in a threatening way. Bad move, when the other guys have machine guns. They were each shot five or six times."

The foursome at the other table was preparing to leave. Marilou could not help but notice that the small dark-haired woman who held hands with the gray-haired newspaper publisher looked about eighteen. Osterman produced an American Express card, and the tall blond waitress smiled automatically at him as he told her to include her tip in the bill. Marilou waited until the group was gone to resume the conversation.

"Wow. So was there, like, a big investigation, and a trial?"

Mimi Anderson shook her head. "They were never charged," she said. "The cops said they acted in self-defense."

"Amazing," Marilou commented.

"And a year or so before that, we had our very own serial killer. Just brutally ripped apart three women and a man. He was never caught."

"Jesus," said Marilou. "I had no idea."

Mimi nodded gravely. "One of the women he killed was a teacher at the school. You've got her old job now. You're the fifth person, I think, who's had it since Patsy was taken from us. Not counting substitutes."

Marilou did not even look at the plate as the waitress set it in front of her. "You mean to tell me you've had five different English teachers in—what, three years?"

"Not counting substitutes," Mimi Anderson said again.

"What happened to them?" Marilou felt increasingly uncomfortable about the direction this conversation was taking.

"They split," Mimi said, taking a big bite of her sandwich and losing most of an avocado slice out of the side of her mouth.

"Why?"

The big woman dabbed at her face with a napkin. "I dunno—various reasons, I guess. Not everybody can take small-town life."

"Or Donna Hurley, I bet."

Mimi Anderson laughed. "You'll get used to her. She'll thaw a bit, once she feels like you've acknowledged her as the matriarch. She's something of a fossil, but she's okay."

"I'll have to take your word on that," Marilou said.

Her companion laughed again. "You have to remember that she's been here forever, and it's only natural for her to think she runs the place. In many ways, she does."

"What does she do with kids who don't do their homework—boil them in oil and eat them?"

"Come on, she's not that bad. Every small school district has a teacher like that. Get used to it."

"I'll try to," Marilou said.

"You'll do fine," Mimi told her. "I see a certain strength in you, behind all that nervous, youthful uncertainty. I'd like to paint you. I'd like to see if I could capture that look of yours. I get the sense that you've been through some sort of trauma, and that it's made you strong."

Marilou gulped, then took a hasty drink of water to lubricate her suddenly dry throat. The second half of her sandwich lay uneaten on the plate before her. She was no longer hungry. She did, however, want a cigarette, and rather badly. Yes, she thought, recalling Gary's final moments on the beach. Yes, I've seen trauma. You watch someone you love get his head ripped off and I guarantee you'll be a little nervous for a while, too.

But strong? At a new job, in a town full of strangers—and strangeness—Marilou felt anything but strong.

5

Scurvy

The room was built in the 1930s, added to the Annex at Drew Bailey Memorial High School, which served Julian and a handful of other small towns in the mountains northeast of San Diego. It was a Depression-era project, its construction mandated more by the need to employ able-bodied men than by any pressing need for space in a rural area whose population was, at that time, declining. When, some fifteen years later, the school's main building burned down and another rose in its place, the Annex, built as the United States prepared to enter World War I and the last of Julian's once-profitable gold mines were closing down forever, became the oldest structure on the small, picturesque campus. The three rooms in the original part of the building were modernized, one by one—new linoleum floors laid, bigger and thicker windows installed, acoustic ceilings put in to absorb the noise—but the added room never was, making it the oldest unaltered learning space in a high school that dated from the 1880s—old indeed for Southern California.

In its early years, the room was sparingly used—one or two periods a day for something like college-prep math or Latin (which finally fell from the curriculum when the eighty-year-old instructor fell from his mountain porch and into an abbreviated, wheelchair-bound retirement). It was not until the sixties, when families fleeing San Diego and Los Angeles began to swell the area's school-age population, that the room saw anything like regular use. Nonetheless, it had by that time begun to accumulate the base layers of identity, much as the first flows of rainwater down the face of a new slope outline the later shape of the mountain. Teachers came and teachers went, subjects varied, stains accumulated in the carpet, and stacks of books disappeared into the huge closet and were never seen again. Teenagers passed through on their way to adulthood and left missives of their youth scrawled on the room's wooden desks.

It was during the sixties that a teacher arrived in Julian to make the room his own. He was Scott Lurvey; he taught English—with a special fondness for American literature—and in a very short time he became a small-town legend. He was old and eccentric when he arrived from some stuffy prep school in Massachusetts, and he was older and even more eccentric when he checked out some two decades later. By the time Marilou McCormick came on the scene, in the fall of 1992, he was eight years gone, but his personality still dominated the room. None of his replacements, male or female, had lasted long enough to erase it.

Marilou learned of Scott Lurvey through Carl Estabrook, the only teacher on the staff anywhere near her age. After lunch with Mimi Anderson, she decided to get started redecorating the room. Robert had attached a new string to the blinds, and she raised them, sending a cloud of dust into the room. She was annoyed to discover that only one of three sections went up; the strings for the other two were apparently missing also. Robert had simply replaced the first thing he'd found and quit, thinking the job done. Marilou loathed laziness. She reminded herself to prod the janitor, gently but firmly, to finish what she had asked him to start.

The windows, likewise, were in three vertical sections, with fixed grids at top and bottom and a center section, which, in theory at least, swung out. Her annoyance increased upon discovering that the section of window she had uncovered was painted shut. Further investigation revealed that only the middle window worked. She managed to get it open about four inches, though she could not raise the blinds in front of it, and she wondered if she would be able to get it closed. The heavy glass grid hung on its aged hinges at an unintended angle, threatening to fall out. "This place ain't long on maintenance," she muttered.

But at least there was *some* light in the room, and *some* movement in the air, both improvements. The closed blind tapped against the open window and the fan clattered softly above her desk. Marilou determined to make the best of it. A favorite Georgia O'Keeffe painting, reproduced on a poster nearly as tall as she was, went up on the wall by the closet, opposite the authors. On the wall behind her desk she hung a map of the world, color-coded to show the geographical distribution of ethnic and religious populations. Two potted plants took spots on the bookshelf and the table. She had some smaller posters, a series of about a dozen brightly colored art pieces—and if any room ever needed a few splashes of color, she thought, it was this one. But she could find no suitable place for them. She could scatter them at odd spots around the room, or . . .

She took another critical look at the wall of authors. What a dour bunch! And the lineup really was, as she had said to Donna Hurley, the old boys' club. Although she had inherited her father's love of literature, she considered her taste in particular authors more modern. This group was, by and large, the same crew of white men she had been forced to read in high school, not knowing that there was a whole world of equally meritorious if less-recognized literature beyond the edifice of "classics" erected by the American educational establishment. These unsmiling renderings suggested an exclusive club whose membership had not changed in decades. Perhaps, as a small school in a small town, Bailey High was simply behind the curve, but despite Donna Hurley's attitude, Marilou had not come to Julian to perpetuate outdated traditions. Nor was she comfortable with the posters themselves—the lines were too harsh, the eyes black and staring.

"Well, you've got to come down sometime," she said to the group at large. "It might as well be now."

She stepped down off the raised area and dragged one of the student desks over against the wall. Standing on the plastic seat, she could reach all but the very highest posters. Faulkner and Crane would be easy to take down, but she would have to stand on the top of the desk to reach Jack London. Then she would move the desk, and remove Poe, Herman Melville, and Sinclair Lewis, repeating this process all the way down the wall until all the faces were gone.

But the desk was less than sturdy, and as she stretched upward to separate the top corner of the London poster from the wall, she felt it wobble beneath her. And the poster was stubborn. She could not tell if it was glued or taped, or attached to the wall in some other way, but it did not seem to want to come free. She thought about just ripping it, but that would leave crappy-looking remnants behind, and besides, her aim was not to destroy the posters, only to get them out of sight.

The heater came on all of a sudden, and Marilou shot it a look of annoyance. As she did so, her hand slipped. With a cry of pain, she jerked her hand away from the edge of the poster. Her weight shifted—and the desk teetered off balance. Marilou pinwheeled her arms in the air, but it was too late. The desk tipped over, and Marilou landed, hard, on her tailbone.

"Ow! Son of a bitch!"

She looked at her hand. Blood streamed from a gash that ran

halfway across her palm. The blood ran down her arm and onto the sleeve of her dress. Alarmed, she wiped at it with her other hand. Several dark red droplets plopped onto the carpet.

The heater shut off.

"You all right?" said a voice behind her.

Marilou's heart nearly jumped out of her chest. She turned around to see Carl Estabrook step out of the closet and into the main area of the room. He came toward her, but something in her face stopped him.

"Remember me?" said the young history teacher.

"What were you doing hiding in my closet?" Marilou demanded.

"I wasn't hiding. The closet connects our two rooms."

"It does?"

"Yeah. I was coming over to say hello, see how you were doing. I heard you fall. Are you all right?"

Marilou exhaled dramatically. "My hand's bleeding all over the place, my butt hurts, and you just about scared me to death, but other than that, I'm fine," she snapped at him.

"I'm sorry I scared you," he said. "Here, let me help you up."

"I'm fine!" she repeated, ignoring his outstretched arms. With her uncut but blood-smeared hand, she pushed herself up and looked at the cut. It was far worse than the other one. The authors seemed to be leering down at her. She glanced at them once, quickly, then looked away.

"Could you please go get me some tissues?" she asked Carl Estabrook. "For this?" She held up her bleeding hand for him to see.

"Wow, that's really bleeding," he said.

"No shit, Sherlock. Now will you please get me something to clean it up?"

Chastened, the young teacher hurried from the room. He returned quickly with an entire roll of toilet paper. Marilou wrapped a bunch of it around the cut and squeezed. She could feel it throbbing. It hurt a lot more than she let on.

She got to her feet, righted the desk, and replaced it in its row. Redecorating could wait for now, she decided. Apparently, the posters were not going to come down without a fight.

"What happened?" Carl Estabrook asked her, concern outlined on his face.

"Oh, I started to take those posters down, and I guess I cut myself on the edge," she said, still holding her injured hand. "I'll be all right."

"I never saw a paper cut bleed like that," he said.

Marilou hadn't, either, but she wasn't about to play the damsel in distress. "That's some sharp paper," she said. She took her hand away and looked at the bloodied tissue. "There. It's pretty much stopped. That's twice I've done that now. Next time, I'll be more careful. Thanks." She forced a smile.

Carl Estabrook was of medium height but built like an athlete; his movements were graceful and self-possessed. Conservative in haircut and dress, he sported a carefully maintained dark beard, neatly trimmed and shaved away from the places Marilou imagined it did not come in quite fully enough. His eyes were hazel and alert, intelligent yet soft. Marilou thought him altogether an attractive man, the sort of which her father would approve. But it was nothing more than an observation.

"I'm sorry I startled you," he said again.

"That's okay. It's not your fault I didn't know about the closet."

"Taking Scurvy's posters down, are you?"

"Scurvy? Who's Scurvy?"

"The correct question," Carl Estabrook said, "is 'Who *was* Scurvy?' Scurvy taught English in this classroom for something like twenty years. I had him when I was a student, and so did all my older brothers."

"You're from here?"

"Yep. So's my mom, and her parents. Three generations of

Julianites." He leaned against the front of her large desk and continued talking. Marilou learned that he had graduated from Bailey in 1984, which made him her senior by only a year. He had gone down the hill to San Diego State, done his student teaching, and come right back home, where his mother lived three houses away and most of his high school teachers were now his colleagues. He was beginning his fourth year of employment at the school.

"It's strange," he said, "But this room has hardly changed at all from the way I remember it—when Scurvy taught here."

"Tell me about this Scurvy," she said. "Why'd you call him that?"

"His name was Scott Lurvey," Estabrook said. "Scott Lurvey, Scurvy. It just evolved. Everyone called him that. Behind his back, of course."

"What was he like?"

"He was a weird old coot," Estabrook said, looking up at the high ceiling and laughing softly to himself. "Most of us were in awe of him. He had this shock of white hair, which he hardly ever cut or combed, and one strand of it used to fall down in front of his face like this." He tugged at a lock of his own short hair, forcing it down toward his eyebrows. "It made him look almost demented. He was a big man—tall, broad-shouldered, definitely a presence. He treated each class like a performance. He'd stalk around this stage here, acting out actual scenes from the books we were reading. Sometimes he'd assume the role of a character, and he'd teach the whole class in that role. He did Tom Joad one day, I remember, when we were reading *The Grapes of Wrath. . . .*"

"Depressing book," Marilou put in.

"Yeah, well, it was one of Scurvy's favorites. We'd just read the part where Joad kills a guy at one of the migrant camps. He hits him with a shovel over and over until he dies. Scurvy was up here with a yardstick, slamming it on this desk as if it were the victim's head, and yelling at us, challenging us to argue that the killing was wrong. He broke the yardstick, as I recall."

"He sounds like a lunatic," Marilou said.

The young history teacher grinned. "He *was* pretty dramatic," he said. "Sometimes he'd do characters, and other times he'd do the authors themselves. He'd talk to the class as if *he* were John Steinbeck, Jack London, Herman Melville, or whoever. He'd yell at us for not appreciating his work, whoever he happened to be at the moment. He intimidated a lot of kids. But he challenged us, too. Made us think. And if you made a good point, he'd praise you for it. All in all, he was a hell of a teacher. You were never bored in one of Scurvy's classes."

"So these are his posters, then?" Marilou nodded at the wall of authors.

"Yeah. They've been here for eons."

"Actually," she said, "they can't have been here before 1968."

"How do you know that?"

"Because that's when Steinbeck died. And the date is on the poster. Salinger's is the only blank date. Of the rest, Steinbeck's death is the most recent."

"That's pretty observant of you," Carl Estabrook observed. "Scurvy especially loved Steinbeck. Jack London, too, and Hemingway—hell, I guess he loved them all. 'The giants of American literature,' he called them. He was always singing the praises of American authors. He thought the Brits were too stuffy and old-fashioned."

"Is he . . ."

"Yeah, Mary Lou. He's dead."

"Too bad. He sounds like an interesting man to know."

"He kicked off during my senior year. We came back from spring vacation, and he was gone."

"How did he die?"

"Who knows? Heart attack, I think. He was old. It wasn't

really talked about, at least not by the other teachers. Times have changed. We just came back from break, and Ms. Hurley was in this room instead of Scurvy. We missed him, but life went on."

"Wait a minute. Ms. Hurley had this room?"

"Yeah. After Scurvy died, she took over his classes for the last part of my senior year, and she moved her own classes in here, as well."

"Why'd she give it up?"

Carl turned his palms upward. "Don't know," he said. "You'll have to ask her, if you're curious. She might tell you. Then again, she might not."

"Not very friendly, is she?" Marilou said.

"She just takes a little getting used to. She's been here an awfully long time, and she's seen a lot of teachers come and go. Give her a year or two to warm up to you."

He slid off the desk and moved toward the closet. "Well, I'll let you get cleaned up," he said. "Tomorrow it begins. Another school year. May it be an interesting one. I'm looking forward to working with you, Mary Lou."

"Just Lou," she said without thinking.

"Beg pardon?"

"It's Marilou—one word, small *l*," she told him. "But my friends call me Lou."

He smiled at her from the closet entrance. "Lou it is, then," he said. "I'll see you later."

"Bye, Carl."

I must really miss my father, she thought. Her hand continued to throb, gently but painfully, under the toilet paper.

"Watch your step in this closet," Estabrook added, now out of sight. "It's awfully dark in here."

6

The First Day of School

The school bus crested Cigarette Hill at the moment of sunrise, and the driver was instantly blinded. Cyrus "Moondog" Nygerski lifted his foot from the gas pedal and let the empty bus coast downhill at sixty-five miles an hour, thankful that the road was straight. On either side of the two-lane highway, away from the glare, knee-high forests of cholla cacti, deceptive in their fuzzy appearance, caught the day's first sunlight, and the contours of the parched hills stood out in stark relief.

Nygerski opened a box next to his seat and pulled out his watch. He was going to be a good fifteen minutes early arriving at his first stop, the tiny desert community of Palm Spring, the easternmost outpost of the Julian school district, nearly forty miles from the school itself. The little hamlet was seldom confused with the more famous resort city to the north—aside from the missing *s* at the end of its name, it lacked swimming pools, golf courses, and anyone as famous as Sonny Bono or Gerald Ford. The town was so small that it did not appear on most maps; it consisted of a campground, a café, and perhaps two dozen weatherworn shelters. Moondog didn't mind being early—it was the first day of school, and the extra time would allow him a cup of coffee at the café and a chance for some small talk with the waitress, the owners' cute twenty-four-year-old daughter, who was already beginning to fret that life had passed her by.

An early Neil Young album thundered from the four speakers Moondog had installed along the sides of the bus; he'd hooked up the tape deck himself, under the dash. In the box was an assortment of tapes he carried to play for the kids: some AC/DC and Alice in Chains for when they behaved, a Billy Graham sermon and some John Lennon/Yoko Ono feedback-and-screaming stuff for when they did not. Armed with these, a thermos of coffee, a bag of trail mix, and a map of his route, he'd set out from the school in semidarkness half an hour ago; the entire circuitous route would take him nearly two hours to complete. He'd done it in an hour and a half in practice, with Doug, but that had been without kids, and he'd allowed himself to be drawn into an impromptu race with a hay truck that had left the big Indian white-faced—no easy accomplishment.

"I think I'm going to like this job," he told the waitress, whose name was Olive. He'd met her at infrequent stops at the café over the years on his way to and from Mexico; they had a casual, conversational relationship. "It's been a long time since I've worked. At any real sort of job, I mean."

"Welcome to reality," the waitress said. "At least you'll be able to sleep in on the weekends. I have to be here seven days a week." Her name was incongruous, for the girl was blond, and despite living in the desert, she looked somewhat washed-out. She served coffee and doughnuts to a handful of regulars, old-time desert rats with skin the color and texture of well-worn leather. Moondog gathered from the indifference with which she served them that they were here every day and had become part of the place's sparse decor. For him, however, she managed a wan smile. She hung over his coffee cup after filling it, obviously eager to talk.

"It's all right," he replied. "I like the mornings. I like the feeling of having a head start on the day."

"You must have to get up awfully early," she said.

"About five," he replied. "I'm on the road before it's even light."

"Just you and the Moon, huh?"

Her casual comment brought Moondog up short, though he was careful not to show her a reaction. The Moon, in fact, had not been up this morning, for it was in the waxing half of its cycle, rising and setting after the Sun, emerging larger and later each afternoon. Moondog kept close track of the phases of the Moon, with good reason.

For Cyrus "Moondog" Nygerski was not your ordinary school bus driver. Unpublished novelist, sporadic newspaper columnist, former Hollywood stuntman, baseball player, dope smuggler, and rock musician, Nygerski also harbored a terrible secret, and had for three years. Though economic necessity had forced him to take the job, he knew he was putting himself in peril, and quite possibly endangering the lives of the area's unsuspecting residents, as well.

"I'm trying to talk my boss into letting me take the bus home at night," he said to Olive. "That's what *he* does with *his* bus. That way, I wouldn't have to drive to the school first, switch vehicles and all that. It'll help a lot when the days get shorter. But he says he's gotta get the board's approval." Moondog took a sip of coffee. "Ah well, as Ted Kennedy once said, we'll fall off that bridge when we come to it."

Olive looked at him quizzically, a half smile on her thin, pale lips, and Moondog realized that she had been born right around the year of the incident to which his joke referred. The generation gap, he thought sourly. Getting old. He shrugged, then drank off the rest of his coffee.

"Your passengers are gathering," Olive said, nodding at the window. "I don't envy you, with that bunch."

Moondog followed her gaze, and he saw that half a dozen teenagers had assembled near the bus in the gravel parking lot. The community of Palm Spring was everywhere within shouting distance of itself; the café and its parking lot were the one central meeting place. The arrival of the school bus had doubtlessly alerted the entire settlement. Two boys playfully pushed each other; a girl preened in the big side mirror by the driver's window.

"I'll be fine," Moondog said as he got up to go. He left her a two-dollar bill for the seventy-five-cent cup of coffee and was rewarded with a smile and a wish for good luck.

But there were no behavior problems on this first morning's ride; Moondog introduced himself to the students at each stop, turned the music to moderate volume, and enjoyed the drive through the high desert as the kids enjoyed one another and the expectations of a new school year. He drove down through Shelter Valley and Scissors Crossing, up the long, leisurely grade past San Felipe, out of the desert and into the scrub trees on the fringes of Ranchita, past the cattlefields around Lake Henshaw, and down the long slope into Santa Ysabel, where he again turned toward the Sun for the final climb to Julian. Most of the stores were still closed when he wheeled the bus through town, but the women in the window of the Apple Pie Bakery were hard at work rolling crusts, a storeowner hosed down a patch of sidewalk, and a few early breakfasters could be seen on the deck of Mariah's. At the far end of town, the bus passed several students making their way to school on foot, their backpacks slung over their shoulders.

His was the last of three buses to arrive. The parking lot swelled with kids. Moondog maneuvered the bus slowly among them as he eased toward his designated unloading spot, at the far end of the main building. Some of the kids leaned out the open windows to greet classmates. Two girls in identical black miniskirt outfits walked by, laughing and oblivious, in front of the rolling bus; a kid with a Mohawk haircut and a school letter jacket ran after them. One of the boys in the back of the bus called out to the two girls. The Mohawk turned around and gave him the finger.

"Schoo-ool daze," Moondog sang softly to himself as he turned the wheel. "When life is worth living."

Marilou McCormick had just finished a cup of coffee in the teachers' lounge and was headed, briefcase in hand, out the back door of the main building, bound for the Annex and her classroom. As Moondog nosed the bus into its parking space, the Sun suddenly flashed into his eyes from the gap between the gym and the agricultural building, and for the second time that morning he was momentarily blinded. "Look out!" someone yelled from outside the bus. Moondog caught a flash of red and hit the brakes. The tires yelped in protest, and some of the kids who had already stood up were pitched forward down the aisle or onto the backs of the seats in front of them. A puff of bluish smoke rose from beneath the hood; a moment later, Moondog realized that an astonishingly beautiful woman was standing in front of the bus, glaring at him through the windshield.

"Fuck, man! You tryin' to hurt somebody?" cried a high-pitched voice from the back.

"Open the damn door, Moondog!" yelled another kid.

"Yeah, let us outta here!"

She glared at him for perhaps five seconds, but to Moondog, it seemed much longer. His passengers squeezed toward the front of the bus, but he did not open the door. The woman's ice blue stare held him captive.

"Come on, dude, let us out."

The Sun was behind her, and when she turned on her heel and tossed her hair back, its redness again caught the light. Moondog watched her stalk purposefully off toward the Annex. She didn't look back once.

"Damn," he said softly. "Who was that?"

"I never saw her before," said the kid closest to the door.

"Me either," said the kid next to him. "Open the door already."

There were mice in the closet.

Robert could hear them scurrying around in there as he unlocked the door to room 13, and when he found the switch that lit the closet's single hanging bulb, he saw their droppings around the bases of the bookshelves. He wondered if the school kept mousetraps among its supplies.

The closet was huge, and it was filled from floor to ceiling with books. Most of them were paperbacks, and for each title, there were at least thirty copies. Some of them, like *The Adventures of Huckleberry Finn* and *Moby-Dick,* he recognized from his own school days, but that had been more than thirty years ago, and he hadn't given their contents a second thought since then. There were more copies of *The Old Man and the Sea,* as well as another thin volume, titled, ironically, *Of Mice and Men.* Many more of the titles were utterly unfamiliar to him. Farther back in the closet, near the steps that led down to Carl Estabrook's classroom, the shelves held a few dusty hardcovers, old dictionaries, old yearbooks, and science and history texts that Robert guessed had been stored in here years ago and forgotten.

He retrieved a dustpan and broom from his closet in the hall, cleaned up the droppings, and then scanned the room itself for any messes that might have been left by mice or other visitors. There were none; the room was as clean as he had left it the day before. He did notice the plants, the Georgia O'Keeffe poster, and the map of the world, which hadn't been there yesterday. One of the map's top corners had come loose and hung down, obscuring Alaska and most of Canada from view. Robert found a roll of Scotch tape and reaffixed it to the wall.

He wandered over to the gallery of authors, picked out

Ernest Hemingway, and began reading the short paragraph next to the scowling face. Robert had made good progress on *The Old Man and the Sea* the previous evening, even though he was a slow reader and his wife had found frequent excuses to interrupt him. He remembered with amusement his wife's reaction to his sudden interest in the book. Was it jealousy? Or just petulance that the routine had changed? She had never seen him absorbed in a book during their entire marriage, and Robert supposed that a little suspicion at his unusual behavior was to be expected.

He was still looking at the Hemingway poster when the heater kicked on. Robert jumped backward, startled. The room would not receive direct sunlight until late afternoon, but this was September. There would be no need for heat in the classrooms for at least another month. Puzzled, Robert checked the thermostat on the opposite wall and saw that it was turned all the way down. He frowned, then looked up at the spinning fan above the teacher's desk. It seemed to be spinning crookedly, dipping to one side and then the other, like an airplane waving to someone on the ground.

A minute later, the heater shut off, and the room felt no warmer. Robert made a mental note to mention it to Doug; then he went off to check the other classrooms.

The teachers began arriving shortly before eight o'clock. Marilou McCormick passed him in the hall, said, "Hi," and kept on walking. Carl Estabrook lugged a desk out of his room, pointed out a piece of blackened gum wedded to the plastic seat, and asked Robert if he could remove it. As he attacked the hardened wad with putty knife and sandpaper, Donna Hurley passed by without a word, glancing down at him as if considering similar projects.

A five-minute warning bell rang, and suddenly the hall was full of kids. They streamed past him, some in western dude clothing, some with strange haircuts featuring bare spots in many of the wrong places, some sporting the bright-colored garb of the surf set at the beach, fifty miles away. To Robert, they all looked impossibly young, much younger than he thought teenagers used to look. Especially the girls. A few of them wore outfits that were quite revealing, and Robert tried hard not to stare.

The kids took little notice of him as he kept working away at the gum. Estabrook and Hurley appeared at the doors of their classrooms, and some of the kids began to drift inside. Others popped back and forth between the hall and the front steps, chased one another, and yelled insults and good-natured banter. Spirits were high; there was quite a bit of noise. One amorous couple leaned against a wall, kissing open-mouthed as their schoolmates passed inches away, unperturbed by the public display of affection. Times had changed a great deal, Robert thought, since his own high school days, when such things had been done in the woods, not in the hall.

Robert finished sanding the spot where the gum had been, placed the desk just inside Carl Estabrook's door, and acknowledged the teacher's thanks with a smile and a little nod. Then the final bell rang and the hall emptied. A moment later, Steve Dakota's voice floated over the public-address system. Robert heard it in stereo, from the classrooms on either side of him.

"Good morning, everyone," the superintendent said. "And welcome back."

Dakota led the student body through the Pledge of Allegiance, which was followed by several announcements concerning school rules—no loud music in the parking lot, no smoking in the bathrooms, hall pass needed from the office if a student is late, et cetera. "And finally," Dakota's disembodied voice proclaimed, "I'd like to extend a warm welcome to the new members of our staff. Ms. Marilou McCormick, our new English teacher; Robert Rickard, our new custodian up in the Annex; and Cyrus Nygerski, our new bus driver. We're glad to have you with us, and we hope you have a wonderful year."

* * *

For Marilou McCormick, the first day was largely an exercise in remembering names. Her classes were large—four of her five class lists contained more than two dozen names—and today they were all strangers.

Her day began with freshman English, a required course for all ninth graders. Second period was an American literature survey course taken by mostly sophomores, some juniors, and two or three seniors who'd put off getting that last English credit they needed to graduate. Third period was free—she could use that time to prepare for other classes, sit in the teachers' lounge and drink coffee, read, or whatever. The other half of the freshman class filled the room for fourth period. After lunch came English III, essentially a follow-up to the American literature course, in which a few British and foreign-language writers (whose works had been translated into English) managed to crack the lineup. And finally, remedial reading. Marilou thought it a poor bit of scheduling to put this class at the end of the day—she would get the less-gifted kids after they'd been through a rigorous gauntlet of wood shop, phys ed, and agricultural classes, and their thoughts would be more on the outdoors and that afternoon's impending freedom than on their own tenuous literacy. It would depend on the kids, of course, but even before she met them, Marilou anticipated a certain degree of difficulty.

She had no idea what form it would take, however, until the massive bulk of Richie Marks shambled into her sixth-period class, took a seat in the front row, and stared at her like a puppy.

He didn't do anything else the whole period. He just sat there and stared. He was one of the largest human beings Marilou had ever encountered at close range. He had to be at least six and a half feet tall, and close to three hundred pounds—most of it muscle. She later found out that he played in the line on the football team and could usually protect the quarterback all by himself, unless he had to run. But though his size was imposing, there was no malevolence at all in his face, which was that of a child. But his eyes never left her, and after half an hour or so, she began to find the relentlessness of his gaze unsettling. She hadn't even seen him blink. The other kids shifted in their seats, looked at the clock, at the posters, at the tops of their desks, and at one another. Richie just stared.

Marilou didn't take much notice of the small, dark, fish-eyed boy seated directly behind Richie until the bell signaled the end of the first day of school, a day that after the fencelessness of summer vacation must have seemed interminable, especially to remedial readers. All but two of the kids grabbed their books and belongings as quickly as they could and bolted for the door.

Richie didn't move. The boy behind him stood up, stopped, and tapped Richie on the shoulder. "Come on," he said. Richie showed no reaction. Then, to Marilou's astonishment, the smaller boy hauled off and whacked Richie across the side of the head with his open hand. In the vacated room, it sounded like a gunshot. Marilou stepped quickly to the front of the raised area, ready to intervene.

But Richie looked more hurt than angry. He looked, in fact, as if he was about to cry. "Ow, Kyle!" he whined, turning around. "Whadja do that for?"

"It's time to go, you big lunkhead," the smaller boy said, exasperated, as though he'd been waiting for Richie to move for thirty minutes instead of thirty seconds. "Didn't ya hear the bell?"

"Sure. Course I heared it."

"Let's go, then," the smaller boy said. "We got a bus to catch. What are ya waitin' for?"

A hint of puzzlement crossed Richie's face, as if the complexity of the question confused him. "I was . . . I was jest thinkin'," he said. "That's all. Jest thinkin'."

"Ha! You ain't had a thought in your whole life! At least not one you could remember five minutes after havin' it. Come on."

The mountainous boy slowly raised himself to his feet, his squarish head with its too-big ears and close-cropped curly hair lolling atop a neck thicker than it was long. He shuffled toward the door, his friend behind him.

"Just a minute, boys," Marilou called out. She stepped down off the raised area and walked over to them. The smaller boy, the one named Kyle, was only small in comparison—he was fully as tall as she was. His eyes darted away from hers and back again.

"Don't strike another student in my classroom again," she said to him.

"It don't hurt 'im," Kyle said defiantly, his prominent Adam's apple bobbing up and down. He was constructed much differently than his friend—thin, long-necked, all sharp angles and jerky birdlike movements. "He's used to it."

"I don't care what you do after you leave here," she said. "But in my classroom, you are not to hit him. You are not to hit anyone. Are we clear on that?"

"Aw," Kyle said, looking at the carpet. "It don't mean nuthin'."

"Are we clear on that?" she repeated.

"Yes, ma'am," Kyle mumbled, still looking down.

Marilou glanced over at Richie and saw that he was still staring at her. His puppylike expression had not changed. She thought of saying something to him, then changed her mind.

"Good," she said to Kyle. "I'll see you boys tomorrow."

She turned and walked back to her desk. Kyle gently tugged at Richie's sleeve; failing to get the bigger boy's attention, he yanked on it harder. "Come on," he said. "Come on, ya big baby. Let's get outta here."

7

September Moon

In America's high schools, September is a crucial month. If the school year is a baseball game, September is the first swing through the batting order. Patterns are established early, and if you see a curve on a 3-2 count the first time up, you're likely to see it again when the game is on the line. Student cliques, which may admit new members in the early fall, will be impenetrable by Thanksgiving, and the kids who draw detention in September will still be sitting there in April. New romances are born, teachers subconsciously select favorites and scapegoats, and battle lines between various social groups are sketched, if not fully drawn, all on the basis of that first month's impressions.

For a new teacher, first impressions are doubly important. Unencumbered by a reputation, Marilou McCormick set about making the strange classroom she had inherited her own. On occasion, this meant getting tough with a few potential troublemakers. Much of it, she had encountered before and expected—the gossipy groups of girls, the pock-faced boy who called her

"Babe," the paper-airplane aviators and graffiti artists, the teenage hoodlum, whom she reported to the vice principal for making repeated lewd remarks in class. All this she chalked up to normal teenage misbehavior. But some things about Julian, Bailey Memorial High, and room 13 were different.

Robert had fixed the other two blinds with some old twine he'd found in the supply shed, explaining that he'd been able to locate only the one legitimate string. The twine was rough on her hands and bent on circling up the wall and tangling with the blinds themselves. The makeshift strings were a pain in the butt and not likely to last long, but she had asked Robert to put through a request for new ones.

It had taken her less than a day to notice the school's lack of ethnic diversity. The high school was at least 90 percent white; most of the remaining kids had Native American or Hispanic genes. There were no Asians at all, and as far as Marilou could tell, there was exactly one black student in the entire school.

His name was Jim Green, and he was one of the four seniors in her second-period American literature class. He was well over six feet tall, and Marilou guessed, with a twinge of guilt at her own racial stereotyping, that he starred on the school basketball team. Like the mountainous Richie Marks, he, too, had an inseparable friend, a skinny little sophomore named Phelps Gayle, who was as short and loquacious as Jim was tall and silent. The Greens must have moved to Julian from somewhere in the Deep South, Marilou thought, for on those infrequent occasions when Jim spoke in class, he did so in an almost incomprehensible dialect that called to mind slaves and cotton picking. Phelps, for his part, called the older boy "nigger" in an offhand, not unfriendly manner that Marilou found jarring.

There were other oddities. A pretty girl, obviously five or six months pregnant, sat every day in the front row of her second literature class, after lunch, and made no effort in either dress or manner to disguise her condition. Marilou admired her automatically—she knew that girls who got knocked up still frequently dropped out. But she also noticed that the girl paid polite attention in class but volunteered nothing, not even an occasional question. And she did not talk to any of the other students, nor they to her.

There was a boy in her second freshman English class who seemed unusually jumpy and afraid of everything, especially her. He sat every day in the desk nearest the door, and he was always the first to escape.

And Richie and Kyle continued to be a source of trouble. Twice more, she reprimanded Kyle for striking the larger boy; both times, Kyle was utterly unrepentant. "See, Ms. McCormick," he told her, his Adam's apple bobbing up and down like the needle on a seismograph, "he's my cousin. An', as you can tell, he ain't too bright. Nothin' but a big baby, really. I'm just tryin' to keep him outta trouble."

"You'll be in trouble the next time I see you hit him," Marilou said, and by the end of the week, Kyle had separated her from her first detention slip.

The disciplinarian at Bailey High, she soon discovered, was the vice principal, Bill Oates, a sandy-haired, granite-hard former Navy SEAL whom the kids, inevitably but not without awe, called "Wild Bill." She disliked him instantly, as she did most military men, but by the end of the week, she was grateful for his presence.

It also took less than a week for Carl Estabrook to ask her out, to a Saturday-night show at the Cedar Mountain Inn, the dinner theater a few miles from town. She turned him down as gently as she could. He really wasn't her type, either, and the night at Pismo Beach was still fresh in her memory. She wasn't up to dating yet.

But when Saturday night arrived and the full Moon rose above the mountains, she felt restless and lonely, and she found herself wishing she'd accepted his invitation. Though she felt little physical attraction to him, he had been friendly and polite, and in a town full of strangers, that counted for something. And she suspected that her father was right about the outlaws she chose for boyfriends. Her past, she told herself, not her future. In Julian, she had no reputation to ruin. Things could be different here. *She* could be different.

With such thoughts, she fought the urge to drive into town and make an appearance at one of the two bars along Main Street, where she knew she could amuse herself watching local toughs compete for her attention. She was getting too old, she told herself, for such dangerous sport. Was it simply loneliness that made her so restless? she wondered. Or something more serious, some fundamental emptiness that she dared not examine too closely and thus disguised with liaisons that diverted her attention and did not last? She poured herself a glass of wine and sipped it as she paced the main room of her cozy little dwelling, feeling small and very much alone. The phone was there on the small bar that separated the kitchen area from the living room. She picked it up and dialed her father's number. She got his answering machine, then hung up without leaving a message.

Unable to relax, she decided to go out for a walk. The night was clear, and the full Moon illuminated the trees and fields around her. The big house next door was dark; her landlord and his Hollywood friends were not at the Julian retreat this weekend. She walked across the sloping meadow behind her cabin, down toward the tiny pond that lay there, hidden by a grove of coastal oaks and a few scattered pines. There were no human noises save her own soft footsteps on the grass, but the air was alive with the sound of crickets, and she could hear the low song of the bullfrogs from the pond. Everything was bathed in moonlight. She had no trouble finding the path through the trees that led down to the pond—more like a bog, really, and no bigger than her living room. Finding a fallen tree trunk, she sat down to listen to the ambient noises of the woods and to admire the play of moonlight on the cattails, lily pads, and the small pool of open water.

What have I done? she thought. She missed the beach, the nightlife, her childhood friends, her father. She had never felt more alone.

Suddenly, from far off in the distance, came the howl of an animal. Her skin prickled; she drew her unzipped jacket tightly around herself, though the night was quite warm. A wolf, she thought. Her heart fluttered high in her chest. No, another part of her brain answered. There are no wolves in California. But it didn't sound like a coyote. Other plaintive voices joined the chorus. Marilou shivered involuntarily and looked nervously around her at the play of shadows among the trees.

"Time to go now, Lou," she said aloud, getting to her feet. "Time to go home." And she walked briskly back through the woods and across the field to her house, where she locked and bolted the door behind her, then poured herself another glass of wine. She had been enjoying the noises of the night, but now she turned on the radio. Eventually, she took both bottle and glass to her bedside table and got under the covers with her latest mystery novel. The radio played softly, and she heard no more howls. Even so, it was hours before she slept.

Robert Rickard was also awake, unable to sleep because of the full Moon. He sat out on the couch in front of the turned-off television, listening to his wife toss and turn in the bedroom as he methodically plowed through the last half of *The Old Man and the Sea*.

His son, Jimmy, wasn't home. The wayward manchild was, in fact, not far from Marilou's house, using the light of the Moon and the assistance of two hoodlum friends to remove an expensive stereo and two televisions from a large vacation home. The owners had insurance but no alarm system, and the job went off without a hitch.

Cyrus Nygerski was not seen anywhere in or around Julian that night, or the following night, when the Moon was still full. But no one kept track of Moondog's whereabouts. And that was just the way he liked it.

Robert returned the book on Monday morning. He had established a routine of cleaning room 13 first, right after putting up the flags and disposing of any obvious disasters in the parking lot. He wanted the room to look good when Marilou first set eyes on it, and she seemed always to be the first teacher to arrive. *She* always looked good. Robert tried to pass her in the hall at least once during his shift, to exchange a quick hello and to see what she was wearing and how she had styled her flaming hair. She usually had a smile for him, and he invariably felt that odd little tingle as she walked by.

But this morning, she was disturbed. "Come in," she said mechanically as he rapped softly on the wood, holding the book in his other hand. She was looking up at the Georgia O'Keeffe poster on the wall by the closet and frowning. "Robert, how did this happen?" she asked him.

He looked at the poster and saw that it had been marred by a big splotch of reddish brown stuff, as though someone had thrown paint at it. "I don't know," he said, feeling stupid.

"Has anyone been in here besides you?"

"Not that I know of." He stepped closer to her and examined the poster. The brown spot was the size of a grapefruit, with spatters radiating outward. The stuff was thick and had dried in lumps; the poster had crinkled slightly around it. And the color looked exactly like . . .

"It looks like blood," Marilou said. "Dried blood. Doesn't it?"

"Well . . . yeah, I guess it does, sort of," Robert said. "But it's gotta be something else. Like . . . like one of those catsup packets or something."

The heater behind Marilou's desk made a coughing sound.

Marilou looked at the heater, then back at Robert. Then she reached up and tore the poster off the wall.

"Well, in any case, it's ruined," she said, crumpling it into a big ball. She walked to the trash can beside her desk and stuffed it in. "I think somebody must have gotten in here over the weekend and done a little creative vandalism. Jerks."

Robert moved toward the raised area. "You need to water these plants more," he said, noticing the drooping brown leaves.

"I've watered those plants every day since I brought them in here," Marilou said. "They're still dying. I don't know what it is. Not enough light, maybe. It's frustrating."

"Here," Robert said, holding out the copy of *The Old Man and the Sea* to her. "I finished it."

Her severe expression softened. "Good for you," she said. "Did you like it?"

"Oh yeah, it was great." He placed the book on the corner of her desk. "I was glad he still had the skeleton of the fish when he got to shore. So the people in the village knew he really caught it."

"Yeah, well, people have read a lot of symbolism into that book." She was at the blackboard now, writing out the week's assignments in chalk. "Really, it's just a halfway-decent fish story. My freshmen are reading it."

"I ain't much of a reader," Robert admitted. "I don't think I've really read a book since high school. And that's nearly forty years ago now."

"Well, it's never too late to start," Marilou said.

"I was looking at the back cover," Robert said, hoping to prolong the conversation. "It talks about how Hemingway killed himself."

"Shot himself in the head," Marilou affirmed, still writing.

"What makes a guy like that kill himself?" Robert said. "I mean, he was a famous writer. He had it made. And he was only sixty-one. He had everything."

"Maybe he couldn't stand the thought of growing old," Marilou suggested. She stopped writing on the board and turned to face him. "He was a very robust man, very athletic, into the outdoors, fishing and hunting—active things. He was very physical—he related to the world in a physical way. And maybe when he saw his body beginning to deteriorate, he couldn't take it."

"But he was such a great writer. He could've written more books."

"Well, some people think he was great. My father likes him a lot. I think he's pretty overrated. There are a lot of better writers who died in obscurity."

"I just think it's a tragedy," Robert said.

"Every suicide is a tragedy," Marilou replied softly.

"But it's worse when you're Ernest Hemingway, or somebody important," Robert insisted. "Just as it's a worse crime to kill a John Kennedy, or a John Lennon even, than it is to take out some punk in some street gang. Killing anyone is bad, but—"

He stopped abruptly, surprised at his own words. This kind of critical thinking was utterly foreign to him. Where had it come from? The book? The room? The young teacher? She was smiling at him, a different smile from those he'd seen before, her lips closed and one side of her mouth raised higher than the other. "You're making a rather profound ethical statement, Robert," she said to him.

"I am?"

"You're saying that some lives are more valuable than others."

"Well . . . they are," he said, confusion creeping in.

"Don't you think there's potential in every life?"

"Well, sure. But it's . . . it's what you do with that potential that counts, isn't it?"

"Is it?" She still had that odd (and ungodly attractive) smile on her face, and Robert realized that she was enjoying herself.

For a moment, he wished he could ask her out to lunch and that they could sit and talk about such things at leisure, his brooms and his washrags stowed somewhere and forgotten. Of course, it was better as a wish than it could ever be as reality—he was, after all, twice her age, and he knew that in fifteen minutes he would have difficulty holding up his end of the conversation. She had been to college and was every bit the professional; he was a high school dropout who had spent his life picking up trash and painting white lines on the freeway. He wasn't in her league and he knew it. He wasn't even in the high minors.

Choosing his words carefully, he said, "I'm not saying that Ernest Hemingway, or any other famous person, was *born* better than the rest of us. It's what he *did* that makes him special. If he hadn't written books, he'd be just another guy who blew his brains out, and me and you would've never heard of him."

"And that would make his death less of a tragedy—that you and I had never heard of him?"

"I dunno. But . . ."

"For every Ernest Hemingway, there are thousands of people who aren't famous, who kill themselves out of the same kind of despair. And in a way, aren't their stories even more tragic? Hemingway at least left his books. Most people leave nothing."

"But think of what else he could've written, if he'd lived."

"We'll never know, will we?" Marilou said, and turned back to the board.

"No," Robert said, feeling dismissed. He could hear people beginning to fill the hall. "No, I guess we never will."

During the first two class periods, Marilou noticed that a good number of her students—perhaps one-fourth of each class—were absent. As she walked to the main building at the start of third period for her break, she found out why.

The bus came barreling into the parking lot, its tape deck blasting something by one of the grunge bands popular with the MTV generation. Marilou hurried to the side of the parking lot as the bus screeched to a stop in front of her. The engine and the music shut off, and a moment later, kids poured off the bus, hustling in all directions to make their third-period classes.

Marilou waited by the back of the main building until the driver emerged. She had seen Moondog around the school, usually at the beginning or the end of the day, usually from a distance. He had not impressed her as anything more than an aging ex-hippie who probably still smoked pot and listened to old Joe Cocker records. On one occasion, she had seen him leaving the parking lot at lunchtime in a pickup truck as old as he was, driving too fast through a crowd of milling students.

Today, she was shocked at how disheveled he looked. He hadn't shaved, and his long hair had not been combed. One of the sleeves of his denim jacket had sustained a large rip near the shoulder. A particle of some kind of food hung off of one end of his thick handlebar mustache.

"Hi," she said. "You're awfully late."

"Yeah, I know." His eyes were bloodshot, the dilated pupils nearly swallowing the dark irises.

"Big night?" she asked.

The bus driver shook his head. His eyes looked beyond her. "I don't remember," he said.

"Is that why you're so reckless with that bus? You look hungover out of your mind. That's the second time you've almost run me over."

"I'm sorry about that," he said, flashing a slight grin. "I guess I've been meaning to say hello."

"With a bus?"

Nygerski shrugged and looked down at the ground. "I don't drink," he said, "at least not to excess. I have a couple of beers sometimes. So, no, I'm not hungover."

"Then how come you're two hours late?"

He looked back up at her and studied her face for a moment

before answering. "It's kind of hard to explain," he said. "Listen, I don't think we've been formally introduced. I'm . . ."

"Cyrus Nygerski," she finished for him. "A name like that is hard to forget."

"My friends call me Moondog," he said, grinning again.

"Marilou McCormick. Mine call me Lou."

They clasped hands briefly. "Does that mean we're friends?" he asked.

"Maybe," she said, and nodded at the bus. "As long as you keep that oversized phallic symbol away from me."

His grin widened. "A chick with a sense of humor," he said. "I like that."

Over Moondog's shoulder, she saw the vice principal emerge from the side door of the main building. He strutted toward the bus. "Here comes Oates," she warned him. "And I don't think he's laughing. It looks like you've got some explaining to do. Excuse me."

She walked quickly to the building's back door and slipped inside, resisting the urge to look back.

8

Robert's Dream

That night, Robert had the strangest dream of his life. In the dream, he was back in room 13. It was early morning, and he seemed to be alone in the building.

He was over by the authors' wall with the carpet sweeper, running it back and forth, when he heard a noise from across the room. He looked up and saw a man step out of the closet.

The man was tall, broad-shouldered, white-haired, and bearded, dressed in a plaid flannel shirt, blue jeans, and heavy black boots. He seemed to be smiling.

"Hello, Robert," he said, his voice deep and full.

The carpet sweeper in Robert's hand stopped moving. Robert stared at the unexpected visitor. He noticed that the Georgia O'Keeffe poster, unblemished, was back on the wall by the closet, and that the plants were healthy and green. The bearded man stared back at him. "How did you get in here?" Robert asked.

"I live here," the man said.

Robert stared at him and said nothing.

"Don't you recognize me, Robert?" The man spoke softly, but his rich baritone resonated in the stillness of the room. "I've been watching you. We've all been watching you." The man nodded at the posters on the wall behind the janitor.

Robert's eyes followed his. They were met by the unmoving eyes of the unsmiling portraits. All looked the same as they always had. Except . . .

Except Hemingway was gone. Robert recoiled in shock, dropping the handle of the carpet sweeper. The words were still in the corner of the poster, but the pen-and-ink face had disappeared, leaving nothing but empty space.

He turned around. "You're . . . you're . . ."

"That's right, Robert," the man said, chuckling. "I'm Ernest Hemingway."

Robert's lips moved noiselessly for several seconds before he was able to speak. "Y—you can't be!" he sputtered. "Ernest Hemingway's dead! He killed him—"

"That's right, bucko," the big man rejoined, his grin broadening. "I took my old shotgun out of the shed, sat down, and blew my fucking head right off! How's that for grace under pressure?"

"What?" Robert said, too stupefied to say anything else.

"At least it was a manly way to go, don't you think? Better than rotting away in the chemical stink of a hospital."

"What do you want?" Robert managed to ask.

"A happy ending," the visitor said. "Or, at the very least, a satisfactory one."

"What?" Robert said again.

"Mr. Lurvey is lonely, Robert. And she's so very, very pretty." Hemingway looked meaningfully over at the teacher's desk.

Robert felt a knife blade of fear stab his heart. "You leave her alone!" he cried.

Hemingway laughed from deep in his belly. "Don't meddle in things you don't understand, Robert. She is not yours, you know. She belongs to Mr. Lurvey. He has already expressed his desire for her. And we intend to take her to him." His eyes swept the pantheon of authors.

"But you're *dead!*" Robert shouted at him. "You're *all* dead! This is all pure bald-headed *nonsense!*"

Robert cut off his protest abruptly when he saw the gun. From somewhere behind him, Hemingway had produced what looked like an old-fashioned six-shooter. He twirled it once around his finger. Then, as Robert watched in horror, he held the gun to his whitened temple, stroking the trigger almost lovingly. He looked at Robert and chuckled.

"Authors never die," he said. "Don't you know that? We're immortal."

He pulled the trigger. The room exploded in sound and blood.

The blast tore at Robert's eardrums and shook the blinds and windows. The slug ripped away half of Ernest Hemingway's head. Blood and brains spattered the Georgia O'Keeffe poster on the wall behind him, the carpet at his feet, and several of the nearby desks. Blood poured from the gruesome, gaping wound, soaking the flannel shirt and jeans, splashing off the top of the boots onto the floor. As he watched the explosion of gore soak the carpet, Robert thought wildly, That's going to be hell to clean up.

Incredibly, Hemingway was still standing, and still laughing. Blood ran into his open mouth and dripped off his beard. The apparition did not seem bothered in the least that half his head was missing.

"See? I told you," said the bloodied but unbowed figure of Ernest Hemingway. "Authors never die."

Robert swallowed hard, unable to take his eyes off the horrific animated corpse in front of him.

"I know she wants to get rid of us, Robert. You can't let her."

"It's her room," Robert said weakly.

"No, it is *not!*" Hemingway bellowed, the side of his jaw flapping crazily where the bullet had torn away the flesh. "It's Mr.

Lurvey's room! She's welcome to stay—in fact, he *wants* her to stay. But she's going to have to accept the fact that it's *his* room. She's going to have to accept *us*." Hemingway's expression—what could be seen of it beyond the gore—had turned grim. He pointed the pistol at Robert. "We could use your help," he said.

Robert's eyes widened. "No!" he cried, backing toward the wall of windows, visually measuring the distance to the door and the time it would take to get there. Hemingway followed Robert with the gun.

"Help us or die," the dead author said.

"No!" Robert screamed again, and he dived behind a desk in the back row. Another report rocked the room. The bullet crashed through the window behind them. As soon as he heard the shot, Robert was on his feet again, propelling himself, low to the ground like a fullback, toward the alcove and the safety of the hall. A second bullet ripped into the wood of the door frame as Robert ran from the room—and he woke up, shaking in terror.

His wife lay undisturbed beside him. The Moon, now past full but still fat and brilliant, shone in on the bed through the unshaded window. It was 2:30; he did not fall back to sleep for the remainder of the night.

The first thing Robert did when he arrived for work the next morning was to check room 13. He flipped on the light and looked at the authors. Hemingway's face peered seriously out from its poster as it always had. A few wadded-up pieces of paper lay around the edges of the room; Robert gathered them up quickly and deposited them in the trash can by Marilou's desk. There were some gum wrappers and pencil shavings here and there, as well as bits of dried yet aromatic dirt brought in on the boots of the agriculture students. Robert went to put up the flags and police the parking lot before returning to the room with the carpet sweeper, happy that his horrific vision of the night before had been only a dream.

He whistled softly as he worked, moving the desks out of the way, row by row, so that he could run the sweeper over the entire floor. In the other rooms, he used a big broad dust mop, for their floors were waxed linoleum, easy to clean. But in room 13, the floor would never be entirely clean until the carpet was replaced, an expense the tightfisted school board had yet to authorize. There were many stains; once a uniform green, it now resembled a camouflage suit. However, Robert did not remember the large and especially dark stain by the row of desks nearest the closet. He frowned. Had somebody spilled a Coke there? He bent down to touch the darkened area. It was dry. The stain looked as if it had been there forever.

Robert flashed back to his dream. Had not Hemingway been standing on this very spot? Robert remembered vividly the image of the man's head exploding, of blood flowing freely onto the floor, spattering the nearby desks and wrecking the poster (exactly as it in fact *had* been wrecked, the day before). But the desks were clean, except for a few lines of graffiti, which he quickly wiped away with his rag and spray bottle. Perhaps he'd simply never noticed the stain. Its link to his nightmare was probably nothing more than a trick on the part of his subconscious mind.

But as he was leaving the room, his spray bottle tucked under one arm and the handle of the carpet sweeper in his opposite hand, Robert made a second startling discovery. A piece of wood, about the size of his thumb, had been splintered off the inside of the door frame. The carpet sweeper clanged to the floor. The gouge in the wood was at eye level, and new—the bare wood stood out brightly against the dulled dark paint, and the edges of the break were sharp and unworn. Robert knew it had not been there yesterday. And the damage was at the exact spot where, in his dream, Hemingway's last bullet had hit, barely missing him as he had escaped the room. But Robert was not dreaming now. This was real, this hole in the door frame, as real as the fear Robert felt as he ran his finger along its ragged edge.

He found the missing piece of wood on the floor at his feet, hard up against the base of the wall, where he had missed it with the carpet sweeper. Though the wood had been smashed, he could still fit it roughly back into place.

Slowly, and glancing involuntarily once or twice in the direction of the closet, half-expecting Hemingway to reappear, Robert moved over to the wall of windows. He wondered now why he hadn't raised the blinds. It wasn't that he didn't trust his own repair job—the thought of raising the blinds had simply not occurred to him. Strange. He raised them now, though the middle section did not go up without resistance. And in that middle section, in one of the fixed lower panes, was a small round hole that could only have been made by a bullet.

Behind him, the heater at the other end of the room suddenly roared into life. Robert jumped, breaking off the piece of twine as he jerked his hand away. The blinds clattered down over the window. Completely unnerved, he grabbed the carpet sweeper and spray bottle and ran from the room.

"Robert! What's the matter?"

Had the voice been a rich male baritone, and had it come from the room behind him, Robert surely would have screamed. But this voice was female, and Robert looked down the hall, to see Marilou McCormick, a good ten minutes earlier than usual, approaching him, carrying a leafy green houseplant fully half her height.

"What happened?" she said as she drew near to him. "You look like you've just seen a ghost."

Perhaps I have, Robert thought, and felt a shudder he hoped she didn't see. She had stopped beside him, her back erect, her lively and lovely eyes looking into his from beneath her hair, which today she wore slightly differently, having drawn it back from the top of her head into a single braid, leaving the bangs to dangle. A pair of wide silver hoops hung from her ears; she wore little makeup, artfully applied. Robert noted anew how pretty she was, and some of his fear faded.

"It's nothing," he managed. "That big heater came on all of a sudden, and it startled me, that's all."

"Yeah, that heater's weird," she said. "It seems to have a mind of its own."

"I've also gotta fix the blinds again," he said. "My repair job broke."

He followed her back into the room, remembering that he had left his washrag in there somewhere. The heater had fallen silent. He watched her as she set her briefcase down on her desk, positioned the plant on the floor near the other wall, and walked purposefully into the closet, where the books were stored.

"I wish there was more light in this closet," she called after him. He could hear her rummaging around among the bookshelves. "Do you think you can get me a brighter bulb?"

"I'll ask Doug about it," he said, loudly enough for her to hear him in there. "Maybe we can hook up another fixture or something."

"That'd be nice. It's hard to—"

Suddenly, Marilou screamed, a short burst of alarm. Robert stiffened, then moved swiftly to the entrance of the closet. Marilou came out half-running, her face white, the paperback books in her arms dropping all around her. One foot caught an upturned edge of the carpet, and she pitched toward him. Robert caught her as she fell. The rest of the books went flying. Her hands gripped his forearms, hard. Had he not been there, she would have fallen on her face.

"Are you all right?" he asked. It was all he could think of to say.

She nodded, looking at the books scattered on the floor, and took a step away from him. Then she abruptly burst out laughing.

"I'm sorry," she said. "God, I'm an idiot. There was a mouse in there—a really big one. And he bared his teeth at me, as if he was going to attack."

She smoothed her skirt in what Robert took for a nervous gesture. "I'm *not* afraid of mice, if that's what you're wondering," she told him. "But this one startled me. He was so . . . so fierce-looking. Usually, they run away."

"Maybe there's something wrong with it," Robert suggested. "Maybe it's sick or something. I'll see if—"

But at that moment, the heater came on again, and they both started. Robert noticed the soft but persistent metallic whine, clearly audible behind the rush of air.

"I'll see if we have any mousetraps," he finished. "And I'll check them first thing in the morning, so you don't have to find any dead bodies. Or maybe I can lay out some poison, if we ain't got mousetraps."

"Robert, really, don't go to all that trouble," she said. "I'm not worried about a few mice. There are probably mice all through this building. They don't bother anyone. This one just startled me, that's all."

The heater shut off. Marilou knelt down to pick up the books.

"Here, let me help you with that," Robert said.

He squatted down to gather the paperbacks nearest his feet. There were perhaps two dozen copies of the same book, a thin volume titled *The Call of the Wild*. The cover featured the head of a snarling wolf, with a full Moon and a sled-dog team in the background.

"What is this?" Robert mused, holding one of the books in his hand. "A werewolf story?"

The look Marilou shot him was stone-cold. "What on Earth makes you say that?" she said. There was no more laughter in her voice at all.

Robert registered that his question had made her angry, or at least tense. "I dunno," he said defensively. "There was a werewolf movie on the tube last weekend—my wife was watching it. I watched a little of it with her. And there's the full Moon. . . ." He showed her the cover.

"It's not a werewolf story," she snapped. "It's about a domestic dog who's kidnapped and sent to the Arctic to work as a sled dog. Eventually, he becomes wild and joins a wolf pack. My freshman are going to begin reading it next week. It's got nothing to do with werewolves at all."

"Oh." They finished picking up the books in silence, but Robert kept glancing at the provocative cover. The author's name was Jack London; Robert recognized it from the wall. He realized that he very much wanted to read the book. What's happening to me? he thought.

They placed the books on the table at the rear of the raised area; when Marilou went back into the closet to get more, Robert quietly slipped one into the back pocket of his jeans. He should have asked, he knew, but her mouth was drawn into a thin and severe line that discouraged conversation. He saw that the map behind the table had sustained a rip that ran from the North Pole to a spot between Iceland and Greenland, and he wondered if she had noticed it yet.

Then he remembered the other poster, and his dream. "Mr. Lurvey is lonely," the bloody Hemingway thing had said to him. "And she's so very, very pretty."

She was indeed, and Robert found himself thinking about her at odd moments during the day—when he was out by the buses having a smoke, or splitting firewood behind his house, or driving to the store for beer. Maybe that was why he had had the dream—that and the book. But where had the other thing come from?

It was time to clean the other classrooms. He picked up his washrag from a desk near the door and paused to look at her once more before leaving.

"Who's Mr. Lurvey?" he asked her.

Marilou, standing at her desk beneath the silent heater,

looked at him indifferently from behind her open briefcase. "He was a teacher here, in this room," she said. "Many years ago. He's dead now. But he was quite a teacher, I'm told. A real inspiration. Why do you ask?"

"Someone mentioned him to me," Robert replied. He felt cold. "I was just curious."

Robert caught up with Doug at the beginning of third period, when he went out behind the gym, where the buses parked, for a smoke break. His boss was hosing down the outside of his bus in a pair of black rubber boots that came up to his knees. Seated on an overturned bucket against the wall, sipping from a can of V-8 juice, was Cyrus "Moondog" Nygerski. Moondog had cleaned up since his tardy appearance the day before, but he still looked a little pale, and his eyes stared straight ahead, seemingly at nothing.

"Robert!" Doug greeted him. "What's up?"

"Well, I think there may be a problem in room thirteen," he said, stepping between puddles as he approached.

"What kind of problem?" the Indian asked.

Robert lit his cigarette and threw the match into the nearest puddle. Nygerski waved his hand at the cloud of smoke. "Man, how can you smoke those things at your age?"

Robert shot him a look of annoyance. "What's it to you?" he snapped.

"Don't you know what they do to your body?"

Robert took a long, satisfying drag and exhaled slowly. "Yeah, and it's my body. Won't last forever, anyway."

"What's the problem, Robert?" asked Doug.

"Well, there's a bullet hole, it looks like, in one of the windows."

Doug walked to the front of the bus, hose in hand, and sprayed down the grille. A long-handled squeegee mop was propped against the chain-link fence that ran outward from the corner of the gym; a bucket of soapsuds stood beside it. "When," he said, not looking at Robert, "did you first notice this?"

"Just this morning."

Doug went on hosing down the bus.

"Thirteen," Nygerski said to nobody in particular. "*Bad* number for a classroom."

"Robert," Doug said, "that bullet hole has been there for years."

"It has?" Robert felt his face redden.

"You fix the blinds?" Doug asked him.

"Yeah. You told me to."

"You ever washed those windows?"

"No."

"You ever even really looked at 'em closely?"

"No, not really."

"So how do you know whether that hole got there yesterday or ten years ago?"

Robert watched the water splash off a hubcap. "I guess I don't," he said. "But . . ."

"But what?" Doug asked when Robert didn't continue.

Robert hesitated. It would be stupid to tell Doug about his dream, he decided, especially with Nygerski right there listening in. They would dismiss him as a fool. Which, he thought, perhaps he was.

"There's other things wrong with the room, too," he said.

"Like what?"

"Well, there're mice in the closet. And the heater don't work right—it comes on when it's turned off, and it don't sound healthy."

Doug moved around to the other side of the bus. "Anything else?"

Robert followed to stay within earshot. "Little things. A chip out of the door frame. Stains in the carpet . . ."

"That carpet needs to be replaced," Doug said. "It needed to be replaced when I first took this job, eight years ago. Hey, Moondog, turn off the water, will ya?"

Nygerski got slowly to his feet, walked over to the outside faucet with the hose attached, and turned the handle. "Is that the new teacher's room?" he asked Robert.

"Yeah."

"Shit," Doug said, "there've been so many teachers in that room the past few years, I've lost track of 'em."

"It's kind of gloomy in there," Robert said. "Spooky, almost."

"Spooky, Robert?" Doug chuckled as he curled up the hose. Robert decided to give up trying to get Doug to take a look at the room. He was clearly getting nowhere.

"I've got a feeling about that girl," Moondog said. "I don't think she's the type who spooks easily."

9

Trouble with Jim

Trouble with Jim Green, the only black among the approximately two hundred students at Bailey Memorial High, was the last thing Marilou McCormick wanted. But by the beginning of the third week of school, she realized it was unavoidable.

"Any of you have Jim Green in class?" she asked during a lull in conversation in the teachers' lounge one day after lunch. Carl Estabrook was there, as were Alan Doucette, the science teacher, Bob Hommel, who ran the computer lab, and Donna Hurley.

Marilou found the small teachers' lounge a place of trepidation. For one thing, it was the only place on the entire campus where smoking was permitted, and Marilou still felt the pull of temptation. For another, the janitors didn't expend much energy on the teachers' lounge—the teachers were, after all, grown men and women capable of cleaning up after themselves. But in Marilou's observation, her colleagues were worse slobs than her students. The lounge was always a mess. Cups with cigarette butts stewing in day-old coffee, haphazardly stacked newspapers, old magazines, and dog-eared books littered the tables and countertops. Crumbs and pieces of uneaten doughnuts and sandwiches attracted various forms of insect life. The trash cans were emptied only when they threatened to erupt onto the floor. Still, it was the one place where she could talk freely with her colleagues, away from the interference of students or administrators. On many days, the dry land of adult conversation was a welcome shore in the sea of adolescence that surrounded her.

"Had him in bio last year," Alan Doucette volunteered. He was a tall, trim man of about forty-five, his dark hair thinning on top and graying at the temples. He wore wire-rimmed glasses and a lab coat and looked almost stereotypically like what he was: a high school science teacher. He was also a heavy smoker, and the worst offender at leaving butts in inappropriate places, like the bottoms of coffee cups.

"What was he like?" she asked him.

"Pretty good student," Doucette said.

"Heck of a basketball player, too," Bob Hommel put in. He was older and thicker than Doucette, and he had been at the school for some fifteen years. "Not a bad wide receiver, either. Too bad we don't have a quarterback who can throw." Hommel, in addition to his teaching duties, was also the assistant football coach.

"Think you guys'll win a game this year?" Doucette needled him. "That game against Del Mar Academy was pretty brutal."

"Oh, we'll beat the Adventists," Hommel assured him. "Even in thin years, we always beat them. They spend more time in church than in practice."

"Did he say much in class?" Marilou asked anxiously. There was little time left in the lunch hour, and she did not want to spend it discussing the misfortunes of the football team.

"Not a lot," the science teacher recalled. "He was very polite and attentive, but kind of shy. Tried like hell not to stand out, which I guess is understandable. But he never gave me any trouble, and he did the work. Not brilliantly, but he passed all the tests and turned in assignments on time. I think I gave him a *B, B* minus, maybe."

"Is there a problem, Lou?" Carl Estabrook asked.

"Well, yeah," she said. "It's him and his little friend, that Phelps Gayle. I suppose they think they're being funny. . . . That Phelps has quite a little mouth on him. It's 'nigger this' and 'nigger that' all the time . . . right in front of the whole class. And Jim . . . well, whenever he does speak up, which isn't often, he talks in this ridiculous slave dialect. It's quite a little act. I know they're just putting me on, but it's annoying."

"That doesn't sound like Jim at all," Bob Hommel said.

"No, it doesn't," Carl Estabrook agreed. "He's a pretty serious kid, pretty straightforward. At least he's always been that way with me."

"Have you talked to them?" Alan Doucette asked.

"I've said a few things. But I haven't really confronted them. I guess I thought if I ignored it long enough, they'd stop doing it. They haven't."

"How do the other students react?" Donna Hurley asked. She had been sitting quietly, nibbling an egg salad sandwich, listening to the conversation.

"That's another thing," Marilou said. "They just sit there, like nothing out of the ordinary is going on. I mean, you'd expect them to laugh, or *something*. But they act as if hearing this black kid talk like a whipped slave from Alabama is the most natural thing in the world, like they're all in on the joke."

"I see." The older woman nodded, and one corner of her mouth twitched upward in the barest hint of a smile. Stop the presses, Marilou thought.

"You don't seem surprised," she remarked.

Donna Hurley rose from the table, leaving her half-eaten sandwich on the napkin in front of her. "After twenty-five years,

Marilou, not very much surprises me." To the group, she said, "I've got to go set up a videotape for my next class. We're watching the first half of *Macbeth*."

Carl Estabrook quoted in a dramatic voice: " 'Macduff was from his mother's womb / Untimely ripped.' "

Donna Hurley stopped just inside the door. "You did learn something in my class after all, Carl," she said. Without waiting for a reply, she opened the door and disappeared into the hall.

"Correct me if I'm wrong, but that sounded like a joke," Marilou said.

Estabrook laughed. "I told you she's not so bad. She'll warm up, once she sees you're going to stay awhile."

"What're you going to do about Jim and Phelps?" Bob Hommel asked.

Marilou sighed. "I don't know," she said. "If it keeps up, I'll have to have a talk with them about it. God knows what they'll say."

Alan Doucette lit a cigarette. The smell hit Marilou's nostrils and made her want one. "It still doesn't sound like Jim," the science teacher said. "What do you suppose has gotten into him?"

"Beats me," Bob Hommel mused. "He seems like a real good kid. Anything but a wise-ass."

"Maybe," Carl Estabrook volunteered, "he's got a crush on you, Lou. Maybe this is his weird, awkward, adolescent way of expressing it."

"Oh, come on." Marilou felt her face redden.

"Why not? You know, you and I aren't that much older than these kids. I've had girls bat their eyelashes at me and make some pretty strange remarks. You know what teenage boys are like."

"He's probably wondering if you've got knees," Doucette mumbled. "No one here's ever seen 'em."

Carl Estabrook laughed, and Marilou forced a smile. She

could tell that the useful part of the conversation was over. And she wasn't about to change her modest style of dress, no matter how much her fellow teachers teased her. Her job was hard enough without deliberately adding distractions.

On the day after this discussion, Marilou went to the office, looked at Jim Green's class schedule, and sought out all his current teachers. They gave her similar reports: that he was a reserved but attentive student, competent but unspectacular, unfailingly well-mannered. She found out that his father had a private chiropractic practice in Julian, his office built onto the family home, and that his mother worked as a receptionist for County Health Services in Ramona. He had three younger sisters, the first of whom would be a freshman next year. They apparently were a California family; there was no mention of an origin in the southeastern United States, or anywhere else. They were a nice middle-class family, and despite their minority status, they seemed to be fairly well accepted in the community.

But the trouble with Jim Green persisted, until it became too annoying to ignore.

The American literature class was reading *The Grapes of Wrath,* a five-hundred-page requirement Marilou couldn't get out of the way too quickly. For if there was an American author she disliked more than Hemingway, it was surely Steinbeck, with his vision of a hardscrabble, unforgiving world dominated by taciturn, inarticulate men. Part of it, she knew, was bias—growing up in San Luis Obispo, she had been Steinbecked to death during her own high school years. In college, a classmate from Vermont had told her that the same sort of regional pride, force-fed to him in school, had left him incapable of enjoying the poems of Robert Frost. "Two roads diverged in a wood," he had been fond of saying, "and I took the one that led the hell away from New England."

The class was in the midst of a discussion on the character of

Jim Casy, the Okie preacher who befriends the Joads and travels with them to California. Jim, as usual, sat quietly in the back of the room, next to Phelps Gayle, his inseparable buddy. As a girl near the front explained her theory that Casy's self-proclaimed role as a "retired" preacher served to reinforce the book's theme of loss—of land, heritage, friends and family, and, as illustrated through Casy, religious values—Marilou saw Jim lean over to Phelps and whisper something.

"Jim," she called, when the girl had finished, "you seem to have an opinion. Why don't you share it with the rest of the class? What do *you* think is the significance of Casy's role in the story?"

The tall black boy looked at his shoes, as he often did when her eyes were on him.

"We're waiting," she said after several seconds of silence.

"I don't reckon I knows," Jim mumbled, still looking down.

"Go on, Jim," Phelps urged. "Tell her what you jest tol' me." This, too, was a pattern; Jim often would not speak until Phelps prodded him.

"If it's good enough for Phelps to hear, it's good enough for the rest of us," Marilou said.

"Come on, Jim," Phelps said. "Spit it out."

"Well," the black youth began slowly, "I's thinkin' as I read dat bit bout Casy goin' off in de wids, en ponderin' things en all . . . I's thinkin', ain't dat jes' what Jesus did, afore dey kilt 'im? En den I thinks, he's got de same name almost. Got de same inishuls—J.C. En if dere's one thing dem poor people needs, it's a feller t' come lead 'em to de promis' lan', like Jesus. So mebbe Jim Casy is s'posed to be Him."

This was the longest speech Jim Green had ever delivered in her class, and Marilou would have expected a normal bunch of kids to be convulsed with laughter, or at least snickering among themselves. But there was barely a smile in the entire classroom. Jim and Phelps had apparently let the whole class in on the joke. It had to be a joke. Nobody talked that way anymore, except as a put-on. And she had been put on long enough.

"That's very interesting, Jim," she said as evenly as possible. "And I'd like to speak with you privately after class, if you don't mind. Does anybody else have any thoughts on Jim Casy as a Christ figure?"

When the bell rang, Jim Green remained at his desk, head bowed. Phelps Gayle remained seated also as the other students crowded through the door.

"I didn't ask you to stay after class, Phelps," Marilou said.

"Jim stays, I stay," the white boy replied. Marilou noticed a good-sized rip in his Mettalica T-shirt and a smudge of dirt streaked diagonally across one cheek. She didn't think that either the rip or the smudge had been there when the class had begun, but how could he have acquired them sitting at his desk? Her mind, she decided, was simply playing tricks on her.

"I'd like to speak with Jim alone, please."

"What for? He ain't done nuthin'."

"I'd like to speak with him alone. You can wait for him in the hall."

"Whatever you got to tell my man Jim, you can tell me, too. I ain't leavin' him git in trouble for nuthin' he didn't do."

She fought the urge to correct his butchered grammar, then sighed. "All right," she said. "Come up here, both of you."

When they were standing in front of her desk, Jim looking down and Phelps defiantly meeting her eyes with his own, she said, "I want you to drop the game. It's gone far enough."

The two boys exchanged a quick glance, and Phelps's eyes returned to hers. "What do you mean, Ms. McCormick?" he asked, all innocence.

"You know exactly what I mean. The master-slave act. The ridiculous dialect. Jim, if you want to be a comedian, do it in the parking lot, not in my classroom. Is that clear?"

Jim looked at his shoes. Phelps said, "Aw, Ms. McCormick, that ain't fair. He can't help the way he talks. He talks that way natural. All niggers do."

"That's another thing," she said, keeping her voice calm. "I find that word offensive, even when you use it in a friendly way. I know Jim is your friend. You can talk that way between yourselves, when you're not in class. Keep that language out of this room. There will be a detention the next time I hear it."

The two boys fell silent. Two students, looking for help with an assignment during her free period, poked their heads in the door. "I'll be through here in a minute," she said to them. "Please wait out in the hall."

She turned her attention back to her class cutups. "Jim, you haven't said a word. You seemed to have quite a bit to say in class, though."

The black youth shrugged and continued to stare at the floor.

"Look, I'm not stupid," she told them, no longer able to keep the anger out of her voice. "I'm new here, and I guess you've decided to have a little fun with me. I guess you've got the rest of the class involved, too. Okay, you've had your fun. The game's over, as of right now. If it continues, you boys are going to find yourselves staying after school on a regular basis until it stops. Is that clear?"

"I still don't know why you're after Jim," Phelps mumbled. "He ain't done nuthin'."

"Would you like me to give you a detention right now?"

"No, ma'am."

"Then drop it." She clenched her teeth; frustration boiled within her.

"How about you, Jim?" she asked the tall, silent youth.

He looked up at her, his eyes dark saucers. "Ma'am?"

"Is it clear?"

"Scuze me, ma'am?"

Marilou stood up and bit down on her lower lip hard enough to draw blood. She flung open her top drawer, grabbed the pad of detention slips, and slapped it down atop the desk. The pen sliced through the pink paper in places as she scrawled their names and the identical reason for punishment—insubordination—on both. "All right," she hissed as she shoved a slip into the hand of each boy. "We'll see how you like staying after school for the next three days. And if it doesn't stop, you can have three days after that!"

Phelps rolled his eyes at the ceiling; Jim just stood there, blinking.

"Get out of here, both of you."

The two unrepentant boys left the room. Marilou sat back down at her desk and took two deep breaths. The two kids who had been waiting in the hall shuffled in, and she forced herself to smile at them. She stole a glance at her hands, underneath the desk. They were shaking, and she couldn't make them stop.

10

The Foul Ball

Cyrus "Moondog" Nygerski kept his past from close scrutiny. Originally from Back East, he had lived on five secluded acres in Mesa Grande for the past seven years, writing occasional columns for the *Julian Nugget* and other small publications and living off the money he'd made smuggling marijuana up from Mexico and as a stuntman in Hollywood. Too old now for either of those high-risk occupations, Moondog spent much of his time writing novels and trying in vain to interest a publisher. Though he had few expenses—he owned his property free and clear and drove a beat-up old pickup truck and an old Yamaha motorcycle he'd won betting against the Red Sox in the 1990 playoffs against Oakland—Nygerski had found it necessary to take a real job, though it cut quite sharply into his cherished anonymity.

For Bailey Memorial High was a center of social activity, where names and faces became stories, and lives inevitably intertwined. It was perhaps inevitable as well that Moondog would make his entry into the strange story of room 13 through the school's baseball field. At one time, baseball had been his life.

Young Cyrus Nygerski had been one of the top high school prospects to come out of New England in the mid-sixties. A left-handed second baseman with cat-quick reflexes who could occasionally hit for power, he had been recruited by half a dozen major-league teams. The Chicago White Sox had offered him a modest signing bonus and a chance to see the American Midwest. A year of minor-league ball against stiffer competition than he'd ever seen had convinced him that his future lay elsewhere, but the years had not dampened his affinity for the game.

Because Moondog kept his senses attuned to what was going on around him, he knew that Julian was a baseball town. He knew that the high school team regularly challenged for regional championships, and he knew of the informal adult baseball league that played its games on the high school field. He observed the pickup games that took place there on an almost-daily basis.

Time hangs heavy for a school bus driver during the middle of the day, while the passengers are in class. Moondog spent these long hours in a variety of ways. There was routine maintenance to do on his bus, of course, and sometimes Doug enlisted his help on various campus projects, such as moving chairs and tables around in the library before a school-board meeting or chalking the lines on the football field. But on other days, he was free to retreat to the tiny Julian Library and write, or to walk in the graveyard overlooking the town, or to linger over an extended brunch at Mariah's, or to find a secluded sunny spot to read a book. Much of the time, however, he hung out with Doug and Robert by the bus parking area, helping out with small tasks and shooting the shit as the shortening days passed.

During one of these idle mornings, after watching Moondog whack golf-ball-size rocks over the chain-link fence with a broken broom handle for most of an hour, Doug suggested that they make use of the deserted baseball field.

"Stuff's in the gym," Doug said, jangling the big ring of keys he always carried. There were at least two dozen keys on it. "In the equipment room—in the basement. Gloves, bats, balls. You coming, Robert?"

Robert looked up from his book. It was fourth period, maybe half an hour before lunch. Robert was done for the day, but he'd told Moondog and Doug he preferred to hang around for a while than to go home to face his unemployed son and the pile of dishes the boy had surely left unwashed from the night before. The janitor got up and followed them.

They surprised three boys in the below-ground area by the basement entrance to the gym, strategically out of sight of the other buildings. One of them quickly snuffed out the joint they had been passing and covered it with his sneaker, but he was holding in a hit and there was no concealing what they'd been up to. Moondog recognized the kid from his bus route; Doug seemed to know them all.

"What's the matter with you assholes?" the Indian demanded. "Ain't you even got the sense to use the woods? Why aren't you boys in class, anyway?"

"Come on, Doug, cut us a break," said the smallest of the three, a dark, beady-eyed boy who blinked rapidly and couldn't seem to stop looking all around, as if they hadn't already been busted. "It's too nice out to be cooped up in that dark room."

"Where are you supposed to be right now?" Doug asked him.

"English. Ms. McCormick's room. Christ, that room gives me the creeps. It's like a morgue."

"And how about you two?"

The tall red-haired boy coughed, expelling a cloud of marijuana smoke. "PE," he said. "We're s'posed to be doin' laps around the football field. It *sucks.*" He looked down at his shoe, with the evidence underneath it, and quickly looked away.

"Hey, we could use a few players," Moondog said to Doug.

"Players for what?" asked the red-haired kid, eager to seize upon a distraction.

Moondog cocked an invisible bat and took a phantom swing.

"I hate baseball," declared the third kid. It was easy to see why—he was chunky and sort of geeky-looking, with black plastic Woody Allen glasses that had slid to the end of his wide nose and would probably fall off halfway to first base if he ever put the ball in play. He had acne and bad hair, shiny and black, that hung over his forehead. The red-haired kid at least had height, and an absence of excess weight—he was, in fact, skinny to the point of scrawniness. Moondog could see right away that they were no athletes. Kids with ability in sports did not skip physical education. Making them chase down fly balls seemed to him an appropriate punishment for their truancy and drug use.

"It's either baseball or the principal's office," Moondog said.

"Aw, man!" the chunky kid cried, not happy with either choice.

"Quit your whining, Raymond," Doug told him. "You're getting off easy. We'll make you catcher, so you won't have to run."

In the equipment room, they located baseballs, two batting helmets, a catcher's mask and chest protector, several aluminum bats, and an old wooden one Moondog insisted upon using. They found gloves for each of them, though the only left-handed one was a first baseman's mitt, its big scoop webbing coming loose on the thumb side. "Hell of a glove for a second baseman," Moondog grumbled. "These places never have the right equipment. Future stars hobbled, just because of their left-handedness. It's a crime."

Ballfield bound, the three adults and their juvenile charges ran into Carl Estabrook in the parking lot, on his way from the Annex to the main building. The young teacher questioned why the boys were not in class, but Doug disarmed him with an invitation to join the game, which Estabrook quickly accepted.

The baseball field was at the front of the school, on the far side of the tennis courts. It was big for a high school field. The third-base line, in front of the visiting team's dugout and the main section of stands, paralleled the highway. Left field went on forever, ending only at a row of trees in the distance, where the road curved on its way toward town. The first-base line pointed to a steep embankment, at the top of which the campus ended and the woods began. These trees were much closer than the ones in left. The Annex, at the foot of the embankment, sat well back from the field. Marilou McCormick's classroom was the closest part of the building to the playing field, though it lay well into foul territory and a good distance from home plate.

The field itself was in miserable shape. Not a blade of grass grew anywhere in the infield, and that which managed to survive in the outfield did so in clumps, a situation that invited bad hops and twisted ankles. Only in spring, during the high school team's season, was the field ever really maintained—the infield raked for large rocks, the outfield regularly watered. The football field, at the other end of campus, was in equally bad condition, and the school rotated its underfunded campus maintenance in keeping with the athletic season at hand. Though the field was used by the Little League, the informal adult league, and the public at large, the school district did not maintain it for them.

"I'll pitch," Doug said when they reached the field.

"Second base is mine," Moondog said.

The others arrayed themselves at various positions and took turns batting. The quality of play was poor—the three kids booted grounders, misjudged fly balls, and whiffed at many of Doug's easily hittable pitches. But Robert managed first well enough, and Carl Estabrook, playing third base, shortstop, and short left field, made a few plays. Nobody managed to get a hit through the middle, because Moondog Nygerski sucked up anything hit anywhere near him.

Doug was impressed. "I never saw a lefty play second before," he said. "I didn't think it was possible."

"It's prejudice," Moondog replied, laughing. "A bunch of right supremacist nonsense."

"You're pretty good with the glove," Doug acknowledged. "Let's see how you hit."

Nygerski stepped into the left-handed batter's box and waved the wooden bat. Estabrook took over at second; Doug told the boys in the outfield to move around toward right. Moondog swung the bat easily back and forth, looking at the trees atop the embankment.

Doug laughed. "I've been here eight years, and I've only seen two people hit the ball over that bank. It's a lot harder than it looks, buddy."

"Show me what you got," Moondog replied.

Doug threw him a fastball. With an alarmed squeak, the young catcher ducked out of the way. Doug had been throwing easily to the other batters, and the speed of the pitch took Moondog by surprise. He did not swing. The ball hit the chain-link backstop and rolled back out past home plate.

"Oh, we're gonna be *serious,*" Moondog said, picking up the ball and tossing it back to Doug.

"I been pitching since high school," Doug said, laughing good-naturedly. "Too fast for you?"

"You kidding? Throw me that shit again."

The catcher cowered tremulously behind home plate as Moondog readied himself for Doug's next offering. Moondog swung but undercut the ball slightly, sending a fly ball out into center field. The red-haired kid looked up, ran in a few steps, then backpedaled hurriedly, too late. The ball dropped onto the grass behind him.

"In a real game," Doug said, "that would've been an out."

"In a real game, I wouldn't have swung," Moondog shot back. "It was about a foot outside."

"Bet you can't hit my curveball," Doug said, bending to retrieve the bouncing throw from the outfield.

"Try me."

It was a lousy curve. Even the kids in single-A ball, all those years ago, had boasted better breaking stuff. It hung up around his eyes, big as a grapefruit. Moondog stepped back as the ball broke lazily in on him, and he sent a towering drive into deep right field.

Nobody even made an attempt to run after it. They just watched it go. Raymond, the catcher, stood up behind home plate and took off his mask. "Whoa," he said. "You got all of that one, dude."

But Moondog had, in fact, gotten too much of it. For as they watched, the ball began to hook, slightly at first and then more dramatically, into foul territory. Doug turned around on the pitcher's mound and watched the ball sail away from home-run land toward the end of the Annex. Moondog dropped the bat; Doug's shoulders sagged as the tremendous blast went foul. And then, in the distance, they heard the unmistakable sound of breaking glass.

"Uh-oh," Doug said. "I think the game just ended."

Marilou McCormick was in midsentence when the ball crashed through the window. The lecture on Jack London, like the author's life, came to a sudden and premature conclusion.

The ball took out the lowest pane in the corner of the window nearest the authors' wall. It bounced three times on the carpet before coming to rest near the back wall. The door to the hallway was open, and a sudden wave of mountain air rushed through the room.

In that first second of startled silence, the poster nearest the window, Mark Twain, tore free from the wall. The wind wedged it into the jagged hole in the window. It crackled there, struggling to get free—the flapping of the dry, decades-old paper every bit as loud as the breaking of the glass a moment earlier.

One of the freshmen in the back row got up and attempted to retrieve it, but he was too late. The poster flapped madly against the broken glass. The kid drew his hand away with a surprised cry of anguish; Marilou saw that his fingers were already red with blood. Impaled on the glass spear, the uncharacteristically stern face of Mark Twain ripped in half and sailed out the window, and then the two pieces of the poster were gone, borne away on the brisk autumn breeze.

Delayed commotion broke out in the room. One kid grabbed the ball and threw it to his buddy in the front row. He threw it halfway back and across the room to another kid, and the game of catch was on.

"All right! Everybody sit down!" Marilou shouted above the din. The kid by the window was holding his bleeding hand with the uncut one; both were covered in blood. Marilou started to go to him, but her way was blocked as a teenager leapt out of his seat to catch his friend's errant throw. She ducked out of the way and looked desperately at the clock. Four minutes until lunch. The spot where the Twain poster had been stood out like a missing tooth, but Marilou noticed that the poster itself had left no mark. The paint surrounding it had not faded at all.

"Give me the ball!" Marilou shouted, turning to face the chaos. But it was no use. She could tell there would be no controlling a group of freshmen whose class had been so unexpectedly interrupted. The game of catch expanded to include nearly every student in the room. Marilou gave up trying to restore order and returned her attention to the kid who had cut his hand. Strangely, she thought, the rest of the class seemed to be ignoring him. She strode purposefully toward the window.

"I think you're looking for me," said a distinctly nonfreshman voice behind her.

She turned around. Most of her students were out of their seats by now. The ball flew through the air. Cyrus Nygerski stepped into the fray and intercepted it with one hand. While the room did not exactly fall silent, the noise level abated considerably.

"I broke your window," Nygerski said. "I'm sorry."

"You!" Marilou glared at him, her eyes a storm.

"Hey, it's our bus driver!" one of the kids shouted.

"Shut up!" Marilou snapped at him. Robert Rickard and Carl Estabrook, each wearing a baseball glove, stood just inside the door, behind Moondog. She could see Doug out in the hall with the bat, holding it in one hand and swinging it gently back and forth just above the tops of his shoes, which he stared at intently.

"He's cut himself rather badly," Moondog said. The boy by the window was now dripping blood on the carpet. He seemed paralyzed, staring in open horror at the deep glass cut across his palm.

"I'll get a towel," Robert said, and hurried out of the room.

"Trevor, are you all right?" Marilou said, advancing to touch the boy on the shoulder. The cut did look bad; Marilou's stomach flipped when she examined it, realizing that he had come within a few centimeters of slicing his wrist.

"Hurts," the boy said.

The bell rang and the students surged out of the room. Marilou watched them go.

"Better get down to the office," Carl Estabrook advised the boy. "You're probably going to need stitches. "Come on."

Robert returned with a clean towel, which Marilou wrapped gently around the cut. Carl Estabrook led Trevor out the door.

Marilou turned her attention to Moondog. "*How* did you break my window?" she asked him.

Moondog nodded toward Doug in the hall. "He hung a curveball. I swung too early."

"You were playing baseball? Out on the field?"

"We were. It was an accident. I'll fix the window."

"No, I will," Robert said. "It's my job."

"We'll have to order a new pane of glass," Doug said from the hall. "In the meantime, let's board it up. We'll do it now, during lunch break, and you can take off an hour early tomorrow. I'll show you where some boards are."

Robert and Doug left, leaving Moondog and Marilou staring at each other in the sudden silence. The building had emptied for lunch.

"Baseball, huh?" Marilou said. "You must be a pretty good hitter to hit one that far."

"I've played some ball," Moondog said. "Look, I'm sorry about your window."

"It's all right. Robert said he'd take care of it. Besides, it's the first time all year I've had fresh air blowing through here. The windows don't work right."

But Moondog was no longer looking at her. His attention had been captured by the pantheon of authors, newly absent one member. Slowly, his dark eyes took in the entire room, beginning at the long wall and moving over the raised area up front, the crooked rows of desks, the dark closet, the wall nearest the door, where the Georgia O'Keeffe poster had been. He took a few steps toward the center of the room, gazing up at the slowly revolving fan hanging over Marilou's desk as he did so.

"Is something wrong?" she asked him.

Moondog took a deep breath; to Marilou, he seemed to be sniffing the air. "We're not alone in here, are we?" he said.

"What? What do you mean?"

"There's a presence in here," Moondog said. "A consciousness. And it's radiating some kind of anger . . . a sense of having been cheated, or betrayed." He turned once, a complete circle, his eyes wide and alert. "Oh, it's strong," he said. "This whole room is vibrant with it."

Marilou tossed her hair back and folded her arms across her chest. "You're a very weird person," she said. "Is everything a joke to you?"

"I'm not joking," he said. "There are definitely supernatural forces at work in here. Big time."

"Are you trying to tell me this room is *haunted*?" she cried. "And do you actually expect me to believe it?"

"Maybe not," he replied. "But I know a supernatural force when I've met one. If I spent some time in here, I bet I could communicate with it, find out what it's so angry about."

"I'm going to lunch," she said, moving to get her briefcase. "I'm sorry, Moondog, but I don't believe in ghosts."

"I do," he said. "I've met one or two in my time."

She fixed him with a stare from beside her desk. "Who *are* you?" she said. "No, don't answer that. I have a feeling I don't want to know. Just don't break any more windows, okay?"

If Moondog was dismayed by this dismissal, he gave no outward sign of it. He shrugged, and without another word to her, he left the room.

Marilou felt her knees weaken. The bus driver scared her with his crazy talk of supernatural forces at work in her classroom. But she had to admit to herself that she found him interesting, as well. It was an interest she determined to resist. Guys like Nygerski were trouble—hadn't she been down that road a few too many times before? And this one believed her room was possessed.

"Well, *I* don't," she said out loud, and lifted her briefcase. On her way out, without thinking about it, she glanced quickly over her shoulder at the authors on the wall. As always, they looked stonily back at her, giving her nothing.

Moondog caught up with Doug and Carl Estabrook outside by the flagpole. "Hey, Nygerski," Estabrook called to him as he approached.

"Kid all right?" Moondog asked.

"Sure, he'll be okay. They took him down to Dr. Sohn's to get it sewn up. Pretty bad cut."

"Yeah. Worse than it should have been. I'm glad he's gonna be okay."

"That was a hell of a poke. You'd straightened it out, that ball would *still* be in the air."

Moondog looked at Doug. "I've played some ball myself," he said.

"I can tell," Estabrook replied. "By the way you handle a glove."

"It's been awhile," Moondog said.

"Yeah, but you can still play. What would you think about joining our team?"

"You need all the help you can get," Doug said with a grin.

"Team? What team?"

"A few of the teachers, couple of kids, plus Bill, the bus driver at the elementary school. Five-team adult league. We play after school. Since you work here, you're eligible. We could use a good bat in the lineup."

"Your team needs a *lot* of help," Doug said.

Estabrook laughed. "These Indians think they're hot shit just 'cause they're on a modest little winning streak. Doug here is eligible to be on two teams, but he plays for his ethnic group rather than his employers."

"Blood is thicker than money," Doug quipped.

"Seriously, we play in the afternoons, after everybody gets out of work. There're about three weeks left in the season. A good time for us to bring in a ringer, wouldn't you say, Doug?"

Doug emitted a low chuckle. "First time I face you in a real game, Moondog," he said, "I'm gonna strike your ass out."

"Board up the windows," Moondog replied, and the three of them parted company, laughing.

11

A Pretty Girl

A pretty girl, Marilou thought, ought to have a lot of friends, in any high school. She should know; she had been one once, not so long ago.

She remembered well what it had been like to be sixteen, attractive, and sought after. Her father's gray hair had been mostly black when she had begun her freshman year. Back then, she had been surrounded by people—dates and wanna-be dates, groups of kids at the beach in the spring, summer, and fall, and girls who wanted to be like her. She had been smart, pretty, and popular. But she had also been lucky enough to have at least three true friends, girls whose loyalty would only have deepened had she fallen into troubling circumstances.

Thus it puzzled her that Heather Monroe seemed utterly alone. The girl was six or seven months pregnant by now, and each day she seemed to grow lovelier. Her heart-shaped face glowed with the radiance unique to impending childbirth; her blue-green eyes sparkled beneath her dark bangs. If only she would smile, Marilou thought, laugh with someone close to her, she would be beautiful indeed.

Heather came into class every day after lunch, never late but never first, and took the same seat in the front row. In class, she paid attention but volunteered nothing, answering politely whenever Marilou called on her. Her written assignments were always turned in on time and were unfailingly well done. At the end of each class, she got up and left the same way she'd come in—alone.

It couldn't be easy, Marilou thought with a stab at empathy. Attitudes toward teenage pregnancy had softened somewhat over the years, but the silent condemnation still lurked not far outside of one's immediate circle of friends. Heather seemed to have no friends. Yet the expression she wore to class reflected a quiet contentment, an acceptance of her situation, which Marilou automatically admired. She saw no fear, no anger at circumstance, no shame. If it was a mask, it was a convincing one.

Marilou wanted very much to see behind the mask, to reach the girl, to hold out a hand to her. Heather had never given her the slightest indication that such an overture was needed or would even be welcomed. Marilou wondered if there wasn't a bit of jealousy in her protective feelings toward the girl. A few of her high school and college friends had children now, and from time to time Marilou received happy three-sentence letters accompanied by photographs that told of busy, messy, joyful lives. Marilou had avoided parenthood as she had avoided other long-term commitments. Any children of her own would come later in life, if at all. She would never know Heather's experience, which, though difficult, promised its share of rewards, as well.

Heather's excused absence from physical education, circulated by memo to all the girl's teachers, finally gave Marilou an idea on how to draw her out. She asked Heather to stay after class one Friday in late September. Taking a folding chair from the other side of the raised area, Marilou set it beside her desk and motioned for the girl to sit down.

Heather's face showed no anxiety—or any other emotion—as she lifted the hem of her full-length dress above her ankles and ascended the two steps. She sat down silently in the chair as Marilou slid behind the desk. Heather Monroe was not a big girl, and even in the last trimester of pregnancy, she could be described as delicate. Her dark hair, the bangs cut just above the eyebrows, framed her angular face; the ends curled forward underneath her jaw and over the embroidered collar of her flowered dress. Marilou liked Heather's modest and somewhat-antiquated taste in clothing; it contrasted with the exhibitionist styles of many of her peers. Her eyes, crystalline even in the dusty light of the room, looked unabashedly into Marilou's, waiting, patiently expectant.

"You do very well in your work for this class," Marilou said. "You must get a lot of support at home."

Heather shrugged. "Enough, I guess," the girl said.

"And your other classes? How are they going?"

"Fine," Heather said in the same noncommittal voice.

"Good. Good. So, how are you feeling? Is everything all right?" Marilou turned on her warmest "I'm your friend" smile, hoping the girl would relax and really talk to her. But Heather just sat there stiffly—primly, almost—and smoothed her dress down over her swollen abdomen.

"Everything's fine," she said.

"When's the baby due?" Marilou asked when it became obvious that Heather wan't going to say anything else.

"Late December. Right around Christmas, the doctor says."

Careful to maintain her smile, Marilou asked, "Are you going to keep it?"

Heather's back stiffened; anger flashed in her translucent eyes. "Of course I'm going to keep it!" she declared. "This child is mine, and no one can take her away from me! They've taken everything else, but they can't take my baby!" More quietly, she added, "They can't take my dignity, either."

Marilou reached a hand across her desk, then withdrew it when Heather did not respond to the gesture. She wondered who "they" were. And what, exactly, had they taken away?

Marilou folded her hands in her lap and looked at the girl. A faint stream of afternoon sunlight glanced through the windows and spotlighted a large stain on the carpet near the back row of desks. The board Robert had nailed in place cast a rectangular shadow. The authors, who Marilou noticed were never in direct sunlight, glared balefully down at them.

"I think that's very admirable," Marilou said, still smiling. "And it's part of why I asked you to stay after class. I have a proposal for you."

Heather looked back at her and said nothing.

"I'd like you to help out with my remedial-reading class," Marilou said. "It's sixth period, when you would normally have phys ed. You could help tutor the slower students, work with small reading groups, that sort of thing."

"Ms. McCormick, I don't want any special treatment," Heather said quietly.

"Don't think of it as special treatment," Marilou countered. "You write very well. You obviously know the material. I'm asking you to share what you know in order to help some students who don't learn as quickly. It has nothing to do with you being pregnant."

"Ms. McCormick, I appreciate the offer, but you're wrong—it has everything to do with my little pearl here." Heather rubbed her stomach in a protective encircling motion. "If I were not pregnant, you would not be asking me this."

"Heather, I . . ." Something in the girl's face made Marilou stop. She was right, Marilou realized; help in remedial reading, while it would be welcome, was really nothing more than an excuse to insert herself into Heather's life and situation. And Heather clearly did not want a helping hand. Marilou had thought she was being clever, but Heather had seen right through the attempt. Her admiration for the girl grew, even as her puzzlement deepened.

"I'm . . . glad you're getting support at home," Marilou said. "Is the baby's father around at all?"

Heather stood up. "Yes, he's around," she said. "And no, I'm not going to tell you his name. Can I go now?"

"Sure," Marilou replied, rising also, as the first two kids in her next class poked their heads in the door. "I just want you to know that I'm here, and I care, if you need anything."

"Ms. McCormick, I'm fine," Heather reiterated. "But thank you."

"Anytime," Marilou said to Heather's back as the girl left the room. It was an exceedingly strange moment. Not many sixteen-year-olds had the poise and self-assurance to make her feel dismissed, but that was what Heather had done. The girl was an enigma. Curiousity raged in Marilou's brain. She thought that maybe she would call the girl's parents, but on what pretense? There was nothing whatsoever wrong with Heather's schoolwork. It would be seen as meddling.

She thought about Heather Monroe all weekend. On Saturday, she made the hour-long drive down the hill to San Diego, where she shopped for clothes at Horton Plaza, browsed the used-book stores along Adams Avenue, and took in a movie—alone—at the Ken Cinema. On Sunday, she spent the morning at home with the newspaper, reading it all, even glancing through the sports section and the vacuous, celebrity-dominated Sunday magazine. In the afternoon, she cleaned the house, which wasn't hard, since it was small and had not seen a single visitor since she'd moved in. When that was done, she took a long walk, admiring the subtle autumn colors of the fields and woods.

Nothing she did could shake her puzzlement about the girl. Most other teenagers in Heather's place would be overwhelmed, or at least frightened, by what biology had thrust upon her. Heather seemed to revel in it. But what of friends? What teenage girl could navigate such a challenge without them? Why did Heather discourage closeness? Why did the other girls shun her? It was like something out of another century.

On Monday, Heather assumed her usual seat in the front row and listened, as usual, attentively but without comment. She left at the end of class as she usually did—without a word. It was as if the previous Friday's conversation had never taken place.

But her remedial-reading class that day provided its own distraction, and it took Marilou's mind temporarily off of Heather and her pregnancy. The day's final class, filled with poor students who did not want to be there, was a daily challenge to her patience and stamina. Marilou could not afford to let her guard down with this bunch for even a minute. Already in the new school year, several outrages had confronted her. Once she had caught one of the juvenile delinquents in the back row taking a Bic lighter to the shirttail of the kid sitting directly in front of him. On another occasion, she had confiscated a pocketknife from a young man who had been using it to cut off the buttons holding up the back of a girl's dress. And there were always the thrown objects, the paper clips and thumbtacks propelled through the air by rubber bands, the crude comments, and the overall level of noise and anarchy. If Marilou could keep the class from erupting into total chaos and maybe impart one new piece of knowledge to those kids receptive enough to take it home with them, she considered the period a success.

Today she was at the blackboard at the beginning of class, chalking up a new list of vocabulary words for the week. The old heater at the front of the room hummed and clicked occasionally, like someone's stomach growling; the ceiling fan clacked lazily above her desk. She had almost stopped noticing the strange small sounds of the antiquated machinery. The class buzzed behind her—midrange social noise that she likewise tuned out, much as people who live near busy city streets cease to notice the sound of traffic. They will, however, notice the sudden screech of braked tires or the crunch of metal, and Marilou stopped in midword when she heard Kyle Tyler's unmistakable voice rise above the others, and she recognized the threat of the open hand behind it.

"Richie! Get rid of that thing! How many times I gotta tell ya?"

She spun around. Kyle had left his seat and now stood over Richie's desk (though not over Richie; even seated, the mountainous boy was taller). Richie cowered away from his wiry cousin, cradling something she could not see in his massive arms, his frightened eyes darting back and forth between the object and Kyle's face.

"B-b-but Kyle," Richie whined plaintively. "You said I could have 'im. You said if I took care of 'im an' gave him food and stuff, you said I could have 'im!"

"Yeah, and look what you done. You always kill 'em. They don't last a day. Then you carry 'em around 'til they stink."

"He tried to run away," Richie whimpered.

"Kyle, get back in your seat," Marilou commanded. She noticed that the rest of the kids in the classroom had grown suddenly quiet and were watching Kyle and Richie like the audience at the beginning of a play. Kyle looked at her but made no move to return to his desk.

"Richie, what have you got?" she asked quietly.

Richie looked up at her, his hammy features quivering. "You won't let him take it away, will you, Miss McCormick? Please don't let him take it away!"

"He's got a mouse, Ms. McCormick!" Kyle cried.

"Sit down!" she demanded. She meant it, and Kyle knew she did.

"Yes, ma'am," he said meekly, returning to his seat behind Richie's.

Marilou moved slowly across the floor toward Richie's desk. The huge youth pulled his arms closer to his chest, hiding whatever it was that he held. The rest of the class had gone utterly silent, as if she had asked him an academic question and they were all waiting for the slow train of his mind to roll ponderously down the tracks to some kind of answer.

"Show me," she said, standing beside him.

"I tol' him not to pick 'em up anymore, but he don't listen," Kyle said from his seat. "He always kills 'em."

"I dint mean to," Richie whimpered in a voice comically small for the huge body. "He tried to run away."

"Let me see it, Richie," Marilou insisted gently. She could feel her stomach begin to loosen up for calisthenics. Slowly, very slowly, Richie uncurled his arms.

The mouse lay along one wide forearm, unequivocably dead. Marilou's stomach began a series of sit-ups. A startled cry formed in her chest and leapt upward. She caught it in her throat, swallowed hard, and forced it down. It looked a lot like the mouse that had scared her in the closet and made her drop the books and embarrass herself in front of Robert. Its bulging, lifeless eyes seemed to stare at her. Its skin was pulled back from its jaw, baring long teeth in its final death agony. Its head had been crushed. Blood and oozy gray-brown material squished through a crack alongside one ear, matting the short gray fur, which Richie had rubbed clean off in one oval-shaped spot along the dead rodent's spine. Its claws raked the air like bird talons. There were spots of dried blood on the ends of Richie's thick fingers.

The sit-ups switched to jumping jacks. Marilou laid a hand on Richie's desk to steady herself, hoping she wouldn't lose her lunch in front of the whole class.

"Kyle," she said softly, not looking at anything, "go down to the bathroom and get some paper towels—a bunch of them."

The boy complied. Marilou stood by Richie's desk until Kyle

returned with a crumpled fistful of paper towels. There were few comments from the rest of the class; those she heard were spoken in hushed tones and audible only because of the eerie quiet that had descended upon the room. She had never seen this bunch so subdued. Certainly these remedial-reading kids never responded this way when she *wanted* them to be quiet. Their silence now struck her as outright weird.

Kyle stood beside her, holding the paper towels. "Richie," she said, still looking at a spot in the air rather than at him or his dead pet, "put the mouse on the towels."

"But Miss McCormick—"

"Do it!" she snapped at him.

Kyle thrust the paper forward. Richie leaned away from him.

"You heard the lady." Marilou, to her surprise, detected the barest hint of kindness, of compassion for his mentally inferior cousin, in Kyle's gruff voice. It was buried deep, but it was there.

"Come on, Richie, give it up," he said. "There're other mice."

Richie cupped the body of the mutilated mouse gently in the too-strong hands that had accidentally killed it. Holding them out over the proffered paper towels, he slowly opened them and let the corpse drop onto its burial litter.

"Now get rid of that thing," Marilou told Kyle. "Put it in the trash can in the hall. And put something over it." She did not want Robert to see it lying there, staring vacantly upward, when he arrived in the morning.

"Richie, go wash your hands," she said.

The strange stillness in the room persisted for the remainder of the period. There was none of the usual verbal volleyball, off-color language, or anxious activity in anticipation of the end of the school day. Richie sat quietly at his desk, eyes downcast, and Marilou did not call on him. When the bell rang, the students filed numbly out of the room.

"Christ," she said out loud to herself as she gathered up her papers and placed them in her briefcase. "I could use a drink."

"An excellent idea."

Marilou jumped. Carl Estabrook stepped out of the closet. "I'll buy you one at Quinn's," he said.

"I wish you wouldn't do that," Marilou told him crossly.

"Do what? Buy you a drink?"

"Come through the closet," she said. "It startles me."

"I'll knock over some books or something next time so you'll know I'm coming," the young history teacher said. "It's a long way to walk around."

She smiled at him and relaxed a little. "I guess it is," she said. "And I'll take you up on that drink."

12

Dinner with Carl

One drink became two, and then three, and eventually segued into dinner, for Marilou found herself in need of adult conversation. At first, they talked of subjects unrelated to their jobs, and Marilou felt relief at being away from the day's work and her workplace, listening to Carl's stories of growing up in Julian and about the turbulent history of the town. But eventually, the talk strayed back to the most obvious thing they had in common: the school, their teenage students, and the strange classroom Marilou had inherited.

"Richie brought a dead mouse into my remedial-reading class today," she said with an involuntary shudder as they ate their salad. "I couldn't believe it."

"Is that why you were so rattled?" he asked her. "When I came into your room?"

"Was it that obvious?"

He smiled at her. "Mm-hmm."

"Well, like I said, you startled me."

"But it was more than that, Lou. Wasn't it?" She had noticed that he made a point of calling her consistently by her preferred nickname, and while she liked it, she also heard the warning bells of encroaching and not-altogether-invited familiarity, an attempt to place himself within her confidence and trust. The bells were muffled by alcohol and the fact that she had, after all, accepted his invitation, but she was aware of them nonetheless.

"Yes," she answered. "He had it in his pocket, like a rabbit's foot. He'd been rubbing it. He stroked it so much that it didn't have any fur left on most of its back. He'd crushed its head—with his fingers."

"Ugh." Carl made a face. "That's not exactly an appetizing dinner table image."

"Sorry." She fell momentarily silent and looked down into her wineglass. She wondered briefly if each of her short-term predecessors had sat in this same restaurant with the handsome young history teacher. But he wasn't a bad sort, really, if a little less colorful than the men with whom she was used to keeping company. She felt a little bit ashamed of herself for not giving him more of a chance.

And the wine had dissolved some of her reserve. "I think they're breeding in there," she ventured. "And God knows what they're eating, but something's making them behave strangely."

"What are you talking about?" he asked.

"It's not the first mouse I've seen. They live in the closet, between our rooms. There's a whole colony of mice in there. You must hear them."

"To tell you the truth, I hadn't noticed. But I don't doubt there are mice in there, though I've never seen one myself. But so what? Mice are mice."

"Not this one," she said. "In my experience, mice are afraid of people. But the one I saw in the closet showed no fear at all.

He bared his teeth at me, which I thought was damn strange. Looked like he was going to attack. Scared the shit out of me, if you want to know the truth. And I'm *not* afraid of mice. But this one looked really . . . well, *mean*, for lack of a better word. I ran out into the classroom, dropped the books I'd gone in to get all over the floor, and very nearly fell on my face. If Robert hadn't been there, I might've."

" 'Your knight in shining armor, coming to your emotional rescue,' " Carl said, quoting the Rolling Stones song in a voice heavy with comic exaggeration.

"What's that supposed to mean?" she demanded.

"Nothing. But it's pretty obvious he's got a wicked crush on you."

"Come on. He's old enough to be my father."

"He has a kid, actually. Not much younger than you are. Managed to graduate, but I hear he was a hoodlum in training even then. He's tweaked most of the time, and he steals to support his habit."

"Poor Robert," Marilou murmured.

"Yeah, it can't be any picnic having a son who's a druggie. He probably has to hide all his spare change, and his wife's jewelry."

"You think he likes me, huh?"

"He spends about three times as long on your room as he does on any of ours," Carl said. "The other day, I had to point out a sticky spot in the corner where some kid spilled a soda. It had been there for most of a week. It was starting to attract ants. And Donna's always bitching about him forgetting to empty her wastebaskets, or taking days to get rid of some graffiti or spitballs stuck to the windows. I'll bet he never lets anything like that slide in your room for very long. Am I right?"

Marilou nodded. "He always takes care of any problems right away. He's been really good. Did you know that he's a high school dropout? Hasn't read a book since he was seventeen? He told me that. But he borrowed *The Old Man and the Sea* from me, and read the whole thing. And the other morning I surprised him reading another book. He put it down when he saw me, but I could tell he'd been absorbed in it."

Carl laughed and shook his head. "Anything to impress you, I guess."

"I don't think that's the reason," she said. "He acted all embarrassed that I'd caught him. Imagine being embarrassed about reading! I think it's neat that a guy with no education takes a job as a janitor at a school and gets interested in books. It's the sort of thing they make movies about."

"*Educating Robert,* starring Marilou McCormick," Carl said lightly but with an edge of sarcasm.

"I didn't have anything to do with it," she retorted, stung by his teasing. "In fact, that very first time I met him, when he was reading *The Old Man and the Sea,* he said he'd found it lying on the floor. Later, we had this big discussion about Hemingway and his suicide. Now, I don't particularly like Hemingway. I don't think he has much to say to women. So if he's taking up reading to impress me, he couldn't have picked an author who was less appropriate."

"I like Hemingway," Carl muttered defensively. "At least I remember liking him—in Scurvy's classes."

Their entrées arrived, cutting short the literary discussion. Marilou had already discovered that restaurant fare in Julian consisted mostly of cowboy food, but the braised chicken breast she'd ordered turned out to be surprisingly good. She thought momentarily of her former life on the coast. It seemed like months since she had tasted a decent piece of fish. Julian, she reflected, was in many ways closer to Texas than to the Pacific Ocean. Carl had buffalo steak smothered with some brick-colored southwestern sauce, which he attacked with gusto.

"How's Jim Green?" he asked as they were finishing. "He and his little buddy still giving you a hard time?"

She leaned back in her chair, her belly full, her head swimming slightly with drink. "No," she said, "and I'm surprised. I'm not sure why they stopped, though I'm certainly not complaining."

"Good old-fashioned discipline," Carl suggested.

"I'd like to think so," she replied. "But I'm not sure *what* happened. "I mean, I gave them detentions, sent them to Oates's office. None of it did any good. Detentions, getting kicked out of class—it didn't seem to faze them. Phelps went right on saying 'nigger this' and 'nigger that' and Jim kept up with that ridiculous affected accent of his. There wasn't a thing I could do about it, and they knew it and took advantage of it. I had just about resigned myself to ignoring it and putting up with it for the rest of the year, or maybe talking with their parents, when all of a sudden they stopped."

"Just like that, huh?"

"Just like that. Jim speaks perfectly enunciated English to me now. He volunteers in class, and he doesn't look over at Phelps first for approval every time he opens his mouth. And Phelps has behaved, too. Hasn't uttered the *n* word once."

"Maybe they just got sick of sitting in detention," Carl suggested.

"Maybe. I'd like to think that *something* I'm doing in that classroom is working."

"Jim's a good kid. Playacting in class doesn't sound like him at all. I'm glad he's gotten over it."

"Me, too," Marilou said. "But now that I think about it, you know what was even stranger? The reaction of the other kids. It was as if they *had* no reaction. I would expect a bunch of kids like that to crack up laughing. But either everybody in the class was in on the joke or they thought it was perfectly normal for Jim and Phelps to be talking like that. They didn't react at all. They just sat there and listened to that crap, day in and day out, and not one of them so much as cracked a smile. If *that* was playacting, it was pretty damn good."

Carl mopped up some of the noxious-looking sauce with a piece of bread, chewed on it thoughtfully, and said nothing.

"It was the same thing today, in remedial reading," Marilou went on. "When Richie pulled out that dead mouse, I would have expected at least one of the girls to scream. I mean, *I* almost did. But the kids—nothing. Everybody pretty much just sat there. It was as if they were in some kind of trance." Marilou laughed self-consciously and took a sip of wine. "Maybe that explains the way the other kids treat Heather."

Carl looked at her blankly.

"Heather Monroe? The pregnant girl?"

"What about her?" Carl said.

"Do you know her?" she asked.

Carl nodded and drank from his glass. "I've had her in class," he said. "Last year."

"Was she as aloof then?"

Carl shrugged and looked down at his now-empty plate. "Yeah, I guess so," he said. "She's always pretty much kept to herself."

"Do you know who the father is? Another student, perhaps?"

He shook his head. "I don't think anybody knows. I don't think she *wants* anyone to know."

"I don't see any evidence of a boyfriend," Marilou said. "In fact, as far as I can tell, the poor girl doesn't have any friends at all. The other kids in class don't even talk to her."

"Hmm." Carl tossed off the last of the wine in his glass and made a show of pouring more for each of them. "You know, Lou," he said at length, "teenage pregnancy isn't all that unusual. It's unfortunate it happened to someone as bright and promising as Heather, but really, thousands and thousands of young girls get knocked up every year. She happens to be one of them. And it's not uncommon for the young guys who are the fathers to make themselves scarce, either."

"It shows a lack of character, though," Marilou said. "If I

were Heather, I'd be pissed. I'd make damn sure the guy took some responsibility. She seems totally unperturbed."

"And you find that unusual."

"Yes! She's what—sixteen? And in a couple of months she's going to have a little human being to care for, with all its needs and demands. That's a hell of a lot to face at that age. At any age. And yet she doesn't seem the least bit worried. She acts as if she's proud of it, lording it over everybody else, including me. Maybe *that's* why she doesn't have any friends. It seems like she doesn't want any."

Carl leaned back in his chair, sipped his wine, and looked at her, waiting for her to continue.

"I tried to talk with her," Marilou said. "I wanted to offer her, you know, a shoulder to lean on. To show her that somebody cared. Not only did she reject the offer; she acted as if the very suggestion that she might need any help was an insult to her."

"I'm sure it's hard for her," Carl said.

"I think she's reveling in it," Marilou countered. "She comes to class every day, she's never late, and she gets *A*'s on everything. She's got no social life that I can see, but she does the work, and she's blithely unworried about the hard times ahead of her. She's more than six months gone by now. She's a good student, as I'm sure you know. But how's she going to keep up when the baby comes?"

"Well, if she's doing the work and getting *A*'s, I wouldn't worry about it."

"I just think it's weird, her attitude. I keep thinking that if I'd been pregnant at that age, I sure would have appreciated a sympathetic teacher, and a network of friends. She doesn't seem to need or want any of that."

"That surprises you?"

Marilou looked momentarily down into her glass, then back up at her dinner companion. "It disappoints me," she said. "And it angers me a little bit, too. Why should everybody shun her, in this day and age? And where the hell is the father? It's probably some kid at school, going happily on with his life, without any stigma, and without taking any responsibility. He should be there for her. It isn't fair."

"Life's not fair," Carl said simply. "Look, Lou, you can't expect every small-town girl to share your college-educated, feminist ideals of social justice. We teachers are only a small part of their lives. There's only so much we can do. Their parents and peers have already had a thirteen-year head start by the time they get to high school. Our influence isn't as great as we sometimes like to think it is."

"I think we can have a great deal of influence," Marilou said. "If I didn't think so, I wouldn't have gone into teaching in the first place. I'll keep trying to talk to Heather, without being pushy about it. If I can get her to confide in me, she'll be better for it, in the long run."

"And your curiosity will be appeased."

"Carl, don't you think it's weird?"

"What? A girl keeping her emotions to herself instead of spilling all to a new teacher she's known for less than a month? No, I don't think it's particularly strange."

"Well, when you put it that way . . ." She trailed off, looking away from him. For several moments, neither of them said anything. Carl refilled her wineglass and his own. He's trying to get me drunk, she thought.

"Hey, Carl," said a big balding man, passing their table on his way out the door with a middle-aged woman Marilou presumed was his wife. "Ready for the game tomorrow?"

The history teacher visibly relaxed, his face breaking into a broad smile. "We're always ready, Don," he said. Introductions were made—although Marilou knew she would forget their names in ten minutes—and the couple left.

"What game?" she asked him.

"Don manages the Corner Market," Carl informed her. "He's also the captain of the chamber of commerce's baseball team. We play them tomorrow, after work. You should come."

"Baseball's not really my thing," she said. "But maybe I'll watch. Are you guys any good?"

Carl laughed. "It depends on what you mean by good," he said. "Most of us have never been anything more than casual players. I'll tell you, though, that new bus driver can play some ball."

"You mean Moondog?"

"Yeah, Moondog. He's a character, but he sure can play."

"I know what you mean," she said, "about his being a character. What's his story, anyway? Who is he?"

Carl shrugged. "Nobody seems to know too much about him. He used to write for the paper, before Osterman bought it. Flamingly liberal columns, mostly, with an offbeat sense of humor most of the locals didn't understand. And weird stuff, about conspiracy theories, and the occult."

"That reminds me," Marilou said. "You know what he told me that day he broke the window? After you and Robert left?"

"No. What?"

"He tried to tell me my room was possessed. 'There's a presence in here,' he said. I mean, can you believe it?"

"Lou, it was probably his idea of a joke."

"He wasn't smiling when he said it."

"He was probably trying to get *you* to smile."

"Who knows? He's weird, and the room is weird. It's so dark and gloomy, even with the blinds open. And it looks like it hasn't changed in . . . well, forever."

"It hasn't," Carl said. "At least not much, not since my own school days, when Scurvy taught in there. He *never* opened the blinds. And the desk is right where it was, and those posters. . . ."

"Those posters!" Marilou repeated. "The ones that make authors look like ax murderers."

Carl Estabrook laughed. "None of the other teachers seemed

to mind them. Why don't you take them down, if you dislike them so much?"

"You know, that's a funny thing. I tried to take them down—twice. They must be made of some special kind of paper stock, because I got the worst paper cuts I've ever had. They wouldn't stop bleeding for the longest time. I mean, I don't believe what Moondog said to me, but it's almost as if those posters have minds of their own and they don't *want* to come down. And yet nothing I put up seems to stay on the walls. And every plant I've put in there has died."

"Weird."

"I thought so. You know, coming to Julian is almost like stepping through a time warp."

"In what way?"

"In lots of ways. The whole town is an antique, or tries to be. I know the people here are really proud of the mining heritage and all—the past is their bread and butter; it gets people to shop in all the junk stores and take carriage rides and all that. But does that mean the school has to be stuck in the past, too? Kids *are* going to grow up and move out of here, and they'll have to live in the twenty-first century. And the authors on those posters are all long since dead. The stuff they wrote is pretty dead, too, and what makes it even worse is Donna's opinion that they're the only authors who've ever written anything important."

Carl laughed again. "I've heard a little bit," he said, "about this ongoing argument. I don't think it's one you're going to win."

Their waiter appeared beside the table and attempted to cajole them into ordering dessert, which they both declined. Carl poured the last of the wine into their glasses as the waiter cleared the plates.

"Donna's got to realize—and the kids do, too—that there's a whole lot of literature that's been written by people who aren't white or male," Marilou said earnestly, ignoring the half-full glass. "I wanted to teach *I Know Why the Caged Bird Sings,* by Maya Angelou. Donna shot me down immediately. Wouldn't even discuss it."

"I've heard of that book," Carl said. "Hasn't it been banned in a few places? Alabama, Mississippi, someplace like that?"

"That's exactly why we should teach it," she declared. "To open students' minds to ideas that may, at some place and time, have been considered dangerous."

When Carl said nothing, she plowed on. "Do you know why some school boards took it off the shelves? Not because it's written by a black woman—although I did notice that Scurvy's icons of American literature are all white—but because it talks about rape and lynching and illegitimate children. In other words, reality! It's too *real* for people like Donna to deal with. *The Grapes of Wrath* was real for its time, for the thirties. But the world has changed. We should change, too. We should at least be open to it."

She stopped, annoyed at the way he was looking at her. "What?"

"You been to a school board meeting here yet?" he asked.

"No. Why?"

"Let me fill you in on something about this community," he said. "You've probably caught it from some of the parents, anyway. If not, you will. Look, the school board has five people on it. Two of them are born-again fundamentalist Christians. They want Alan to teach creationism in biology class. They want any mention of sex outside marriage expunged from the English curriculum. They want all girls to take home ec and all boys to take auto shop. And Lou, they represent the town. They got elected *because* of their views, not in spite of them. And they almost got a third guy elected last year, which would have meant a fundamentalist majority. And then, let me tell you, you could've thrown all those ideas of yours about liberal education right out the fucking window."

Marilou sat silently for a moment. "If that's the case," she said finally, "I'm surprised I was hired at all. The other three must have liked me."

"Dakota liked you," Carl said. "The board pretty much defers to him when it comes to making actual decisions. They're terrified he'll walk. They had four superintendents in two years before he came along. But the other three members of the board aren't any progressives, either. Julian may be in Southern California, but it's closer in spirit to Kansas."

"In other words, I'm new, I'm young, and I'm not to be trusted," she said. "And Donna's ideas of what constitutes good literature would get a whole lot more support than mine."

"I think you understand," Carl said.

"But it's so *stupid!*" she exclaimed. "All great writers, especially the ones we put on pedestals after they die, were once mavericks. That's *why* writers write—because they have something new to say. They go against the status quo. They *question* the accepted wisdom of their time. It's only years and years later that they become part of the status quo themselves. Like the authors on my wall."

"Lou, what are you railing at *me* for? I agree with you."

She heaved a sigh, then smiled. "I'm sorry," she said. "It gets frustrating sometimes."

The waiter returned, cleared the remaining dishes, and plunked the check down in front of Carl. He immediately grabbed it, knocking over the salt shaker.

"Better throw some of that over your left shoulder," she said.

"Oh, sure." He laughed.

"I mean it, Carl," she said, smiling. "You can't be too careful about these things."

"You're superstitious, huh?"

She nodded. "It's from my mother. It's silly, I know, but just humor me." She nodded at the salt granules on the table.

He rolled his eyes, but he took a pinch of the spilled salt and tossed it over his left shoulder. Then he returned his attention to the check.

Marilou reached for her purse. "Here, let me help you with that."

"No, no, it's my treat," he said. "I invited you."

"Let me pay half," she said. "We ordered all that wine, and the drinks before dinner."

"Think of it as one of *my* superstitions." He smiled at her and placed a fifty on the tray that had come with the check. She sighed and didn't press the matter further.

Their cars were parked side by side on the street behind the restaurant. Darkness had fallen over the town. There were no lights on Julian's side streets, and the Moon was not in the sky. She knew he would try to kiss her, and she did not resist. He curled an arm around the small of her back; his tongue ran gently along the edge of her front teeth and slid behind them. She made no move to pull away until she felt the upper part of his leg press slowly but firmly forward against her dress. Breaking the kiss—a little bit reluctantly—she looked into his face and said, "It's too soon, Carl. And I'm a little drunk."

"Want me to follow you home? Make sure you get there all right?"

She smiled kindly at the obvious ploy. "Thanks, but no. I'm all right. And it's a school night. Got to get plenty of rest."

She squeezed his hand momentarily as they stepped apart. "Well," he said, "thank you for your company, and the conversation. Let's do it again sometime."

"Okay."

"Maybe on a Friday," he said. "Or any other night that isn't a school night."

You're pushing your luck, she thought. But his interest amused her. As she got into her car and turned the key, she decided that even though he wasn't really her type, she might eventually be persuaded to become interested. It had now been almost two months since that awful night on the beach, and

Marilou reflected that in recent years she had seldom gone that long without a man. Let him push, she said to herself as she steered carefully out of the tiny business district. If nothing else, she was flattered by the attention. She supposed she didn't mind being nudged a little.

13

The Dog

The dog was poking around by the side of the gym, jabbing its snout into a discarded paper bag to investigate the contents, when Robert got in. He tossed a glance at the mutt before unlocking the Annex. The sight of a dog on campus was not unusual. Julian was full of strays, many of them former pets of city dwellers who had driven them to the mountains and abandoned them there, and the school grounds offered easy repasts for canine foragers in the form of half-eaten doughnuts, discarded sandwiches, and unfinished bags of Doritos. Robert, whose job it was to pick up the mess before school started, didn't mind seeing a stray dog from time to time. He appreciated the help.

But this one was mangier-looking than most, and old, old. Robert took one look at the bedraggled thing and concluded that it was probably heading into its last winter. The once-black muzzle had gone entirely white, and it limped pitifully on emaciated legs that wobbled with each step. Part husky, mixed with something stockier—Newfoundland or Great Dane perhaps—

it had been a big, robust dog once, but now its skin hung on its ribs like a wet overcoat. Its black-and-tan fur was matted in patches and missing in others. Scabs the dog had no will or energy to lick festered all along its flanks; the once-proud head drooped as if in apology for not giving up the ghost before it had come to this. The dog was a pathetic sight, and Robert wondered briefly how long it had managed to survive in the wild without a doting human family and a private carpeted corner in which to curl up.

The old dog continued to scrounge as Robert opened up the classrooms and turned on the heat. Now that it was mid-October, the mountain nights were growing considerably colder, and the Sun's warmth took several class periods to penetrate the thick stone walls of the Annex, even with the help of the larger windows in the newer rooms. In room 13, which faced west, the Sun was no help at all—the heater, which sounded more metallically angry with each passing day, had to do all the work itself.

When it *wanted* to work, Robert amended his thoughts. For its functioning seemed only loosely connected with the thermostat. It must have some automatic mechanism, Robert guessed, that had gone bad over the years. On several occasions, he had been startled by the suddenness with which the heater announced its presence, and he wondered if its outbursts disturbed Marilou McCormick's classes, as well. When he turned it on each morning, it shrieked in protest, and the air it blasted into the room was at first as cold as the morning beyond the walls. It warmed up eventually, and the scream mellowed to a dull whine, but to Robert, it still sounded like metal on metal.

One recent morning, he had gotten a Phillips screwdriver and taken off the front panel, but that was as far as his scant mechanical knowledge had gotten him. He had shone a flashlight between the metal slats and seen the fan behind them, and he had poked around with a yardstick, but he had not been able to find anything grossly out of place. Doug had put him off every time he'd mentioned it, until he had given up asking for the big Indian's help. Robert had put the panel back in place, telling himself that if it got much worse, he'd go directly to the superintendent.

As he did on most mornings, Robert lingered in room 13, enjoying the atmosphere of the room and looking it over critically for anything amiss. Ever since the Georgia O'Keeffe poster had been mysteriously destroyed and the world map had ripped, first in one corner and then entirely in half, the teacher had apparently given up putting anything else on the walls. The authors, though, continued to greet him with their silent stares every morning, and Robert nodded at Hemingway, London, and Poe, who had become, if not his friends, at least acquaintances.

His introduction to Poe had been curious. He had stepped on the book one morning after unlocking the door. The book had gone sliding across the carpet, taking Robert's foot with it. Robert had hit his elbow on the windowsill when he fell, and days later it still hurt. The front cover of the book had been nearly torn off. Worried that Marilou McCormick might be upset with him, Robert had lovingly repaired the book with Scotch tape. But instead of putting it back, he had begun reading it, even before finishing *The Call of the Wild*. Never a reader, Robert now had two books going at once. He kept the Poe book in his janitor's closet, and during slow times when classes were in session, he would often find himself thumbing through it, reading stories or parts of stories at random. In this way, he had read the last half of a story called "The Tell-Tale Heart," most of "The Cask of Amontillado," and, just yesterday, the first few pages of a captivating yet horrifying tale entitled "The Pit and the Pendulum," which he had put down only because Doug had come into the Annex, looking for him to help set up bleachers in the gym for a school assembly. The short stories in the book were much harder reading than either London or Hemingway, but Robert felt himself drawn into them, despite the vague feeling of dread that lingered when he steered his eyes away from the page and back toward work and real life. Had he thought about it, Robert would have realized that he didn't so much *want* to read the stories as he felt *compelled* to read them.

And he had been jolted when Marilou had asked him, just yesterday morning, after several days of nothing more than brief encounters and murmured hellos, how he liked the Poe book.

Robert had been taken aback, because, as with *The Call of the Wild,* he had not mentioned the book to her—he had simply borrowed it. *The Call of the Wild,* which he had similarly "borrowed," now sat on the side table in his living room. He only had about thirty pages to go, but somehow had not gotten around to finishing it.

"How did you know I was reading that?" he'd asked her.

She had looked at him guilelessly and said, "I gave it to you, didn't I?"

"No. I found it on the floor. I was gonna ask, but . . . well, I just started reading it."

"Oh. Well, feel free." Then it had been Marilou's turn to look puzzled. "I must have seen you reading it," she said. She had shrugged, then turned her attention to the chalkboard behind her.

But Robert knew that she *hadn't* seen him reading it, because he had taken pains to conceal it from her. Again, it was something he felt he *should* do, without knowing why. He'd watched as words took shape on the board in her crisp, rounded handwriting, his eyes anticipating the shapes of letters before she made them. He could hear the clicks and sighs of the heater as it waited to interrupt the next conversation. He could hear other sounds, as well—the wind whistling around the board he'd nailed up against the broken window, water in the pipes that led to the art room, and the soft shuffling within the walls that betrayed the presence of mice. *All* his senses seemed to be heightened when he was in this room. He could smell Marilou's perfume, though they had nearly the entire length of the classroom between them; he could taste the air's chalky dryness. He had already noticed how much easier reading was for him here than at home, and he guessed that that was why *The Call of the Wild* lay unfinished. It almost seemed that the room itself increased his awareness. And if this could happen to him, he thought, couldn't something similar be happening to the young teacher, who was that much smarter to begin with? Should it surprise him that she could read his mind?

"The cover calls Poe 'the father of the modern horror story,' " Robert had said to prolong the conversation.

Marilou had stopped writing on the board and turned to face him. "I'm sorry, what did you say?"

"Edgar Allan Poe," Robert began again. "It says he's known as the father of the modern horror story."

Robert remembered her laugh—short and cynical and unlike any expression she'd shared with him before. "As if horror stories can't have mothers," she had said. "What about Mary Shelley, who wrote the original *Frankenstein*? Poe's awfully wordy and pompous. He may be historically important, but I'd rather read a good Anne Rice novel."

"Who?" Robert's eyes veered toward the wall of authors.

"You won't find her up there, Robert. She's a modern writer, and still very much alive."

"I see. You gotta die to rate a poster."

"Unfortunately, that's the way it works for a lot of writers," she said. "Or artists of any kind, for that matter."

Robert had gone about his business then, glad for whatever snippet of conversation she made available to him. He supposed he would never entirely lose his infatuation with her as long as they worked in the same building, but it had faded to a small glow that warmed him when he saw her, although it did not interfere with his work. He still watched her, but without the impossible longing. He had seen her walk across the campus with Carl Estabrook at lunch, and he had spotted her car and his outside Quinn's on a couple of afternoons after school. He also noticed that she had started to drop by the baseball field on the days when the teachers' team played; Robert liked to hang around for some of the games, too, rather than go home to his shiftless son's dirty dishes and his wife's soap operas. He speculated about the budding friendship between the two young teachers, but he would not have admitted to being jealous.

The teachers' team was competent, if a bit aged. Alan Doucette pitched and Carl Estabrook played third. Their best players were the two students who played in the outfield, and their new addition, the long-haired, left-handed second baseman, Cyrus "Moondog" Nygerski.

On a baseball field, Moondog seemed utterly in his element. He dived for sure base hits and turned them into outs. He completed double plays effortlessly. And he could hit, too—though, since their impromptu game, Robert had not seen him drive a ball as far as the shot that had broken the window in Marilou's classroom. But Moondog used the whole field, slapping outside pitches down the third-base line for extra bases, advancing runners when needed with ground balls to the right side, getting enough distance for the sacrifice fly with a runner on third and less than two out. Robert guessed that Moondog was around forty, but on a baseball field, he seemed years younger. So far, he had played in three games, and the teachers had won them all.

By the time Robert completed his preliminary sweep of the rooms, the dog was on the field, sniffing at something on the ground by first base. The creature had moved clear across the parking lot and around the tennis courts in the few minutes Robert had been inside the Annex—no great trek for a healthy dog, but quite a journey for an animal so obviously on its last legs. It still looked as if it would collapse at any moment, but the creaking canine evidently had a few flickers of life left.

After all, Robert realized as he went to get the flags, the dog had walked here from *somewhere.*

By now, Robert had memorized the routine. The flags went up. The Sun rose over the hill behind the main building as Robert policed the parking lot, picking up Coke cans and other debris and putting it all into the large plastic garbage bag he carried in one hand. Soon he was interrupted by the buzz of a small engine, and Moondog, in a black leather jacket and matching helmet, streaked through the parking lot on his bike. The bus driver waved as he flashed by, skirting the stone wall surrounding the flagpole on his way to the buses out back. Robert tied the bag, deposited it by the side of the gym for later disposal, and returned to the Annex to start cleaning the classrooms.

A few minutes later, the vice principal, Bill Oates, pulled up in front of the main building in his spiffy white Porsche. Oates liked to start the morning by finding fault with some aspect of the night janitor's work; the secretaries in the front office had told Robert that this was usually the first thing they heard when they came in. Oates usually arrived before any of the staff, and Robert knew that he damn well better have the flags up and the most glaring trash out of sight by the time the Porsche came through the gate. His job was to keep the kids in line, but Oates, who kept his body in tiptop physical condition, was so at home in the role of disciplinarian that he intimidated everybody, the teachers and staff included.

At around 7:15, Moondog's bus fishtailed around the corner of the gym, barreled through the parking lot, and entered the California highway system. The elementary school's buses followed shortly, at a more subdued speed. Robert could expect Marilou McCormick to arrive sometime after that, and he made sure to have her room cleaned before she set eyes on it. By the time he heard her purposeful footsteps in the hall at around 7:40, he was sweeping the floor of the art room, whistling softly to himself.

"Robert, could you help me a minute?"

She stood in the door to the art room, one hand on the wooden door frame, several silver bracelets hanging loosely on her wrist. She wore pants today, black, gathered at the waist, and a red blouse with a matching red ribbon wrapped around the ponytail in which she'd put her hair. He stopped pushing the broom and looked at her.

"I need to bring the TV and VCR from the library up here," she explained. "It's on a stand, so I figure the two of us can just roll it."

"Sure," Robert said, leaning the broom against the nearest wall. A minute later, they were walking across the parking lot together to the main building. Robert basked in her presence as much as in the deepening morning. A slight breeze had come up with the Sun, but it was still warm; Marilou remarked on how much she liked mornings in the mountains, and Robert replied that he liked them, too. Half a dozen cars belonging to teachers and staff dotted the parking lot. No kids had arrived yet. The dog was nowhere in sight.

Valerie let them into the library, and they slowly wheeled the television stand, which was taller than Robert, out the side door and onto the asphalt. He pushed and she guided, and they had reached the base of the Annex steps when a familiar vehicle turned into the parking lot. Robert's heart sank as he recognized his son's old Datsun pickup.

Jimmy parked next to Marilou's car and adjusted his Chicago White Sox cap as he approached his father. He smelled redolently of marijuana. Christ, Robert thought, it's not even eight o'clock.

"Hey, Dad," Jimmy said, ignoring Marilou completely, "can I borrow twenty bucks?" The youth thrust his hands into the back pockets of his jeans and looked expectantly at Robert.

"Jimmy," Robert said sternly, "where are your manners?" He looked at Marilou, who had paused with her hand against the TV stand, in the same position as it had rested on the art room door. "My son, Jimmy," he said. "Marilou McCormick."

"Hello, Jimmy," Marilou said, flashing a smile even the surly youth could not ignore.

"Please to meetcha," Jimmy mumbled.

"What do you need the money for?" Robert asked warily.

"There's a construction job down in Ramona that's hiring. Bertie told me about it. I gotta get there today, and I don't have the gas."

Robert regarded his obviously stoned son, dressed in torn jeans, boots, and a T-shirt that hadn't been changed for two days. His hair needed cutting and he could use a shave. He hadn't seen the kid for two days, and he guessed that some all-hours party was responsible. He quickly evaluated the boy's chances of being hired and mentally kissed the twenty dollars good-bye forever. Hell, the story about the job was probably bogus, anyway—the money was more likely to be spent on beer or dope.

"All right," Robert said, reaching for his wallet. "But as long as you're here, why don't you give me a hand with this?"

"Dad, I gotta be down there by nine."

"Relax, you'll make it. Now, help me get this thing up the steps."

"It's easier to go around, isn't it?" Marilou asked. "Take it through the back door?"

"Good idea," Robert said. And with Marilou navigating, they wheeled the stand up the bumpy incline that led around to the back of the Annex. As he guided it through the back door, Robert thought he saw something move—down the hall, near the alcove outside Marilou's room. But when he turned to look, there was nothing there.

"Can you take it from here, Dad?" Jimmy whined. "I gotta run."

"Come on, help me get it in the classroom." Robert tried hard to conceal his irritation.

Heaving an exaggerated sigh, Jimmy pushed the stand as Robert steered it toward room 13. At the spot where the alcove joined the room, it was necessary to lift the front wheels over the lip of the carpet. Jimmy was in front when they entered the room. He tilted up his end of the stand and then abruptly set it down again, short of the carpet.

Robert heard low growling noises.

"Uh, Dad . . ."

The TV stand took up most of the doorway, but between the top of the VCR and the bottom of the shelf on which the monitor sat, Robert could see into the room. And he could see the dog, the same wretched mutt that had been scrounging in the parking lot when he arrived. Only now the dog looked different. It had its hackles up, and its eyes were alert. Its flesh still festered, but it stood on legs no longer unsteady, teeth bared in a snarl.

"Easy, boy," Jimmy said. "We're just gonna bring this old TV in, and—"

The dog barked at him, once. Jimmy stopped, and the dog began to growl in a more menacing tone than before.

"How did that dog get in there?" Marilou put a hand on Robert's shoulder and tried to see around him and the TV stand. He felt a stab of pleasure at her touch.

"I don't know," Robert said. "Go slow, Jimmy."

They eased the stand partway into the room. The dog continued to growl. "It's all right, boy," Jimmy cooed. "You just stay there. That's a good—"

With a roar, the heater behind the desk came on. Robert felt a jerk on the TV stand as Jimmy jumped in surprise. The dog's growl suddenly rose in pitch, and it advanced toward Jimmy.

"Hey now! Easy!" Jimmy cried in real alarm. With one last snarl, the dog sprang at the youth, teeth flashing. Jimmy shouted something incoherent and threw up his arms. Robert heard him cry, "Ow! You son of a bitch!" and then the dog went flying backward, crashing against the authors' wall. Robert pushed the TV stand out of the way and squeezed into the room.

The dog was momentarily stunned, but it got quickly to its feet. But that moment was all Jimmy needed. As the dog coiled for another attack, Jimmy swung a well-aimed boot and kicked the dog just below the muzzle. There was a sick cry of pain as its head flew upward. Eyes blazing with fury, Jimmy advanced on the dog and kicked it again, in the side of the head. The dog's entire body jumped, then slumped onto the carpet. Its tongue lolled out of its mouth, followed by a slow but steady stream of blood.

The heater shut off with a protesting clank.

At some point, Marilou had screamed, but now the only sounds were Jimmy's heavy breathing and the labored clacking of the fan above the desk. Robert noticed that his son was bleeding from a wound on his forearm—a dog bite. The boy would have to see a doctor.

Stunned, the three of them stared at the inert body of the dog for several seconds, unable to speak. It was Robert who finally broke the silence.

"I think you killed it," he said to his son.

"Goddamn, it almost killed *me!*" Jimmy's voice was shaking.

The dog was indeed dead, as Robert confirmed with a cursory look. It was now bleeding from the nose and mouth, and Jimmy's first kick had broken its jaw. It had shat itself, and its eyes were open and lifeless.

"Jimmy, are you all right?" asked Marilou. Her voice was not altogether steady, either.

Jimmy flexed his arm and looked at the wound, which consisted of several bleeding puncture marks. "It's not too bad," he said, his bravado returning. "I'll get it cleaned up and put something on it."

"You should see a doctor, Jimmy," Robert said.

"Aw, Dad . . ."

"He's right, Jimmy," Marilou said. "You don't know what diseases that dog might've had."

"Dad, I gotta go to Ramona."

Robert sighed and cursed anew the never-ending nature of parenthood. He pulled his wallet from his jeans and took out some money. "Look, here's another forty bucks. While you're down there, go to the clinic and have somebody look at it, okay?"

Jimmy snatched the money from his father's hand. His face softened for a moment. "All right, Dad," he said. "I really gotta run."

"Don't spend it on dope," Marilou said.

Jimmy, who was almost out the door, stopped and turned around. He and Marilou glared at each other for a long moment. Robert watched them, sensing his son's surprise at being seen through. It was almost incomprehensible to him that they were peers, this accomplished young teacher and his lazy, unambitious son. And yet they could have been high school classmates.

Now he saw that Jimmy and Marilou were grinning slightly at each other, as if acknowledging some mutual understanding. Abruptly, his son broke the standoff, turning to Robert. "Thanks, Dad," he said, and disappeared down the hall.

They both looked at the door. "He will, probably," Robert muttered.

"What?"

"Spend it on dope. You must think I'm an idiot."

"I'm sorry I said that, Robert."

"Don't be. It's probably true."

"It was a flip remark that just came out. I was . . . kind of in shock, I guess. I mean, that dog—"

Marilou's breath stopped as suddenly as her words. Robert had turned at the same moment, and he'd seen it, too.

"Oh my God!" Robert murmured, his voice small with disbelief.

The body of the dog was gone. In its place was a dark stain slightly larger than the dog had been.

Marilou and Robert looked speechlessly into each other's faces. Slowly, Robert bent down to touch the stain. It was dry.

14

The Championship Game

The informal Julian men's baseball league finished its season in the week before Columbus Day. The days were growing increasingly colder and shorter, and by that time, it was obvious which the best two teams were. With Moondog Nygerski batting fourth and anchoring the infield at second base, the teachers won four of their last five games, losing only to the Indian team, whose members came mostly from two reservations north of Santa Ysabel. Moondog and his teammates, whose strong finish had earned them second place, were looking forward to one last rematch.

The championship game was set for four o'clock on the second Wednesday of October. Moondog's bus was half-empty on the homeward route, as many of the kids had opted to stay for the game. Without the usual ballast, Moondog skidded around several of the curves on the way down the mountain, causing a moment of concern for one grandfatherly driver whose RV, lumbering closer to the center of the road than the sheer drop on the side, barely escaped a head-on collision. "I wish I had a photon torpedo," Moondog grumbled as he steered the bus skillfully into the next downhill curve. "Those things shouldn't be allowed on the road."

By game time, a crowd of several dozen spectators had gathered at the field. Most of the students sat in the stands on the first-base side—the home side when the high school team played there in the spring. The Indians, by virtue of their first-place finish, got the home dugout and the last at bat. They also had the larger cheering section, nearly filling the stands behind third.

Marilou McCormick was surprised to see Heather Monroe in attendance. The pregnant girl sat by herself at the end of the first-base stands, a knitted shawl wrapped around her shoulders. Other nearby students boisterously ignored her as they watched the teams warm up. Marilou waved to Carl Estabrook at third; he smiled and nodded at her as she took a seat beside Heather. Though she was not really a baseball fan, her tentatively growing friendship with Carl had brought her to a couple of games. She had joked with him afterward that her presence must have been bad luck, because he had gone hitless in both contests. He had laughed, his lack of individual accomplishment having been overshadowed both times by team victory. Meanwhile, she had unexpectedly begun to admire the play of the bus driver with the strange name.

"Hello, Heather," she said as she sat down. The girl looked at her with a flicker of surprise, and Marilou guessed that for however long Heather had been sitting there, no one had spoken to her. "How are you feeling?" she asked.

"I am feeling fine," Heather answered, brushing a dark brown curl back from her forehead and looking out at the field. "Really, you needn't concern yourself."

Marilou noted the girl's striking profile—the straight line of the nose, the small rounded chin, the elegance of the thin neck on which she held her head high and unashamed. She had meant to say something else, but everything in Heather's manner discouraged conversation. It's as if she *wants* to be alone, Marilou thought, once again torn between admiration for the girl and puzzlement at her behavior.

A paisley skirt whirled at her other side. "Hey, Lou, what's up?" Mimi Anderson asked as she sat down heavily on the wooden bleacher. "Did you put any money down on this thing?" The art teacher hoisted her ponderous purse into her lap and rummaged around until she came up with a tube of Chap Stick, which she began applying liberally to her pale lips.

"I don't bet on baseball," Marilou said.

"What's good enough for Pete Rose is good enough for me," Mimi Anderson said. "You know, there's quite a bit riding on this game, actually. Doug and Alan were in the teachers' lounge for about an hour today, haggling over the odds. They finally agreed on three-to-two in favor of the Indians. A lot of people are in on the action. I invested fifty bucks on our team. Thought about cutting Doug in for half if he'd throw a couple fat ones, but he's probably got a few weeks' pay on the line." She finished with the Chap Stick and fished into her purse again. "You want a banana?"

"No thank you."

"Suit yourself." The big blond woman peeled the fruit halfway down and wrapped her lips around the tip, slowly severing the first bite. Marilou watched her chew and swallow it, marveling anew at what a physically present person the art teacher was. Even her simplest actions seemed sensuous. Perhaps that was why she was an artist, because she was able to commune with clay, chalk, paint, and stone with the same primal energy other people brought to eating, drinking, and making love. She had observed that Moondog Nygerski played baseball the same way, with ease and uninhibited grace, as though bat, ball, and glove were extensions of his body, itself an unconscious instrument of some larger life force. She had come to the games to watch Carl Estabrook and had shared drinks with him afterward, but he had not been in the erotic dreams that had accompanied her solitary sleep on those nights.

Marilou surveyed the crowd and spotted Steve Dakota standing behind the batting cage, his hands in the pockets of his sports jacket. Correctly neutral, she thought, here to represent the school without an overt show of partisanship. Carl had told her that the superintendent secretly wanted to play on the team; he had, in fact, participated in batting practice once or twice at the outset of the season. He had been discouraged from joining the squad, Estabrook had said, because he wasn't all that good, and because he was the boss and his presence made everybody uncomfortable.

Robert Rickard was here, too, she saw, also alone, standing near the far end of the first-base stands, almost in right field, as if guarding against another foul ball that could threaten the distant Annex. From the field, the building really did look far away; in the games she'd watched, no one had come close to hitting it. It had been an extraordinary accident, by a good hitter, that had broken her window. She wanted to tell Nygerski that all was forgiven, but at the same time she was wary of the strange bus driver who had told her, in apparent seriousness, that her classroom was haunted. Even if it was, how did *he* know, on the basis of a few seconds in the room?

Marilou watched the crowd as much as the game as Barry Curtis, the faster of the two students on the team and the center fielder, slapped Doug's first pitch past the third baseman and Carl Estabrook hit into a double play. Angel Martinez, the other student, flied out, and two girls hung a zero on the manual scoreboard behind third base.

The Indians loaded the bases with nobody out in their half of the inning. Alan Doucette, who taught physics and could explain how a curveball curved (which did not mean that he could throw a good one), was the pitcher. Big Jim Elliot hit a screaming line drive, but he hit it too close to Moondog Nygerski, who dived to his right, speared the ball on the fly, and doubled the runner off first. There were admiring whistles from the crowd. "The man can play, can't he?" Mimi Anderson remarked to Marilou. Marilou nodded without taking her eyes off him.

The next batter hit a routine grounder to Carl Estabrook at third, and Marilou clapped with the rest of the school team's rooting section when he threw to first for the third out, keeping the game scoreless.

Moondog belted a triple to deep left field to lead off the second, and he scored the game's first run on a sacrifice fly by Wild Bill Oates. After that, there were a few scattered hits, but the score remained 1-0 until the Indians, with the help of a bad-hop ground ball past Carl Estabrook at third, pushed across three runs in their half of the fourth. The school team got one back in the fifth when Angel Martinez doubled, stole third, and scored on Moondog's single up the middle. But Big Jim Elliot hit a tremendous home run into the hinterlands of left field the following inning, and when Moondog came up again in the seventh, with two out and Martinez on second, the score was 4-2 Indians, the Sun was sinking toward the trees beyond left field, the air was growing colder, and, to the huddled crowd on the first-base side, it felt very much like the last chance.

Marilou had been chatting with Mimi most of the game, between attempts at striking up a conversation with Heather. But now as Moondog came to bat, her attention returned to the field. Nygerski sent a foul ball over the stands and into the fence surrounding the tennis courts. The next pitch was at the knees. Moondog let it go, and Danny Taylor, the chamber of commerce president, who always seemed to be pressed into umpiring duty for the most important games, called it a strike.

Doug broke off a curve in the dirt, then wasted a fastball outside, evening the count. The Indians' first baseman trotted over to the mound, said something to Doug, and returned to his position. The Sun was above the trees in left field, and in Moondog's face, as he was a left-handed batter. Doug threw the ball. It arced toward home plate, then dropped suddenly down and away. Moondog swung and missed.

A cheer went up from the stands behind third base. Doug pumped his fist in the air and stalked triumphantly off the mound.

"Check his glove for Vaseline," Carl Estabrook yelled as he grabbed his glove from the bench.

"Damn," Mimi Anderson said. "Looks like I'm gonna be out fifty bucks."

"So much for heroics," Marilou murmured, trying to sound as if she didn't care.

When the Indians added another run in their half of the inning, making it 5-2, many of the school team's supporters decided it was time to stop squinting into the setting Sun and to retreat to the warmth of their cars and homes. Heather Monroe was among this group; she got up and walked off without looking at Marilou or saying good-bye.

The pessimism seemed justified when the eighth inning passed quickly with no more scoring. More people left as Bill, the catcher, and Barry Curtis made quick outs in the top of the ninth. The wind had picked up, the Sun was almost into the trees, and the remaining fans pulled their coats and sweaters tightly around themselves to wait out the impending end of the local baseball season.

But Carl Estabrook, who hadn't had a hit all day, slapped a ground ball past shortstop. Angel Martinez then hit a solid line drive down the left-field line. Estabrook beat the throw into third, Martinez wound up on second, and a small buzz of anticipation rose from the handful of fans near Marilou and Mimi. Cyrus Nygerski hefted the wooden bat and advanced to the plate as the tying run.

" 'But Flynn let drive a single, to the wonderment of all,' " Mimi Anderson chanted gaily, " 'and Blake, the much despised, tore the cover off the ball.' "

"Huh?" said Marilou.

"Don't you recognize it?" the art teacher asked.

"No."

"It's from 'Casey at the Bat.' Don't tell me you teach English and don't know 'Casey at the Bat.' "

"Baseball's never been one of my big interests," Marilou said apologetically.

Anderson recited the next two lines of the poem. " 'And when the dust had settled, and they saw what had occurred, there was Jimmy safe at second, and Flynn a-hugging third.' " She smiled at her younger colleague, then raised a hand to her forehead to shield the Sun as Moondog walked up to the plate.

The Sun was almost sitting on top of the pine trees now. The shadow ended between the pitcher's mound and home plate. Moondog cast an anxious eye momentarily in the other direction, toward the school's main building and the arid mountains beyond. Then he stepped into the batter's box.

Doug threw three pitches low and outside, each one missing the strike zone by more than the last. "It would have been a shitty poem," Mimi Anderson muttered, "if they'd walked Mighty Casey with first base open."

"What really happens?" Marilou asked.

"Mighty Casey strikes out."

"Well, I wish they'd get it over with," Marilou said. "I'm freezing."

The crowd had dwindled to less than a quarter of its original size, but those who had stayed were abuzz at the last-ditch rally. Marilou saw that Steve Dakota had remained, but Robert Rickard had not. Moondog swung the bat back and forth, waiting for Doug's next pitch.

It came inside; Moondog could probably have let it go and taken the walk. But his timing was perfect. Taking a small stutter step backward, Moondog whipped the bat around. There was a loud crack as the sweet spot connected with the ball.

Moondog did not even attempt to run. The ball rocketed into the dying sunlight of right field. It was still rising when it cleared the embankment, well west of the Annex and solidly in fair territory. The right fielder, like Moondog, simply watched it go. It came to rest somewhere far back in the trees behind the school.

"Yes!" Mimi Anderson leapt to her feet, toppling the huge purse she had been cradling into Marilou's lap as the rest of the crowd reacted to the tremendous home run. The teachers' team streamed onto the field to welcome Estabrook, Martinez, and finally Nygerski to home plate with the runs that tied the game. Doug, on the mound, just stared out at the distant woods in disbelief.

"It's tied!" the art teacher cried, shaking Marilou excitedly by the shoulder.

"So what does that mean?" Marilou managed to ask. "Extra innings?"

"Probably. Unless we wrap it up right here. You can't tie for a championship."

"Well, I'm about ready to go home," Marilou said. "It's going to be dark soon, and I'm getting colder by the minute. I'm not used to these mountain nights."

"I'm sure they'll turn the lights on," Anderson said. "I'm gonna stay to the bitter end. Fifty bucks is fifty bucks."

"You're *not* leaving *now!*" came an angry voice from the field.

Marilou turned. The voice belonged to Carl Estabrook. The young teacher's anger was directed at Moondog, whose home run had just tied the game.

A tight little circle of players jostled near the home plate end of the stands, by the gap in the fence through which players entered and left the playing area. Nygerski was closest to the exit. Estabrook, she saw, had hold of his shirt, physically preventing him from leaving the field. Alan Doucette, Barry Curtis, and several other players stood around them. Wild Bill Oates, whom Marilou would have expected to be at the center of any confrontation, was still at home plate, holding the bat and watching, along with the players in the field, to see what would happen.

"Let me go," Marilou heard Nygerski say softly.

"You can't leave *now!*" Estabrook shouted at him. "Not when we've got a chance to win! I won't let you go!"

"You'll be very sorry," Moondog said.

"And what the hell is *that* supposed to mean?" All the anger in the standoff belonged to Estabrook, whose grip on Moondog's shirt tightened. "Are you threatening me?" he demanded.

Moondog nodded toward the trees beyond left field. "The Sun's almost down," he said. "I have to go. Now."

Estabrook did not release his grip. "We've got lights," he said. "Come on, we've got a *tie game* here, man! We need you!"

"I've done all I can," Moondog said. "Now, I'm telling you, you better let me go. Otherwise, I can't be responsible for what happens."

Marilou had left her seat; she was now standing directly behind Carl Estabrook, separated from him by several players. She could see Nygerski's face. It bore a look of desperation and controlled insanity. She knew he wasn't joking. For whatever reason, he *had* to get away. And she thought of the morning, almost a month ago, when he had shown up late for school with something of the same gaunt, haunted look. Moondog was making an effort to keep his voice calm, but his agitation was evident. His hands were shaking, flecks of foamy white spittle clung to the corners of his mouth beneath the dark mustache, and a vein throbbed visibly near one temple. Marilou thought crazily that there could be a real fight here—over a game of *baseball,* for Christ's sake—and that Carl would probably get the worst of it.

"Let him go, Carl," she said.

Estabrook turned around at the sound of her voice. She saw surprise in his eyes. "Don't you want us to win, Lou?" he croaked.

"It's just a game. Let him go if he wants to."

"Better do what she says," Moondog growled. "You're all in danger."

"What the hell?" Estabrook looked wildly back and forth between Moondog and Marilou, and then at all the players gathered around. His hesitation gave Moondog the chance he needed. He crashed a forearm into the teacher's chest. Estabrook staggered backward and loosened his grip. There was a short ripping sound as Moondog twisted free. He sprinted for the parking lot. Moondog had evidently planned his escape, for his motorcycle was parked just beyond the tennis courts. It roared to life. Moondog raced out of the parking lot, barely slowing down as he took the turn onto the highway, tilting so far over, it appeared for a moment that he would lose his balance. Seconds later, he was gone, disappearing beyond left field into the gathering twilight.

Marilou watched him go, her emotions in conflict. It was the first time she had seen him on his bike.

Danny Taylor, his umpire's mask in his hand, was the one who broke the silence. "What do you suppose got into *him?*" he asked no one in particular.

"Dunno," said Alan Doucette. "You okay, Carl? He smacked you pretty hard."

"Son of a bitch," Estabrook muttered, rubbing his chest. "Yeah, I'm fine. Damn, I can't believe he abandoned us like that!"

"He's strange," Doucette agreed. "But at least he stayed long enough to tie the game. Now let's win it."

"Play ball," Danny Taylor said, pulling his mask back on. "We'll turn on the lights at the end of the inning."

"The son of a bitch," Estabrook muttered again. He looked sullenly at Marilou.

"You guys can win without him," she said. She gave him a smile she did not feel, then returned to her seat next to Mimi Anderson. The confrontation had made her uneasy, and the cornered-animal look in Moondog's eyes had actually frightened her. It was a relief that he was gone. And yet she felt that a moment of near understanding had passed between them in the half second that their eyes had met when he had been in Carl Estabrook's grip. That, too, was unsettling, and she didn't know why.

"I hate sports," she said to the art teacher. "They turn men into pugnacious little boys."

"Which is their true nature," Mimi Anderson replied. "Underneath all the career and family stuff, games are what really make them tick. It's what makes them so exasperating—but it's also a part of their charm."

"Maybe you're right," Marilou said, feeling herself relax a little. "But you know what? I don't really give a damn who wins."

"Good for you," Anderson said. "Of course *I* care, but that's because I've got fifty bucks invested. Tell you what. I'll take you to dinner if we win."

"And I'll buy if they lose," Marilou said, feeling her shakiness begin to dissolve.

The big woman reached out and rubbed Marilou's back with the palm of her hand. "You're all right," she said.

The game went eleven innings. The last two innings were played under the lights, and the baleful eye of the full Moon, which rose above the hills soon after Moondog's sudden departure. Bob Hommel, pressed into service at second base, might have caught the Moon in his eyes when he misplayed Doug's ground ball and allowed the Indians to score the winning run; in any case, it would serve as a convenient excuse later, during several rounds at Quinn's with members of both teams.

Marilou gladly paid for dinner with Mimi Anderson at Bruno's, a quieter and more expensive restaurant at the other end of Main Street. The peace was worth the price. She was happy that the game and the season were over, and that her classroom windows would be safe until spring.

15

The Earth Is Unstable

The Earth is unstable in California—every school-age child in North America knows that. So are some of the people. Every so often, goes one joke, God picks up the United States by the Eastern Seaboard and shakes it, and everything loose rolls to California. For Moondog Nygerski, originally from Boston, the day of the earthquake—the day after the championship game—would turn out to be one of the pivotal days of his life.

The day began badly enough. Moondog's bus arrived at Palm Spring more than an hour late. There was no flirtatious small talk with Olive, the waitress, this morning, nor any of the usual banter with the kids, who weren't too happy to be kept waiting in the chilly dawn of the high desert.

"Man, where have *you* been?" said a kid named Hodge, a junior of medium height whose fondness for doughnuts and Twinkies would likely lead to a desk job with a private security company. "You look bad. You got a hangover?"

"Sit down and shut up," Nygerski growled at him. "And hang on. We gotta make up some time."

Moondog indeed looked terrible. He hadn't shaved, and his bloodshot eyes drooped above gray semicircles. Odd bits of leaves and twigs stuck to his clothes, which were torn in several places. Small cuts lined the backs of his hands; his fingernails were dirty and dark. At each stop, the students looked at him strangely. He picked up Kyle Tyler and Richie Marks, and even the lumbering, slow-witted boy's usually expressionless face registered surprise at Moondog's shoddy appearance. Several other students tried snide remarks; they were cut down with a glare and told to be quiet. Moondog was not in a mood to be trifled with this morning, and his passengers quickly got the message.

Moondog felt as bad as he looked. Though he had little memory of the night, he knew he hadn't slept. Exhaustion squeezed his brain; his bones ached with a feeling akin to metal fatigue. And he worried about possible fallout from the previous evening's incident on the baseball field. He had a vague image of himself punching a teacher, a teammate, and he wondered what clout, if any, Carl Estabrook carried with the superintendent. Whatever happened, there would be questions, and his answers would be awkward, at best. Marilou McCormick's car had already been in the parking lot when he'd arrived, late, on his motorcycle. He thought he'd caught a glimpse of her face at the Annex door in his rearview mirror as he wheeled the bus quickly through the parking lot, having skipped all the daily state-required safety checks. She was the one, he remembered now, who had extricated him from danger. I wonder if she knows, he thought. He felt nauseous, the inside of his mouth tasted terrible, and he was dying for a cup of coffee. The thermos beside him was empty and needed to be washed.

Still, he drove with assurance, albeit excessive speed, and would likely have been at the school not more than a few minutes into first period had not Kevin Byars, one of the Sheriff's deputies, picked that morning to lay a speed trap just beyond

Lake Henshaw on the long downgrade into Santa Ysabel. Moondog didn't see the cop car, cached behind a small grove of manzanita trees, until it pulled out far behind him and turned on its red-and-blues. A fully loaded school bus traveling downhill at more than eighty miles an hour cannot just stop. Moondog rolled almost all the way to the intersection at Santa Ysabel before Byars, lights pulsing and siren wailing, caught up with the bus.

The kids, predictably, went nuts. "Shut up!" Moondog roared above the hoots and raucous laughter. He stood up and glared at them.

"You're busted, Moondog!" somebody yelled from the back.

"Shut *up!*" Moondog shouted again, and it was clear from the tone of his voice and the murderous look in his eyes that he meant it.

Moondog opened the door as the officer approached the bus. Byars was a no-nonsense cop, stockily built, with granite features and a crew-cut sprinkled with gray. "You in the habit of running from the police?" he demanded.

"I stopped," Moondog said.

"Took you long enough," the officer growled. "You know how fast you were going?"

"I'm late," Moondog told him.

"Well, you're gonna be later. *And* poorer. Lemme see your license and registration."

"Look, I know I was speeding," Moondog said. "But I couldn't help it. You know any physics?"

"What's that got to do with the price of apples?" Byars snapped.

"How steep would you say that hill back there is? Fifteen degrees? Twenty?"

"Who the hell cares?" the officer said. "You're getting a ticket, and it ain't gonna be cheap." Byars had one foot on the bottom step of the bus, his hand palm up on his knee. He wanted documents, not debate.

Someone made a comment in the back of the bus, inaudible up front, setting off a burst of laughter. Moondog quieted it with a glare and a slashing hand motion across his throat.

He returned his attention to the officer. "The force propelling the bus down the hill," Moondog explained with exaggerated patience, "is equal to the sine of the angle, times the acceleration due to gravity—which is a constant nine-point-eight meters per second squared—times the mass of the bus, which, when it's full like this, is huge. What's the sine of twenty degrees? It's up around a third; it's not insignificant. So you take one-third of the total weight of the bus, me, and all these kids, and multiply it by ten. It's a humongous number. The only force opposing it is friction, from the tires on the road and from the air. It's way imbalanced. I can't *help* but speed. I'd wear out the brakes if I didn't."

The officer's stony expression did not change. "If you think this fancy talk is gonna get you out of a ticket, you're sadly mistaken," he said. "My partner's on his way. We'll see that you get to the school safely, so these kids can get to class. Then I'm gonna write you a ticket and have a little chat with your boss."

"Put the cuffs on him!" one student cried gleefully. The hubbub started up again, for many of the kids thought this was the coolest thing that had happened on the bus all year.

"Use your stun gun!" yipped another.

"Shut up!" Moondog cried into the rising foam of voices.

"You goin' to *jail*, sucka!"

"Shut *up!*"

"I can't believe you were doing eighty-three with a school bus full of kids," Byars said, shaking his chiseled head. "You're a maniac."

The first class of the day had just ended, and Marilou McCormick had stepped out the front door of the Annex for a breath of fresh air when Moondog's bus, escorted by two cop cars, one in front and one in back, pulled slowly into the parking lot.

Most of the bus windows were open, and he had the stereo on, not loud, but loud enough for her to recognize Mick Jagger singing "Satisfaction." The kids poured off the bus, laughing and joking and making goo-goo eyes at the officers, who sat stiffly in their cars and watched them disperse. Nygerski remained behind the wheel, awaiting his fate.

Bus and driver were still there forty-five minutes later when Marilou again emerged from the Annex and headed toward the main building for her break. One of the cop cars remained also, parked behind the bus. It was empty.

Moondog opened the bus door as she approached. She looked at him questioningly, then stopped.

"I want to thank you," he said. "For sticking up for me yesterday."

"Baseball is a silly game," she said.

"Did we win?"

"No."

"Too bad," Moondog said softly. "I wish I could've stayed."

"Why didn't you?"

"Bad timing." His mouth smiled, but his eyes did not. "It's a somewhat complicated story," he said. "But if anyone here would believe it, it would be you."

"We need to talk," she told him.

His expressionless face concealed his surprise. "About what?" he asked.

"About my classroom, and what you said about it." She paused, and they looked at each other for several seconds. "And about the other stuff, too. Your weird behavior last night. And how come you're late again? You look like you've been in a fight or something." She let his eyes follow hers back toward the cop car. "Are you in trouble?"

"Don't know," he said. "I got a speeding ticket." He reached into the pocket of his jacket and held the ticket out for her to see. "The cop told me to wait here. He's in talking to the boss right now."

"What time do you bring the bus back? After school?"

"Depends on how fast I drive the kids home." He grinned at her; she did not smile back.

"I'll wait. I'll be in my classroom correcting papers. All right?"

"All right," he said automatically. He was staring at her, probably too intently, but she did not look away. The bell rang for third period, and still she made no move to leave.

Moondog had not had his morning coffee, and Marilou must have found his stare disconcerting, for she cocked her head to one side and said, "What?"

"You're very beautiful," he said to her before he could stop himself.

She blinked twice, rapidly. His dark eyes held hers a moment longer, and then she whirled on her heel and stalked off toward the rear door of the main building. Moondog watched her knee-length plaid skirt flare outward; his eyes followed her as she walked away from him, her back erect and shoulders squared. Only after she disappeared into the door did he close his eyes and put his hands to his temples. He had had a headache all morning, but now it was worse.

Winter announced its impending arrival in the Southern California mountains that afternoon. By the time Moondog returned from his route, the wind had acquired a bite. A thick bank of clouds, shepherded by the fast-moving air, had moved in from the north and blocked the Sun. Brown leaves swirled around the nearly deserted parking lot. The wind buffeted the bus, which Moondog had driven at reasonable speeds along the whole loop.

For the first time in weeks, the baseball field lay deserted. The Bailey High football team, under the brusque encouragement of its bundled coach, shuffled around on the football field in front of half a dozen onlookers, preparing for the next loss in a dismal season. Homecoming was less than two weeks away;

this year's squad had thus far managed four touchdowns in five games, and the battle-weary coach had been heard to remark in teachers'-lounge candor that it was a good thing the game was against Borrego Springs, one of the few teams in the area anywhere near as bad as Bailey.

Moondog parked the bus in its usual spot behind the gym and did a cursory job of sweeping its interior before ambling over to the Annex.

He knocked on the side of the open door, and the heater, which had been running, shut off immediately. "Did you make it do that?" Marilou asked as he entered the room.

She was seated at the big desk, her briefcase open on her left, a stack of papers on her right. Her small black purse sat beside the briefcase. She kept her desk cleared of most extraneous material—no family pictures, no sentimental trinkets or paperweights, no flowers, no snacks, and no books. It was almost too neat.

"I don't know," Moondog said lightly. "Maybe I did."

She shifted the stack of papers into the briefcase and snapped it shut. Moondog moved toward the front of the room, but he did not go up onto the raised area. The chair in front of the huge desk—the "conference chair" in which Heather Monroe had sat during Marilou's ill-fated attempt at gaining her confidence—he ignored.

"Why do they call you Moondog?" she asked. "You don't much look like a surfer."

He shrugged and looked over at the wall of authors. "It's my nickname, that's all."

"But it must come from *somewhere*."

He turned, and his dark eyes met hers. "Why do you want to know?"

She looked down at the backs of her hands, fumbling for a coherent answer. "I guess I want to know more about you," she said finally. She looked up. "You've acquired something of a reputation as a mysterious dude around here."

He laughed. "Mysterious dude, huh? I wish it were that simple."

"Why exactly do you think my classroom is haunted?" she asked him. "And by what?"

Moondog moved toward the authors' wall and scanned the posters. "There's a presence in here, some sort of supernatural entity," he said. "I felt it the first time I was in here, and I feel it now. And it's got . . . something . . . to do with these posters."

"How do you know this?" Marilou said, pushing her chair back from the desk.

Moondog drifted down the row of authors, looking into each pen-and-ink face. "Nathaniel Hawthorne," he murmured in warm recognition. "Good old Boston boy. A puritan, just like me."

Marilou laughed. "You? A puritan?"

But Moondog didn't answer. He moved slowly down the wall. Something about the posters captivated him.

"Papa Hemingway," he said, nodding to the grim, bearded face. "And Stephen Crane. Sometimes the good die young. My man Ed Poe! Eddie, *baby*." He turned briefly to Marilou. "You know that some guy puts a bottle of brandy on Poe's grave every year on his birthday? Comes to the cemetery all dressed in black, and nobody knows who he is."

"I didn't know that," Marilou said.

But Moondog had moved on. "John Steinbeck," he said. "He would never trade intensity for longevity. Neither would I."

"You haven't answered my question," Marilou reminded him.

He turned to face her. He had wandered almost all the way down the wall; nearly the whole classroom stood between them. "Do you like these posters?" he asked her. The dreamlike quality was gone from his voice.

"No," she said. He thought he saw an involuntary shudder. "In fact, I hate them."

"Why haven't you taken them down?"

Marilou's face went blank for a moment. Nervously, she looked down at her hands again. "I guess . . . I just haven't gotten around to it."

"Two months, and you haven't gotten around to it? Come on."

"I've been busy!" she snapped at him. "It's my first year here, and all these new kids . . . You don't know—you just pick them up and drive them home, and the way you drive, they probably just shut up and hang on for dear life!"

He grinned. "My driving style does have its advantages."

"You're not responsible for anything but getting them here—you don't have to make them want to learn. You don't have to deal with parents, and homework, and the office. . . . You don't expend one-quarter the energy I do. I'm exhausted by the end of the day. You don't think I'm busy? You don't know what busy is!"

"I think you've tried to take those posters down," Moondog said, "and something's prevented you from doing it."

Marilou's jaw dropped. "How did you know that?" she asked in a husky half whisper.

"Because they don't want to come down." He walked slowly back along the wall, toward the front of the room. "These posters," he said, "these authors, are part of the presence I feel. Something of them and of their work is in this classroom, and not just in books. I know it sounds far-fetched, but I can feel it as clearly as I can see you. Whatever supernatural force is in here is using these posters to manifest itself."

Marilou stood up and walked to the center of the raised area. "That's the most ridiculous thing I've ever heard," she said. "They're just posters. They're not even very good ones."

"But you *have* tried to take them down."

"Ye-es." She took another few steps toward him, stopping at the top step. She threw a sidelong glance at the authors, then quickly looked away.

"What happened?"

"Twice I got paper cuts, and once I fell on my ass," she said, not looking at him.

"Do you think the selection of the authors might be significant?" Moondog asked her. "I mean, there are a lot more writers who *aren't* up there. It might help to look for things these authors have in common."

"They're all dead, for one thing," Marilou said. "Except for Salinger."

"And he might as well be, for all he's written the past thirty years," Moondog said. "What else?"

"Well, they're all white. They're all Americans. And except for Edith Wharton and Willa Cather, they're all men."

"Willa Cather—she almost counts as a man, anyway," Moondog remarked.

"Why is that?"

"Well, she was a dyke, right?"

"God, you're obnoxious." Marilou stepped off the raised area and walked toward him. She stopped just far enough away from him that they could not touch each other. He saw anger creeping in behind her confusion. "Look, who *are* you?" she demanded. "You almost run me down with a bus, you tell me my room is haunted, and now you're trying to lecture me about literature. And you drive a bus! You show up late, for God knows what reason, and then you come in here and start talking to the posters! They're just pictures on paper, for God's sake! I can take them down any time I want to!"

"Do it, then," Moondog said quietly.

"I haven't had time!" Several veins stood out on her neck.

"You're scared," he told her.

"I'm not," she insisted, lowering her voice with an effort. But she made no move toward the posters.

"Tell you what," he said. "*I'll* do it. You want 'em down, we'll take 'em down. Pick an author. Whom do you want to get rid of first?"

She blinked, then stared silently at him for several seconds. Her face was flushed. She looked over her shoulder at the authors and then away again. "Steinbeck," she said. "He looks like the devil, with that goatee. Take him down first."

The poster of Steinbeck was well above the blackboard, near the far end of the wall. Moondog dragged one of the desks over. "Is this what you did?" he asked Marilou. "When you fell?"

"More or less. One of the legs was wobbly, I guess. I wasn't being careful."

Moondog wiggled the desk to assure himself it was sturdy. "What's holding the posters up?" he asked.

"Don't know. Tape, some kind of glue. They've been up there a long time. Carl says they've been there since *he* was a student."

"Well, we'll cut 'em down if we have to." Moondog pulled a buck knife from the pocket of his jeans but did not open it. Testing the desk one more time, he placed a foot on the seat and hauled himself upward. He curled his fingers around the top edge of the blackboard and lifted his other foot onto the top of the desk. His eyes were now at the same level as Steinbeck's. With the knife in one hand, he reached for the corner of the poster with the other—

And God stamped his foot very near them.

Moondog felt the desk lurch underneath him. He jumped backward onto the floor and fell to one knee. The light fixtures high above him swayed crazily; the fan above Marilou's desk danced and rattled; the heater screamed into life. Marilou's briefcase slid off the desk and bounced on the carpet steps, springing open and spilling papers. Her purse fell to the floor and overturned. Books tumbled off the shelves behind her desk. From the closet came the sound of more chaos as volumes fell from their resting places. The blinds slapped against the rattling windows. Dust flew everywhere. The door to the room slammed shut with a report like a rifle shot.

Marilou screamed and pitched forward into his arms. Dust,

powder, paint chips, and small chunks of plaster rained down from the ceiling. They clung tightly to each other as the room shook all around them.

"My God!" Marilou cried. "It's the big one!"

"It's quieting down," Moondog reassured her, his mouth close to her ear. The smell of her was immediate and intoxicating, even in the midst of disaster.

The earthquake lasted less than sixty seconds. Its epicenter would later be pinpointed on the Elsinore Fault, just north of Julian, a scant five miles from the school. It registered 5.7 on the Richter scale—powerful enough, for those in the immediate area—but it was not even the strongest quake in Southern California that year. In Julian, cans toppled from grocery store shelves and boulders rolled out onto the highway, but there were no injuries and little substantial damage beyond the boundaries of the town. It would make the evening news and serve as a topic of conversation for a day or two, but it was in reality a routine California quake, as much an accepted part of life in that part of the world as summer sunshine and blondes in convertibles. As with every earthquake, it would be seen as an act of God, its precise location a crapshoot, its timing utterly random.

Marilou McCormick and Cyrus Nygerski would not see it that way, however. Belief in coincidence has its limits. Someone—or something—wanted the portrait of John Steinbeck to stay on the wall and could command powerful forces to keep it there. Neither of them would ever really doubt this again.

They were still holding each other when the shaking stopped. A heartbeat later, the heater shut off. Though the room was a wreck, they both noticed immediately that not a single poster had been torn or dislodged.

Moondog picked a paint chip out of her hair and tossed it onto the carpet, which looked like it had been snowed on. Several of the desks lay on their sides; a trash can near the top of the steps had overturned, as well. "It's over," he said. "Looks like Robert's got his work cut out for him, though."

She laughed nervously and dislodged herself from his arms. He stood up and, taking her hands, helped her to her feet.

"We should get out of here," she said. "There could be aftershocks."

"Especially," he said pointedly, looking at the wall and the upside-down desk beside it, "if we try to take down any more posters."

She flashed him a quick, unreadable look and moved to the front of the room to gather the spilled contents of her briefcase and purse. She jammed the papers roughly into her briefcase, not bothering to straighten them, and snapped it shut. Moondog noticed that her hands were shaking.

"Here, let me help you."

Her eyes froze him on the first step. They were moist and confused. More than that—they were terribly frightened.

The heater roared suddenly and she jumped, respilling her purse. Moondog moved to collect the odds and ends that littered the carpet. She pulled the purse away from him, took the package of tissues and lipstick case wordlessly from his hands, dropped them on the floor again, picked them up, and shoved them into the purse. "Let's get out of here," she said.

But the door was jammed. The doorknob wouldn't turn. Marilou jiggled it furiously, and then, losing all pretense of composure, she dropped the purse and flailed at the closed door with her fists. "Let me *out!*" she screamed.

Moondog put a hand on her shoulder and drew her gently away. "Ssh," he said. "Calm down. Let me try."

"Let go of me!" she cried, pushing him away roughly.

"Will you calm down?" he snapped at her. He took her shoulders in both his hands and turned her around to face him. She bit her lower lip and looked into his eyes. Her face was streaked with tears. He thought of kissing her but didn't.

"It wants to keep us here," he said. "And I think I know why."

"It?" She was still shaking, and his hands were still on her shoulders.

"Whatever's calling the shots in this room," he said. "We may have to use the windows."

She swallowed and shook her head. "There's another way," she said. "Through the closet."

Marilou moved unsteadily to the light switch just inside the closet and flipped it, with no result. The bulb had blown, leaving the closet in near-total darkness. Ignoring the protests of the equally unnerved mice, they climbed through it anyway, picking their way hand in hand through knee-high stacks of books and supplies that had fallen and now blocked their way. Twice she stumbled, and Moondog caught her against himself. Both times, they separated slowly, drawing courage from the contact, feeling for each other's presence in the absence of light. Three narrow steps led down into Carl Estabrook's half of the closet, where large stand-up maps and folding chairs had fallen all over one another, making navigation even more treacherous. The heater came on again in the room behind them, as though infuriated that they were getting away. At any moment, Moondog expected an aftershock to rock the building and bury them in the stuff that remained on the closet's shelves. But at last, they emerged into Carl Estabrook's classroom, which was well lit through unblinded windows. Pieces of acoustic ceiling tiles lay smashed all over the floor amid desks, books, and papers—the room was as trashed as Marilou's. They unlocked the door from the inside and stepped gratefully out into the autumn air.

Hers was the only car remaining in the parking lot; his motorcycle was stashed by the buses behind the gym. The sky was steely gray, and cold for October, filled with the unidle threat of winter. Moondog and Marilou stood on the Annex steps and embraced.

"It's true, isn't it?" she said when the hug was over. "Something *made* that earthquake happen. Something in my room."

"It's true," he said.

"And you knew. You knew from the first time you set foot in there, the day you broke my window. How?"

He looked up at the gray sky as if searching for an answer. "It's a long story," he said finally. "And I think you might recognize some of it."

She studied his face. "You're a puzzle."

"I don't mean to be," he said. "At least not to you."

She shook some of the dust off her skirt. "Do you want to come over?" she asked after a moment's hesitation. "We could talk about it there. I could make you dinner."

It was the second time that day she had surprised him. Moondog studied her face. "That's . . . very nice of you, but I can't," he said.

"Just for a while? We still have a lot to talk about."

"I can't," he said, and looked away.

"Why not?"

His eyes returned to hers; he took a deep breath. "Look, Marilou, I know who you are. I know where you came from. And I know what happened to you on the beach last summer."

Marilou recoiled as if she had been slapped in the face. She stared at him hard. Her mouth moved, but no sound came out.

"Last night, when I left the baseball game, didn't you wonder why?" he asked her.

She swallowed. "I . . . figured you had your reasons," she croaked. "How did . . ."

"Last night the Moon was full," he said. "And it's still going to be pretty full tonight. Full enough, I think, unless we get totally socked in by the cloud cover. And I can't take that chance."

Marilou looked utterly confused. "What do you mean, 'full enough'?" she asked. "What are you *talking* about?"

His eyes looked intently into hers. She did not look away. "You mean you really don't know?" he said.

"How do you know about the beach? About . . ."

"Gary," Moondog said. "His name was Gary, wasn't it? Gary . . . Brown, some ordinary name like that."

"Burns," she whispered, still held by his eyes. A shudder ran through her.

"It was in the newspaper," Moondog explained. "I pick up all the major newspapers in California after the full Moon. I make note of any unexplained violent deaths—and there usually are a few. When you were hired here, I recognized your name from the article."

"But . . . *why*?"

He studied her agitated face. "You really *don't* know, do you?"

"What?"

Moondog felt his palms beginning to sweat, as they did when he was nervous, and when the Moon was full. Doubt prickled at the back of his mind, but he had told her too much already.

"Three years ago," he said slowly, "something horrible happened in this town. Several people were brutally killed. There was another teacher—I knew her briefly. She was one of the victims."

Marilou stared at him. "Go on," she said.

"Each full Moon, there was another murder. I was the one who first realized what was going on. I was able to stop the killings, but I was, uh . . . injured in the process.

"If you talk to the people around here, eventually they'll tell you about it, even though it was pretty traumatic, and even though this is a pretty closemouthed community. The victims were mangled, as if they'd been attacked by a wild animal. The crimes were never officially solved, and most likely they never will be. I'm the only one who knows what *really* happened—me and a guy who's hiding out in Mexico, last I knew. And I'm paying a terrible price for it."

Marilou shook her head. "What does any of this have to do with me?"

"The last victim," Moondog went on, "wasn't mauled like the others. He was shot through the heart. And I know who shot him, because I was there. My friend shot him—with a silver bullet, fired from my gun. On the night of a full Moon. Unfortunately, he bit me first."

Marilou's eyes widened in either disbelief or dread. "Are you trying to tell me that you're a . . . a *werewolf*?"

Moondog nodded solemnly. "And so was whatever killed Gary Burns."

Marilou took a step away from him, her blue eyes wild and unfocused. "I *really* don't know how to take you," she said.

"Not many people do," he admitted.

"I can't believe you're telling me this. Like you're serious!"

"I *am* serious! You didn't believe me about the presence in the classroom, either," he reminded her. "It took an earthquake to convince you! You asked me how I knew. I know because part of *me* is supernatural. The force inside my body comes from the same plane as the entity in that classroom—the one that's trying to kill you."

"*Kill* me?" Her voice was a squeak.

He nodded. "I sensed that, too, today. Whatever it is, it harbors a great desire to see you dead. I don't know why, but I can feel its anger, its lust for death—your death."

Her jaw moved up and down before words came. "You're *crazy!*" she screamed at him. "You're trying to frighten me!" She took several quick steps away from him, into the middle of the empty parking lot.

"Lou, I'm not!" he called after her. "I'm trying to *warn* you! Please!"

She stopped and glared at him. "What am I supposed to think?" she cried. "You say you're a werewolf. Okay, where are the people you kill every month? Why haven't I heard about *that*?"

"As far as I know," he said, taking a step toward her, "I haven't killed anyone."

"As far as you KNOW?"

"I'm not one hundred percent sure, because there's a memory loss that happens when I transform, but I haven't heard of any werewolflike murders around here lately. And I take precautions. That's why I left the game—and just in time, too. There's a place I go, to make sure people are safe from me."

He took another step forward; she matched it with a step away from him. "You actually expect me to believe this?"

"Look, why do you think I was so late this morning, and that other morning, a month ago? Why do you think I looked so wasted on those mornings?"

"Maybe you're a druggie," she shot back. "Maybe you were coming down off an all-night acid trip or something."

"I wish that were true," he said. "It would be a lot more fun than being a werewolf, believe me! And a lot less dangerous. Do you think I *wanted* this to happen? Do you think I *asked* for it? It's *hell* going through all that every month. It wastes me for *days!* But it happened, and now I need to go on with my life. Unfortunately, I also need a job. I'm handling the problem as responsibly as I know how."

Marilou had almost reached her car. "I . . . I think I need to go home now," she said.

"And I need to go to the place I go when the Moon is full," he told her. "Lou, trust me. I'm telling you the truth. And I think you know that I am."

"I don't know anything anymore," she said as she opened the car door. "And to think I came to this town for peace and quiet! You are without a doubt the strangest person I've ever met."

"I'll see you," he said as she got in and turned the key. He watched her wheel out of the parking lot and make the turn toward town. Then he was alone.

The gray sky was already beginning to darken. His heart

throbbed against the inside of his chest. Sweat ran freely across his palms. He wiped them on his jeans as he walked toward the back of the gym and his motorcycle, wishing that the weather would worsen, and that he had kept his awful secret to himself.

16

No School

No school today, Robert," Doug's voice said at six in the morning over the phone. "But you gotta come in anyway. Everything's all fucked up from the earthquake. We got a lot of work to do."

Robert was already up. He'd slept badly—the quake had set him on edge. His wife, a native Californian who was nonetheless afraid of earthquakes, had kept him up moving breakable things from shelves, filling plastic gallon jugs with fresh water, and checking inventories of canned food.

His son had not come home at all, nor had he called, but Robert had stopped worrying about the boy's absences years ago. It was his son's *presence* that annoyed him. Jimmy would show up when he got hungry, or needed money or a shower or a change of clothes. His wife would feed and fuss over him while Robert stewed in silent anger. Chrissakes, the "kid" was going to be twenty-four next month, didn't do any kind of steady work, and still lived with his parents. He smoked dope in his room when Robert wasn't home, and Robert had learned not to leave more than one beer in the refrigerator, hoarding his private stash in an ice chest in the garage—a fact that Jimmy had yet to discover. Jimmy did all right for himself, his father thought bitterly. He ate the food Robert bought, wore the clothes his mother washed, and got laid regularly—his latest girlfriend was a trampy type who hung out barefoot in front of the liquor store. Robert had seen them together many times but had not been formally introduced. He supposed she had a place where Jimmy stayed during his increasingly frequent absences, but his son's chronic unemployment, drug use, and devil-may-care attitude toward life so incensed Robert that they barely talked at all anymore. If I had more backbone, Robert frequently told himself, I'd kick his butt the hell out of here and let him fend for himself.

"I'll be there in half an hour," Robert said.

"The rooms are a mess," Doug told him. "It's gonna take awhile to get everything cleaned up. Could be some OT in it for you."

"I can stay as long as you want," Robert replied instantly. "See you in a few."

Robert's spirits were high as he packed himself a lunch and prepared to leave. The extra money would be nice, though Jimmy would likely eat it up, but even better was the prospect of spending an entire day at work, away from his less-than-ideal family. He left his sleeping wife a note, then walked gratefully out the door.

Thank God for the job, part-time though it was. At least it got him out of the house. He had little feeling for his wife beyond the comfort that she was there, and he suspected that the reverse was also true, for she displayed more interest in Phil Donahue than in him.

He drove easily up Banner Grade, not too fast and not too slowly, undismayed that the early-morning weather seemed to worsen with altitude. At the bottom of the hill, it had been breezy, with patchy clouds against the clear blue sky over the high desert. But the clouds were holding court in Julian, sitting atop the mountains in a cold gray clump, unmoved by either the wind or the early-morning Sun. As Robert ascended, he drove into the clouds themselves; by the time he arrived at the school, he was immersed in wet fog, his headlights and windshield wipers working against it.

He parked directly in front of the Annex, since the parking lot would not be in demand. He was still in a good mood when he unlocked the building, despite the mist and the wind that whipped at his thin jacket. Once inside, he would have shelter, and, when he got the heaters on, warmth.

His mood lasted even as he opened the two lower rooms and surveyed the damage—the toppled desks, the fallen ceiling tiles, the scattered books. In Donna Hurley's room, a flourescent light tube had fallen to the floor and exploded. The art room was worse, with smashed ceramics projects, spilled paint, and scattered supplies. Robert could see that he had at least a full day's work ahead of him, and the prospect made him happy. The good feeling of impending accomplishment lasted until he unlocked the door to room 13. It seemed to stick, but with a little bit of effort, he got the key to turn.

"Well, hello there! It is indeed a pleasure to have some company, finally."

The man stood by the back wall, leaning against the table where Marilou McCormick kept extra books and papers, most of which were now on the floor. In one hand, he held a bottle. Robert, one step inside the door, blinked and then stared, his mouth partially opened. He was dimly aware of the chaotic condition of the room—desks tipped over, books and plaster and paint chips on the carpet—but his attention was on the visitor. The man was small, with a hollow, somewhat pained expression, though the lips twisted upward into a humorless grin. His dark hair was neatly combed back from his high forehead, but one lock had escaped and dangled distractingly above one eyebrow. He was well dressed; a frilled white shirt and black trousers were topped by a heavy black overcoat that reached his knees, its thick collar turned up to give him something of a regal look despite his short stature. The man swaggered forward, tipped up the bottle, and took a healthy slug, then held it out toward Robert. "Share a drink, old chum?"

Robert didn't move. The man stumbled and almost fell on the steps as he descended into the main part of the classroom. "Come on, Robert, do imbibe with me," he said. "It's most exceptional potage—from Scurvy's private stash. Found it in the closet, concealed among the books." He took another swig. "Ah! Fine sippin' whiskey like this only improves with age."

Robert found his voice. "Who *are* you?" he demanded. "How do you know my name? How did you get in here?"

And who the hell, he wondered, was Scurvy?

"I'm shocked—indeed, I am profoundly grieved—that you don't recognize me," the man said. "Maybe I should put you in the closet and brick it up? Have you perchance perused that little tale yet? It's one of my best. Of course they're all pretty good, even if *she* doesn't think so. Uncultured wench."

Robert just stared.

"I could hit you over the head with this bottle, and by the time you came to, you'd be in a room with no doors and no windows, and only a few hours' air to breathe." The strange man looked at the bottle as though seriously considering the idea. "Be a shame to waste good booze, though."

"Who *are* you?" Robert cried.

The man bowed theatrically. "Edgar Allan Poe, at your service," he said.

Robert's eyes whirled to the authors' wall. Poe's poster was blank, except for the words. The author's face was gone.

Just like Hemingway, he thought. But Hemingway had appeared in a dream, when he was safely at home in his bed. And Robert was sure that he was wide-awake. He had the wrecked room to prove it.

Robert took a step backward, toward the door. "What do you want?" he croaked.

"Your help." Poe smiled with all the warmth of a hundred-year-old corpse.

Robert took another step backward. "I've got . . . classrooms to clean," he said.

"Have a drink, Robert. Relax." Poe advanced toward him, offering the bottle.

This can't be happening, Robert told himself. It's just some guy, been drunk all night, snuck in here to play a joke. Maybe Doug put him up to it, or that crazy bus driver.

But the poster was empty.

"C'mon, chum, join me for a drink." The man held the bottle in front of Robert's face. He could smell the liquor. He took another step back and shook his head.

"Suit yourself." Poe tipped the bottle, then wiped his mouth with the sleeve of the long black coat. " 'Twas quite an earthquake yesterday, was it not? Enough to wake the dead." The author cackled at his own joke.

When Robert didn't answer, Poe continued. "Here's what I want you to do," he said. "See that fan up there? Right above where that lovely young teacher sits? I'm afraid I lack the physical stature necessary to reach it. But you can, if I position myself on the desk and you stand on my shoulders."

"I don't know anything about fixing a fan," Robert said. "I'm not even sure it's broken. It just makes noise."

The dead author grinned conspiratorially. "Who said anything about fixing it? What I want you to do is loosen the nuts on the bolts that are holding the thing up there. I've got a wrench in my coat, though there is the possibility that the earthquake loosened them enough that you won't need it."

Robert only stared, and Poe laughed again. "Do you not grasp my intent? It's beautiful! Though time may have dulled its blades, they should have sufficient mass and speed to cut quite deeply. You loosen the nuts until they're almost but not quite ready to come off. The next good aftershock should shake them loose. If that fortuitous event should happen during the day, and she's sitting there—*swack!* No more teacher's dirty looks."

Robert's eyes widened. "You want to *kill* her?"

"Not me, old chum," Poe said with a wink. "I don't care about her. It's just sport to me, that's all. Entertainment. But for Scurvy, it's different. Between you and me, I think Scurvy's in love."

"Who's Scurvy?" Robert blurted.

Poe's expression became suddenly serious. He fixed Robert with his bottomless dark eyes. An involuntary shudder ran through the janitor's body. "You're in Scurvy's room, my friend," the dead author intoned.

"Mr. Lurvey," Robert said, suddenly understanding. "Scurvy and Mr. Lurvey are—were—the same person."

"Scurvy brought me here," Poe said. He took in his fellow authors with a grand sweep of his arm. "He brought us all here, breathed new life into all of us. He's our master." Poe took a long swig from the bottle. "It's a shame old Mark Twain got away. But he was always a contrary sort. Myself, as long as Scurvy keeps a supply of this stuff on hand, I am quite content to serve him."

Robert started to back away again, but Poe sensed his intention. "Don't try to leave," the author snapped. "You can't leave. Not when we have work to do."

"What makes you think I'll help you?" Robert said.

"Refuse, and it will go hard on you."

"Why do you even *need* my help?" Robert wondered aloud. "Why don't you loosen the nuts yourself?"

"Not tall enough," Poe said. "Neither are you. But if you stand on my shoulders . . ." Poe gave Robert an exaggerated wink. "We little guys have got to stick together, right?"

"What about your friends?" Robert asked, nodding toward the literary pantheon.

Poe took another drink.

"They can't help you, either, can they?" Robert said, the triumph of the realization edging into his voice. "You're all ghosts! You need a living human being to do your dirty work. That's it, isn't it? You can show up and talk and try to scare me, but you can't actually *do* anything."

"You're very wrong," Poe said, and the room filled with a blinding flash of light.

Robert threw his hands up to protect his eyes, and he heard the door slam shut behind him. When he opened his eyes again, Poe was gone. The heater roared to life.

Dazed, Robert looked around the room. Perhaps the flash had momentarily blinded him, because everything seemed too dim, even though the lights were on. They glowed weakly from high, high above, like the feeble sunlight of a winter's day eking its way into a well. Robert saw that Poe's face was back on its poster, scowling as always, fixing him with a malevolent stare. The heater's pinched, unlubricated voice whined in his ears. And the fan had changed. Its four blades still rotated slowly, clattering softly in syncopation with the steady whir of the heater, but they were no longer parallel to the floor. They were, in fact, very nearly perpendicular. And as Robert watched in astonishment, the thing began to move!

The fan swayed forward, not as it had in the earthquake, but with a purpose. For a moment, Robert feared that what Poe had predicted was about to happen—that the fan would fly from its fixtures and decapitate him. He watched in captivated fascination. The metal post holding the fan to the ceiling stretched and bent. The fan swung forward, back, then forward again—and Robert could *see* the metal stretch, allowing the fan to descend with each swing. Yes, it was impossible, but there could be no doubt that the thing was coming closer to him with each swing. Robert could see the whirring fan blades spinning faster and faster, egged on by the heater's hysterical whine. Robert edged toward the rear of the room as the fan swung forward, back, forward, back. In a few more swings, Robert—not that he would want to—would be able to reach up and touch the lethal blades as they passed overhead.

And now the room itself began to contort. The walls pressed inward, and the ceiling retreated to a dizzying height. The arc of the approaching fan encompassed the entire area between the walls, and Robert realized in stark terror that he would soon have no place to run. He ducked away as the fan hurtled toward him at head level. What was happening was clearly impossible, and yet all his senses told him that he would soon be sliced to pieces if he didn't get out of the classroom in the next few seconds. Rolling away as the silver-gray blur swung toward his chest, Robert made it to the door and tugged at the doorknob. It was jammed.

"Help!" he screamed, pounding on the door with his fists. "Somebody help me!"

But the noise from the heater overpowered his words. The metallic shriek had become earsplitting. Robert covered his ears and watched from the floor in disbelief as the fan blades came toward him again, slicing the air less than a meter above his prostrate body. The fan stopped just short of the wall of windows, against which Robert cowered, swung back toward the far wall, and came forward again, neatly sawing an overturned desk in half as it homed in. Shaking and hyperventilating, Robert pressed himself against the floor along the back wall. He could smell sawdust and burning oil as the demented machine barely missed him. In another pass or two, the stench would be augmented by the smell of his own blood as the fan blades sliced him as efficiently as they had the desk. He looked desperately at the picture of Poe, high above him in the metamorphosed room. The author's cruel pen-and-ink expression had not changed.

"Please," Robert cried hoarsely. "I'll do anything! Make it stop!"

His words were drowned out by the shrieking heater. Robert could do nothing but lie helplessly against the back wall and wait for the fan, its blades promising butchery, to make its next pass. He felt as though he was seeing the room through a trick camera that distorted distance and dimension. But if all this was an illusion, why was the bilous taste of fear on the back of his tongue so real? Robert felt his throat constrict; there was no saliva in his mouth to lubricate another futile cry for help. On this pass, or the next, the deadly pendulum would surely cut him in two.

The swinging agent of death came toward him—and Robert heard something on the other side of the door. It was the sound of a key being inserted into a lock. He gathered his breath. *"Help!"* he cried with all the strength that remained in him. The heater's crazed whine jumped an octave or two. Robert covered his ears in pain and closed his eyes. The door swung inward, banging Robert in the head—and the agonizing noise abruptly ceased.

He opened his eyes to see a pair of green elf shoes, attached to legs in black tights that disappeared into a plain red skirt just beyond the knees. There was a black briefcase beside the skirt, a pressed white blouse beyond that, and a concerned face framed by wavy red hair looking down at him from what seemed a great height. "Robert!" Marilou McCormick exclaimed. "Are you all right?"

The fan was above the teacher's desk, where it had always been, its blades once more horizontal and circling lazily. The room, though still a disaster, had reverted to its normal dimensions.

He sat up and rubbed his head where the door had hit it. She knelt beside him, and as his sense of proportion returned, she no longer seemed so tall. What the hell was going on here? Had he fallen asleep and had another dream? Or was he losing his mind? He looked into Marilou's face, searching for a clue.

"What are you doing here?" he asked her, trying to keep the shakiness out of his voice. "There's no school today."

"I came in to clean up," she said. "After the earthquake."

"That's *my* job."

"Oh, I know. But you don't know where everything goes—the books and papers and so forth. Robert, what happened in here?"

"We had an earthquake." Robert's heart was still doing gymnastics in his chest, but he did his best to conceal his fright from her. He knew his answer sounded inane, but it was the most ostensibly normal thing he could think of to say at the moment.

"I mean just now," she said. "I *know* we had an earthquake, but that was yesterday. Just before I opened the door, I heard you scream. And then I find you on the floor. What happened?"

Robert looked at her hard. She seemed much older than she had on the day he had first met her, not quite two months ago. There were worry lines around the youthful mouth, and an animal wariness in the eyes that he had not seen before. Was the room working its perverse magic on her, as well? What sort of strange things had *she* seen? How much did she know?

He decided to risk confiding in her. "Do you remember the dog?" he asked her.

A cloud crossed her face. They had thus far avoided discussing it. "I remember," she said softly.

"Ms. McCormick . . ."

"Lou, Robert."

"All right, Lou. Do you believe in ghosts?"

She said nothing for several seconds. He got groggily to his feet and sat down at the nearest upright desk. She sat in the desk beside it, turning it to face him. "Tell me what happened," she said.

And he did. He related the entire incident, not leaving out Poe's plan to sabotage the fan so that it would come crashing down on her. He related how the room had become his pit, and the fan his pendulum. After he finished, neither of them said anything for what seemed like a long time. Finally, Robert said, "You probably think I'm crazy."

"No, Robert," she said quietly. "I know the room is haunted."

"You do? How?"

"Moondog told me," she said. "And I believe him. Last night—"

There was a loud crash from deep inside the closet, and a moment later, Carl Estabrook's voice floated out to them from the darkness. "Goddamn, where did all these frigging chairs come from?" They clanged about as he pushed them aside, and then he emerged into the room. He grinned at Marilou, ignoring Robert. "What a mess, huh?"

"At least this time you had the manners to announce your arrival," she said.

"How could I help it?" He spread his hands out to his sides, and they both laughed.

"I had to use that closet as my escape route last night. After the earthquake, that door slammed shut, and the latch jammed."

"You were *here*?" Eastabrook said, echoing Robert's surprise.

Marilou nodded. "I had some work to do."

"Boy were *you* lucky." Carl Estabrook whistled softly as he surveyed the room. Robert didn't care much for the way the young teacher, dressed for action in sweatpants and a short-sleeved preppy pullover shirt with an alligator nibbling at his nipple, had taken over the situation. Unnoticed, Robert took a few steps toward the door.

"This room's even worse than mine," assessed Estabrook, hands on hips. "You're lucky you didn't lose any windows. That desk got split right in half." He nodded at an overturned desk near the door.

Marilou looked at Robert. He looked at her—and there was

no need for words. They both knew the desk had not been broken in the quake. Marilou knew because she had been in the room then. Robert knew because he had watched the fan blades saw through the desk on the last pass before it would have cut through him.

He would have liked to talk more with her about the bizarre things they both had witnessed in this strange, strange classroom, but Estabrook's presence precluded further conversation on that subject.

Perhaps Marilou sensed that, too. She turned to her colleague. "Anybody been in to make coffee?" she asked.

"Alan's here. You know what a caffeine freak he is."

"Let's go see," she said, steering him toward the door.

Robert followed them into the hall. Later that day, after the paint came grudgingly off the floor of the art room and the other classrooms had been straightened and swept, he would screw up enough courage to make a pass at cleaning room 13. He worked quickly, with the door open, keeping well away from the authors' wall. It was a lousy job, but he could live with it. He could *live*.

17

Moondog's Hearing

Moondog's hearing before the superintendent and vice principal took place the following Monday, during third period. Most (but not all) of the earthquake damage had been cleaned up, and school went on, though there was a giddy sense of trepidation among the students that an aftershock could send them scurrying for the doors at any moment. For many of them, any break from the routine was welcome, and it would be a day or two before things returned to normal.

Steve Dakota's inner sanctum, behind and out of sight of the two secretaries who stood as the first line of defense when visitors entered the school and who handed out late slips and hall passes to wandering students, included a conference room with a long table. Moondog's accusers—Dakota, Bill Oates, and Doug—arrayed themselves around one end. Marilou McCormick, attending the hearing at Moondog's request, sat neutrally along one side. Moondog took a seat at the end of the table nearest the door, which he feared might be held open at the conclusion of the meeting for his permanent exit.

Moondog looked and felt a good deal better this morning. He had showered and shaved and donned clean clothes, and he had driven his route without incident, arriving at the school on time. The outfit was his usual one: blue jeans, boots, a denim jacket, and one of the hats from his collection, this one a white fedora with a black band. The hat lay on the table in front of him.

"We've had a number of complaints," the superintendent began, "about your driving. Specifically, about excessive speed. And now this . . ." Steve Dakota's large hands grasped Moondog's citation. He waved it lazily in the air.

"Plus, you've been late on at least two occasions, as far as I know," Oates said. He rested his hands on the edge of the table and drummed lightly with his fingertips.

"I'll pay the fine," Moondog said quietly. Avoiding a court appearance would cost him $169, so the ticket said. Bribing the officer, he had decided after Friday's impromptu physics lesson, was out of the question.

"That's not the point," the superintendent told him. "You were clocked on radar, with a bus full of kids, going eighty-three miles per hour. That is totally unacceptable."

Moondog looked around the table, sizing up his position. Doug, in his usual uniform of blue jeans and a red T-shirt with one pocket (the colors varied from day to day, but not the style), sat impassively, arms folded across his chest, his long back and legs in a straight line sloping downward from the top of the reclining office chair to the carpet beneath the table. Bill Oates looked ready to spring. He sat erect at the front of his chair, and his fingers continued their soft tapping on the tabletop. Both Steve Dakota and Marilou McCormick looked ill at ease. The superintendent did not like matters of discipline, and Marilou did not really know the reason for her presence. "Moral support," Moondog had told her without elaboration when she had asked why he wanted her there, and she had reluctantly agreed to accompany him.

"Is there anybody who could take his place?" Bill Oates asked Doug. In his turtleneck and military haircut, Oates looked a little like Steve McQueen. "I'd say eighty-three miles an hour merits at least a good long suspension, if not outright dismissal."

"What I'm more interested in," Dakota said, "is the safety of the students. *And* getting them here on time." He looked pointedly at Moondog. "Not just most days. Every day."

Oates tugged at the front of his turtleneck and cleared his throat. "I think we should fire him," he said. "Doug, how soon can we get a new bus driver?"

"Hard to say," the big Indian said, looking at a spot in the air between Oates and Moondog. "We'd have to train someone. I suppose I could talk old Paul into coming out of retirement for a few weeks while we break in someone new. Then again, he's seventy-five years old."

"And drives at reasonable speeds," Dakota put in.

"His pacemaker won't allow him to drive over fifty-five," Doug quipped.

"Do we have anyone else?" Oates asked.

Doug shook his head. "Not who could start right away."

"Well, I don't want to send this guy out another day, if we can help it," Oates said, addressing his words to Dakota, even though Moondog was sitting right there. "A sixteen-year-old kid should know better than to drive a school bus eighty-three miles an hour when it's full of kids. We've got to let him go."

"I don't think that's necessary," Marilou said quietly.

They all turned to look at her.

"Everybody makes mistakes," she said. "I don't think it's fair to fire someone without giving him a second chance. I know I would think it unfair if you fired me with no warning for something *I* did."

"*Anyone* should know better than to drive a fully loaded schoolbus at eighty-three miles an hour," Oates maintained.

"I agree," Doug said.

"And what about the lateness?" asked Dakota, leaning forward. "I live on the coast, better than an hour away, and I manage to get here on time every day. Is there some reason you can't?"

"There is," Moondog said. He tried to catch Marilou's eye. Failing, he spread his hands palms down on the table in front of him. The fingernail on the right index finger was entirely black.

"And what would that be?" Oates demanded.

"I'm afraid I can't tell you."

"Why not?" Oates pressed. "It's your job we're talking about here. And you are answerable to this office."

"You wouldn't believe me," Moondog murmured, looking down at his hands. The index fingers were indeed growing longer, month by month, just as the gypsy woman in Ojai had said they would.

"He's only been late twice," Marilou said.

"That's twice too many, as far as I'm concerned," said Steve Dakota. "I'm sorry, Cyrus, but if you're not willing to cooperate with us and follow the rules, I'm afraid I'll have to take Bill's recommendation and find someone who will."

Moondog looked at Marilou. Her translucent blue eyes gazed back at him, but he could read no message there. He was on his own.

"I think your driving is irresponsible and dangerous, and I think you set a bad example for the students," Oates said.

"I'm not sure the sound system you have on that bus is appropriate, either," Dakota added. The superintendent had been in the parking lot one recent morning when the bus had come in blasting a raucous tape by a heavy-metal girl group called Cycle Sluts from Hell.

"And I don't like the way you dress, or comport yourself," Oates added. "It's not the proper image for the school."

"I see," Moondog said acidly. "So, in addition to speeding,

I'm now in trouble for my clothes and my taste in music. Anything else?"

"You're in trouble all over," Oates shot back. "And unless you tell us why you were late and had to speed to make up time, you're gonna be out that door at the end of this meeting."

Moondog's eyes sought out Marilou's for reassurance. "Your baseball team would suffer," he said, turning back to Oates.

"I don't care about that," Oates said. Apparently humor, so often an effective tool for defusing tense situations, wasn't going to work with the vice principal.

Moondog leaned back in his chair. "Let me get this straight," he said. "The status of my employment at this school is going to be decided here, today, at this meeting?" He looked at the superintendent.

"That's right," Steve Dakota said.

"And the three of you will decide?"

Dakota nodded.

"And as of right now, you want to fire me?"

"I know *I* do," Oates interjected.

Moondog looked from him to Dakota. "At this point, I would have to say that I'm leaning toward dismissal also," the superintendent said. "The speeding by itself is not so bad, but I'm troubled by your refusal to be honest with us about the reason you were late."

"You would be more troubled," Moondog said cautiously, "if I told you."

"What's *that* supposed to mean?" Oates no longer made any attempt to hide his hostility.

Moondog turned in his chair. "Doug, you haven't said much. You agree with them?"

"It ain't up to me," the big Indian said. "They tell me to find another bus driver, I'll go find one."

"You're still sore about that home run, aren't you?" Moondog mumbled.

"I told you, baseball has nothing to do with it," Oates snapped. "Can we stick to the subject?"

Moondog folded his arms across his chest and scowled. "I really feel that I'm being judged unfairly here. One speeding ticket, and you're threatening to show me the door. I'm sure you've had other bus drivers who've gotten speeding tickets."

"I can't remember one," Dakota said.

"I got a ticket once," Doug volunteered. "About six years ago."

"See?" Moondog said to Dakota and Oates. "And he's still here. Thank you, Doug, for that small show of support."

"That still doesn't answer the question of why you show up so late," Oates snapped.

"That's only happened a couple of times," Moondog said.

"It shouldn't happen at all," said Steve Dakota. "And until you can explain the reason for it, and assure us that it won't happen again, I'm not inclined to trust you with our kids."

Silence fell on the room. Moondog looked at Marilou, who looked back at him impassively.

His eyes returned to the three men. "Can I assume that what's said here at this meeting will be treated as confidential? That it will go no further than this room?"

Oates frowned, but Dakota folded his hands on the table in front of him and said, "Yes, you can assume that."

"Good." He glanced again at Marilou, who was looking down at her hands, and sucked in his breath. "It's a bit of a long story," he began. "And like I say, you probably won't—"

Marilou spoke up suddenly. "It's all right, Moondog. You don't have to protect me."

"What?" He looked at her in confusion.

She turned to Oates and Dakota. "He was late those mornings because he was with me," she said. "It's my fault. I wouldn't let him leave."

Silence descended on the conference room. Moondog knew

when it was best to simply shut up, and he recognized this moment as one of those times.

He noticed that Doug's expression had not changed, but Steve Dakota's face had gone red, and Oates looked like somebody had punched him. The vice principal's jaw worked itself up and down several times before he recovered enough of his composure to speak.

"Do I understand you right?" Oates said, glaring at the young teacher. "You . . . and him?"

"Yes," Marilou said.

"Well . . . I . . . He should at least have the sense to get up and come to work on time!" Oates sputtered in indignation. The look he flashed Moondog was white with jealousy.

"There's no rule against . . . ah, fraternizing among school employees," Dakota said awkwardly. Moondog couldn't help noticing the effort the superintendent made not to look in Marilou's direction. "However, I do not expect your social lives to interfere with the school schedule."

"It won't happen again, Mr. Dakota," Marilou said. "I'm sorry."

"I still say we fire him," Oates grumbled. "And you, Ms. McCormick, should use better judgment."

"Let him stay," Doug said.

Everybody looked at him. "Even a dog's entitled to one bite," the big Indian explained. "He got caught once for speeding. Nothing terrible happened. Anybody can make one mistake. I think we're making too big a deal out of this."

Steve Dakota sighed, a clear signal that he wanted the meeting to end. "All right, I think I've heard enough," he said, futility edging his voice. He turned to face Nygerski. "I want no more speeding," he said. "And I want you to keep the music in your bus at a reasonable level, especially in the parking lot and driving through town. Consider this an official warning. I believe the fine you're going to have to pay will be punishment enough. But if it happens again . . ."

"I understand," Moondog said quietly.

Marilou McCormick stood up. "Can I go now?" she said. "I've got a class to prepare for."

"By all means," said Dakota, avoiding her eyes. "The meeting's over."

Moondog got up quickly, meaning to follow her. He was halfway through the office door when Oates's voice stopped him.

"Nygerski!"

Moondog turned around.

"I'll be watching you," the vice principal said, holding himself militarily erect. Moondog noticed that his fists were clenched at his sides; Doug and Dakota were still seated at the table, chatting amiably about a subject undoubtedly unrelated to the just-concluded meeting. "You screw up in even the slightest way, and you can be sure I'll take notice. And I'll let *him* know, too." Oates aimed a sharp, angry nod at the superintendent, who wasn't paying the slightest attention.

"I'll remember that," Moondog said, and hurried from the room.

"Hey, Lou! Wait!"

She had almost reached the Annex steps. Members of a third-period gym class laconically swatted balls back and forth across the tennis courts. Donna Hurley's voice, in mid-lecture, floated out into the parking lot through an open window.

"Why on Earth did you do that?" Moondog asked her, a bit out of breath as he caught up. "Why did you cover for me?"

She brushed away a strand of hair the wind had pushed in front of her mouth. "Moondog, I wasn't about to let you sit there and tell them that you're a werewolf! Can you imagine what Oates would have said?"

"I would've told him that he can't fire me for that," Moondog said. "It's discrimination. It'd be like firing Doug because he's an Indian."

At this, she laughed, and he felt a little better.

"Besides," he went on, "the word *werewolf* conjures up too many negative images. I would've told him to refer to me as 'lycanthropically challenged.' "

She shook her head, still laughing. "Oh, Moondog," she said, "you really are a character."

"You still don't believe me, do you?"

Her laughter faded to a puzzled smile, and she studied his face. "It's a lot to ask me to believe," she said. "That you're a werewolf, that my classroom's haunted . . . all of it."

"Believe your eyes," Moondog said. "Lou, you *saw* a werewolf! And you've seen what the force that's in your classroom can do. You've seen it! What's stopping you from believing it?"

"Oh, nothing except about eighteen years of education, all of which reinforces the idea that we live in a rational universe—a universe where things like werewolves and ghosts are nothing but myths, made up when people were much more superstitious and ignorant. I'm sorry, Moondog, but I'm not willing to simply throw that whole belief system away because of something I thought I saw. Yes, I've seen some strange things, things I can't explain. You're trying to explain them to me. I'm listening. But I'll make up my own mind. I've got one, you know."

Moondog saw that she was no longer smiling. "Well, you certainly took a big risk for something you don't believe," he said.

"I didn't say I disbelieved it, either," she retorted.

"But now you've got Oates and Dakota convinced we're sleeping together."

She looked at the ground. "I didn't want you to lose your job," she said.

"I didn't want *you* to lose your reputation."

She laughed again, but this time there was an undertone of bitterness. "My reputation is for me to worry about," she said. "If I had worried more about it in the past, I wouldn't even be here."

"Still . . . thank you."

"I didn't want you to lose your job," she said again.

"You be careful in that classroom," Moondog replied.

They stared silently at each other for several seconds. "You *are* serious," she said finally. "Look, I'm not completely convinced that my room is haunted, and I'm even less convinced that you're a werewolf, or that Gary was killed by one. But I'm pretty sure that *you* believe these things. I don't see any insincerity in you. That's why I said what I said."

Moondog was formulating a reply to this when the bell rang. Seconds later, students spilled down the Annex steps and streamed past them. "Class in five minutes," she said. "I gotta go." And before he could say anything else, she drifted into the crowd of students and disappeared into the building.

He found Doug and Robert out by the buses during the slow part of the following morning. "Thanks," he said to the big Indian.

"For what?"

"Letting me keep my job."

"Shit, I didn't do nothin'. It's Ms. McCormick you should be thanking." Doug grinned at him. "You sly dog."

"I've never even kissed her, Doug. She made it up on the spot."

Doug's smile thinned but did not disappear. "Now why would she do that?"

"You superstitious?" Moondog countered.

"Why?"

"Room thirteen—her classroom. I've never seen you go in there. Not even when I took out the window. Robert went in, Carl went in, but you stayed in the hall. How come?"

Doug's features clouded. "Call me superstitious, then," he said coldly.

Robert spoke up. "I've never seen you in there, either."

"Not my job," Doug said.

"I think it's more than that," Moondog said. "There's something in that classroom that isn't right, and it scares you. Do you believe in the supernatural, Doug?"

Moondog was aware that Robert was staring at him.

"Look, Moondog, I just work here," Doug said. "I got a good job I intend on keeping. I don't need to get messed up in anyone's personal problems—yours or hers."

"What happened to the other teachers?"

"What do you mean, what happened to them?"

"The other teachers in that classroom? Carl tells me there's a new one every year, sometimes more than once a year. He says there have been five teachers in that room in the last three years. What happened to them?"

"They quit," Doug said. "Not everybody can take small-town life."

"You don't really believe what you're saying, do you?"

"What's not to believe about it?" Moondog saw that Doug was growing irritated at his line of questioning.

"She's in danger, Doug."

The big Indian's response was to kick the front tire of his bus, examining it for nonexistent leaks.

"You *know* there's something in that classroom, damn it. And I know that it's after her."

Robert spoke up suddenly. "I do, too. I've been seeing strange things in that classroom since the day I started working here. And that heater keeps coming on, and those posters—"

Doug cut the janitor off before he could elaborate further. "Leave it alone, Moondog," he said. "You're messing with something bigger than you."

"What about the other teachers?"

Doug walked to the front of the bus and stood close to Moondog. "I've been here eight years," he said. "I've seen teachers come and teachers go. She'll go, too, and after not too long a time, but *not* because of anything in that classroom. She's young, nice-looking, and smart. What the hell's going to keep her in Julian?"

"A lustful ghost?" Moondog said.

"Look," Doug said, "I'm gonna keep this job. Don't make trouble for me, or the next time there's a full Moon, I won't stick up for you." Doug glared at him hard, and Moondog understood his meaning exactly.

"So you know," he murmured.

"I don't know anything," he said emphatically, "except that good bus drivers are hard to find, and that there are times when the best thing to do is keep your mouth shut. I don't care if there's ten ghosts in that room—shit, I don't care if there's a hundred! When I go home at night, they can't hurt me! I don't waste my time thinking about it, and neither should you." In a kinder, gentler tone, he continued: "She'll be all right. She strikes me as a chick who knows how to take care of herself. Nothing happened to the other teachers. They left, but they lived. She will, too."

"I wish I could be sure of that," Moondog said.

"Well, I'm sure that if I don't get that oil spill by the auto shop cleaned up, the teacher's gonna be pissed," Doug said. "Come on, Robert."

The diminutive janitor got to his feet. Doug was already walking away. Moondog caught Robert's arm and the janitor looked at him questioningly.

"Come in early tomorrow," Moondog said. "We need to talk."

18

The Closet

A week after the earthquake, Marilou McCormick and Carl Estabrook had their respective halves of the closet restored to reasonable order. Some of the odds and ends in there had broken, and many of the old books hadn't made it back to their original shelves, but the floor was clear. One could walk into the closet in search of needed material and have a pretty good chance of finding it.

Marilou's half was much better organized than Carl's, for the excellent reason that she seldom used it. Carl stored baseball equipment, board games, maps, overhead projectors, Halloween costumes, and other assorted junk on his side. Marilou's half was filled mostly with books, which she would not bring out until later in the year, if ever. She kept current materials out on the shelves in the raised part of the classroom by her desk, where she could get at them easily, for she did not like to venture into the cavernous dark closet unless it was absolutely necessary.

She had asked Robert to replace the single uncovered bulb

that hung from the ceiling after it had blown out in the earthquake, and the janitor had done so (telling her afterward that the mice had chattered at him the whole time). Still, the closet remained a dark and forbidding place. It had had a window once, but the spot where the window had been was now boarded over by an oaken panel, installed when room 13 had been grafted onto the building. The floor of the closet was bare wood, stained dark brown, and it swallowed light that a friendlier surface would have reflected.

Even with the light on and the floor cleared, the closet was not easily navigated. Marilou knew it better by feel than by sight. Her feet and hands remembered every tentative step in the pitch-black after the earthquake, as she and Nygerski had picked their way through the narrow passage, down the three steep steps, and around the ninety-degree turn into Carl's storage area. Her skin remembered and prickled anew each time she went in there. Her heart remembered as well, and it pounded at the inside of her chest, though Marilou could not recall ever having suffered from claustrophobia.

Thus, she seldom went into the closet. More often than not, she would ask a student, or Robert, to get something for her. She wondered how much of her uneasiness was due to Moondog Nygerski and her growing belief that the strange bus driver was right—that some sort of supernatural presence inhabited both classroom and closet. In her professional moments when a lesson was moving along and most of the class was paying attention, she confidently put such notions out of her mind, but increasingly, between classes, she made up excuses not to be alone in the room. And since the earthquake, little things like the capricious behavior of the heater or a squabble between back-row students distracted her more than they should. Some of the more observant class cutups sensed this immediately, and over the past few days, her jumpiness and their behavior had worsened.

Though the situation with Jim Green and Phelps Gayle had

mysteriously resolved itself, Richie and Kyle continued to disrupt the remedial-reading class. And there were quite a few other disciplinary problems, the most unusual of which involved a bright but timid boy in her English III class who had taken to running out of the classroom at odd times and refused to turn in assignments. She had become so exasperated by his behavior that she had finally scheduled a lunchtime conference with the superintendent.

Had that conference not taken place, she would not have returned to the classroom ten minutes before the start of fifth period that Friday, intending to chow down the sandwich stored in her desk drawer. The boy's parents had been there, and Steve Dakota had spent the entire meeting murmuring vague reassurances while they shrilly accused Marilou of carrying out some imagined vendetta against their son to prevent him from getting into college. Carl had told her more than once that their boss was a spineless figurehead. Pissed off at Dakota's utter failure to back her up, she unlocked the door from the alcove and stalked into the empty classroom.

The voices coming from the closet were soft and indistinguishable. At first, she could not make out the words. Two students doing a drug deal, or engaging in some extracurricular biology? It disturbed her that because of the walk-through closet, her room could never be totally secure.

She stopped by the light switch and listened.

"You don't have to worry," a girl's voice said—and Marilou was pretty sure she recognized it. "Everything's coming along fine."

"I just feel so . . . unnecessary," said another voice. "Almost as if I don't exist for you anymore."

Marilou took an involuntary step toward the closet when she heard the man speak. She put a hand to her heart, which had suddenly begun to beat very fast. The voice belonged to Carl Estabrook.

The girl laughed softly, pleasantly—it was a heartbreaking

sound because it was lovely, and Marilou had never heard joy from this particular voice. "But you do," the girl said. "Right here."

"Is there much pain?"

Marilou took another stealthy step toward the closet, listening for the girl's answer. She swallowed, forcing a wayward heartbeat back down into her chest. "I don't get sick in the morning anymore," the girl said. "My back gets tired, but that's about all. Really, this is the best time. Although it's been kicking more lately, which is—"

At that moment, the heater kicked on. The sound of metal on metal behind the rush of air was unmistakable. Its wail obliterated the conversation in the closet.

But Marilou had heard enough. She walked in. Carl Estabrook stood in the closet's lower half, one foot on the lowest of the three steps. The girl stood on the top step, and she turned around as Marilou entered. She was not at all surprised to see that the girl was Heather Monroe.

Carl jumped visibly upon seeing her. His foot came off the step and he swayed backward. Recovering, he ran a hand awkwardly through his short hair and looked wildly at the supplies around him, as if trying to find an excuse somewhere on the shelves. Finally, he looked at her—but not at her eyes. "Lou, I . . . uh . . . Hello, Ms. McCormick! Looking for something?"

Heather backed against a bookshelf, her eyes like those of a scared fawn, and clasped her hands protectively over her swollen belly.

For several seconds, no one said anything more. Marilou looked from one face to the other. Each evinced a different kind of fright.

"Heather," she said in a low, controlled voice, "why don't you go get ready for class? I need to speak with Mr. Estabrook in private."

Wordlessly, Heather left the closet. She slid down the stairs past Carl and exited through his classroom, though her next class was with Marilou.

Carl watched her go, and it seemed a very long time before he turned to face Marilou. His eyes still would not meet hers.

"So," she said tonelessly. "It's you."

"What do you mean?" he said.

"You know damn well what I mean. *You're* the father."

"Lou, listen to me. If you'll let me explain—"

"You pig," she spat out at him in utter contempt, without raising the volume of her voice. Outside the closet, the heater continued to wail. "Everything you said was a lie, wasn't it? And if that wasn't bad enough, you've got that poor girl covering for you. How'd you do it, Carl? Threaten her with a coat hanger?"

"Lou . . ."

"You see her every day," she hissed. "You see how she has no friends, no support, no respect. And yet life just goes merrily on for you, doesn't it? You're Mr. Fucking Popularity! You teach your classes; you play in your baseball games; all the kids like you. And they shun her. You've got it made, don't you? As long as she doesn't say anything, your dirty little secret's safe!"

She was working herself into a lather of righteous indignation. The heater's rising wail backed her surging anger. And a part of her was enjoying it.

"How old is she, anyway, Carl? Fifteen? Sixteen? My God, they have *laws* against that! But that doesn't matter to you, as long as she keeps her mouth shut! You're safe, while she suffers."

"Look—Lou," Carl stammered. "You said yourself that Heather doesn't seem to be suffering. You said—you told me she acts like she's *happy* about it."

"Oh, you bastard," Marilou spat out in a half whisper choked with rage. "And that's what everyone's going to call your child: a bastard. Only in their minds it'll be *her* child, because you aren't man enough to take responsibility for it!"

"Let me explain, Lou," he practically begged. "It's not what you think."

"What do you mean, it's not what I think? Are you trying to deny that you're the father?"

He hung his head. "No," he said. "No, I'm not trying to deny it, exactly. It's just . . ."

"Then what is there to explain?" she said, her voice several degrees colder than the stale air in the closet.

"I didn't mean for it to happen," he said pitifully.

Marilou stared at him incredulously. "You . . . didn't . . . mean . . . for it to happen," she repeated slowly. "Of all the *asinine* things to say! You mean that you didn't mean to get her pregnant, or you didn't mean to fuck her?"

"Both," he said, spreading his hands out to his sides in a gesture of innocence. Marilou wanted to smack him.

"You know, I liked you." she said. "You were nice to me, right from the first day. You struck me as a decent guy. Now I find out it was all a facade. I wonder what Oates and Dakota will say when they find out. And the born-again school board—I'm sure they'll have some—"

He was up the steps and upon her with alarming speed. His right hand flew to her neck; his thumb pressed hard against her windpipe. She had no time to cry out. She was dizzily aware that he had slammed the back of her head against a shelf of hardcover textbooks. Starry, sharp-edged pain swam all around her.

"Now you listen to me, chick," he hissed at her, his bearded face very close to hers. "If you tell anybody—*anybody*—about this, I'll twist your pretty little neck until it breaks. I'll kill you! I don't want to. You're very attractive, and I had hoped we could be friends. But if you squawk, you'll die. I guaran-damn-tee it! I'm not going have my career ruined over some high school floozy and a moment's passion. You understand me?"

Marilou felt his grip tighten around her neck, and she gasped for breath. "Are you nuts?" she managed to croak.

His bulging eyes offered no assurance to the contrary. She felt as if she might black out at any moment. She flashed on Robert, the janitor, and imagined him finding her strangled body, with oversized mice nibbling at her flesh, here in the closet when he came in to work on Monday morning. "Carl, let go of me!" she rasped.

"Will you listen to me for a minute, and not make any noise?"

Desperately, she nodded. He relaxed his grip on her neck but did not let go of her completely.

"That's better," he said, his eyes retreating partway into their sockets. "It happened last spring. And when I say it happened, that's what I mean, because it wasn't anything either of us planned, or anticipated. I think we were brought together for a purpose, by forces beyond our control."

Marilou stared at the contorted face at the other end of the strong arm that held her pinned against the bookshelf. "You are *such* a shit," she whispered.

His hold on her neck tightened momentarily, making her wince, and then relaxed again, though not enough to allow her to squirm free. "Shut up, you fucking cunt," he spat out at her. "You *know* there's something weird in that room. I'm not the most sensitive guy in the world, but even I can feel it. So don't pretend you don't know what I'm talking about!"

Marilou said nothing. She wanted no more, at this moment, than to get out of the closet unharmed.

"It was after school one day," he went on. "I came in here, either to get something or to put something away, and she was in your room, even though the teacher had left for the day. That teacher didn't like to spend much time in there after school—I guess you know why.

"Anyway, Heather was in there, working on some assignment. It was cold, and she'd turned on the heat. When she heard me rummaging around in here, she looked in and asked me what I was doing. I went into your room, we started talking, and—"

"Oh my God!" Marilou exclaimed. "You mean you . . . right in the classroom?"

"Yes!" he cried, and although his voice was not loud enough to be heard outside the closet, its volume startled her, for they had been whispering. "Yes! I fucked her, right on top of that big desk of yours! I don't know what came over me—came over *us*. All of a sudden, I was just overwhelmed by lust. I had to have her! It was as if someone had sprayed some highly potent chemical into the air, some sort of super-aphrodisiac. We couldn't keep our hands off each other. I mean, we knew it was wrong, but we did it anyway. And it was strange, because that big heater started running louder and louder. . . . I'm sure we made a lot of noise, but the building was empty, and even if it hadn't been, no one would have been able to hear us over the heater."

Marilou stared at him. She could hear the heater now, wailing away. It did seem to have a mind of its own sometimes, though she had attributed its uneven volume to the vagaries of age and poor maintenance. She realized that there could be no more than ten minutes before the next class. Someone would surely come into the classroom soon, and Carl would have to let her go.

"That was the first and only time, Lou," he said pleadingly. "I swear it! And I've . . . I've had a hard time living with myself ever since."

She swallowed once, hard, feeling his strong hand against her throat. "You raped her!" she whispered in disbelief.

His hand dug into the soft flesh of her neck, cutting off her breath. An involuntary squeak escaped from her, like air from a balloon before it's pinched into silence.

"I did *not*! She was ready and willing! More than willing—hell, *she* seduced *me*! I absolutely did *not* rape her, and if you tell or insinuate to anybody that I did, you feminist bitch, you will die! I'll kill you! Are we clear on that?"

His face was very close to hers, and tiny droplets of his saliva sprayed her cheeks and chin. She remembered with revulsion that not long ago she had allowed this man to kiss her. She was very glad her judgment had been sound enough that night not to invite him home, and she was horrified that she had even imagined him as a lover. His grip tightened, and blackness swam around the edges of her peripheral vision. Had he let go of her just then, she would have fallen to the closet floor.

Numbly, she nodded. There was little else she could do.

"That's a good girl," he said. He relaxed his hand, and Marilou sucked in air. "Don't think I'm bluffing, either. I could snap your pretty little neck right now if I wanted to."

What *she* wanted to do was hike a knee as hard as she could into his groin. It would almost be worth dying for, but not quite. And she did not doubt that he was capable of murder at this moment.

"I'm going to let you go now, Lou," he said. "As far as anyone knows, this conversation never happened. You never saw Heather and me in here together, and you never discovered our secret. If I hear differently . . ." He squeezed her neck for a painful second to make his point. "Okay?"

She nodded again. "Okay," she managed to croak. "Just let go of me."

He dropped his hands to his sides. Gingerly, she felt her neck, wondering if it was red, and if someone would notice. "God help you," she muttered, before she could stop herself.

But he made no move toward her. Instead, surprisingly, his face softened, and a touch of human emotion, resembling either regret or sorrow, came into his eyes. He looked like a man just awakened from a trance, unsure of his whereabouts. "It's the room," he said hollowly. "And the child . . . it's not really mine."

Marilou backed away from him slowly, edging toward the opening to her classroom.

"It's Scurvy's kid," Carl Estabrook said in a voice suddenly drained of passion. "It's Scurvy who—" Abruptly, he stopped, and she could see his face close itself off to her. "Go teach your class," he said. "Go on, get out of here!"

She stumbled against the shelves in her eagerness to get away from him. She certainly did not want him to touch her again. Two dozen pairs of eyes accosted her from the authors' wall as she staggered out into the classroom. The clock showed that she had been in the closet for only five minutes.

She sat down at her desk and forced her shaking hands to remove the notes she had prepared for her next class from the top drawer, next to the sandwich. From the same drawer, she took a light scarf and wrapped it loosely around her neck. She was no longer hungry at all. The heater behind her had fallen silent. Now it was her mind that was racing.

19

Remedial Reading

The remedial-reading class followed English III, but Marilou found it difficult to concentrate on anything after the confrontation in the closet. Fortunately, Friday was the day she had the underachieving students in her last class do a writing assignment based on whatever piece of dumbed-down literature they had struggled through during the week. The assignment always took up most of the forty-five-minute class period. Every Friday, Marilou was grateful for the end-of-the-week respite in her most difficult class. Today, she had numbly gone through the motions in English III, looking as infrequently as possible at Heather Monroe, seated placidly, as usual, in the front row. She simply wanted to get the week behind her and get the hell out of there. Surely it had been one of the strangest weeks of her life.

Now she walked slowly up and down between the rows of desks as the students bent over their work. A bevy of jumbled thoughts clamored for attention behind her calm exterior. Carl Estabrook, she now knew, was caught up in the haunting of the room, and she did not doubt that he could do her harm. She could still feel his thumb against her windpipe, and she would not be able to relax again, not ever, as long as he was in the same building. And yet how was she to take the man who had warned her about the room, the mysterious Moondog Nygerski? Her father would have taken one look at him and told her to run as fast as she could in the other direction—even if he didn't know that the bus driver claimed to be a werewolf. *Was* he one? Could there possibly be any truth to those gothic legends that had inspired so many bad movies? She wanted badly to disbelieve him, as she had wanted to deny the evidence of her eyes that something inhuman had killed Gary. And from that thought grew a more sinister one: Could it be that *Moondog* had been on Pismo Beach that night, under the full Moon? If what he said about being a werewolf was true, he would not remember whether he had killed or not.

She entertained the thought of quitting. She would merely become the latest in a long line of teachers to be frightened away by the room and its strange spirits. Perhaps that was the prudent thing to do—get a job in another town somewhere, move far away from Julian, and let someone else deal with the weird room and its savage posters, the personality changes, and the half-human hired help. But Marilou McCormick did not look upon herself as a quitter. Besides, she *liked* this odd little town. She liked the brilliant night sky and the open mountainsides. She liked living on a narrow country road without streetlights, with a national forest behind her. She liked Julian's preoccupation with its past, and the moody weather that swept over the mountains in autumn. She liked the people who recognized her by name and said hello on Main Street. Until recently, she had liked her job, and she silently vowed that it would take a hell of a lot to frighten her away from it.

She was beginning to like this Moondog character, too, weird though he was, and she wanted to stick around long enough to find out if the things he said were true.

She glanced absently down at the work of some of her students but did not linger beside any one desk for long, remembering how she, as a student, had found it impossible to write a word while the teacher was watching. Writing was difficult enough for this bunch, anyway. The assignment was to compose a single page, and many of the students attempted to fill the space by writing as large as possible and employing huge margins at both sides of the paper. Most of them wrote very slowly, laying down each word like a brick in a wall. No one, however, appeared to be concentrating more fiercely on the task at hand than Richie Marks.

The huge boy hunkered over his desk, his broad back bent in a semicircle, his face very close to the paper. The pen moved slowly, steadily, meticulously. She knew from previous assignments that even the simplest words were difficult for Richie. Many times, his papers came back nearly blank, two or three half sentences filled with inverted letters and punctuated by unrecognizable shapes and squiggles straining to reach halfway down the page. Often he stared blankly at the desk for most of the allotted time. Marilou was both pleased and curious to see him working so hard. She glided over to his desk. Her pleasure dimmed when she peered discreetly over his shoulder and discovered that he was not writing, but drawing.

He had drawn a single shape—a simple line drawing—at the top of the page, and was now lovingly duplicating it, one under the other. He was working on the third figure in the column, taking pains to make it identical to the first two. It took her a minute to recognize the shape. It was a mouse.

Marilou had some time ago come to the realization that the boy would have to be passed, whatever the quality of his work—it was either that, or a special school for the retarded. He could read, albeit stumblingly, and he could write his name and an occasional coherent phrase or two, but none of what she tried to teach him was ever going to stick for very long. Mainstream schooling was largely wasted on kids like Richie, and Marilou and many of her colleagues wished that the bureaucrats in Sacramento would yield to that conclusion. Until they did, he was here, and she would do what she could for him.

She slipped quietly back behind her desk ten minutes before class ended; when the bell rang, she positioned herself in front of the steps to collect the papers as they were passed forward. She glanced at Richie's paper as it came in. Four mice, and not a single word.

"Richie," she called, as the big boy rose slowly to his feet, "I want to see you for a minute before you go."

A worried expression crossed the boy's blank features. "I'll be late for the bus," he said. His cousin Kyle, who would not be riding the bus home with him because he was serving the equivalent of a life sentence in after-school detention, stood by his side. Richie looked over at the smaller boy for support, but Kyle said nothing.

"You won't miss the bus," Marilou reassured Richie. "It'll just take a minute."

"But . . ." Richie looked again at Kyle, and then back at the teacher.

"It's all right, Richie," Kyle said. "You know where the bus is. I'll see you later, okay?" Kyle slapped Richie on the back, a bit hard for a gesture of friendship, Marilou thought, and trailed the rest of the students out the door, on his way to the detention room in the main building.

"Okay, Kyle," Richie said weakly as he watched him go. He sank back down in his seat.

Marilou pulled Richie's paper from the stack and placed the rest on the front of her desk. "Richie," she said softly as she approached him.

"Huh?" The boy cast puppyish eyes upward at her.

"You seem to like mice an awful lot."

The blank expression gave way to a beatific smile. "Oh yes!" he cried. "I do! Mice are the nicest animals in the world. Kyle says maybe I can get a couple of 'em, and make 'em a cage, an' git 'em a wheel to run in, and . . . and . . . and feed 'em, and pet 'em when they git lonely, and . . . and . . ."

"That's fine," said Marilou, concealing the sudden queasiness she felt in her stomach. She held out his paper to him. "But this was a *writing* assignment, not drawing."

His smile faded. Confusion clouded the eyes. "You don't like my mice?" he said in a small voice.

"I like them fine," she said gently. "I think Ms. Anderson might like them a lot if you showed them to her in art class. Your drawing is really quite good."

Much of the smile came back. "Yeah! I sure like mice, by God, especially the ones with big ears an' real soft fur. Sometimes I . . ."

"Richie."

"Huh?"

"I don't see how I can give you a grade on this. Didn't you pay any attention to the week's writing assignment? I don't recall that it had anything to do with mice. And besides that, in this class we use *words* to communicate, not pictures."

Richie looked at the top of his desk. For several seconds, he stared blankly at the bare wood, etched with grafitti, without speaking. The other classes had funneled out of the building; it was almost unnaturally quiet. "I like to pet soft things," he murmured. "Mice are soft."

Marilou flashed back to the mouse that had turned up dead in Richie's huge hand; her stomach did a small flip. "You were supposed to write a page on this week's reading," she said to him, "not draw pictures of mice. You need to learn to follow directions."

Richie didn't raise his head. He looked, in fact, as if he was about to cry. "I done a bad thing," he said, his voice barely audible. "I been bad."

His hangdog attitude was so pitiful that Marilou moved closer to him and placed a hand on one of his massive shoulders. "No, you haven't been bad," she assured him. "I'm not angry with you. I just want you to do the assignment. To write something—not draw pictures."

He looked up at her, his eyes all childlike innocence. "Gonna give me detention?"

Perhaps I should, Marilou thought. At least he'd be with Kyle then. Though his cousin treated him roughly and bossed him around, he seemed to be Richie's sole source of comfort and security. Richie seemed lost without him.

Marilou sighed. "I want you to write something," she said. "Anything—as long as it has something to do with the story we read in class. Work on it over the weekend. Have Kyle help you with it if you need him to. Bring it—"

She was leaning partially over the desk as she spoke to him. Suddenly, the heater came on with a noise like a car wreck. Startled, she whirled around. Her long hair moved with her, brushing against Richie's face. Instinctively, he reached up with one of his huge hands and grabbed a handful of it. There was a lot to grab, and it felt soft, like the fur of a mouse.

"Ow!" she cried. "Richie, let go of my hair!"

The heater keened furiously. Richie looked at his hand, and at the strands of red hair snagged between his fingers. He twisted his hand this way and that, his face blank and mesmerized. Slowly, he raised the hand to his cheek.

"Richie," she cried sharply, unable to stand because of the hold he had on her. "Let go! You're hurting me!"

But Richie did not relax his grip. The boy seemed to be in some sort of trance. He ran the fistful of hair across his cheek, a contented smile spreading over his hammy face. "You have soft hair," he murmured.

"Let *go*!" she shouted at him as she tried to pull herself away. Some of the hair ripped away in a burst of pain. But most of it remained attached both to her scalp and Richie's thick fingers. He tightened his grip and reached for her with his other hand.

"Richie, let go of me!" she screamed.

Behind her, the metallic wailing of the heater grew still louder. Richie's eyes widened. His other hand went not for her hair but for her mouth. "Don't scream," he whispered huskily to her. "The others'll come. They'll think I've been bad. His hand covered all of her face but her eyes; she could feel and smell the sweat on his palm. Really frightened now, she tried to cry out again, but Richie pressed down harder, pushing her screams back down her throat. She thrashed her head from side to side, pulling out more hair; the boy wrapped his hand in it more tightly, keeping his other hand glued to her face. She gasped for air, and in a moment of true panic, she discovered that she could not breathe.

"Quiet now, *please*!" the equally frightened boy said pleadingly. The heater shrieked, mocking her inability to do so. Marilou felt her legs give way beneath her. She fell to the floor. Richie sank to one knee, still not loosening his grip. She kicked out at him in desperation but connected with nothing but air. Her shoe flew off and hit a desk. She balled a free hand into a fist and swung wildly. Her knuckles collided with the side of Richie's skull. Pain rocketed up her arm.

The boy was not even fazed by the blow. "Miss McCormick, please!" he whimpered. "Be still! Don't want no trouble."

She was on the floor now, the room spinning and closing in around her, the heater screaming in her ears. She realized that she was about to lose consciousness. Her lungs cried out for air, but she could not draw a breath. The door to the hall was still open; it looked miles away, high above her. Richie's eyes were no longer frightened—rather, they appeared lifeless and automatic, like a robot's. Through the legs of the desks, she could see several of the posters. The authors' faces leered down at her. Her eyes fell on the face of John Steinbeck, her father's favorite writer, and the scourge of her own high school years. In her last moment of lucid thought, she noticed that the dour, devilish face seemed to be smiling.

* * *

Moondog's bus idled in its spot next to the main building as the last of his passengers boarded. Oblivious to the yammering all around him, Moondog drummed his fingers on the large steering wheel and watched students, in groups of two or three and occasionally more, stream past the bus on the way to their cars, the main building, and the world outside the school grounds. He recognized Kyle Tyler, who for disciplinary reasons had not ridden the bus home for several weeks now, heading for another afternoon of detention. He checked out a few of the better-looking girls, and thought through a short list of possible musical selections for the ride down into the desert.

Donna Hurley exited the Annex immediately behind the first wave of students, heading purposefully toward the main building. Moondog had noticed that she was always the first teacher to leave—as if she did not want to spend any more time in the building than was absolutely necessary. Carl Estabrook, chatting amiably with a group of female students, came out a few moments later.

Doug's bus pulled out from its spot in front of Moondog's and lumbered toward the highway. Moondog's left foot depressed the clutch. His right hand moved to the gearshift—and stopped.

Something was wrong. The instinct was not specific, but it was there. Over the past three years, Moondog had learned to trust such feelings.

"Hey, Mooner, how 'bout some tunes?" somebody yelled from the back.

Moondog ignored him and tried to let his intuition crystallize. Kyle Tyler had walked Richie Marks to the bus most afternoons since the beginning of his long sentence in after-school detention. The bony, weathered-looking kid had told Moondog early on in this ritual, and only half in jest, that he doubted Richie had the brains to find his way to the bus by himself. Yet today Kyle had walked to the main building alone, and

Richie had not appeared, though both boys had ridden the bus that morning.

"Come on, driver, let's boogie!" came another cry from the back of the bus.

"Yeah, let's move out already!"

Moondog pulled up the lever for the parking brake and turned in his seat to face his passengers. "Where's Richie?" he asked no one in particular.

"Who cares? Let's go!"

Moondog didn't move. "No football practice today?"

"Uh-uh," said a boy who was on the team. "We got a game up in Indio tomorrow. Gotta leave real early."

"Richie's still in class," volunteered a girl near the front. "Ms. McCormick said she wanted to talk to him."

Moondog reached over into the glove compartment, where the tapes were, and pulled out a pocket watch on a long string. "He's five minutes late," he said.

"Leave without him," someone suggested.

"Yeah, let the big lug walk home."

"Shut up," Moondog advised his charges. He turned the key, and the idling bus fell silent. Pocketing the key, he stood up. "You all wait here," he said. "Anyone who's not on the bus when I get back gets left behind. I'll just be a minute."

At the outer edge of consciousness, she heard his footsteps in the empty hall. But she could not be sure they were real. She was spiraling downward into unconsciousness, and her senses had the ethereal quality of dreams. She no longer had the strength or the will to resist. The room had almost been sucked away into blackness. The pain in her lungs, the smell of Richie's smothering flesh, and the sound of the heater had merged into a single flickering sense of a reality she felt slipping away.

But her eyes *were* open, and in the moment before sight, too, was engulfed, she caught a wavering glimpse into the face of Cyrus "Moondog" Nygerski.

He stood in the doorway, impossibly far away. Then she saw him move, incredibly slowly, like a slow-motion film. She saw his arm reach back and come forward, like a baseball pitcher's, and then something silver flashed through the room, tumbling end over end in a lazy parabola. It seemed to hang in the air for minutes. Marilou saw quite clearly that the object was a knife. She watched its every tumble, the blade in perfect focus. The knife struck the far wall with a loud *thwang* and stuck there, vibrating like a tuning fork.

The heater shut off. The great mass of suffocating flesh lifted from her face. She sucked desperately at the air, coughing and wheezing. The room swam around her.

Moondog Nygerski was already in motion, following the knife to where it had stuck in John Steinbeck's left eye. Moondog leapt upward, his fingertips gripping the top of the chalkboard, his feet on the metal chalk tray which ran along the bottom. With one hand Moondog grabbed the handle of the knife and raked the blade downward, ripping the goateed pen-and-ink portrait in two. Richie screamed and flung his hands in front of his face.

A second later, the chalk tray gave way under Moondog's weight. He tumbled backward onto the carpet. The knife bounced off of one of the desks and landed in the middle of the classroom floor. A section of the tray now dangled limply from one end below the blackboard. The ruined poster, split not quite all the way down the middle, hung limply against the wall above it.

Reality came slowly seeping back to Marilou as she filled her lungs. She was on her back on the floor, her skirt up around her thighs. Richie stood dumbly over her, his hands shaking uncontrollably, his face white and unreadable. Several strands of her hair hung from Richie's hand.

Wordlessy, Moondog bent down next to her, slipped an arm around the small of her back, and helped her to her feet. She smoothed her skirt down around her legs and felt her hair where Richie had pulled it. The boy stood, waxen and statue-like, beside his desk, his hands hanging at his sides.

"Are you all right?" Moondog asked her.

Marilou drew several deep breaths and swallowed twice. "I . . . I think so," she said, looking at Richie. She thought that if someone pushed the boy ever so slightly at this moment, he would topple to the floor. His eyes were glazed and unfocused.

Not taking her eyes off him, Marilou took a couple of steps to where the knife lay on the carpet. She bent to pick it up, her eyes never leaving the immobile Richie. "I believe this is yours," she said, holding it out, handle first, toward Moondog.

"Thanks." He closed the knife and pocketed it.

"Lou? What's going on?" Mimi Anderson leaned into the room, a streak of green paint highlighting her loose blond hair. "I thought I heard somebody scream." The art teacher looked at each of the three people in the room in turn. Richie took no notice of her.

"N-nothing," Marilou said. She looked meaningfully at Moondog, her eyes imploring him to keep silent.

"You sure?" Anderson looked doubtfully back and forth between teacher and bus driver.

"Yeah," Marilou said weakly. "It must have been the heater. That thing makes an awful racket sometimes. When it first comes on, it sounds like a scream. Robert says he can't get anyone to fix it."

The art teacher glanced over at Richie, who still stared blankly into the air. She looked at Moondog and then at Marilou, who was adjusting her scarf around her throat. "Are you *sure* everything's all right?" she asked skeptically.

"I'm sure," Marilou said. "Richie, you're late for your bus."

"Huh?" The boy blinked as though awakening.

"Your bus," Marilou repeated.

"Wha—where's Kyle?" The boy swiveled his bull neck, searching the empty room.

"Richie, everybody's waiting for you," Moondog said. "Let's go."

The boy stared at Moondog but did not move. Moondog walked over to him and gently took hold of his arm.

"Wait," said Marilou. "Mimi, could you walk him to the bus? I need to talk to Cyrus here alone for a minute."

As if on cue, the bleat of a bus horn sounded from the parking lot.

"Damn kids," Moondog muttered. "I told 'em to sit tight."

"You better take 'em home," Mimi Anderson said.

Marilou could see the art teacher's intelligent eyes take it all in: the dangling chalk tray, the ripped poster, the dumfounded Richie, and her own frightened, dissheveled appearance. For a moment, she considered confiding in the older woman, whose awareness that something was being concealed from her was all too apparent on her face.

"Lou . . ."

"I'll talk to you about it later, Meems, okay?" She hoped she didn't sound too desperate.

The bus horn sounded again.

"I'll be out there in a minute," Moondog said, pulling the keys from his pocket. "It's not like they can go anywhere."

"Okay," Mimi Anderson said, casting a final doubtful glance at Marilou. "Come on, Richie."

The towering youth docilely allowed the art teacher to lead him from the room. When they were out of earshot down the hall, Marilou turned to Moondog. "I thought he was going to kill me."

"He almost did," Moondog said gravely.

"How did you know to do what you did? To throw a knife at the poster? Anyone else would have jumped Richie."

"He's much bigger and stronger than I am. He would have thrown me off."

"But why did he try to kill me? And why did wrecking the poster stop him? Moondog, what did you do?"

"It's part of a theory I've been forming about this room," he said. "It'll take some explaining."

"Explain, then. Believe me, I'm listening."

The horn sounded again. "I've got a bus to drive," he said.

"Give me the short version. Please, tell me what's going on!"

He looked down at his hands. "I can tell you what I think, anyway," he said. "I don't have all the information I need, but . . . Okay, what literary character does Richie remind you of? A Steinbeck character."

She tilted her head and looked at him in puzzlement for a second, until the light of comprehension clicked on. "Oh my God!" she cried. "He's Lennie! Lennie, from *Of Mice and Men*. Is that it?"

He smiled at her crookedly. "You *have* read some of the old books."

"Fuck you," she retorted, her manner belying the harshness of the words. "I happen to hate Steinbeck, but everybody's read *Of Mice and Men*. I don't think they let you into college until you do." Suddenly, she felt ill. "Moondog, these posters . . ."

"They are part of the presence I warned you about," he said.

"Lennie . . . breaks a woman's neck . . . in the book."

Moondog nodded. "And whatever entity has set up shop in here was able to use him to attack you."

"I've got to take these posters down," she said weakly.

He shook his head. "You could hurt yourself," he said. "You already have. Lou, my advice to you is to be careful."

"Moondog, what should I do?"

"Go home," he told her. "Forget about it over the weekend. That's all you *can* do for now. Meanwhile, I'll do some research. There are ways of dealing with these things. I've really gotta go."

"Don't leave me behind," she said, hastily grabbing her briefcase and purse. "I'm not staying here another minute. I'm not sure I even want to come back."

* * *

But when he returned from his route, he found that she had waited for him. She had pulled her car around to where the buses parked and was seated on the overturned milk crate where Moondog had passed many school mornings shooting the shit with Robert and Doug. She stood up as he wheeled the bus into its designated spot. He opened the door and looked at her in surprise.

"We still have a lot to talk about," she said.

The school grounds were completely deserted. The late-afternoon Sun peeked over the roof of the Annex. The wind kited brittle brown leaves in the air and whistled through the chain-link fence, rippling Marilou's skirt and swirling little dust storms around her feet. He saw worry in her face, but there was something hard there, too. She would make a worthy ally.

He smiled down at her. "Do you want a ride?" he said.

20

A Talk with Donna Hurley

Robert sliced open his hand in three places removing the ruined Steinbeck poster from the wall. When he was through and the crumpled remains of the poster were tucked safely inside a plastic garbage bag that Robert deposited outside the Annex door (to take later to the Dumpster out where the buses parked), Marilou helped clean the cuts and apply a butterfly bandage and several Band-Aids. One corner of the poster had stubbornly refused to come off the wall, but it was now just a shard of paper no larger than a dollar bill, and Marilou anticipated no threat from it. Moondog's knife had scarred the wall, however, and over the weekend a gooey black substance had begun to ooze from the ragged slash in the plaster.

"What do you suppose *that* stuff is?" he asked her as she put the last Band-Aid in place.

"Hell if I know," she replied. "It looks like tar."

"I'll get a putty knife and take care of it for you," he said.

"Don't touch it, Robert!" she said quickly, the alarm in her voice surprising them both. "I mean, it could be acid," she explained in a more normal tone. "Or some kind of poison. Let it go, unless it gets worse. Please, be careful in here. This room is dangerous."

Robert looked bemusedly at his bandaged hand. "Yes," he said. "I've learned that."

But the ripped poster *had* come off the wall, albeit with difficulty. And he had managed to vacuum the floor that morning without any electrical surges or other strange incidents. The vacuum cleaner was now parked in the corner where the authors' wall met the windows, and the heater had remained silent all morning. Perhaps the power of the entity in the room had limits.

Marilou McCormick seemed to sense this, too, for although she remained alert to the room's potential to harm her, she was more relaxed than Robert had seen her in many mornings. She moved confidently to the chalkboard at the back of the raised area, a sheet of paper in her left hand. Her hair was braided down her back, and she was dressed in a simple pair of blue jeans and a mannish white shirt with rolled-up sleeves that was a couple of sizes too big for her.

"Robert, would you do me a favor?"

"Sure," he said instantly, delighted that she would ask him for anything. "What is it?"

"Would you stay while I put the assignments on the board? I get nervous when I'm alone in here."

"Don't blame you," Robert said. "There's a lot to be nervous about. Sure, I'll stay." He had already cleaned the room, and the other three rooms awaited his attention, but Robert was more than happy to watch Marilou instead. He sat down at one of the desks in the front row as she began writing, her chalk letters rounded and feminine, and as neat as if they had been written with pen on paper. He half-expected the heater to come on and send her hand jerking, ruining the flow of the words. But it didn't even click.

Feeling a bulge in the back pocket of his jeans, opposite the one in which he carried his wallet, Robert pulled out a thin paperback and set it on the desk in front of him. Marilou happened to glance over her shoulder at him just then. "What are you reading?" she asked, turning away from her work.

Robert held up the book. "*The Great Gatsby,* by F. Scott Fitzgerald," he said. "I found it on the floor of the closet, after the earthquake."

"How are you liking it?"

"It's okay, I guess. It's kind of slow. And . . . I don't know . . . it strikes me as a little stuffy, too."

She looked at him strangely, as if he had made some sort of inappropriate remark, and it was a second or two before she turned again to the board. She kept glancing back at him every few seconds, and Robert felt suddenly self-conscious. He opened the book and attempted to read it, though he found more pleasure in watching her. Besides, he really did think *The Great Gatsby* something of a bore, even though he remembered sort of liking the movie version with Robert Redford when he had seen it years ago with his wife. Marilou didn't say anything else to him, though he noticed that her letters were no longer so perfectly rounded.

He's certainly become more sophisticated, Marilou thought, to be criticizing a book for being "stuffy." She doubted that he would have made such a criticism at the beginning of September. It occurred to her that Robert had changed a great deal in the two months she had known him. The most notable change was in his speech. He spoke in grammatical, complete sentences now, not the shy, halting mumbles of someone embarrassed by his lack of education. And he always had a book nearby—a book written by one of the authors on the wall. *They* were educating him, she realized, and it occurred to her that *they* might have a more sinister purpose in mind.

But Moondog had told her she could trust the janitor. He had taken Robert aside, he'd said, and, though he had not revealed his lycanthropic nature, they had discussed the haunting of the room. Robert had told Moondog about his dream of Hemingway and his encounter with Poe; Moondog had filled in the janitor about the cause of the earthquake and the efforts of the "presence" to control the hearts and minds of some of the students. Robert had pledged his support in any plan to rid the room of its evil spirit.

It was Moondog's shirt she was wearing now—he had pressed it for her the previous evening with one of those old-fashioned irons one heats on top of a woodstove. And it was Moondog who had convinced her to come back to work first thing Monday morning after Richie had nearly killed her on Friday afternoon. "Don't interrupt the routine," he had told her. "Don't let it suspect that you know anything." Over the weekend, he had given her back her strength, and whatever the room tried to throw at her next, she felt that she would be prepared for it.

He had taken her home with him on the bus; on the dirt road down to his place from the defunct store at Mesa Grande, he had even let her drive it. She had laughed as she wheeled the behemoth vehicle around the washboarded turns at fifteen miles an hour, never having driven anything larger than a pickup truck. He had lightly touched the back of her neck and laughed with her, and the tension that would take two days to dissolve had begun to crumble then.

She loved his place. Everything inside was wood, and the house itself exuded openness, as kitchen and bedroom merged doorlessly into the central living space. There were two massive desks, piled high with papers, magazines, coffee cups, beer cans, calculators, small sculptures, and other junk; a computer peeked out from amid one of the stacks. Around the room lay assorted musical instruments, from guitars to an old accordion and several flutes, and a Jew's harp on top of the computer. There were posters of art and pop culture, including an earless

Van Gogh and a shot of a sixties rock group she'd never heard of called the Bloodhounds. Her favorite piece of decoration by far was a set of wooden Russian dolls, one fitting inside the next, of twentieth-century Russian leaders. Boris Yeltsin, the largest doll, swallowed Gorbachev, who swallowed Brezhnev, who swallowed Khrushchev, who swallowed Stalin, who swallowed Lenin, who swallowed Nicholas, the last of the Tsars. Over the course of the weekend, she took the set apart and reassembled it several times.

And over the weekend, gradually, she had felt the gripping fear of the deadly classroom ease, so that it no longer held her so tightly. The isolation had helped. Moondog's five acres were sandwiched between two sprawling ranches, so that from his wide south-facing porch he had an uninterrupted view of rolling, half-wooded hills. And he had cooked for her, braided her hair, and showed her something she had almost forgotten: how to relax. He had played a guitar and sung to her under the stars; when the night grew colder, he had built a fire for her to warm herself. He had read to her from one of his eight unpublished novels, this one a comedy, and she had laughed at the funny parts without analyzing them. Toward dawn on the second morning, he had made love to her, slowly and expertly, and she had responded with an ardor that had been tightly bottled up inside her since that night on Pismo Beach. When the nightmares of the classroom floated upward into her consciousness in the wee hours of the night, he had been there to hold her. She had been in his arms a few hours ago, before they had risen in the predawn darkness and driven to the school. There she had waited in her car behind the gym until she drove it around to the parking lot at her usual time of arrival.

They had barely discussed the classroom. That had not been the point. But it was the central thing that had brought them together, and it could not be avoided indefinitely. On Friday, after the confrontation in the closet and, later, Richie's attack, Marilou had never wanted to see the room again. The weekend with Moondog had given her the courage to return, to face Scurvy's ghost—and Donna Hurley.

"Somehow, she knows something," Marilou had told him as they sipped coffee on his porch on Sunday morning. "She taught in there, you know, right after Scurvy died. And she doesn't go in the room. She poked her head in once, on the first day, and she couldn't wait to leave."

"You need to talk to her," Moondog had said. "Find out what you can about the room's history. Something happened in there—something to do with literature and death. Doug's afraid of it, too, though I doubt if he knows exactly what it is. Donna Hurley might."

"Have *you* ever tried talking to her? I don't think she's smiled at me once since the beginning of the year."

"What have you got to lose?"

"My sanity," Marilou had said, and he had let her long pause stretch into a contemplative silence. "You know, Carl told me that the only significant turnover at that school over the past ten years has been in the superintendent's office—and Dakota's been there four years now—and in my classroom. Since Scurvy, nobody's spent more than a year in there."

"Doug told me the same thing."

"I think I'm beginning to understand their reasons."

"Talk to her," Moondog had said. "About Scurvy. Find out what you can about him. Somehow, he's the key."

They had dropped the subject then, but Marilou already knew that she would not run away. Moondog had given her back her confidence. This morning, the room, like a class of teenagers, seemed less like a sinister menace than an adversary, one to be fought with experience and cunning. She finished putting up the assignments, then turned, to see that Robert was watching her over the top of his book. She wondered who else was watching her.

* * *

Donna Hurley's other job, besides teaching the upper-level English classes, was to oversee the school library in the main building. She went there at the conclusion of most school days. It was there Marilou found her, after a remedial-reading class in which Richie and Kyle had behaved unusually well, and Friday's incident had not been mentioned. She waved at Moondog in his bus on her way to the main building; he flashed her a smile and a thumbs-up sign.

The school, in Marilou's opinion, had a woefully inadequate library. Next to the office, but separated from it by two sets of lockable double doors and a short stretch of hallway, it doubled as an all-purpose meeting room (though really large public gatherings were held in the cafeteria). The collection was outdated, incomplete, poorly arranged, and dominated by the white male authors who, to Marilou's ongoing annoyance, still ruled the curriculum. The rectangular room was laid out in the most user-unfriendly way imaginable. Near the door was a tiny glass-encased cubicle, which Donna Hurley used as an office. Most of the shelves were squeezed toward the near end of the room, so close together that a person could barely squeeze between them. Long rectagular tables dominated the far half of the room, with an assortment of uncomfortable plastic and metal chairs pushed up close to them. These chairs faced away from the door and toward three tables laid end-to-end, with chairs facing out. Behind the tables were more shelves, the Stars and Stripes and California Republic flags, and an appallingly bad mural of a western town that was supposed to look something like Julian. It was here that Julian's ultraconservative school board faced the public and dispensed policy at its monthly meetings.

Donna Hurley was alone in the library, up near the flags and tables, shelving books. The older teacher looked up as Marilou entered, nodded curtly, and returned her attention to the bookshelves. Steeling herself, Marilou advanced toward the far end of the room and set her briefcase down on one of the tables.

"I need to talk to you," she said.

Donna Hurley turned around. The electric streak of white hair against black accented the severity of her unsmiling expression. Her dark brown eyes met Marilou's light blue ones. "Why?" she asked.

"It's . . . it's about my classroom," Marilou said nervously. "And . . . it's about Scott Lurvey."

For several seconds, Donna Hurley simply stared at her, and Marilou wondered if the other woman intended to say anything at all. Perhaps it had been a mistake to come, she thought. She had heard that the senior English teacher had few behavioral problems in her classes, and she thought she knew the reason. It wasn't just that she handpicked the more academically capable students (which she did); it had more to do with that *look* of hers. The witch who boiled children in oil in the story of Hansel and Gretel could not have appeared more intimidating.

Slowly, Donna Hurley set down the armload of books she'd been shelving, stacking them neatly on the table next to Marilou. "What exactly do you want to know?" she asked.

"Well . . ." Marilou fumbled for an answer that would make some sense. "It's just that . . . there have been some . . . strange things happening in my classroom. . . . His classroom, I'm told."

"Scott Lurvey is dead," Donna said stiffly. "He's been dead now for almost ten years."

"I know that," Marilou replied. "But he *did* put up those posters, didn't he?"

The muscles in Donna Hurley's face visibly sagged. "So you know about the posters," she said softly.

"I don't *know* about anything in that classroom," Marilou retorted. "But I have witnessed some strange things, things I can't explain. I was hoping that you could enlighten me."

"What sort of things?"

"Things like an old dog being kicked to death and then disappearing, leaving nothing but a dried bloodstain. Things like a desk being cut neatly in half, and my plants dying, and everything I try to put up on the walls being ruined. Things like one of my students turning into a character from a Steinbeck novel and trying to strangle me."

Donna Hurley showed no reaction. "Have you talked to the superintendent about these things?"

"I . . . Well—I've tried—sort of," Marilou stammered. "But I'm afraid he'll think I'm nuts." Marilou looked over her shoulder toward the door to the hall. She wished Moondog could have been there instead of out driving his bus. "*You* probably think I'm nuts," she muttered.

"No."

Pulling out one of the rigid wooden chairs by the table, Donna motioned for Marilou to sit down. "No, Marilou, I don't think you're nuts," she said, and sat down herself. "But how did you know to come to me?"

"Carl told me you had that room," Marilou said. "You took it over, right after Scurv—Mr. Lurvey died."

"That's right," Donna said.

"Why didn't you keep it?"

"Can't you guess?"

"I don't want to guess. I want to know. Donna, it sounds silly, but I'm scared. That classroom is dangerous."

Donna Hurley said nothing.

"And I think you know it," Marilou plunged on. Too late to back out now. "You never go in there. I haven't seen you set foot in that room once. Not even on the first day, when everybody stopped by to wish me luck."

The older woman took out a pack of cigarettes, lit one, and placed the pack on the table beside her. Smoking was not allowed in the library, but Donna Hurley was high enough in the school's pecking order that such regulations did not apply to her. She blew a cloud of smoke toward the ceiling and said, "You have a lot of spirit. There's an inner strength in you that you keep hidden from the world. I didn't see it at first. But you're strong. I really didn't think you'd last this long."

"God, Donna, it's not even Thanksgiving yet."

"One woman quit before the end of September."

The smoke hit Marilou's nostrils and made her feel queasy. She stared down at the table and said nothing.

"It's been musical chairs in there since Scott died," Donna told her. "A few teachers lasted the year. Most didn't. We covered with substitutes."

"Have there been male teachers?" Marilou asked anxiously.

"Oh yes," Donna Hurley replied. "Interestingly, at least a couple of them seemed rather accident-prone. As I recall, one teacher, a man named Overton, burned his hand on an electrical outlet. And poor Matt Walsh had a bookshelf fall over on him. Broke his leg; then he fell again, trying to get up to that desk on crutches." She took a puff on her cigarette, then exhaled. "One way or another, though, they all quit."

"I have no intention of quitting. I just want to find out what's going on."

"That's what I mean. You're tough. You look so young and vulnerable, but you don't back down easily. You're not afraid to argue with me, for instance, about the curriculum. Most of your predecessors didn't have the nerve. It's a good quality, your independence. I admire it in a person. Scott did, too."

"What exactly does he have to do with all this?"

Donna Hurley took a long drag off her cigarette before answering. "Tell me," she said, "about the boy who turned into a Steinbeck character."

Briefly, Marilou recounted Richie's attack on her, and how Moondog Nygerski had come into the room and saved her by destroying the poster. Donna listened, nodding occasionally.

"You don't seemed surprised by any of this," Marilou remarked.

"Only about the bus driver," Donna said. "That was remarkably perceptive of him, the way he sized up the situation."

Marilou looked down at her hands. "I've found him to be a rather remarkable person," she said.

"Didn't you lose one of those posters, earlier in the year?" the older teacher asked.

"I did," Marilou recalled. "The one of Mark Twain. It flew out the broken window."

"And the young black man who was giving you a hard time—he stopped acting up right after that, did he not?"

Marilou's mouth opened, but no sound came out of it immediately. "I never . . . put the two things together," she said finally.

"But you did find out about Heather Monroe, and who impregnated her?"

Marilou was thunderstruck. "You *know* about that?"

The corners of Donna Hurley's mouth twitched ever so slightly upward. "My dear, Nathaniel Hawthorne wrote the blueprint for that little scenario nearly a century and a half ago. Haven't you ever read *The Scarlet Letter*?"

Marilou stared at her older colleague in naked amazement. "You mean—"

"Yes. Carl and Heather were made to act out parts in that book. Jim Green was possessed by the character of the runaway slave in *Huckleberry Finn*. You've already figured out about Richie. I'm sure there are others."

"So the posters . . ."

"Are windows between literature and reality. *That's* what's haunting your classroom, my dear. The classics you so disdain."

"My God," Marilou whispered. "That's why I can't take the posters down."

"Actually, you probably can," Donna Hurley said. "You might hurt yourself trying, but they're just posters. Scott likes them, but he has other means of self-expression. He's very, very clever."

Marilou noted the use of the present tense. "Were you . . . close to him?"

The older teacher snuffed out her cigarette on the tabletop and reached for another one. "Closer than anyone," she said as she lit it. She shook out the match and deposited it on the table, next to the butt. Smoke curled from her mouth and nostrils. "We were lovers, he and I."

Marilou felt all the muscles in her face go slack with utter and complete astonishment. She looked across the table at her fellow English teacher and simply gaped.

"I was mad for him," Donna Hurley remembered. "And he was mad for me, too. Though at the end, everybody just said he was mad, period."

Marilou tried hard to imagine Donna Hurley in love with anyone, but the image wouldn't jell. She couldn't recall ever having seen the woman smile. Perhaps her capacity for love had died with Scurvy.

"He hated his nickname," Donna Hurley said, as if reading her thoughts. "Scurvy. Some of the worst kids called him that to his face. He didn't like it that people laughed at him. But he didn't try to change."

"I'm told he's something of a legend," Marilou said quietly.

Donna exhaled slowly, lengthily, watching the smoke waft toward the light fixtures. "Scott Lurvey was the best teacher this school ever had," she said. "The best teacher, in all likelihood, that it will ever have. This school did not deserve him."

Marilou sat silently, waiting for her to continue.

"For most of us, what we do here is a job—a job we care about, certainly, but a job nonetheless. But for Scott, teaching literature was a passion. He devoted himself to it entirely. And, oh, how the other teachers hated him for being good! I cringe when I think of the abuse he had to take, just because he did his job better than any of the rest of us could ever hope to do ours. They reacted as if he was deliberately trying to make the rest of us look bad, when the truth was simply that he loved his work and excelled at it. And his students learned. Some of them were afraid of him, and some thought he was a buffoon—

but they *learned*. They learned. Because for Scott, the classics of American literature were living, breathing things. His passion made them real. He honestly believed that he had ongoing relationships with those authors on the wall, and the characters they created. He *willed* them to life."

"And they're *still* alive," Marilou murmured. "Aren't they?"

"Yes. Scott's dead, but his passion lives."

"But why am I in danger?"

"Because Scott is lonely."

Marilou stared at her colleague. "He has all those authors, and their characters. How can he be lonely?"

Donna snuffed out her cigarette on the tabletop, next to the first one. "A book is but paper and ink without someone to read it. And Scott's authors, for all their greatness, are just dead men. Their characters are simply compilations of words. By themselves, without an audience, literary creations can do very little. But you, my dear, have an imagination. I've noticed that it has been the more imaginative teachers who have had the most trouble in that room. You may be in more danger than any of them."

Marilou sagged against the back of her chair. "Can I have a cigarette?" she asked.

Donna looked at her in surprise. "I didn't think you smoked," she said.

"I . . . quit before I came here," Marilou said. "It's just . . . well, this is all so . . . overwhelming. It's too much."

"I understand." Donna lit one for each of them.

"So if I am Scurvy's audience," Marilou said slowly, "why does he want to do me harm?"

For the first time, the older teacher's face took on a kindly expression. It wasn't quite a smile, but it was close. "All of us want to achieve some kind of immortality," she said. "Death is the one certainty we all face, and because it cannot be beaten, it is the adversary against which we struggle the hardest. Writers and artists try to do it through work that outlives them. I suppose teachers try to do it, too, through students who remember them and pass along their teachings. But Scott was not satisfied with that. He used to say that the entire universe can fit inside the soul of a human being, and that for each person, the universe is different. He said that literature was a bridge, and that if you freed your soul from your body, you could cross that bridge into a separate but equally real reality. Scott wanted to cross that bridge. But he didn't want to make the trip alone."

"And now he wants . . . me . . . to join him?"

Donna Hurley nodded slowly.

"And the only way I can do that is . . ."

"Death," Donna finished for her.

Marilou sucked hard on her cigarette, swallowing too much smoke, and coughed. She felt momentarily dizzy, the way her first smoke at the age of thirteen had made her feel. But her nerves were less on edge than they had been a minute ago, and her hands had stopped shaking. Thanks a lot, Scurvy, she thought, you've got me smoking again. But she realized that if Scurvy really wanted to kill her, he had faster and more efficient methods at his disposal.

"He tried to convince me to come with him," Donna Hurley said. "And a part of me wanted to. But I was afraid." She looked down at the table. "I'm still afraid," she confessed. "And I fear that he's very angry with me for betraying him. You see, I don't think he got what he wanted. I think he traded the passion and vitality he had in this life for some sort of hellish purgatory. He can't get out of the classroom. He can't interact with the dead. All he can do is bring grief to the living."

"What a selfish existence," Marilou said.

"Born of bitterness," Donna rejoined. "In life, over rejection by his peers. In death, over the certain knowledge that he made a mistake and that it can never be undone, until the end of eternity. Every major religion has a taboo on suicide. No good can ever come of it."

Marilou's eyes widened. "He killed himself?"

"You didn't know?"

"No. . . . How?"

Donna Hurley blew a stream of smoke at the far corner of the ceiling. "It was a gruesome death," she said. "I was the one who found him. Apparently he'd gotten it into his head to slit his wrists, but he couldn't find anything sharp enough in the classroom. So what he did was, he took the panel off the heater and stuck his hands in there, with the fan going."

Marilou winced.

"It was a mess," Donna said, nodding. "And it must have been excruciatingly painful. One hand was completely chopped off. The other was a mass of bloody pulp with missing fingers. He staggered around the room until he bled to death."

Marilou felt the color drain from her face. A column of smoke drifted upward from the cigarette in her hand; she sucked on it gratefully.

"I'll never know why he didn't just hang himself on that fan over your desk," Donna said. "Or why he had to kill himself at all. I'm sure he regrets it in his soul."

Marilou smoked and said nothing.

"We used to make love on that desk, during lunch break," Donna said, her eyes still off in the far half of the room. "And on the floor, and on top of that heater . . ."

"My God!" Marilou snuffed out the half-finished cigarette. "It *is* his child."

Donna looked at her with immediate understanding. "Oh, he has more."

"You mean . . . other girls like Heather? In . . . in other years?"

Donna Hurley nodded. "And teachers, too, on a few occasions. Scott enjoyed the sexual part of literature. I'm sure he enjoys seeing it acted out."

Marilou simply stared at the older teacher in astonishment.

"If I were you," Donna Hurley said, taking a last puff, "I'd be careful around that room with your bus driver. You could be next."

Marilou gripped the edge of the table and pushed her chair back, getting to her feet. "Thank you," she said. "You've been very helpful." And before Donna Hurley could say anything else, Marilou had stalked from the room.

Marilou walked out into the cool autumn afternoon, her head spinning. She badly wanted another cigarette. And she needed to talk to Moondog. He had been right—Donna Hurley *had* known more about the classroom than she had let on. And the older teacher also knew about their relationship. God, it was all falling apart. Ever since the earthquake, and the disastrous meeting with the superintendent. It must be all over the school by now.

So what? she thought defiantly. She was all grown up now, and her father was hundreds of miles away. She could do what she wanted.

Still, she was badly shaken by the possibility that her relationship with Moondog might not have been her idea, but Scurvy's. And what about Heather, and those "others"?

The wrongness of it! Her shoes clattered over the parking lot, slapping out her anger with each step as she strode purposefully toward the Annex and her classroom. There was nothing intrinsically evil, she thought, about the dead watching over the living; she could have even been cool with a little benign intervention. But to manipulate lives deliberately, inducing unwanted pregnancies, mental retardation, and the willingness to commit murder—that was wrong!

She was not religious. Though she had never believed in most aspects of the supernatural, she thought herself at least open-minded enough to acknowledge its existence when it hit her in the face. But the twisted morality that allowed for the use and abuse of real people for selfish, perverted purposes—*that* was evil. *That* had to be fought.

The outer doors were still open, though the hallway lay deserted. Moondog had not yet returned from his route. Anger building steadily within her, she stalked down the empty hall, the staccato of her hurried footsteps echoing through the building. She pulled her keys from her purse and opened the door to her classroom. Without hesitating, she walked to the author's wall. Nathaniel Hawthorne's picture was at the end of the board, by the steps to the raised area, she did not need a chair in order to reach it.

"Now, you Brahmin son of a bitch, you're going to leave that poor girl alone!" She grabbed the top of the poster and yanked downward. There was a loud ripping sound as it came away from the wall. Sharp pain stabbed into her hand, but she held on.

And then the metallic scream of the heater overwhelmed the room. Half of the poster was in Marilou's bleeding hand; the other half was still on the wall. Marilou grabbed for it—and the vacuum cleaner Robert had left in the corner suddenly growled and came toward her!

Marilou raked the remainder of the poster from the wall, feeling a fingernail bend backward as she did so. Ignoring the pain, she turned toward the door. But the vacuum cleaner blocked her way. Its furious whine harmonized with the heater's. At once, the thing surged forward, slamming into her, and knocked her against the wall.

"Stop it!" she screamed, pushing the vacuum away from her. She tried to run for the door, but the thing was on her again. An electrical cord whipped around her neck and dragged her down. She crawled toward the nearest desk, but the vacuum cleaner knocked it over, roaring. She felt the searing heat as it rode up over her back, pressing her to the floor. The heater screamed encouragement. Marilou rolled, knocking over another desk, and the vacuum cleaner fell over onto its side. Gasping in pain, Marilou crawled across the room, inching toward the door. The vacuum cleaner righted itself and charged again.

With the last of her strength, Marilou raised herself to her knees, moving a desk between herself and the attacking machine. The cord whipped at her head and she ducked. Her chest heaving, she lifted the desk and threw it as hard as she could at the thermostat. The vacuum cleaner growled again and charged.

The desk crunched into the wall. Bits of plastic and metal went flying. The desk bounced off the wall and the wrecked thermostat and rolled back onto Marilou, knocking her to the floor, directly in front of the vacuum cleaner. Her head hit something hard, and the room went suddenly silent.

21

Absent

Marilou came fully awake in an unfamiliar, darkened room. She lay on her side, on a bed that smelled like new plastic. Light spilled into the room from a hallway with a white linoleum floor; she could hear footsteps and muffled voices coming from somewhere beyond the room. Her bed had a metal railing, and it folded in the middle, so that her head was slightly higher than her feet. Next to it, a man-made tree sprouted several plastic bags and tubes, one of which ran down underneath the sheets and into a vein at the inside of her elbow. She could feel the faint soreness even before she looked to confirm that the needle was there, taped to her skin. A digital clock on the small bedside table read 10:15.

The hospital—she was in the hospital.

She saw that her hands were bandaged, and she remembered cutting them on the Hawthorne poster. Had she succeeded in taking it down? And how had she gotten out of the room? Her memory of returning to the classroom after speaking with Donna Hurley was blurred by pain, drugs, and the anger she had felt. How long had she been here? And how badly was she hurt?

Slowly, she turned onto her back—and gasped in pain. She could feel the bandages there under the hospital gown someone had put on. What had happened?

Her cry brought a nurse scurrying into the room, a pretty, if slightly plump, blonde about Marilou's age, with her hair bobbed under her ears. "So you're awake at last," the nurse said brightly. "I wouldn't go trying to lie on your back just yet. Those are some nasty burns you got there."

Marilou eased herself back onto her side. There was a glass of water on the table. She reached for it with her swathed fingers.

"Here, let me help you," the nurse said, and sat down on the bed. Marilou raised her head, and the woman held the glass to her lips. She took a small sip and let the water slosh around the inside of her mouth before swallowing.

Now she saw that her room was really half a room, partitioned off from the other side by a rigid curtain that ran from floor to ceiling. There was a window on the opposite side of her bed, its blinds drawn tightly shut. Sunlight poked around its edges.

"Where am I?" she asked, her voice dry and raspy.

"You're in Pala Meadows Hospital," the nurse told her. "Marilou, is that right?"

She nodded. "Can I have some more water?"

The nurse held the glass to her lips again. "I'm Jennifer. As soon as you're feeling up to it, they'll send someone along to take down your insurance information," she said. "Then, if you're hungry, we'll see about some lunch."

Lunch? "How long have I been here?" Marilou asked.

The young blond woman smiled kindly. "It's Tuesday morning, a little after ten," she said. "They brought you in last night—around five-thirty. So you've been here about sixteen hours."

"God." Marilou let her head fall onto the pillow and stared out into the hall.

"You were in pretty bad shape when you came in," said the nurse. "I checked your chart. All those cuts, and those awful burns on your back. And you split your head open, too. What happened?"

Marilou felt the back of her head with a bandaged hand. There was a square bandage there, with some sort of cloth wrapped around it.

"I . . . had an accident," she said, and she guessed her answer was partially true. Shards of memory, like pieces of a wrecked ship washing up onshore, floated back into her consciousness. She remembered being pinned to the floor and being unable to get up. She did not remember how she had escaped the room.

Jennifer frowned. "It must have been some accident."

Oh, it was, Marilou thought. A whole string of accidents had led from Pismo Beach to this hospital room in the suburbs of San Diego. She had certainly never set out deliberately to go to work in Julian, in a haunted classroom whose murderous spirit sought someone just like her. She hadn't planned on finding a lover who claimed to be a werewolf. It had not been on purpose that she had walked in on Heather and Carl in the closet. Moondog had not intended to break her window with a fly ball, nor had Robert deliberately left the vacuum cleaner in the room so that it could attack her. It had *all* been an accident, and it could just as easily have happened to somebody else.

"I've never seen someone with their hands all cut up like that," the nurse said. "It'll be a day or two before we can take those bandages off. How did it happen?"

Marilou shook her head. "I don't remember, not very much," she said. "How long will I have to stay here?"

"That'll be up to the doctors. I'd say a few days at least. You lost a lot of blood, and had a concussion besides. And they'll want to keep an eye on those burns." The nurse looked at her watch. "Now that you're awake, I'm supposed to take your vital signs and update your chart. Then there's some paperwork to take care of, and after that, it should be time for lunch. I'll be right back."

"Nurse . . ."

Jennifer turned around.

"Has anyone been here to see me? A Mr. Nygerski, perhaps?"

"Not that I know of," the nurse replied.

"Did anybody call?"

"I'll check. Get some rest."

Jennifer's white uniform disappeared into the white hall. Marilou noticed that there was a television set mounted in a corner of the room, on a high shelf. A remote lay on the bedside table near the clock. It was useless to her now, she realized, because her hands were mummified. The darkened screen glared down at her, mocking her, like the authors on her classroom wall.

She stayed in the hospital for the rest of the week, reading, watching TV, and doing a great deal of sleeping. For the first day and a half, she suffered the humiliation of being spoon-fed by the nurses and requesting help each time she wanted a glass of water or to change the channel. Twice each day, the burns on her back were washed and dressed, and by late Wednesday, to her immense relief, the bandages on her hands came off, revealing a network of cuts. When the partition in her room opened, she met Mrs. Galloway, a small elderly woman in for an operation to alleviate her severe glaucoma. "My doctor's trying to get me some of that government-certified marijuana," she told Marilou, a wry smile on her face. "I hope it works, because nothing else has." Since Mrs. Galloway could not see very well, she shunned books and TV, preferring instead to talk. This made Marilou tired, and she felt guilty at the implied rebuff each time she asked Jennifer or one of the other nurses to close the curtain.

The doctors questioned her several different times on how she had sustained her injuries, but she was able to provide them with only vague, unsatisfactory answers. Marilou wondered whether she had lost her memory of the incident or consciously suppressed it. She knew it would be useless, and possibly dangerous, to talk to the staid AMA-certified physicians about Scurvy's ghost, or anything else too elusive for their electrodes and thermometers.

She did, however, have visitors.

On the afternoon of her first full day in the hospital, while the bandages were still on her hands and she could not yet sit up comfortably, Robert Rickard showed up with his wife. As the nurse showed them into the room, Marilou lifted herself up on one elbow, taking pains to keep her back out of contact with the mattress. Upon seeing Robert, she managed a smile, which he gamely returned. His wife's face remained dark and clouded.

She was both taller and heavier than Robert, and clearly unenthusiastic about this visit. Her mostly gray hair was cut short, and she had developed frown lines angling downward from the corners of her mouth to the sides of her chin. Her dark eyes regarded Marilou coldly.

Robert made introductions. Marilou felt too weak for social niceties. "I'm glad you came," she said to both of them.

"How are you feeling?" Robert asked her.

"Like I've been run over by a truck," Marilou said. "How's my classroom?"

"It's still there," Robert answered. "Oates taught your classes today. I had to do some extra cleanup in there this morning. That goo on the wall is getting worse, and it looks like someone smashed the thermostat. There's a whole chunk of plaster out of the wall."

"Me, Robert," Marilou said quietly. "I'm pretty sure it was me."

"Then you tore down the poster, too, I take it."

In answer, Marilou held up her bandaged hands. Robert smiled and held up the hand that still bore two of the bandages she had placed there only the previous morning. It seemed like a week ago.

"Robert, what's going on?" Judy demanded.

"Ms. McCormick teaches in a dangerous classroom," Robert told his wife. "I don't know why, but accidents just seem to happen in there."

"Perhaps people aren't being careful," Judy murmured in a pointedly offhand way.

"Robert," Marilou said, "could I speak with you alone for a minute?"

Judy sniffed and squared her shoulders. "What do you have to say to him that I can't hear?" she said, her voice heavy with suspicion.

Marilou slumped against the pillow. She was far too tired for a battle with this woman; she simply wanted to talk to Robert about the room and all its weirdness. "It'll just take a minute," she said weakly.

Judy glowered at each of them in turn. "Go on, Judy, why don't you wait out in the hall for a minute?" Robert said.

Judy sputtered in indignation. "Well, I . . ."

"*Please,* Judy," Robert reiterated. "I'll be out in a minute." He touched his wife's shoulder, intending to guide her out of the room. Judy turned and gave Marilou a withering look.

"Well, make it quick," she snapped at Robert. "It's a long drive back up that hill. Honest to Christ, why you insisted on coming all the way down here . . ."

"I'll just be a minute," Robert pleaded, steering his wife toward the door.

Judy sniffed again. "I hope you feel better," she said to Marilou in a voice that had all the compassion of a brick.

"Close the door," she said to Robert when Judy had left the room.

"I'm sorry," Robert said. "Wives can be a pain sometimes."

Marilou managed a weak smile. "Thank God I'll never be one."

Robert smiled back at her. "You're awfully young to sound so sure about that," he said. "Things change."

"Not everything, Robert. Where's Moondog?"

"Well, right now he's probably driving his bus."

"He's all right, though, isn't he?"

"Well, sure. Why wouldn't he be?"

She looked away from him, at the wall. There were several seconds of awkward silence. "I'm really sorry I left that vacuum cleaner in your room," Robert said. "I can't believe I could be so absent-minded."

"The vacuum cleaner! I remember now—the vacuum cleaner attacked me."

"When you tried to take down the poster," Robert said.

"I succeeded, though, didn't I?" Marilou looked at her bandaged hands. "After all that, I sure hope I did."

Robert nodded. "The poster's gone. There're some new stains on the carpet, over by the wall. Bloodstains, no doubt."

"No doubt," she agreed. "Robert, don't feel bad about the vacuum cleaner. It isn't your fault. It's Scurvy's. He's trying to kill me. I know more than I used to, thanks to Moondog. Scurvy *wanted* you to leave that vacuum cleaner there."

"Still . . . I should've put it away."

"Let me guess," Marilou said. "You got caught up in your book, and you forgot about it."

"Yes!" Robert said. "That's exactly what happened."

"Scurvy distracted you," Marilou said. "Remember the first day, when you found that Hemingway book, and you told me you hadn't read a book since high school?"

Robert nodded.

"And now you're happily plowing through the so-called classics of American literature, even though you've never liked to read. Doesn't that strike you as strange?"

"Well, I've got a lot of catching up to do," he said defensively.

"But that didn't bother you for years. Not until you stepped into that classroom."

"What are you saying, Lou?"

"I'm saying you should be careful—for my sake as well as for your own. Don't be manipulated. Don't let the spirit in that room use you for its own purposes. Fight it. It *can* be fought."

"You saying I should stop reading?"

She smiled weakly up at him. "Robert, I'm an English teacher. I'll never tell *anyone* to stop reading. But have an open mind. And read something by someone who's not on the wall. Don't be a slave."

Robert glanced involuntarily at the door. Marilou wondered if Judy's ear was pressed against the other side of it.

"I know you have to go," she said. "I'm glad you came. I know it cost you something."

"I'll come back tomorrow, if you want," Robert said.

She smiled again, then shook her head. "Thank you, Robert. But I'll be all right. And you have other responsibilities. Tell me something before you go."

"What?"

"I still don't remember much of what happened. I remember talking with Donna after school, and being very angry that the ghost had messed up so many people's lives. I remember going back to the room, and the building being empty but unlocked, and I remember cutting my hands and the vacuum cleaner attacking me. And then, nothing, until I woke up here. Robert, how did I get here?"

Robert hesitated, then looked out the window, which the nurse had opened to allow sunlight into the room. "Moondog found you," he said. "He saw your car in the parking lot when he came back from his route, and he checked the classroom. He drove you down here in his bus. Said he could get here faster than an ambulance could."

"Tell him I'd like to see him," Marilou said.

"I will," Robert replied.

Moondog did not visit her the next day, but Mimi Anderson did, bringing a card and flowers from the rest of the teaching staff. The art teacher also brought a little clay figurine of a dolphin standing on its tail, which she placed on the bedside table. The thing was no bigger than Marilou's hand; it was glazed vanilla white, with colorful specks of something embedded in the material. "I made this last year," she said. "I find it soothing to look at."

Mimi prattled on about inconsequential things: a clay fight in that afternoon's art class, an upcoming exhibit at a new gallery in Santa Ysabel, and the refusal of her Volkswagen bus to climb steep hills at over thirty-five miles an hour. It was definitely intended as a feel-good mission, a cheer-up visit. But Marilou thought the time had come to confide in her friend about the classroom.

She approached the subject gingerly. "What are they saying about me?" she asked. "About how I got hurt?"

"That you tripped over the vacuum cleaner and hit your head," Mimi said. "What I don't understand is why you were vacuuming your classroom after school was out for the day."

Marilou looked at the closed partition; she heard no noise from Mrs. Galloway's side. She decided to take the plunge. "I wasn't," she said. "And I didn't trip. The vacuum cleaner attacked me, after I ripped down Nathaniel Hawthorne's poster."

"Lou . . ."

"The classroom's haunted, Meems."

"Oh, come on, Lou!"

"I mean it. Look at my hands." She held them up. The bulky

outer bandages had been removed, but her hands and fingers were still heavily taped. "I didn't get these cuts from falling and hitting my head, or the burns on my back." She turned, hiked up her hospital gown, and showed Mimi the extent of her injuries.

The art teacher observed a respectful moment of silence. "How did all that happen?" she asked finally.

"Scurvy attacked me," Marilou said, easing herself back into a semicomfortable position.

"Scurvy? Who's Scurvy?"

"You honestly don't know?"

Mimi Anderson shook her head.

"How long have you been teaching in that art room?"

"This is my seventh year."

"And hasn't anything weird ever come to your attention?" Marilou asked, her voice quavering. "Like Richie attacking me the other day, or . . . or kids acting like characters in a book? And all those teachers who left—didn't they have problems? Didn't any of them talk to you?"

Marilou was aware that she sounded less than fully rational, and she hoped that her confused mental state would not come to the attention of the doctors and nurses. That's all I need, she thought. Psychiatric evaluations, questions about my sanity. She wondered if she had said too much already.

But Mimi Anderson sat down beside her on the bed and gently took one hand in hers. "Lou, I'd be lying if I said I'd never seen anything strange associated with that room. I hear funny noises from there sometimes, and there have been occasions when kids have done things that have . . . well, quite frankly, frightened the teachers. But . . . but no one ever got hurt before, except that one klutzy guy who knocked a bookcase over on himself."

"So you *did* know," Marilou muttered. "Why didn't you warn me?"

"Warn you about *what*? It all seemed so harmless. I mean,

everybody who's been in that room knows it has a strange energy—it *feels* different. In a way, it's a mirror of the town. Julian's an old gold-mining town with a lot of dark history. It was basically settled by bandits, and the typical way of resolving disputes was murder. The place has a *lot* of ghosts."

"So you don't think I'm crazy?"

Mimi laughed. "Lou, have you ever taken LSD?"

Marilou shook her head. "But you have, I take it."

"About two hundred and fifty times," the art teacher affirmed. "Although it's been years since the last one. The acid out there now is mostly speed. But real acid—it opens doors in your mind you wouldn't normally use. It changes you—makes you more open to things you can't rationally explain. I mean, I've seen things that would make *you* think *I'm* crazy. And they weren't hallucinations."

"What kinds of things?"

"Well, the first house I lived in when I moved down here was this little Quonset hut, out on Whispering Winds Road. I think someone must have died in there, a long time ago, because that place was *definitely* haunted. I used to wake up in the morning and find glasses cracked in the cupboard. One evening, I stood across the living room and watched a tape deck fall off a shelf, by itself, and break a glass tabletop. But, Lou, it didn't chase me away. I did some of my best art in that house. It *inspired* me! All of Julian's like that. The town has its oddities, but it's a great place to be an artist. Maybe the muses like it there. I don't know."

"Scurvy was a teacher," Marilou said, "who committed suicide in my classroom. I'm surprised nobody's ever mentioned him to you in seven years."

Marilou was also surprised by the lack of surprise her colleague showed. "In Julian, seven years is nothing," Mimi said. "In many ways, I'm *still* new. Except for you and Carl, and the superintendent and vice principal, everybody's been there longer than I have."

"And they know the room is haunted, and not one of them told me." Marilou closed her eyes as the enormity of the betrayal sunk in.

"It's not that they *know*," Mimi Anderson said. "I mean, they sort of know, but they choose not to *know*. You have to understand the way things are in a small community. Your classroom's one of those things that's a little bit strange, and everybody knows it's a little bit strange, but they don't talk about it, except around the fringes. We've all heard some weird things about that room. I didn't know until you told me just now that there was a dead teacher involved. But like I said, Lou, you're the first one that's ever gotten hurt."

"Except for that one guy."

"Except for him."

Marilou thought for a moment. "Maybe no one's ever tried to take the posters down before. Maybe he doesn't like my attitude." She squirmed into a more upright position, grimacing with the effort. "All the weird guys I've been with," she said, "and a fucking *ghost* puts me in the hospital."

They both laughed, and Marilou discovered, to her delight, that it did not hurt to do so.

A personal get-well card from Steve Dakota arrived in the next day's mail, and that afternoon, to her surprise, Bill Oates showed up in person, with progress reports on all her classes. By now, she was beside herself that Moondog had not come. She thought about calling the school, but she knew that Valerie would answer at the main office and she would have to leave a message. What was wrong with him? Didn't he know how badly she needed to see him? She grew angrier with each passing hour.

"We couldn't find a substitute," Bill Oates told her when she asked why he had been pressed into service. "All our regular ones had other commitments."

My God, she thought. The whole town knows about that room!

"The nurse says you'll be out of here by the weekend," he said cheerfully. "I'm sure the little terrorists will be happy to see you next Monday."

She smiled and flexed her fingers. The tape was off; red lines that weren't veins crisscrossed both hands. Her back still hurt, but she could now sit up in bed. "Have they been giving you much trouble?" she asked him.

"Everything's been quiet," he told her. "But it's kind of chilly in there. We got the window to close all the way, finally. I think it got knocked off track by the earthquake. And Robert replaced that pane of glass. But now the heater seems to be broken."

For a moment, Marilou considered leveling with him about Scurvy's ghost and the things she had learned from Donna Hurley. But she wasn't sure how much he knew, and more important, she did not know that she could trust him. "No discipline problems?" she asked.

"Nope. Well, there was one little spat one day—two boys and a girl. A love-triangle thing. Some words thrown back and forth, threats of a fistfight. I sent 'em all to the office and gave 'em detention for the week."

She closed her eyes. "Tell me their names," she said. As he did so, she remembered the latest book that Robert had been reading: *The Great Gatsby.* A love triangle. Edith Sanders was the daughter of a wealthy Los Angeles movie producer who had built a home in Julian. Marilou had not made the connection when she had heard the girl's friends call her Daisy. Jeff Matlock was her boyfriend; Brian Layton had moved to Julian that fall, and he had known Edith in L.A. It all fit.

The heater might be broken, she thought, but Scurvy's ghost is still at work.

"I'm very glad you came," she told the vice principal.

* * *

Friday arrived, and still Moondog did not call or visit. Mrs. Galloway checked out, and although the woman's ceaseless tales of woe had wearied her, Marilou felt a wave of loneliness wash over her when her roommate was gone. She called her father, told him she had fallen and sustained a concussion, and that she would be released the next morning, after a final night of observation. The conversation failed to cheer her up.

On Saturday, Marilou was discharged from the hospital. She was wearing a long, loose-fitting dress over her bandaged back, and a Los Angeles Dodgers baseball cap to cover up the one-inch square where they had shaved her hair to sew up her scalp. She still had not heard from Moondog. Mimi Anderson had brought the clothes, and it was Mimi who picked her up. "I can't understand why he didn't come see me," Marilou said in the elevator. She felt betrayed, abandoned.

"Maybe he's one of those people who hate hospitals," the art teacher said.

Marilou did not reply, but inside she was fuming. She had been here five days, and he had not contacted her once. She had thought that he cared for her. Now she wasn't sure.

At the front desk, there were some forms to sign. Marilou waited while the woman gathered the required paperwork. On a clipboard next to her was a sheet headed by a single word: ADMITTED. There were fewer than a dozen names on the sheet. The second name from the bottom caught her attention: MONROE, HEATHER.

"Excuse me," she said to the receptionist. She pointed to Heather's name on the list. "What's she in for?"

"I'm sorry," the woman answered, "but we're not supposed to give out information on patients without approval from upstairs. If you'd like to wait a few minutes, I can check for you."

"No, that's all right" Marilou said. "I can call later. Thanks."

On the way up the hill, Marilou asked Mimi to stop at a store, where, for the first time in more than two months, she purchased a pack of cigarettes. As she lit one up, Mimi raised an eyebrow at her across the seat.

"I quit once. I can do it again," Marilou said, blowing smoke out the window. "Right now, cancer is the least of my worries."

22

Moondog's Lair

Moondog and Marilou literally bumped into each other at the start of third period the following Monday, her first day back. She was headed out toward the buses; he was coming around the corner of the Annex, hoping to catch her in the classroom before she took her break. Both were paying more attention to their own thoughts than to the space immediately in front of them. He grabbed her shoulders as they collided.

She pulled roughly away. "I'm pissed at you," she said.

"For what?"

"For not coming to see me! I lay in that hospital for five days, and all I could think about was how badly I wanted to talk to you. You didn't even call!"

He looked at her face as if studying it for bruises or other abnormalities. "How are you?" he asked her. "You look all right. It's good to see you."

"I'm better," she said, drawing a deep sigh. "And I suppose I ought to thank you for rescuing me again. But I missed you!"

"I missed you, too," Moondog said.

"Then why didn't you come see me? Robert managed to come. Mimi came twice. Even Bill Oates visited me. So where were you?"

Kids streamed between the Annex and the main building, navigating the break between classes. Several of them stopped to watch what looked like the beginning of an argument.

"Come on," she said, encircling his arm with her hand. "Let's go somewhere we can talk in private."

She led him around by the back of the gym, toward the buses. Doug was not there, and Robert was still cleaning the bathrooms in the Annex. When they were out of sight of the parking lot, she took a cigarette from the pack in her purse and lit it.

"When did you take *that* up?" he asked in surprise.

She answered with a short, bitter laugh. "Moondog, how little you know about me," she said. "Until I came here, I was a pack-, pack-and-a-half-a-day smoker. It's one of the things I wanted to change about my life, you know, starting over in a new place. But you gotta admit, the past couple months have been pretty damn stressful."

"You've got a point," he conceded. "It's pretty bad for you, though."

Irritation flickered across her features. "Fuck! Don't you think I know that? I failed, okay? Give me a break!"

"Sorry," he said. "You don't have to get defensive."

"I'm still waiting to hear why you didn't come see me."

"I'm a werewolf, Lou," he said. "I wish to God I wasn't, but I am. Hospitals aren't good places for me. Do you know how much silver there is in a hospital? Or all the strange combinations of chemicals, a lot of them that have exotic elements—even radioactive ones? Even when it's not full Moon, all those things can weaken me. I can't afford to be weak."

"How could you have taken me there, if that's true? Robert said you found me unconscious in the classroom, put me on the bus, and drove me to the hospital yourself."

Moondog nodded. "I carried you to the front desk, and I nearly collapsed myself before they brought the gurney. That's when I knew I had to get out of there."

She continued to stare at him, puzzled.

"And the thing is, my senses are raw," he added. "I feel things most people don't. You know I felt the evil presence in your classroom, and that I knew it was connected to the posters. That's how I could save you from Richie. In the hospital, even in the lobby, all I could smell was blood. And it draws me, Lou, like a bug light draws a moth before it zaps it. Although it's dormant between full Moons, there's still enough werewolf in me to be drawn by blood. I could *feel* that smell, pulling me on into that metal and chemical jungle! If its effect on me was that strong in the lobby, I knew I could never go up into the rooms without becoming violently ill. And then, who knows? They might have kept me there, started doing tests. . . . I might *never* have gotten out."

Marilou looked at the shrinking cigarette in her hand and emitted another short laugh. "I've met people who hate hospitals," she said. "But yours is the most unique excuse I've ever heard."

"You still don't believe me, do you?"

"That you're a werewolf?"

"Mmm."

"Moondog, I believe that *you* believe it. As for the rest of it—let's just say I'm not one hundred percent convinced."

"I can prove it to you," he said.

"How? By asking me out on the full Moon?"

He shook his head. "That would be far too dangerous. But there's a place I go when the Moon is full. No one else knows about it. I'll take you there this weekend, during the day, and then you can make up your own mind."

She took a last drag and dropped the butt on the dirt. "I know, it's litter," she said to him. "Just one of many things to hate about the habit. Moondog, why didn't you call me at least?"

"I don't have a phone," he said. "I realize I could have found a pay phone sometime during the week and called. But like you say, it's been stressful for you. I thought you could use some time away, from me, from the . . . situation—to think. If I was wrong, I'm sorry."

"I could have used a friend," she said. "But I accept your apology. Do you want to hear what Donna told me about the classroom?"

Heather Monroe was not in class that afternoon. The following morning, Marilou arrived to find Robert replacing the thermostat she had broken. Several screwdrivers and pairs of pliers lay on a desk beside him.

"What are you doing?" she asked him.

"Fixing this thing so the heater will work," he said. "It gets awfully cold in here on these November mornings."

"I don't mind," she said, a little alarmed at this unexpected development. "It keeps the kids more alert."

"Almost done," the janitor said cheerfully, crimping a tiny wire with a pair of needle-nosed pliers.

"Robert, I'm not sure I *want* the heater to work," she said. "I *like* it cold." And how, she wondered, had he gotten so handy all of a sudden?

"It'll work the way it's supposed to now," he said, putting down the pliers and reaching for a screwdriver and a plastic cover. His thumb eased the switch forward.

The heater made a few preliminary rattling sounds and then there was a whoosh of air, accompanied by an irregular drumbeat of metal clanks. Scurvy's fingers, rattling around in there? she wondered.

"It sounds just as bad as it did before," she called out above the noise.

Robert frowned, then moved the switch back to the off position. The heater clanked a few more times and then, to Marilou's surprise, fell silent. "Just use it when you need it," Robert said. "I know it makes a god-awful racket." Quickly and efficiently, he put the new plastic thermostat cover in place with a single screw.

Heather did not show up on Tuesday, or on Wednesday. Marilou inquired at the office and was told that Heather had taken an excused medical absence. A phone call to Heather's parents, under the guise of a homework update, yielded little more information. The switchboard operator at Pala Meadows Hospital would tell her only that Heather had been discharged on Monday.

Marilou did not find out what had happened until Thursday, when Heather—looking pale, tired, and, most noticeably, thin—came into class accompanied by two girls who had done nothing but ignore her all year.

Heather walked slowly to her usual desk at the front of the room, and one of the girls held her books as she eased herself into her seat. The radiance in her face had been replaced by a gray mask worn to conceal physical and psychic pain. Marilou's heart sank. Obviously, the girl had miscarried.

For most of the week, Marilou had avoided looking at the authors' wall. Now Hawthorne's empty space, with the dry spatters of blood her determined hands had left there, mocked her from the gallery of dead writers.

After class, Heather gathered her books slowly, giving Marilou the chance to approach her. "Heather, what happened?"

"I lost the baby," Heather said, her voice low but her eyes dry. "Mr. Oates brought everything to the hospital for me, though, so I'm all caught up with the homework."

"Never mind that," Marilou said. "How do you feel?"

Heather looked at Marilou as though trying to discern the hidden meaning behind the question. "I'm not sure," she said.

"These past few months, it's been like living in a dream. I'm sad, of course. But perhaps it's for the best. . . ."

"Heather, come on!" Maggie Featherly, one of the girls who had come with Heather to class, now urged her toward the door.

Heather gave Marilou a thin smile. "I'll see you tomorrow," she said as she moved to go.

"Take care, Heather," Marilou murmured as the girl disappeared into the hall with her friend. The eyes of Nathaniel Hawthorne, gone from the wall, burned in her brain. What had she done?

Saturday came, and Moondog picked up Marilou midafternoon. He parked the pickup truck by a small picnic area near the northern end of Lake Cuyamaca, ten miles from town. He shouldered a small knapsack, and he helped Marilou with hers. They were dressed similarly in blue jeans, boots, and sweaters, for the slanted sunlight of these short late-autumn days brought diminished warmth at high elevations. Marilou wore her long red hair in a simple ponytail. Moondog noted approvingly that the curves she tried to deemphasize when she dressed for work filled out her sweater quite nicely.

They crossed a small earthen dam, from which several men were attempting to catch fish. In spring, if it rained sufficiently, there was water on both sides, but this was November, and the valley to their left was high and dry and covered with red-and-yellow wildflowers. At the other end of the dam, a hilly wooded peninsula thrust into the small lake, nearly dividing it in two. Years before, Moondog had watched a nesting pair of eagles here, but they were gone now, driven away by the ever-increasing numbers of human visitors. Other birds still flourished here, though, and sometimes Moondog amused himself by carrying on whistling conversations with them.

On the other side of the peninsula, a small wooden footbridge crossed over a lazy stream that fed the lake. Then they were in the woods, on a narrow but well-marked dirt trail that began to climb gradually as it looped around toward the western flank of Stonewall Peak.

Stonewall Peak stood guard over the southern end of Lake Cuyamaca, rising to just under six thousand feet, an easy fifteen-hundred-foot climb from the valley floor. The bare outcropping of rock that marked its summit, giving the peak its name, was a favorite area for local rock-climbing enthusiasts practicing for Yosemite or other challenges, but one was more likely to encounter families of picnickers with babies in backpacks along the gradual, well-maintained trail. Hardly anyone ever left the trail; periodic signs along the way cautioned hikers against doing so.

"This is all state park land now," Moondog said. "We have to park across the lake, because otherwise they make you pay for parking. They take down your license number and everything. The last thing I want to do is arouse suspicion. Usually, I come out here on the bike, 'cause I can hide it in the woods."

"You come here every month?"

"That's right," he said. "Sometimes two or three nights in a row, during the time of the full Moon."

The Moon was already in the sky, low over the valley east of the lake, an imperfect oval needing several more days to grow round. Moondog noticed Marilou looking at it.

"I still don't understand," she said, "how the mountain keeps people safe from you."

"You'll see when we get there," he told her. "It's not just the mountain. There's a special place about halfway up. It's well off the trail. I don't think anybody knows about it but me, and maybe a mountain lion or two."

Marilou fell in with Moondog's brisk pace. Pine needles and crackly brown oak leaves carpeted the dirt trail beneath their feet. The Sun peeked through the trees from its spot just above Cuyamaca Peak, immediately to their west. Twice they encountered groups of hikers coming the other way; they nodded and exchanged one-sentence pleasantries.

A squirrel darted across the path in front of them. At the edge of the brush it stopped, fixed small beady eyes on Moondog, and bared its teeth before bounding off.

"That was strange," Marilou remarked.

"Not really," he said. "The Moon's waxing. I'm probably starting to give off vibes."

"Are all animals afraid of you?"

He laughed. "I used to think that most *people* were afraid of me, even before I became a werewolf. There's something about me that makes most living things want to keep their distance."

At that odd remark, Marilou again fell silent. The path emerged onto an unmarked paved road. Another path led off into the woods from the road's other side; a small wooden signpost indicated that it led to the Los Cabreros Horse Camp.

"Moondog, where are we going?" Marilou asked.

"There's another trail that branches off this one behind the horse camp," he told her. "We'll have to be kind of quiet for a while. Sometimes the horses can hear me on my bike, when I'm in a hurry to get up there. Animals can sense things. They freak."

He had not told her everything. There had been a nasty incident two years ago in which three horses from the camp had died in gruesome fashion. The resulting uproar among the equestrian users of Cuyamaca Rancho State Park had cost an innocent female cougar her life, though privately, rangers said that no lone mountain lion could have inflicted that kind of carnage. Moondog was pretty sure he'd been responsible. He had awakened in the woods that morning, dangerously close to the lake, with blood all over his clothes and the taste of raw meat in his mouth. He had taken pains to slink back to his bike unseen. The mountain lions made good cover. Deer hunting was not allowed in the park, and thus lions—and werewolves—had a ready and abundant food source. Moondog had been jolted this past summer, however, when the park reported its first fatal mountain lion attack in more than fifty years. The woman had apparently been killed in the daylight, a few days off the full Moon, so Moondog was pretty sure he hadn't been responsible.

They skirted the camp, and turned off onto a trail that soon began to climb quite steeply. Marilou struggled to keep up, for while she was not out of shape and felt few ill effects from her stay in the hospital, Moondog set a prodigious pace. They stopped twice to pass his canteen and for her to catch her breath. "It's not much farther up," he said at the second stop. Then he smiled as she brushed a wayward strand of hair from her forehead, on which, despite the cool temperature, sweat had formed. His smile broadened when she took off her sweater and tied it around her waist, for she looked fine in a T-shirt.

They stood on a rocky outcropping, looking northward over the lake. "Look," he said, pointing. "You can see the truck."

"It looks awfully far away," she said. "How long do you suppose we've been walking? An hour?"

"About forty minutes, actually. I've timed it before."

"You never wear a watch, do you?" she said. "I've noticed that. Not even on your bus route. You must have a pretty good internal clock."

"Well, I do keep a watch on the bus," he replied. "But it's true—I hardly ever use it. I can get up without an alarm clock, and I can usually tell when I'm on my route whether I'm running early or late. I've learned to tune into natural timekeepers, like the behavior of animals, the angle of the Sun, the phases of the Moon." He grinned. "As you know, that's pretty important to me."

"I look at the clock all the time," she said, "when I'm in class. It's a lot to ask some of those kids to concentrate for forty-five minutes. Other classes seem to fly by. Maybe it would be better if each class was allowed to determine its own natural length."

"Like baseball," Moondog said.

"What do you mean?"

"A baseball game determines its own natural length. You can't run out the clock. Time is measured only in outs, by what happens on the field. It's self-contained."

"And that's why you like it."

"One reason." He pointed to a steep ledge at the side of the trail. Several large cracks ran across it; patches of moss dotted the surface of the rock. "Do you think you can get up that?" he asked her.

She looked at him doubtfully.

"We have to leave the trail now," he explained. "We've got to work our way around to the other side of the mountain. Don't worry, I know the way."

Moondog removed his sweater as well, securing it, like Marilou, around his waist. He leapt at the face of the ledge, grabbed a handhold, and got one booted foot into a large crack. He hauled himself up onto the granite perch above her. "Throw me your pack," he called down. "I'll help you up."

With a nod of understanding, she did what he said. The cuts on her hands, though still red, did not trouble her. He grasped her wrists and hauled her up easily.

"The Moon makes you strong, I guess," she murmured, leaning against him atop the ledge.

"Dangerously so," he said. "Come on."

She looked around. The ledge was utterly hemmed in by oak trees, dwarf manzanitas, and assorted bushes. Only down the trail below did the way look clear.

"Come on where?" she asked him.

"We've got to bushwhack a little," he said. "There's a series of ledges leading off in this direction. See that big dead tree? That's our first marker."

Moondog, accustomed to coming here alone, plunged forward into the underbrush. He soon found that he had to stop periodically, for the branches grabbed at Marilou's face, hair, and clothes, slowing her down even though he did his best to clear the way for her. He ignored the scratches on his arms and neck as he forged onward. The Sun poked out briefly between the trees on Cuyamaca, and then they were in the mountain's lengthening shadow. Moving across the slope now more than upward, they followed Moondog's markers—first a tree, then a pile of boulders, then a large ledge over which a huge oak had fallen and died. They emerged again into the slanted sunlight in front of a huge moss-covered rock outcropping. Here Moondog stopped.

The plateau of boulders towered above them between the trees, looking like an altar, a natural ziggurat that protruded from the side of the mountain itself. Trees sank twisting roots into the fissures and gaps; smaller rocks formed stepping-stones up the steep sides to a high, flat area backed by more rocks and thick old-growth trees. The size and shape of the outcropping gave it the appearance of a stage, a huge stage, like the ones used in stadiums for rock concerts. "Here we are," Moondog said.

Marilou caught a glimpse of something white, not far from them in the bushes. She took a few steps to get a better view, then stopped and gasped, realizing that she was looking at the skeleton of a fairly large animal.

Most of the rib cage was still intact, and there were other scattered bones that had once been legs, shoulders, and other body parts. "It's a deer," Moondog said quietly, standing behind her.

Marilou saw other bones around her on the forest floor. "Did you . . ."

"I think so," Moondog said. "When I revert back to human form, there's no memory—at least no conscious memory—of what I did as a beast. But sometimes I can taste the blood."

She was silent for several seconds. Gently, Moondog took her arm and led her away from the pile of bones. They climbed over the stepping-stones to the flat area atop the ledge. It proved to be quite wide, and it was carpeted with soft, spongy bright green moss that was cool and comfortable to the touch. Moondog sat down, removed his knapsack, and motioned for her to sit down beside him, which she did.

"This is where you come?" she asked him. The forest floor fell sharply away in front of them. To their sides were layers and layers of trees—Moondog had not selected this spot for its panoramic views. Behind them stood an imposing wall of rocks, piled haphazardly atop one another, with gaps between them, dark holes that looked like inviting hideouts for snakes, squirrels, and other creatures of the woods. One of the gaps, at the base of the wall, looked just large enough for a human being to crawl into.

"Don't see the Moon, do you?" he countered.

She searched the small part of the sky that she could see. "We lost it quite a while ago," he said. "Soon after we left the trail. It's now on the other side of the mountain. We're facing due west."

Understanding dawned on her face. "So when the Moon rises . . ."

"The mountain's in the way," he finished for her. He nodded at the large gap in the rocks. "That cave goes a hell of a long way back, believe it or not. It widens out beyond the entrance, and there's room at the end to turn around and even lie down pretty comfortably. It's damp, and in the winter it can get pretty damn cold, but at least it puts a good chunk of real estate between me and the Moon."

"But if that prevents you from becoming a werewolf, then . . ." Marilou paused and looked down at the scattered animal bones.

"It doesn't protect me all night," he said. "See, when I first became a werewolf, I was fortunate in that I knew what had happened to me. Most werewolves don't know what they are, because of the memory loss. They just wake up all groggy, with no memory of what happened during the night. Since they don't know, they can't take precautions, and the results are usually tragic. I took precautions. If I was rich, I could just get on a plane and keep flying west for three days, staying on the daylight side of the Earth. Because obviously if you've got a big enough chunk of the planet between yourself and the full Moon, the transformation doesn't happen. It only happens when the Moon is in the sky. Then I got to thinking about mine shafts. And then I discovered this cave."

"But you said it doesn't protect you all night," she said. "Why not?"

"After midnight, the Moon moves around to this side of the mountain, and I change," he said. "Unless there's a really thick cloud cover. I've discovered that really thick clouds can block the effect. If I lived in a rainier climate—like the Alaska panhandle, for instance, where it's cloudy a lot of the time—I wouldn't go through it as often. There would be months where I'd be unaffected. But it'd be a roll of the dice."

"What's it like—when you change?"

"It's very painful at first. And I'm always sore afterward. Maybe that's why you lose your memory, because of the pain. And then just a blank until the next morning."

"No memory at all? So you don't know whether you've killed anybody or not!"

He smiled wanly. "I think I would have heard about it if I had," he said. "And I have been working at breaking through the memory loss. I've been reading Jung, and doing some dream analysis, trying to get in touch with my unconscious mind. Sometimes I have these dreams filled with images of blood and death, and feelings of ravenous hunger. Other times, I have conventional dreams. Quite a few of them lately have starred a certain red-haired female. . . ."

She laughed. "I'm touched."

"You should be," he said. "You're the first person I've ever brought here. I haven't been . . . close to anyone since this happened to me."

He turned from her and unzipped a small side pocket on his knapsack. "I have something to give you," he said, handing her a small box. He pulled out a small shiny object on a thin metal chain and held it out to her. She leaned closer to examine it. She saw that it was an exquisitely crafted wolf's head, no larger than a thimble, its mouth half open in an unmistakable snarl.

"I got this in Alaska several years ago, from the Indians. It's pure silver."

"It's beautiful," she said.

"So are you. Here."

She lifted the object from his hand, pulled her hair out of the way, and allowed him to fasten the clasp behind her neck. She noticed that a small red welt had formed on the palm of his hand where the silver had touched his skin. She traced it with her finger. "Moondog, what's this?"

The corners of his mouth curled upward. "The Moon's waxing. Silver is poison to werewolves. The closer it gets to full Moon, the more severe the reaction. I hang a silver pentagram in front of the cave when I go in, and sometimes it prevents me from getting out. If you wear that, you'll be safe from me."

"I am not afraid of you," she said softly.

"You should be. I'm dangerous."

"I guess," she said, smiling, "that I have always been attracted to dangerous men."

He kissed her then, and he felt her responding. Their lips parted only when Moondog's stomach growled loudly. She laughed and looked into his eyes. "Is that the beast in you emerging?" she asked him.

"No, no, that's all me. Unfortunately, I didn't bring any food."

"What *did* you bring?" she asked, nodding at the knapsack.

He grinned, then freed his hands to pull out a large plaid

blanket. He began to unfold it on the moss beneath them. She laughed again.

"I like a man who comes prepared," she said.

She kept the totem around her neck when she removed her clothes. Her back still bore the scars of the burns that had sent her to the hospital, bright red against her fair skin. The coolness of the oncoming evening raised gooseflesh on her bare breasts as she bent down to let him take one rigid nipple and then the other into his mouth. The silver wolf's head brushed against his neck, and he tensed.

"Does it hurt you?" she asked him.

"It hurts, but in a good way," he said, his muscles twitching involuntarily.

"Hmm." She licked the side of his neck, kissed her way down to his chest, and ran the silver wolf's head along the flesh of his stomach. He felt the thin line between pleasure and pain as the metal touched awakening nerves. His short breaths whistled in his constricted throat as she circled her tongue into his belly button. The potent totem grazed the inside of his leg, beside his hardening erection. He gasped; she chuckled deep in her throat as she took him into her mouth, moving her head slowly up and down in tandem with his hips.

The condom slipped on easily (for Moondog had, indeed, come prepared). She straddled his hips and took him slowly inside her. Moondog lay on his back and reveled in the sight of her body against the woods and the late-afternoon sky as they began to move together in an unhurried rhythm. He had been very gentle with her in their previous sexual encounters, but now the nearness of the full Moon was upon him. Had it not been for the scars on her back, he would have turned her over and fucked her as hard as he could. But she was in control; the silver totem danced between her breasts as she rode him with ever-increasing velocity, and her cries of pleasure as they climaxed together could be heard far into the surrounding woods.

* * *

It was almost dark by the time they came down off the mountain and emerged from the trees on the shore of Lake Cuyamaca. The lights of the Fisherman's Friend restaurant winked at them across the water. When Moondog suggested dinner, Marilou readily accepted.

They sat at a table by the window and shared a carafe of red wine. Marilou had lasagna; Moondog ordered a steak, cooked extremely rare, which he devoured with obvious relish. The not-quite-round face of the Moon rode high over the lake, reflecting off the still water and making shadows of the trees on the far shore.

Moondog looked out at it as he chewed his last piece of steak. He had said little during the meal, devoting most of his attention to his hunger. Marilou was content to sit in his presence without saying much, either. Her legs were rubbery and weak from the hike and her lover's passion.

"Three more nights," he said now, gazing at the Moon. "Then it'll be my time of the month."

Marilou had her wineglass to her lips as he said this; her sudden laugh sent a spray of Burgundy onto her plate and the table.

"What's so funny?" he asked her.

"N-nothing," she said, dabbing at her face with the napkin. "I've just never heard a guy talk about his 'time of the month' before."

"You know what I mean."

"Yeah. It still sounds pretty weird, though."

He looked down at his plate; she wondered if he was contemplating ordering another almost-moving slab of animal flesh. "The lunar cycle," he said, "does not belong exclusively to women."

"What are you going to do about your bus route?" she asked him.

"I don't know," he said. "Do you think if I told Robert I'm a werewolf, he'd fill in for me?"

She smiled at him. "Well, aside from the fact that he probably doesn't have a bus license, he probably wouldn't believe you."

"He knows about the classroom, though," Moondog said. "I've discussed it with him."

"So have I. And I trust him . . . to a point. But, you know, if Scurvy's ghost can manipulate students, why not a janitor? He *has* helped me, though. I think in a pinch he'd be on my side, not Scurvy's. He's had plenty of opportunity if he wanted to do me harm. Since Richie attacked me, he's the only person who's been alone in that classroom with me. Excluding you, of course."

"And how is Richie behaving of late?"

"As if it never happened," she said. "Like the first two months of school never happened. He's even been doing a little of the reading, and the last writing assignment he handed in was actually passable. I'm beginning to wonder if he's even retarded at all."

"Maybe he isn't. Maybe once the Steinbeck poster came down, Lennie let go of him."

"Like Heather and Hawthorne," Marilou murmured. "I'd like to take down every single one of those posters."

"Yeah, and win another all-expenses-paid trip to the hospital," he said. "You be careful. Besides, you said that Donna told you Scurvy doesn't need the posters. He can manifest himself in other ways."

She nodded. "Like the heater, and the vacuum cleaner. And the mice in the closet, and who knows what else. But damn, Moondog, I need this job. I got here just a little over two months ago, and I don't want to go through a whole job search all over again—not right away. Julian seemed so quiet and peaceful when I first saw it. I had no idea it was such a strange place. I mean, a ghost of a dead teacher in my classroom, a boyfriend who's a werewolf . . . I hear about witch's covens, and spirits of long-dead miners. What, is this whole *town* haunted?"

"Could be," Moondog said. "You'd have to ask one of the old-timers, and they won't talk to you until you've lived here for twenty years or so. I'm an outsider, like you. I got wrapped up in it by accident. I sure didn't *ask* to become a werewolf. It just happened. Like meeting you just happened."

"As I recall, you almost met me with the front of a school bus."

"A gross exaggeration." They laughed together at the memory of their first encounter.

"Moondog, what should I do? Seriously?"

"Well," he said, leaning back in his chair, "I do have a suggestion. I'm not sure you're going to like it."

"I'm listening."

"You're dealing with a supernatural phenomenon," he said. "Attacking it logically and scientifically isn't really going to help you, because historically, science has shied away from the supernatural. Science tends to dismiss things like ghosts, possession. . . ."

"Werewolves," she added.

"Right. Most of what we know—or think we know—about the supernatural comes from the more mystical side of the human experience. From folklore, and religion. Especially religion."

"Go on," she said.

"Remember the old werewolf and vampire movies, where someone whips out a cross or some rosary beads or holy water and the beast is kept at bay?"

"Sure," she said, giving him an amused look.

"And why do you think exorcisms are performed by priests rather than by doctors?"

"What's your point?" she asked him.

"Enlist some outside help," he said. "Decorate your classroom with religious icons. Put up a big ol' crucifix behind your desk. Drive down to Tijuana and get a couple of those velvet pictures of the Virgin Mary. Put some Bibles around. You might even want to pick up a menorah, or a bust of Buddha—you know, to cover all the bases."

"Moondog!" She stared at him as if he had slapped her. "I can't do that! Bailey Memorial High is a public school. Haven't you ever heard of the separation of church and state? Even if I didn't personally object, which I do, what you're suggesting is totally unacceptable."

"And a ghost who wants to kill you isn't?"

"Look, I won't do it," she said, and the finality in her voice was unmistakable. "There has to be another way."

Moondog twirled one end of his mustache in his fingers as he thought. "Well," he said at length, "I suppose we could torch the place. Fire has been known to purify."

She reached across the table and touched his hand. "They put arsonists in jail, love," she said. "I don't think jail would be a good place for you."

"No," he agreed. "First full Moon, there'd be a riot that would make Attica look like a Sunday-school picnic."

They ordered Boston cream pie for dessert, and Moondog ate most of Marilou's piece as well as his own. This was followed by two rounds of Irish coffee, over which Moondog told her that in the days leading up to full Moon, no amount of alcohol could get him drunk. "I tried it once, hoping to pass out when the Moon rose," he said. "But it didn't work. I'm super aware, both physically and mentally. It's part of the curse."

It was nearly midnight when he drove her home, where he would make love to her twice more before dawn. The Moon was in the western half of the sky by then, shining on the face of Stonewall Peak, marching inexorably toward the point in its orbit opposite the Sun—a rendezvous no power on Earth could prevent.

23

The Break-In

The liquor store closed at nine, and after that, there was no reason for most people to go into town anymore. Jimmy Rickard waited out the Tuesday night closing-time line to buy his twelve-pack, which he shoved roughly against the thigh of his friend Pete Sutherland, who occupied the middle of the seat of his well-worn Datsun pickup. "Move over, dude," the youth growled. "Make room for the beer."

Sutherland edged over, pushing Bobby Bauer more tightly against the passenger door. A former high school football player whose generous build had softened into flab since he'd stopped playing, Bauer grumbled as he shifted his center of gravity. "Shit, Rickard, whyn't you get a Jeep or something?"

"Shut up," Jimmy replied as he climbed in behind the wheel. "At least I got wheels. Which is more than I can say for either of you."

He started the engine, then performed a neat U-turn in the nearly empty Main Street. His free hand ripped open the twelve-pack and doled out a cold beer to each of his friends. A minute later, they had left the tiny Julian business district as Jimmy aimed the pickup in the direction of the desert, the Moon full and bright ahead of him.

When he reached the school, Jimmy turned into the parking lot and immediately extinguished his headlights. He knew where he was going, and the Moon provided plenty of light for him to find the way. No cars passed by on the highway in front of the school as Jimmy steered the vehicle around to the back side of the Annex, out of view of the road. He parked in the gravel area behind the building, facing out, and cut the engine.

The school board, which prided itself on its fiscal conservatism, had declined over the past few years to budget money for either a gate or a night watchman—small savings that would this night pay disastrous dividends. The three young men were entirely alone. Jimmy was their leader, not only because at twenty-three he was the oldest of the group, and the only one with a vehicle, but because the break-in had been his idea. "It'll be a piece of cake," he'd told them earlier, dangling a large and heavily laden key ring in front of them. "Look, I got my old man's keys."

"I dunno, Jimmy," Pete Sutherland had said. "What's in the Annex worth stealin'?"

"You know, computers and stuff," Jimmy had replied with enthusiasm, if not accuracy. "Money in desk drawers. Maybe a TV and VCR. And other stuff we don't know about 'til we get in there and look around."

During the course of other nocturnal adventures, the three of them had honed their skill at burglary. In Julian, they had a fair number of peers, for the area has a lot of weekend homes, and a lot of youths with a surplus of time and a dearth of money. Jimmy Rickard and his companions had learned how to pick their targets, how to tell which houses were vacant on a dependably regular schedule, which ones had alarms and which did not, which neighbors kept dogs that might bark. Jimmy kept a tarp in the back of his truck, and he used it to cover big-ticket items like television sets and stereos. He took them to outlets in El Cajon and San Diego that weren't too vigilant about determining the origin of the merchandise. The trio had enjoyed a successful little career—supplemented, in Jimmy's and Pete's case, by dealing a little weed and crystal. Bobby Bauer tagged along because he was basically too incompetent and unimaginative for most work that did not involve theft. Though the three had had their brushes with the law, none had spent a single night in a jail cell, and in their youthful optimism, they may have imagined that thievery would support them forever.

The school, however, represented a different kind of challenge. It represented authority. To these three overage juvenile delinquents who had, like Nolan Ryan and Willie Mays, extended their careers past their proper conclusion, it would not be enough simply to rip the place off. They would have to leave a calling card. It was a matter of honor, of professional pride. To that end, Bobby Bauer, the only one of the three who had actually attended Drew Bailey Memorial High School as a student, had brought along a can of red spray paint.

They spilled out of the truck, tossing their emptied beer cans onto the ground. Let the old man pick 'em up, Jimmy Rickard thought bitterly as he cranked open another can and passed the twelve-pack to Pete. *He* sure as hell wouldn't be picking up other people's garbage when he was in his fifties. He might be in jail, but even jail had to be better than sweeping floors and washing out toilets while other people watched. Picking trash off the freeway was bad enough, but in the eyes of the son, Robert Rickard's new job had even less dignity. Vaguely, Jimmy imagined a villa in Costa Rica, paid for by drug money, from which he would be able to thumb his nose at his father and all the teachers, bosses, cops, and other authority figures who had sought to run his life.

Pete Sutherland's motivation was likewise more focused on his family than the school. A navy brat who'd ended up in San

Diego, he'd moved to Julian the previous year with his mother after his father had left both her and the military to run off with a dancer he'd met at one of "those" bars down by the Sports Arena. In Julian, he had quickly fallen in with Jimmy and his petty-criminal pals. Pete had tried the service himself; the only souvenirs he kept from those turbulent six months were a large tattoo of a mermaid on his left biceps and an expensive crystal meth habit he supported through stealing.

Bobby Bauer was more or less along for the ride—a bored local kid who had hated school and the few jobs he'd managed to get after graduating with a *C* minus average.

Jimmy drained his second beer, then tossed the can in a long, lazy arc toward the far corner of the building. The moonlight glinted off the shiny aluminum as the can tumbled end over end in the air before striking the side of the building and coming to rest. Jimmy let out a long, loud burp, which resonated in the night and which his two partners in crime found hilarious. "Come on," Jimmy said, opening another can. "You guys grab another brew, and let's get to it."

"It seems awful wimpy to use a key," Pete Sutherland said. "Can't we at least break a window or something?" Pete was into violence and destruction—the more senseless, the better.

"Maybe when we leave," Jimmy promised him. "We don't want to do nothin' to attract attention."

But Bobby Bauer had already moved away from them, onto the small concrete patio outside the back door of the Annex. He had the can of spray paint out, and with a studied look on his round face, he moved the can slowly back and forth, holding it in both hands as he inscribed his message. Jimmy and Pete drank their beers in silence and watched him. When he finished the last letter—like the rest, a good three feet from top to bottom—Bobby stepped back to admire his handiwork. SKOOL SUKS proclaimed the huge red letters.

"I can tell it didn't teach *you* much," Jimmy said, stepping past him. In another minute, he had the door unlocked, and the quiet, empty hall of the Annex lay open before them.

"Whooo!" Bobby Bauer shouted impetuously, getting in return not the echo he anticipated but a poke in the chest and a fierce look from Jimmy.

"Quiet down, asshole!" the older youth whispered.

"Come on, Jimmy, we're the only ones here," Bobby squealed.

"Never assume that," Jimmy said. "Assumption is the mother of all fuckups."

"Hey, I like that," Pete said in the dark. "Say that again—assumption is the motherfuck of . . ."

"Assumption is the mother of all fuckups," Jimmy said in a low voice, through his teeth. "Come on."

They went first to the art room, at the very end of the hall. The art room had windows on three sides, including a row of east-facing windows, from which they could see the patio and the truck. These windows also faced the full Moon, admitting more than enough light for their purposes.

"Wow, there's a lot of stuff in here," Pete Sutherland said, looking around at the painting supplies, the potter's wheel, the sculptures made of metal, wood, plastic, and clay that seemed to fill every available corner, top shelf, and out-of-the-way spot along the countertops. The long tables were arranged in a large rectangle around the edges of the room; student paintings displaying a wide range of talent covered the walls.

"Yeah, none of it worth a shit," assessed Jimmy.

"Look at all this paint!" Bobby Bauer exclaimed, opening a supply closet containing stacks of gallon cans.

"What the fuck are we gonna do with paint?" Jimmy snorted.

"Hey, Jim, think quick!" Something dense and cold smacked his cheek and plopped to the floor. He turned just as Pete Sutherland fired another missile at him from the far corner of the room, over by the sinks. Jimmy blocked it with his hand. Clay. Pete had found the clay.

"Fuckin'-A, man!" Jimmy exclaimed, irritated at his friend's playfulness. "Leave the fuckin' clay alone. It ain't worth nothing'." He rubbed his cheek. "Besides, that hurt."

"Aww!" Pete and Bobby chorused in unison.

Bobby had the top off one of the paint cans. In the moonlight, it was impossible to tell what color the paint was. But it would make a nice contrast on the white floor. Standing up, he cried, "Look out!" and splashed the paint into the center of the room, laughing gleefully. "Hey, dudes, it's modern art! Let's add some other colors!"

"Let's find another room," Jimmy suggested. "We're wasting time."

Another piece of clay zipped past his head; he ducked away from it. "Hey!" Bobby Bauer exclaimed as Pete caught him with a good-sized chunk in his ample stomach.

"Come on, let's get outta here," Jimmy said. "Bobby, forget the paint." He nodded toward a higher shelf in the same cabinet. "Let's bring those cans of turpentine, though. That's useful stuff."

"Just a minute," Bobby said. He grabbed a large paintbrush from a jar and dipped it into the pool of dark paint on the floor. Advancing to the blackboard on the far wall, he scrawled another message: FUCK ART.

"Very good," Jimmy said. "You spelled both words right. Now let's grab that turpentine and go find the computers."

Had Jimmy Rickard done his homework, however, he would have known that there were no computers in the Annex—they were all kept in the main building. There was a television and VCR in Donna Hurley's room, at the opposite end of the building, and the sports equipment in Carl Estabrook's half of the walk-through closet was probably worth some small change, but the next door Jimmy unlocked was to room 13, because it was the closest. Bobby and Pete set the cans of turpentine down in the hall outside the alcove. "Man," Pete said with a chuckle. "Your old man's gonna have a lot of cleaning up to do tomorrow."

"Good for him," Jimmy said tightly as he found the right key and unlocked the door.

Room 13 was very dark. The wall of windows faced west, away from the Moon, and the blinds were down and drawn completely shut.

"Where the fuck's the light switch?" Jimmy wondered aloud as his hand searched the wall by the door.

"I can see a little," Pete volunteered.

"What are you, an owl?" Jimmy shot back. "I can't see a fuckin' thing."

"I got good night vision," Pete said. "Open your eyes wider; let 'em get used to the dark. You can see."

"I can see a couple of desks, right here next to me," Jimmy said. "And I can see you guys. That's it. What do you see?"

"Faces," Pete said.

"Quit yankin' my chain," Jimmy scoffed at him.

"No, really, over there. On the wall."

"I see 'em, too," said Bobby. "A bunch of 'em, lookin' right at us."

"Gimme a break, you guys, willya?" Jimmy moved slowly along the near wall. He missed the light switch, but his eyes picked up the steps, the monstrous desk, the heater on the back wall, and, to his left, the black hole of the closet.

"Hey! You guys!"

"You find something, Jimmy?" Pete said.

"I think so. There's a big closet here. Looks like it goes a long way back. Closets are where the good stuff usually is. Damn, I wish we had some light!"

"I don't like this room," Bobby said suddenly, in a queerly small voice.

"Shut the fuck up, Bobby," Jimmy counseled him.

"What's in there, Jimmy?" Pete asked anxiously.

"I can't *see*!" Jimmy said, from inside the closet. His hands danced in front of him, feeling for valuables. His shoulder bumped roughly against a bookshelf, and several paperback volumes tumbled noisily to the floor.

"What was that?" Bobby cried.

"Don't soil your drawers," Jimmy said. "It's just some books." He felt around some more with his hands. "Seems like that's mostly what's in here, books. Maybe in—"

The heater cut him off in midsentence with a metallic snarl that sounded like two horny tomcats in a fight. Jimmy jumped, slamming into the bookshelf and sending more paperbacks raining down around him. "Shut that thing off!" he shouted above the keening wail.

But the heater's shrill whine seemed to accelerate, increasing in volume and pitch until it became physically painful. "Shut it off!" Jimmy cried again.

"Where's the switch?" Pete yelled, equally unnerved. "I can't find the fucking switch!"

"Jesus Christ!" Jimmy cried. The sound was really too much to bear, and it was building, building—like a phaser on overload on the old *Star Trek* series. Jimmy Rickard pressed his hands to the side of his head and stumbled toward the entrance of the closet, nearly losing his balance on the pile of fallen books beneath his feet. Groping blindly, he pulled a paperback from the nearest shelf and staggered out into the room. He could see a little better now; there was more light in the room than in the closet, and his eyes had begun to adjust. He could see the faces on the opposite wall, and he could see the hulking heater, the object of his torment. He took aim and threw the book at the heater with all his strength.

It did not bounce off. There was a groaning sound as the book struck the panel in front of the fan and stuck there. Jimmy could hear the paper being ripped apart and chewed up in animal fashion. The high-pitched metallic sound throttled back, taking on a more guttural quality, almost as if, Jimmy thought wildly, the heater were choking on something.

And then it roared, and Jimmy Rickard saw the last astonishing sight of his short, wasted life.

The huge beast seemed to come out of the wall itself. It crouched on all fours and leapt directly at the young burglar. The room was dark; the shapes were a vague gray on gray. Jimmy did not know that the teeth that ripped out his larynx and severed his jugular vein belonged to an animal that was not gray but brown, with a streak of white running down its chest. He barely registered its size, or its unmistakably canine nature. There was no time for recognition. There wasn't even time to scream.

Pete Sutherland was the one who screamed. The huge dog stood over Jimmy as the young man's lifeblood gushed onto the carpet. The beast flicked a piece of Jimmy's flesh off its snout with its tongue, at that moment meeting Pete's astonished eyes with its own. Pete pressed backward against the wall in terror. By sheer luck, one of his hands landed on the light switch. Instinctively, he pushed it upward—and he stared into the fully illuminated face of impending eternity.

The dog was immense, bigger and more powerfully built than any dog he had ever seen. Its teeth gleamed from behind drawn-back lips; its face and chest were covered with Jimmy's bright red blood. And the eyes, the eyes . . . There was nothing in them but the hunt. Pete Sutherland opened his mouth and began to scream. He did not stop screaming until he died, as swiftly and painfully as his friend.

For Bobby Bauer, closest to the door, that first second of light, in which he saw Jimmy already dead and bleeding on the floor and the dog turning its murderous attention to Pete, was all it took. He turned and ran into the hall. He ran out the opened back door. He ran across the patio and past the truck. He ran out over the parking lot and onto the highway, and he kept running. He was quite some distance from the school when he realized he was no longer hearing Pete Sutherland's screams, but his own.

24

Crime Scene

Moondog knew something was wrong the minute he wheeled his motorcycle into the school parking lot, an hour late for the start of his bus route, and saw three cop cars and a Sheriff's Department ambulance in front of the Annex. A ribbon of yellow tape cordoned off the door to the building.

Marilou was already there, and Robert and Bill Oates, he noted, as his eyes swept the parking lot. He didn't recognize the other vehicles arrayed in front of the tennis courts. A less observant person would not have noticed the other vehicles at all, for the cop cars formed a phalanx in the middle of the lot, arrogantly eschewing regular parking places.

He didn't bother going to his bus. Parking the bike next to the cop cars, he ducked under the tape, bounded up the steps, and hurried down the hall to room 13, expecting the worst.

But Marilou was alive and unhurt, standing numbly by the thermostat on the near wall. She flashed him a look he had not seen from her before—like a cat at a safe distance regarding a kind master who has unexpectedly struck her. The room was full of cops. In addition to the half-dozen uniformed officers, Bill Oates and Robert Rickard were in the room, over by the wall of authors. In the far corner, a man in city clothes conferred with a distraught-looking young man who sat at a student desk, an older man's arm draped protectively around his shoulders. Beside them, Harry Osterman stood with a notebook in one hand, a pen in the other, and a 35-mm camera hanging from his neck.

The centerpiece for this gathering lay at their feet: two sheet-draped bundles that could only be the bodies of two human beings.

One of the officers by the bodies looked up as Moondog appeared in the door. "Who the hell are *you?*" he demanded.

Moondog quickly assessed the situation. Robert's face was ashen. Oates maintained tight-lipped military control. The plainclothesman, obviously a detective, looked up and stared at Moondog with frank curiosity.

He could not read Marilou's face at all, and Moondog was good at reading faces. She averted her eyes when he looked at her. He wondered if she had found the bodies upon her arrival. He looked at Robert. Wouldn't the janitor have gotten here first? Robert looked as though he had been punched in the solar plexus. His eyes were blank and unfocused. Osterman's face held pure hatred.

"There's no school today," Oates said in clipped syllables. "We didn't know how to reach you."

"Who *are* you?" the cop repeated.

"Cyrus Nygerski," Osterman said, as though the name itself were a curse. "Former columnist for the *Julian Nugget.* I fired him two months after I bought the paper."

"I drive a bus here," Moondog said.

"You're also trampling all over a crime scene," the plainclothesman snapped. "Didn't you see the tape?"

"This guy's not big on rules," Oates remarked acidly.

"Obviously," the detective said. "Now, would you do us all a big favor and get out of here?"

Moondog didn't move. He tried to catch Marilou's eye again. She jerked her head away. He looked at the janitor. "Robert, what happened here?"

"My son," Robert said, his voice choked. "Someone killed my son."

"We're in the middle of a double homicide investigation," said the detective. "And unless you can shed some light on the situation, I'd appreciate you staying out of the way."

"You always show up for work like that?" one of the uniformed cops asked.

Moondog looked down at himself. His blue jeans were torn at the knee and smeared with dirt. His denim jacket was unbuttoned, and although he had changed his shirt, he still looked rather rumpled. No doubt his hair looked disheveled, for he had not taken time to comb it, and his last shave had been more than thirty-six hours ago.

"I was late," he said. "I didn't have time to wash up."

Oates was staring at him, but when he looked again at Marilou, she averted her eyes. The plainclothes detective took a few steps toward him, pulled a pack of cigarettes from a breast pocket, and tapped it on the upturned palm of his hand. "Guy Taylor, Sheriff's Department, Homicide. Cyrus Nygerski. I believe we've met before. They call you Moondog, isn't that right?"

"Most people, yeah," Moondog replied unemotionally.

Taylor smiled without humor. "I remember what a clever son of a bitch you are. Seems you have a way of turning up around violent death. Now, why is that?" He shook a cigarette loose from the pack and pointed it accusingly at Moondog's face.

"You're the detective," Moondog said softly. "You tell me."

For a second, the only sound in the room was Bill Oates sucking in his breath. Then two cops grabbed Moondog's arms.

"Come on, buddy," one of them growled. "Let's go." Moondog did not resist as they muscled him toward the door.

"Wait," said Guy Taylor and Marilou McCormick almost simultaneously.

Homicide detective and English teacher looked at each other in surprise. The cops relaxed their hold on Moondog. Taylor lit his cigarette and blew a cloud of smoke in Moondog's general direction.

"Harry, why'd you fire this guy?" Taylor's eyes never left Moondog's face.

"He was useless to me," said the small, balding newspaperman. "All he ever wanted to write about were werewolves and vampires and wild conspiracy theories. And when he did write about something real, it was always from a left-wing point of view. The guy's a Communist, if you ask me."

"Untrue," Moondog said. "Anarchist, maybe, but not a Communist."

"I think he's a lunatic," Osterman said to the detective. "I aim to put out an honest, responsible newspaper. This guy's a loose cannon. That's why I got rid of him."

"And how did he react?" Taylor asked.

"As I recall," Osterman said, "he threatened to rip my lungs out."

"I was just kidding, for Chrissake," Moondog said.

"You've got a strange sense of humor," Taylor told him.

"I'll say," murmured Marilou.

Taylor favored her with a long look. Osterman, Oates, and Moondog looked at her, as well. The detective turned his attention back to Moondog. "You know anything about this?" he demanded.

Moondog took in the hostile faces around him. "How would I know anything about it?" he cried. "I just got here!"

"Where were you last night?" Taylor asked.

"That's none of your business," Moondog replied evenly. "I wasn't here, though."

Marilou stepped forward. "He was with me, Mr. Taylor," she said. "We . . . spent the evening together . . . at my place."

Taylor looked back and forth between teacher and bus driver, and Moondog saw in his face that he was trying to make up his mind whether or not to believe her. It was the second time she had lied for him in a pinch.

"Since it's against the rules in here, I'd like to go outside and have a cigarette, if I may," Marilou said, looking pointedly at the one in Taylor's hand. "May I talk with Cyrus alone for a minute?"

The detective took one last unapologetic drag on his smoke, dropped it on the carpet, and squashed it like a bug. Then he nodded at the two cops beside Moondog. "See that they don't go anywhere." To Moondog, he said, "I'll want to talk with you later, after I question this young man." He turned to two other cops. "I think we can get these stiffs out of here," he said, dismissing the bodies with a wave of his hand.

"Anyone I know?" Moondog asked.

Taylor visibly started. "I don't think you want to look," he said.

"You don't," Marilou declared, stalking past him and tugging on his arm. "Come on."

The two uniformed officers followed them out into the hall. Marilou led him toward the back door. "We can talk out here," she said.

The truck remained where Jimmy Rickard had parked it, and Moondog noticed Bobby Bauer's spray-paint message on the cement. "What happened?" he asked as Marilou lit a cigarette.

"Robert's son and two of his friends broke in here last night," she told him. "They trashed the art room, and then they got into mine. That was one of the kids, with his father, back in the room. He's the only one who survived."

"But . . . how?"

Marilou blew a long stream of smoke out the side of her

mouth. "Apparently," she said, "they were attacked by some sort of wild animal." She stopped talking and looked searchingly into his eyes. "Moondog, how could you?"

So that was it! He recoiled as if she had slapped him. "Lou, you don't think . . ."

"What am I *supposed* to think? The Moon was full, and there were two cans of turpentine outside the door. Just last weekend, you talked about burning the room."

"I was joking!" he said.

"You ought to be more careful what you joke about. Where *were* you last night?"

"Oh, come on, Lou, not you, too."

"Moondog, I *saw* what happened to those two kids. I was lucky to make it to the bathroom before I lost my breakfast. They were ripped apart. Like they were attacked by a . . . a werewolf. And you're going to tell me you don't have any memory of last night, I bet."

"You think *I* killed them?" he asked incredulously.

She looked at the ground. "I don't know," she murmured in a barely audible voice. Her eyes returned to his face. "I guess I'd like you to convince me otherwise."

"I went to the cave," he said. "Some time after midnight, I changed, and no, I don't remember anything after that, until I woke up in the woods. But I know I didn't come over here."

They stared at each other in silence for what seemed a long time. "What killed them, then?" she asked, still practically whispering.

"I don't know," he said. "Let's go see if we can find out."

Bobby Bauer swallowed hard and looked at his father for courage. John Bauer was a thickset, hard-drinking construction contractor who, like his son, had disdained formal education. He had a shock of dark curly hair, a wide face that displayed a five o'clock shadow before noon, and big hands with thick, stubby fingers. He had five other kids, the raising of whom he left largely to his harried wife. Bobby was not the only wayward youth in the family.

"It's all right, son," the father said awkwardly. "Tell them what you saw."

"How did you get into the building?" Guy Taylor asked.

"It was Jimmy's idea." The rotund youth looked miserably at Robert for a moment, then quickly drew his eyes away. "He had the keys. We went in through the back door."

"Out by where the truck is parked," Taylor said.

Bobby nodded.

"And you vandalized the art room, too, didn't you?" Bill Oates said, but with a notable lack of his usual harshness.

Bobby nodded again, then wiped furiously at unsummoned tears as Moondog and Marilou reentered the room. The two cops who had gone out with them remained in the doorway. Two other cops had left the scene, and the bodies had been removed, replaced by crude chalk outlines on the bloodied carpet. Steve Dakota had arrived, and the shaken superintendent stood by the windows, arms folded across his chest, trying to disappear into the blinds.

"Jimmy thought there'd be computers and stuff," Bobby said. "Me and Pete, we were just messin' around. I spilled the paint. He started throwin' the clay. . . ."

"Little thieves got what they deserved," Harry Osterman muttered.

"Shut up," Robert said suddenly and forcefully. "That's my son you're talking about. He may have been an asshole, but he was still my son." He turned away from the group to hide his sorrow and shame.

"Go on, Bobby," Guy Taylor urged the youth. "So you went to the art room first, is that right?"

Bobby nodded, his eyes on the floor.

"And then you came in here?"

"Yeah." Bobby sniffed, and his father patted him awkwardly on the shoulder.

"Go on," Taylor said.

"Well, it was awfully dark. And we couldn't find the light switch. . . ."

"Who went into the room first?"

"Jimmy," Bobby said. "We were both followin' Jimmy."

"And he came over here, like this?" Taylor walked slowly along the wall by the door, eyes on Bobby for confirmation.

"Yeah, I guess so. I was by the door. It was real dark. Spooky. I didn't wanna go in."

"So you didn't hear anything, is that right? You had no idea there was anybody else in the room?"

"Didn't hear nothin'." Bobby brushed at his face again. "Didn't see nothin', either. It was pitch-black. I could see a few desks, and the windows . . . and these faces here." Bobby pointed at the wall of authors.

"How could you see the posters in the dark?" Moondog interjected.

"I'll ask the questions, if you don't mind," Taylor snapped.

"It's a valid point," Marilou said quietly. Moondog noticed that her expression had thawed a bit. With the ebb of anger, a surge of dread had risen to take its place. Still, she avoided his eyes in the same way that she seemed to be shying away from everything in the room that could hurt her—the heater, the closet, the posters, and Moondog himself.

"Did Jimmy go into the closet, Bobby?" the detective asked. The pile of paperbacks, many of them spattered with blood, remained on the closet floor, spilling outward into the room.

"Uh-huh. And then that thing back there came on, real loud." He looked at the heater, which had been resolutely silent since the discovery of the bodies. "It freaked us out. Jimmy yelled at us to shut it off, but we didn't know how. He threw something at it. And that's when the dog attacked him."

"Dog?" Moondog said, startled.

"What did it look like, Bobby?" Bill Oates asked.

"It was hard to see it too clearly. But it was big. God, it was huge. And I could see its face. . . . Its eyes were yellow, I think. I saw it lookin' at me, before I ran away. It was . . . standin' over Jimmy . . . after it killed him." Bobby Bauer shuddered and buried his face in his hands.

"It's all right," John Bauer said. "Take your time."

Bobby lifted his head and looked wildly around the room. "The thing is," he said, "I don't know how it got in here. An' it was totally quiet 'til that . . . that heater went on. When it came on, none of us could stand it. It came on real sudden, and it sounded like . . . like it was gonna blow up."

"It does sound like that," Robert affirmed. "It races like hell sometimes. Something scrapes against something else in there, and I mean it makes a racket. It sounds awful." He looked over at Steve Dakota. "I told Doug about it a few times."

"Did he look at it?" the superintendent asked.

Robert shook his head. "To my knowledge, he's never been in this room."

"I want to hear more about this so-called dog," Guy Taylor said. "Where did it come from?"

"Back there somewhere," Bobby said, pointing to the area behind Marilou's desk.

Taylor threw a quick glance at the heater, then fixed his eyes on Bobby. "You're saying this dog was here in the classroom, waiting silently to pounce on whoever came in? That sounds pretty damn unbelievable." The detective turned to Marilou. "You lock your classroom when you leave?"

She nodded. "Always."

"Was there a dog in here yesterday when you left?"

Marilou shook her head.

"Anyone else have cause to come in here after school is out for the day?"

"No," Steve Dakota said.

"Who else has a key?"

"There's a set down at the office," the superintendent said. "And Doug, our head custodian, has keys to all the rooms. Beyond that, we issue individual keys to the teachers themselves, and to the janitors."

Taylor paced thoughtfully. "And we've already established that the kid used his father's keys to get into the building," he said. "So who let the dog in?"

Bobby looked confused. "All I know is what I saw. I seen it kill Jimmy . . . and then it went after Pete, and I was out the door! I didn't wait around for it to come after me!" Bobby's lower lip trembled; he looked as if he was about to cry again.

"Easy, son," his father said.

"Dogs don't just appear out of nowhere," Moondog noted.

"Not real dogs, anyway," Marilou said. Moondog threw her a quick glance, which she would not meet.

"Real dogs bleed, too," Robert said suddenly. Marilou's eyes widened and fastened on him.

"What do you mean, Robert?" Moondog asked.

The janitor turned to his dead son's friend. "Bobby, do you remember anything of what this dog looked like, aside from its size? What color it was, maybe? What breed?"

"Well, it was dark in here," the youth said after a moment's hesitation. "And after it killed Jimmy . . . like I said, I ran away as fast as I could. But it . . . didn't seem like it was black. It was lighter-colored, sort of brown, maybe. And big, with big shoulders an' jaws and everything."

"Did it by any chance have a blaze of white down its chest?" Robert asked.

Marilou let out a small gasp, then clamped her mouth shut.

"What are you getting at, Robert?" Guy Taylor asked.

"I think I understand his general drift," Moondog said. His arm swept from the heater to the floor to the open door to the hall. "Some sort of dog jumps out from behind the desk and rips out two guys' throats. We have no way of explaining how it got into the room, or why it waited quietly while these three guys trashed the room across the hall. It doesn't make a move until the heater comes on. Bobby here turns and runs away before the dog can attack him, too. Now, how does the animal leave the room?"

"The door was wide open," Taylor said. "Both doors, to this room and to the outside. It simply walked off into the night."

"Wrong," Moondog said.

"What do you mean, 'wrong'?" the detective challenged him.

Moondog nodded at the blood-soaked carpet. "Those two kids had their throats torn out," he said. "Blood must have gotten all over the place. Look—it got all over the wall, in the closet. . . . There're even spatter marks on the front of Lou's desk. There was blood everywhere."

"What's your point?" Taylor said.

"Well, whatever killed them would've gotten pretty bloody itself. Yet I don't see any bloody footprints—or paw prints, if you will—leading to the door. And I didn't see any blood in the hall, either. The windows are all closed. So how did the killer leave the room?"

"Maybe it never did," Robert said softly. "Maybe it's still here."

"What?" Taylor and Osterman exclaimed in unison.

"Scurvy's ghost," Marilou murmured. "It was Scurvy's ghost that killed those boys."

"What are you people *talking* about?" Taylor railed.

"The beast left the room the same way it got in," Moondog said. "Through a portal between dimensions, owned and operated by Scurvy's ghost."

When no one responded immediately, Moondog continued. "There's a supernatural presence in this room," he told the detective calmly, as the expressions around him grew more and more disbelieving. "I've known about it for some time, and Marilou and Robert here know about it, as well. It hasn't killed, until now, but it has proven itself to be quite dangerous."

"Oh, this is bullshit!" Osterman said, stepping into the physical center of the discussion. He stabbed an accusatory finger at Moondog. "This man," he said to Taylor, "is the source of your problem. He loves doing this, making up outlandish stories and trying to convince rational people that they're true. He's a nut."

"I agree," Oates said. "This has gone far enough."

"Hear him out," Steve Dakota said.

Oates whirled. "You're not serious! A ghost? Look, we had none of these problems until we hired this asshole. We had—"

"We've had five teachers in this room in three years," the superintendent reminded him. "Obviously, they thought something was wrong, too."

"I don't believe this," Osterman exclaimed.

"Nobody's asking you to believe, Harry. Just to listen."

"Tell us about the dog, Lou," Moondog said.

"It was . . . over a month ago," she said haltingly. "Robert saw it first, in the parking lot. . . ." As Osterman glowered and Oates listened in obvious disbelief, Marilou and Robert related how the dog had come into the classroom, how Jimmy had kicked it to death, and how the body had disappeared without leaving any blood or palpable remains of death to clean up from the carpet. Taylor raised an eyebrow as he jotted down details of their story on his notepad. Osterman didn't make so much as a scribble.

Steve Dakota turned to Marilou. "Why didn't you report this?" he asked her.

"Would you have believed me?" she said softly.

"Neither of us would have believed you," Oates said. "It's the kind of thing you don't believe until you've seen it for yourself."

"So you believe that this dog who disappeared and didn't bleed is the same beast that killed your son?" Taylor asked Robert.

The janitor looked involuntarily at the swamp of real, human blood where his son and Pete Sutherland had met their deaths.

"I don't know what I believe anymore," he said in a voice barely above a whisper. "I mean, I like to read now. Before I took this job, I hadn't read a book in almost forty years. This fall, I've read five." He raised his head and looked at Marilou. "Was it you, or was it Scurvy?"

Marilou smiled thinly, tenderly. "I'd like to think that I had something to do with it," she said. "But truthfully, I think it was mostly him. Donna told me that the reason I was in danger was because of my imagination. She said that without the help of an imaginative audience, literary characters remain two-dimensional, bound to their stories. Imagination is what makes them come alive. I think Scurvy wanted to spark your imagination as well, to get at me from another angle."

"Excuse me for being dumb," Taylor said, "but who the hell is Scurvy?"

"Scott Lurvey," Marilou told him. "He taught here in this room for many years. He committed suicide eight years ago—in this room."

"Oh, this is ridiculous!" Harry Osterman exclaimed.

"Maybe not," said Robert, who had spent more time looking at the physical details of the room than anyone else. "Look, there's something stuck in the heater."

And so there was. Protruding from the panel in front of the fan blades was a charred fist-sized object that had not been there the last time Robert had cleaned the room. They had not noticed it before because the heater, as old as the room itself, sported a fair number of stains and dings from its many years of service, and because the unpredictable box had been silent all morning.

"Looks like burnt paper," Moondog observed.

Bobby Bauer spoke up. "Jimmy threw something at it when it came on. He yelled for us to shut it off, and then he threw something. You wouldn't believe how loud it was."

"What did he throw?" Moondog asked. "A book, perhaps?"

"Makes sense," Guy Taylor said. "He was in the closet. And

look at all these books. He probably grabbed the first thing handy."

But Moondog was already in motion, bounding up the steps to Marilou's desk and then kneeling in front of the huge heater.

"Stop!" Guy Taylor barked at him. "You're destroying evidence!"

"I'm *gathering* evidence," Moondog replied. "Perhaps the crucial piece. It could be the key to everything."

"Be careful, man!" Robert warned him.

"Moondog, really!" Marilou cried. "Stay away from that heater!"

But he already had his fingers in the heater, working the charred thing loose. "I'm guessing that Scurvy's ghost is dormant right now," he said. "My sense is that he used up all his energy killing those two kids, and now he's gotta lie low and recharge his batteries. That's why we haven't heard the heater, and that's why his boys"—he indicated the wall of authors—"have behaved themselves this morning. I think Scurvy's asleep. If I'm wrong . . ."

"Yes, what if you're wrong?" Marilou demanded.

He grinned down at her. "If I'm wrong, I'll never play guitar again."

Marilou swallowed hard. "There's a . . . a ruler . . . in the top left-hand drawer of my desk," she said.

She made no move to go up onto the raised area. Surprisingly, it was Bill Oates who retrieved it, then walked over and handed it silently to Moondog.

Everyone watched intently as Moondog began prying at the object sticking out of the heater. He worked it in and poked the tip of the wooden ruler in behind it. He turned it this way and that, being careful not to break it off, and managed to move the object a little. The big heater remained silent. Moondog poked at the object several more times. Finally, he dislodged the blackened clump; it tumbled to the floor, wisps of burnt paper floating down behind it.

Everyone could see that it was a piece of a paperback book and that it had not completely burned.

Moondog stood up, then squatted down to retrieve the ruined book.

Robert took a tentative step toward it. "Stop," Guy Taylor commanded. "I'll handle this."

The detective pulled a small plastic bag from one pocket and a handkerchief from another. Advancing to the raised area, he leaned down to pick up the clump of paper that had once been an intact paperback novel. Moondog stood behind Marilou's desk, the fan clicking softly in its lopsided orbit above him. "Can you read the title?" he asked.

Taylor frowned at the burnt object in the handkerchief. "*The Call of the Wild*, by Jack London," he said.

Moondog stepped slowly off the raised area. He looked first at Bill Oates, then at the glowering Harry Osterman, and then at Marilou and Robert, who were standing very close together. Finally, his eyes returned to the detective's.

"There's your beast," he said simply. "Buck, the dog who becomes a wolf. Scurvy brought him to life, thanks to Robert's son. And he and his friend paid with their lives."

25

Wolves in Collision

The cops didn't finish with the room until late afternoon. "We won't have much time," Moondog told Marilou, Robert, and Bill Oates, who, surprisingly, had agreed to help them. They had gathered at Mariah's to eat and plan strategy; because of the unusual hour—4:00 P.M.—they were the only customers in the restaurant. As the waitress and cook busied themselves in the kitchen, the four of them went over their plans.

"The posters have got to go," Moondog said. "They're the key." He produced a plastic shopping bag from underneath the table. "I went to the hardware store and bought four pairs of heavy-duty work gloves. There's wire mesh in these puppies. It should be pretty damn hard for the edges of the posters to cut through them."

"What about the heater?" Robert asked.

From the same bag, Moondog produced a hammer and three putty knives. "Lou was able to extricate herself from a dangerous situation by smashing the thermostat," he said. "We'll do a more thorough job of it. I don't guarantee it'll work, but it might buy us some time."

"Which you say we won't have much of," Bill Oates said. "How come?"

Moondog and Marilou exchanged a meaningful look. "Two reasons," Moondog said. "I don't expect Scurvy's ghost to remain dormant forever. He killed those boys. I'm quite sure that by the time the Sun goes down, he'll be rested enough to kill again."

"What's the second reason?" Oates asked.

"If we get out of there before dark," Moondog said, "the second reason won't matter."

From Mariah's, they took a dirt path that ran behind Main Street and came out behind the baseball field. After a day in which cops and county officials had paraded in and out of the Annex like busy ants and curious onlookers had milled around the entrance to the parking lot, the school finally lay deserted. Classes had been canceled for the remainder of the week. The yellow tape remained in place around the front entrance of the Annex, but the back was clear, and Robert had the key. The cop cars had finally gone.

Moondog had made a few preparations. When the cops had finished questioning him, he and Marilou had made a quick trip out to his place, where he had pointed out the drawer in which he kept his silver pentagrams and his pistol, loaded with silver bullets. "If it all falls apart," he'd told her, "and we're trapped there when the Moon rises, you'll have to shoot me in order to protect the others."

"Moondog, I can't do that!" she had protested several times, but in the end he had convinced her to take the gun, and it sat uncomfortably in her purse as they entered the deserted Annex and their footsteps echoed down the hall toward room 13. His motorcycle was now stashed in the trees along the path they had followed, ready for his getaway. The second night of the full Moon was the second reason for haste. He hoped he would not need to divulge it to Robert and Bill Oates.

They donned the gloves as Marilou unlocked the door to the room and turned on the lights. The blinds were down; a quick inspection revealed that all three drawstrings had broken.

They had planned the assault, and now they swung into it quickly. Moondog dragged a desk over to the wall and stood atop it as he had on the day of the earthquake. Marilou took the hammer and walked purposefully to the thermostat.

She did not hesitate. Swinging the hammer, she struck the thermostat dead center. Bits of plastic, metal, and plaster flew from the wall. The heater emitted several sharp clicks. She backed away slowly, but the thing did not come on.

There was a loud rip as Herman Melville came down off the opposite wall. Oates crumpled the poster and tossed it onto the floor. One finger of his glove dangled loosely. Oates shook his hand in pain and several drops of blood flew off. He grimaced silently and reached for the next poster.

Robert raked Willa Cather from the wall, then Faulkner, then climbed on a chair to take down Sinclair Lewis. Moondog took down Poe, Crane, Wharton. Their gloves sustained cuts with each effort. Scurvy, it seemed, would not give up without a fight.

One by one, the severe pen-and-ink posters came down as Moondog, Robert, and Bill Oates moved methodically along the wall. Neither Moondog nor Oates noticed that Robert trembled slightly, as if trying to shake off some unseen pain, with each famous face he removed. The janitor was breathing heavily as well, but they were all working on extra adrenaline, not knowing the exact nature of what it was they confronted.

All at once, Robert stopped working. Moondog scraped Ralph Waldo Emerson off the wall in two pieces. Oates tore down Kenneth Roberts.

Robert stood away from the wall, shoulders slumped, breathing heavily.

Marilou lay the hammer on a desk and approached him. "Robert, what is it?"

Oates ripped Hemingway's bearded face in half, then reached for Jack London.

"No!" Robert cried in a voice the others did not recognize.

The janitor threw Marilou against a row of desks and grabbed the hammer. Oates turned as Marilou screamed and fell. Robert swung the hammer and crashed it into the vice principal's face. Oates went down like a stone.

"Robert!" Marilou screamed.

And the heater screamed, too, a banshee wail of battle. Robert's eyes were flame. He jumped on top of Oates and began pummeling the prostrate man with his fists. The heater screamed encouragement.

"Robert!" Marilou cried. "Fight it! You can think! You can read! Don't be a slave!"

For the briefest of moments, a look of confusion crossed Robert's tormented face. Sensing his chance, Moondog jumped on Robert's back and attempted to pull him off. Robert sent him staggering with a backhand blow. The janitor delivered a savage kick to the side of the vice principal's head. Bill Oates slumped unconscious on the floor, his face a bloody mess.

"The gun, Lou!" Moondog cried. "Get the gun!"

Marilou fumbled in her purse and produced the pistol. Her hand trembling, she aimed it at Robert, who stepped over Oates and grinned at her madly.

"Stay where you are," she warned him. He stopped, still grinning.

The heater clanked into silence.

"Well now, my pretty thing," Robert said in a voice that wasn't his own. "Who are you going to use that on—me, or Mr. Wolfman here?"

Moondog stood near the windows, his arms loose at his sides. Marilou's eyes darted between him and Robert.

"That's right," Robert said with a sinister chuckle, addressing Moondog but keeping a watchful eye on Marilou. "You sensed *our* presence. Did you really think *we* would fail to recognize *you*?" The janitor looked at his watch. "And what do you know? It's almost moonrise."

"Moondog, should I shoot him?" Marilou's voice was as unsteady as the gun.

"That would be a bit anticlimactic, don't you think?" Robert sneered. "Not to mention bad literature. I can't stand bad literature." His eyes bored into Marilou's with an otherworldly glow. "Besides, that gun's too hot for you to handle."

Marilou screamed and dropped the suddenly searing weapon. Red blisters rose on her hand. Robert laughed with uncharacteristic heartiness.

Outside, they heard the sound of gravel crunching under tires, and then two car doors slammed, one after the other. "Well, well," Robert said. "Sounds like someone's planning to crash the party." Calmly, he walked over to where Marilou had dropped the gun; he picked it up. The teacher backed away from him.

Footsteps sounded in the hall. Robert grabbed Marilou's arm and pulled her toward the wall next to the Jack London poster, which until a few minutes ago had enjoyed the company of other renowned American authors. Now most of the other posters lay in ruins on the carpet. London was utterly alone on this part of the wall. Down by the windows, Salinger hung by a corner, and James Fenimore Cooper remained untouched. Otherwise, the wall was empty.

Sheriff's deputies Frank Blaisdell and Kevin Byars appeared in the doorway, but they stopped when Robert placed the gun against Marilou's temple. "Try anything and she dies," Robert snarled.

On the floor, Bill Oates stirred slightly and emitted a faint groan. Robert waved the gun at the officers. "Get him out of here," he ordered them.

"We've got backup," Byars growled. He was a big, powerfully built man, with craggy features below a salt-and-pepper crew cut.

"So do we," Robert said. He pointed the gun at Oates. "Now, are you gonna take him out of here, or do I put him out of his misery right now?"

Byars hesitated for only a second. "Come on, Frank," he said to his younger, smaller partner.

Robert now positioned himself by the thermostat, his back to the wall, as the the two cops lifted the vice principal's body. Blood dripped from Oates's broken face as they carried him toward the door. "You and your buddies try anything funny," Robert said, pulling Marilou closer to him, "and I'll blow her fucking brains out."

"Robert," Marilou pleaded, "be strong. Don't let him do this to you!"

"Shut up," the janitor snarled. To the cops, he said, "Anyone tries to enter this room before sunset, we'll kill her." He laughed, then nodded at Moondog, who still stood motionless by the windows. "After sunset, you'll have to deal with *him*. Now go on!"

"We'll be back, motherfucker," Byars promised. The two cops carried Oates from the room.

Robert let go of Marilou's arm. Chuckling, he pulled from the wall the pieces of twisted metal and smashed plastic that had been the thermostat. "Did you really think that breaking this trivial device could stop us?" he said to Marilou. "How you have underestimated our versatility. As you have underestimated our entire body of work. We have powers that you can barely imagine."

"Is that the editorial 'we' or the imperial 'we'?" Moondog asked.

Robert turned his possessed face in the bus driver's direction. "In your case, Wolfman, it should be the schizophrenic 'we.' I'm looking forward to meeting your other personality. It should only be a matter of minutes now."

Marilou could see that Moondog's face had broken out in sweat and that one eye twitched. "Moondog . . ."

Nygerski lifted the corner of the blinds, revealing darkening twilight. "That's right, Wolfman," Robert said. "It's almost dark. The Moon will be rising momentarily." He patted the gun. "And I know you take precautions. Like keeping a supply of silver bullets handy."

"Why not shoot me now and be done with it?" Moondog said flatly.

Marilou gasped as Robert leveled the gun at Moondog's chest. For several seconds, no one moved. Then Robert began laughing.

"Bad literature," he said again. "Why didn't George shoot Lennie right at the beginning, before he had a chance to kill the girl? Why didn't Huck and Jim just hop a freight? There wouldn't have been any *drama*, that's why! It wouldn't have been any *fun!* Let's have some fun, shall we?"

Keeping the gun poised, Robert knelt down and picked up a bloodied copy of *The Call of the Wild* from the floor by the entrance to the closet. Marilou glanced over at Moondog and saw that sweat was now running in little rivulets down his temples and that his hands were shaking noticeably.

"I love a good dogfight," Robert said as calmly as if he was talking about last night's Movie of the Week. "Let's see what you're made of, Wolfman."

He turned and hurled the book at the heater.

Marilou watched it sail end over end through the air, remembering the knife Moondog had thrown at the Steinbeck poster. Robert's aim was utterly accurate, but then Scurvy probably controlled that, too. The book struck the heater with a groan, and the heater seemed to swallow it up.

Then it roared, and as Marilou watched in disbelief, the heater began to shake violently, and a large brown animal shape took form where the fan blades were—growing, growing. . . .

The dog sprang onto the carpeted area by Marilou's desk. It

crouched, ready to attack. It bared its teeth at Moondog and growled menacingly, low in its throat.

Marilou knew in an instant she had seen the dog before. It was the same dog she had seen Jimmy Rickard kick to death on the floor of the classroom, and Marilou realized that the dog had indeed exacted its revenge. Only the dog was no longer old and frail. This dog was muscled and mean; its fur shimmered in the fluorescent light of the room. It was young and strong again; Scurvy had rejuvenated it.

As he would have done to Donna Hurley, Marilou thought. As he had wanted to.

"Come here, boy," Robert called, slapping his thigh. "Come on, Buck."

Still growling, hackles raised, the dog obeyed. Robert hooked two fingers underneath its leather collar. Saliva ran from the dog's mouth. Its eyes never left Moondog. A half bark, half snarl rose from its throat as it struggled against its collar. Robert held it back.

"It's about time, isn't it, Wolfman?" the janitor said softly.

And indeed Moondog was already changing. His hands clawed the air, and his gnarled fingers were visibly growing longer. Sweat poured from his face—and hair sprouted from his cheeks, beneath the eyes, on his hands and arms, and around the collar of his shirt. *"Gaaaah!"* he cried, and fell to the floor, writhing. Fabric ripped as his shirt tore up the back. Marilou watched wide-eyed as the transformation overwhelmed his limbs. His hips became haunches, his arms forelegs. There were terrible claws where there had once been harmless fingernails, kept short for playing guitar. Long pointed teeth surged forward from his gums, dripping blood as they ripped the inside of his mouth. He raised his head to the ceiling and let loose a howl that momentarily eclipsed the heater's.

Marilou's heart rose into her throat until she could not swallow. She had thought she had believed him. But now she knew she hadn't, not in her gut, not in the place where words, thoughts, sounds, and reasons did not penetrate and where primitive truths held sway. She had not believed him with the center of her being, not until now.

"Excellent." Robert beamed. "Now *this* is drama." He motioned Marilou to stand back. "Give them room, my love," he said. "The middle of a dogfight's no place for a dame."

The dog snarled at the beast that Moondog had become. The beast bared its teeth and snarled back.

"Ready, Buck?" Robert said to the dog at his side. The dog barked and strained forward against the collar. "Okay, boy," Robert said. "Okay. Go get 'im!"

Robert let go of the dog's collar. With a cry of fury, it leapt at the werewolf. The heater shrieked excitedly. The black-furred thing that had been Moondog moments ago slammed a forepaw against the side of the dog's head. The dog tumbled to the carpet and staggered to its feet.

"Oh, this should be good," Robert said as he took a seat on the steps in front of Marilou's desk. He pulled a cigarette from a pack in his shirt pocket and touched a lighter to it.

Dog and werewolf circled each other among the student desks, each looking for an opening. Marilou saw that Moondog (for she still thought of the creature into which he had transformed as Moondog) could stand upright on his hind legs, but the dog was slightly larger, and it had the desperate viciousness of an animal defending its territory. She watched helplessly as the dog leapt at the werewolf's throat. At the last possible second, the werewolf turned. The dog's teeth closed on its shoulder, and the werewolf roared. In their deadly embrace, the combatants staggered across the room, knocking over several desks. The werewolf reared upward and threw the dog against the blackboard. It slumped to the floor, momentarily stunned. The bleeding werewolf advanced toward it. The heater keened crazily at a suddenly higher pitch. The dog lunged, fastening its jaws around the werewolf's hind leg. The beast that had been Moondog howled in agony.

The dog backed off, feinted, looking for another opening. Robert watched the action with a wide smile on his face, like a redneck at a cockfight.

And Marilou had an idea.

Robert brandished the gun as she came up to him and crouched beside him on the steps. "Relax, old chum," she said in as calm a voice as she could muster. She pulled a pack of cigarettes from her purse. "I just wanted a light for my smoke." She gave him what she hoped was a convincing conspiratorial smile.

He grunted and produced the lighter. "Go on now, get back," he said as he gave it to her. "I told you, a dogfight's no place for a female."

"Thanks, mate," she said, and stood up. Dog and werewolf grappled in the middle of the room as she backed slowly now toward the authors' wall. The werewolf was bleeding from several wounds. Marilou could tell that Moondog was getting the worst of the fight.

Slowly, taking care that Robert did not notice her, she eased over toward the poster of Jack London. Robert watched in rapt attention as the dog lunged again. The werewolf ducked away, and the dog's claws raked the carpet. Robert was focused entirely on the fight. She raised the lighter to her cigarette. The corner of the poster had come loose from the wall. She touched the lighter's flame to it. A tiny wisp of smoke rose toward the ceiling as the poster caught fire.

The werewolf crashed a paw down onto the dog's back. It bit into the dog's hindquarters, and the dog yelped and jumped away—toward Marilou. "Hey, get away from there!" Robert yelled at her, rising to his feet. She hurried back to the safety of the raised area.

Light strobed against the blinds. "We have the building surrounded," came a voice over a bullhorn. "Come out with your hands up and no one will be hurt."

Robert brandished the gun. "That's what *they* think," he said menacingly. "Let them try to come in here! I'll sick my dog on 'em."

Marilou snuck a glance at the London poster. A tiny piece of the corner was barely smoldering. Her heart sank. It looked as if it might go out at any moment.

The dog leapt at the werewolf's throat again. Moondog staggered backward, and in an instant the dog was on top of him. Its teeth dripped blood. It roared in impending triumph.

Its cry was answered by the sound of breaking glass. A canister crashed through the window. It landed on the carpet, spewing a thick cloud. Tear gas, Marilou realized instantly. And in the sudden rush of air into the room, the London poster burst into flame.

Robert rocked back on his heels as if struck. With a throaty cry of desperation, the werewolf threw off the dog. The heater wailed with a pitch that made Marilou's head reverberate with pain.

"Nooooo!" Robert screamed, grabbing his temples. The gun dropped to the floor. The dog screamed, its pitch nearly matching the heater's. With one tremendous lunge, the werewolf leapt atop the dog. Its terrible jaws opened; Marilou could see the pointed teeth. They snapped shut against the helpless dog's throat. Blood spurted halfway to the ceiling. The dog's head rolled lifelessly onto the carpet.

Flames consumed the London poster and licked up the side of the wall. The heater whined unbearably. The room filled with gas. It was becoming difficult to breathe, and to see.

"Come out *now!*" the voice boomed over the bullhorn. Marilou could barely hear it over the furious scream of the heater. The werewolf, its black-furred face covered with blood, looked up from the dog's twitching corpse and fixed its dark eyes directly on Robert. The janitor backed toward Marilou's desk, all the haughty confidence gone from his face.

"Moondog, no . . ." Marilou said.

But her voice was lost in the heater's agonized wail. Robert opened his mouth, but no sound emerged. Marilou coughed as she staggered through the smoke toward the center of the classroom. The werewolf advanced on Robert. The janitor screamed.

His scream was cut short as a furry forepaw tore open his throat.

Fire now engulfed the authors' wall from floor to ceiling. Robert's lifeless body crumpled against the front of Marilou's desk and slumped to the floor. The werewolf—Moondog—her lover—turned toward her; in two halting steps, he descended from the raised area. Marilou stumbled against an overturned desk and fell to the floor.

The heater's scream was now too much to bear. The werewolf advanced on her, blood flowing from many wounds. The beast bared its horrible teeth, and time seemed to stop.

Through the swirling gas, she saw the pistol on the floor by her desk, impossible to reach. The werewolf looked at her as if trying to reach a decision. Then, with a terrible roar, it bounded past her to the windows, gathered itself, and leapt directly into the center section. It gave way and crashed to the concrete outside as the werewolf escaped the room.

The sound of shattering glass and crunching metal was followed by a barrage of gunfire.

"Son of a bitch!" she heard a male voice yell. "After him!"

The heater screamed in raw fury. Outside, above its din, she could hear the wail of sirens and more gunfire. Marilou crawled through the tear gas and the overturned desks, heading toward the door to the hall. She struggled to her feet and stumbled toward it. She felt the searing heat of the room on her flesh and in her lungs. Tears streamed down her cheeks. She coughed violently. Her lungs felt as if they were ready to burst. Flames engulfed the room behind her as she reached the alcove. Then she was lifted off her feet and slammed against something hard as the heater exploded.

26

Don't Look Back

After making sure that no one was following her, Marilou aimed Moondog's motorcycle into the woods along a trail marked HORSES ONLY. At a safe distance from the horse camp, she found a thick clump of trees, concealed the bike, and continued on foot. She remembered the way.

Moondog lay on the moss in front of the cave. His gaunt face showed no surprise as she climbed up on the ledge and sat down wordlessly beside him. Perhaps he had been expecting her.

He looked terrible. Scars from the previous night's battle crisscrossed his naked torso, though she could not help but notice how quickly the wounds had begun to fade. His torn jeans were splotched with dried blood, and a shiny purple half-moon puffed below one eye.

This time, her injuries had been superficial. Today, she suffered nothing more than a stiff back, mild burns on her hand, and a slight headache, to go with the emotional hangover that follows any physical trauma. The ambulance personnel had checked her out, then deemed it unnecessary to take her to the hospital. Bill Oates had not been so lucky. And Robert was dead. She would never forget his last moment as long as she lived, nor the look in the eyes of the beast that killed him. She looked into Moondog's eyes now, searching for a hint of that look, fearing more than anything that she would find it.

Moondog seemed to sense this. "What happened?" he asked her. "Were we successful?"

Numbly, she nodded. "Yes," she said. "We were successful. Scurvy's ghost is gone."

"And Robert? Did he make it?"

Tears sprung into her eyes. She shook her head.

"Oh my God." He sank back on the moss.

"Moondog, I . . . I know it isn't your fault."

But she would never be able to look at him the same way again, and she sensed that he knew it, too.

She opened the backpack she carried and pulled out a clean white shirt. "Here," she said, handing it to him. "I've been meaning to return this."

He put on the shirt with obvious pain. "Did you bring anything to eat?"

She shook her head, then reached into the backpack again. "But I did bring this," she said, handing him a can of beer. It was cold and covered with condensation.

He managed a weak smile. "That's even better," he said.

"Moondog, every cop in the county is looking for you," she said several minutes later. "What will you do?"

He finished the beer and crumpled the can. "Well, obviously I can't go back to work," he said. "I can't stay in Julian, either, not after last night. I guess I'll get my strength back, then sneak out of town under cover of darkness. I'll find a new place and start over."

They lapsed into silence again. After awhile, he said, "I want you to know something."

"What?"

"The werewolf you saw up in Pismo Beach, the one that killed your friend—it wasn't me."

She looked at him in surprise.

"I know you thought that," he said. "I know you wondered how I knew. I was telling you the truth when I said I researched werewolf attacks through the newspapers. You've seen the clippings I keep. See, the only way to remove the curse is to trace the bloodline back and kill the werewolf at its head. I know who bit me, and he's dead. If I can find the werewolf that bit *him,* perhaps I can be normal again. It may be an impossible quest, but it's the only hope I have."

She said nothing. It was small comfort, after all. She had seen his other side kill Robert without a second thought.

"What about you?" he asked her. "What will you do?"

"Stay," she said. "Stay and do the job I was hired to do. They'll get me a new classroom—hopefully one without ghosts."

"Do me a favor?" he asked after another long silence.

"What?"

"Look after my place. You can even move in there if you want. If you've got some paper and a pen, I'll sign over the truck and the bike to you right now. Perhaps one day it will be safe for me to contact you."

She was aware that she was crying. She wiped at her face with her hand. "Yes, I can do that," she said. "But I didn't bring any paper, and Moondog, I don't want your things. I'll keep them for you, just as they are, until you come back."

"Don't wait for me," he said. "It could be a long time. You could be an old woman."

There seemed to be nothing more to say. It was over.

She rose to go. "Bill's in the hospital," she said. "Robert—or should I say Scurvy?—beat him up pretty badly. I'm going to go see him."

Moondog stood also, and, tentatively at first, they embraced.

They held each other for a long time. "Don't look back," he said.

And she didn't, not until she reached the trail and Moondog's lair was out of sight.

She drove the motorcycle toward town, her hair streaming behind her in defiance of California's helmet law. She did not feel much like following rules today. The wind had come up, and mare's-tails streaked the clear mountain sky. The light jacket she wore did little to keep out the cold. She didn't mind. Though her life had been torn apart again, she felt an incongruously joyful sense of liberation.

The school lay along her route, and on an impulse, she steered the bike into the parking lot. She parked, dismounted, and walked up to the yellow tape. The fire had been extinguished. Though the rest of the Annex had not been touched, all that remained of the domain of Scurvy's ghost were the burnt remains of desks, beams, blackboard panels, and electrical fixtures, and a blackened hole that once had been a closet. A thin plume of ash and dust rose from the wreckage.

Absently, Marilou took a pack of cigarettes from the backpack and shook one loose. There were six or seven left in the pack. She looked at it in her hand, and then, reaching a decision, she threw the entire pack into the rubble.

The fire had been stopped just as it had reached the closet, and a pile of blackened paperback books lay there in a heap. For a very long time, Marilou could not take her eyes off them. As she watched, several charred pages dislodged themselves from their parent volumes and floated away on the breeze.